AQUILA BOOKS

THE FIREWALKERS

CHRISTINE MANGALA was born in Tanjore District, Tamil Nadu, South India, into a Brahmin family distinguished for five centuries as devotees of Shiva, as Sanskrit scholars, writers and composers, and tracing its descent from the sixteenth century scholar Appaya Dikshitar, a noted commentator on the ninth century philosopher and saint, Shankara.

Educated at the University of Delhi, where she topped her honours year in English Literature, she then went to the University of Osmania at Hyderabad for her M.A., and in 1968 became the first woman to win the Nehru Memorial Trust Scholarship, which took her to Cambridge for research. Her doctorate from that university was for a thesis on 'The Problem of Evil in Jacobean Drama'.

Since 1968, CHRISTINE MANGALA has lived largely in the west: first in England (where she married a Cambridge don and raised four children), more recently in Newcastle, Australia. She has taught literature in the Universities of Cambridge and of Newcastle, New South Wales; but of late she has put her unique experience of eastern and western religions to promoting a better understanding of both—through lectures and broadcasts, and now in this first novel.

THE FIREWALKERS

Christine Mangala

AQUILA

CAMBRIDGE - SYDNEY - NEW DELHI

First published in Great Britain in 1991
by Aquila Books Limited
P.O.Box 293, Cambridge CB5 8AU

Aquila Books,
42 Homebush Rd., Strathfield, Sydney 2135

Aquila Books,
23 Ajit Arcade, New Delhi -49

Distributed in the United Kingdom by
Vine House Distribution,
Waldenbury, North Chailey,
East Sussex BN8 4DR
Tel. (082) 572 3398
Fax. (082) 572 4188

Distributed in Australia by Schepp Books,
2/40 Leighton Place, Hornsby, NSW 2077
Tel. (02) 476 3712
Fax. (02) 476 2766

© Christine Mangala

All rights reserved

Printed and bound in Great Britain by
Billing & Sons Limited, Worcester

A CIP catalogue record for this book
is available from the British Library

Hardback: ISBN 1-872897-02-9

Paperback: ISBN 1-872897-03-7

FOR LESSLIE NEWBIGIN

CHAPTER ONE

Ekk Dum. . . . Ekk Dum. Up—down. Up—down.

The steady sound of iron hitting the pappadum-dough on the granite slab.

'Right! Time to pull it out!' At Lakshmiyamma's command, Rukku grabs the yellow dough glistening with oil, stretches it to a long rope, winds it round, and shoves it back to receive more blows from the mallet poised above.

'Come on, girl! At this rate, *Kali-yuga* will come to an end before we sit down.' Lakshmiyamma is a little irritable. With her bare arms raised high, clutching the mallet, biceps tightening, blue veins knotting, like a boxer ready for another round, she stares at the dough. Rukku grabs the shiny, slippery creature and feeds it to the descending mallet. One slip and her fingers will be gone, her delicate wrists pounded to powder. Yet Rukku continues, risking all.

Foreign daughter, by no means a favourite of Lakshmiyamma, has come home. Aunt Malini has come home: in her late forties, rich in rustling silks with wide *zari*-borders, her triple-chinned neck struggling above rows of gold chains and necklaces sparkling with rubies, her ear-lobes flashing sets-of-seven diamonds, all proclaiming her foreign affluence—AMERICAN, not DUBAI. Malini's foreign-bred, slacks-disporting (but today saree-clad) pretty daughter Nitya has also come home, to marry a brahmin boy from a good Hindu home, who is also travelling from another part of foreigndom. Washington? Cincinnati? No. Silicon Valley, California.

'Silicon-chillicon-chee-cheecon,' sings Nitya's younger brother, twelve-year-old Seenu, in an attempt to ruffle Nitya, to rouse her from her reverie; while Nitya, the bride-to-be, lounging on the wide-planked hall-swing, swings; swings all day, to and fro, to and fro, ignoring the bustle around her, impervious to the pappadum party in her honour, swings to and fro, apparently absorbed in *The Catcher in the Rye*. And as she swings, she waits, waits for her cousin Aparna.

Aparna-Gauri, when will she come? Why is she so late? Every now and then, Nitya lifts her pretty head and, tossing a mass of curls, looks towards the doorway.

Malini Subramaniyam has come home all the way from America to this country town, Kuchchipuram. Lakshmiyamma's house is not what she was used to in Washington—or was it Cincinnati? What's in a name? 'Foreigndom is foreigndom' as Lakshmiyamma would say. But it wasn't Dubai. That's what matters, not being Dubai. Dubai, even among Kuchchipuram folk, is mentioned with a certain sneer and smile. 'Think of the shame of good brahmin boys cleaning latrines! What if they earned crores? Shiva! Shiva!' Here in Kuchchipuram, Malini and her family find the toilets most inconvenient, though Lakshmiyamma boasts about her 'modern toilets': they have to squat, peasant-fashion, and pour down buckets of water. The only time Nitya's brow darkens is when she thinks of this ordeal. Everything else she is determined to sit out, biding her time, and packing up as soon as the ceremony is over, to a 'civilized city' in the north where flushes are said to work. Meanwhile, where is Aparna? If only she would arrive . . .

'Dear Nitya agreed to the match,' Malini whispers proudly. 'And without any protest, made it so easy for us, her father and me. Kumar is such a pleasant boy. They had met, you know, at a ski-resort, she never told me till all was settled. It was so fortunate that their horoscopes agreed, and his family is not our *gotra*!' Lakshmiyamma recognizes the honour of her foreign daughter coming home, to this dirty country town, to celebrate her only daughter's wedding. What better way to tell the town than a pappadum party? So she has summoned her troops for this solemn occasion, for every stage has to be prepared with great care, with great *sraddah*—and there is such protocol to be observed! Deaf Rajam-mami from next door is allotted pride of place with the best of rolling-pins, big-mouth Seshi has to have the white marble slab, and she is the fastest despite all her chatter—and as for Pattu, the ever-pregnant wife of the temple priest, well, Pattu is allowed to participate only out of kindness; she is a mere novice at pappadum-making and has so much to learn and she could if she didn't keep running back and forth after that nose-dribbling toddler of hers. They are loyal and can be counted on to produce a fine batch of pappadums in a trice! And they are beginning to assemble.

It is getting on to eleven o'clock. Rukku alone has been there since the crack of dawn: Rukku, whose family lives in genteel brahmin poverty, and who was taken up by Lakshmiyamma at the age of ten. Rukku, now twenty-one, but still submissive and quick to divine the mysterious thought-processes of this intrepid old woman, stops before the command falls.

'Let's test.' Lakshmiyamma halts. Rukku grabs the pounded dough, a rubbery, yellow, slithering snake, neatly pinches it into walnut-size balls, and rolls them rapidly in the palm of her hands until they emerge glistening as large marbles, yellow, flecked with grey-black cumin and smelling strongly of castor oil.

'None of these over-spiced, hot, not-to-be-endured-garlic-stinking-northern-nonsense you get in your biriyani-hotels, but pure brahmin, melt-in-the-mouth variety only made here! If you want anything else you can go to your filthy non-brahmin cafés where heaven knows what those *bidi*-smoking fellows fry in pig-fat—or is it snake-fat?' Lakshmiyamma's lips curl in such disdain that no one dares speak.

'Seems ready for rolling,' Rukku ventures. Rukku knows her place. She never speaks in any but the mildest of tones, and always in the tentative mode. Rukku is family and yet not family. Pretty well everything is discussed in her presence, but it is always assumed that she never listens, let alone gossips. Rukku is not family, nor is she an orphan, though the old woman sometimes treats her as one. Rukku knows her place. When her brother Pichchu, a thin, wiry lad of eleven, in immaculate *veshti* and sacred thread, calls on Lakshmiyamma on sacred and semi-sacred days, on Fridays and Tuesdays, when he holds out his brightly polished brass bowl and awkwardly recites the approved sacred formula for brahmin begging—'*Bhavati bhiksham dehi*, lady! May food be given!'—Rukku ladles out the hot rice without a flutter of acknowledgement, no, not a glance or smile. 'Is he really your brother?' asked Seenu when Pichchu appeared that morning—but Rukku chose not to reply.

'Let me see!' Lakshmiyamma takes one of the dough-marbles and pushes her index-finger through, and seems satisfied as the dough springs back with suitable resilience.

'—Come on, give me a hand! I am getting too old for this game. Once I sit, I can't get up. Not long to go before my final trip. Not long, then I shall have a jolly good ride on four shoulders!'

Everyone is used to Lakshmiyamma referring to her funeral procession in this manner. She seems to relish the prospect of herself lying prone on the bamboo pallet, and of being carried by her strong-shouldered son and grandsons. She speaks of it as others would speak of a car-ride or a plane-trip. And she speaks of it in the same spirit as she speaks of the days before this independence-nonsense, days of the British who knew what was what, and how to treat an orthodox brahmin-judge as he ought to be treated, of garden-parties where even the hatted white-memsahibs were polite to him because he kept horses, of the phaeton that bolted at a gallop before the peon could jump on it—could it be he deliberately dawdled so that he could show off? And then there was their motor-car, the first in town. How its hoots and screeches scared even the temple-bull, which never budged from the middle of the street, no, neither for god nor man. Oh, what days they were, and what it was to be the wife of a district judge! Bless his memory! Poor soul! Long-dead, long forgotten! She didn't need these new-fangled foreign madams to tell her what was what.

'Where is that Aparna? She could take charge and I could shut my eyes, but where *is* she? Rukku! Hey, Rukku! Stretch out my mat by the granary, will you? Don't let the gossip-gang trouble me till I have had a nap.'

Foreign daughter Malini appears, spreading out a bright green-and-gold saree. Lakshmiyamma has already turned her face to the ochre-striped wall. She doesn't seem to hear.

'Mother!' Malini tries again. 'What do you think of this for Nitya for the reception?'

No reply.

Is she really deaf? Malini's fleshy face crumples as she hears the old woman mutter to the wall: 'Sarees indeed! Does that girl know how to wear one, walk in one, or keep it falling off her shoulder? Always going around in skirts like a gipsy, and in boys' clothes too! What a shame that poor child Aparna has to see this buffoonery!' Malini retreats to the hall.

'Shall I fan you, grandma?' Nitya has got off the swing as the gossip-gang arrives. Anything to avoid their prying questions.

'Don't come too close! You are not *madi*.' Then Lakshmiyamma relents, mollified by her granddaughter's solicitude. 'Go, get the big palm-fan. There—Aparna keeps it under that bamboo-rafter. Go, go.'

After a jump or two, Nitya dislodges the palm-fan from under the sloping roof, and squats by Lakshmiyamma. 'When is Aparna coming, grandma? I can't wait to see her. It has been so long—five years! Is she still as beautiful as ever? I remember how her long plait swirled when she danced. I can't wait to see her, but mummy wouldn't let me go on my own to uncle's.'

'Your mother is quite right. A bride-to-be shouldn't be roaming the streets on her own, no, not here in Kuchchipuram. I see I am not going to get any shut-eye.' She slowly pulls her bony body upright, and heaves a sigh. 'And what if she is ugly or beautiful? Poor child! It's all over for her. As for dancing, you know what I think of it. It should never have come out of the temples. Now good brahmin girls are cavorting around like *devadasis*!'

'Grandma! You are too severe!'

'It was all a mistake, a terrible mistake! And what a terrible price to pay. . . . Ah, look! They are all here! I might as well get up. —Rukku! Where are you? Is the coffee ready? Did you get the marble slabs out? —Nitya, dear, do you know how to stretch a pappadum?'

'Alas, no. I know how to eat them!'

'Ah! You will see today! Nothing like marble to roll dough on—so smooth, so effortless, so paper-thin! On marble you can't go wrong, the pappadum never sticks, no, not once! Call Rukku, my dear. I need a hand.'

Nitya moves to help, but Lakshmiyamma throws her hands up in horror. 'No, no, no. You can't touch me, you are not *madi*, how many times do I have to tell you? Shiva, Shiva!'

Rukku is there in an instant, having poured out several tumblers of coffee for the women surrounding Malini, who, seated on the plank-swing, is sorting out wedding-sarees, much to everyone's delight.

'How good of you, Malini! Come all the way, eh?' Deaf Rajam invariably shouts. She advances towards Nitya. 'So this is your girl! May the gods bless her!'

Fan in hand, stranded by the granary, Nitya cannot escape Deaf Rajam's overbearing good wishes. The old woman peers into Nitya's face, and cracks her knuckles over Nitya's forehead to ward off evil eyes, all the while proclaiming, 'May the gods bless this child! Such plump, rosy cheeks! May goddess Sivakami protect her! Such shining, curly hair!'

Malini beams in response, and Rajam continues: 'How sensible of you to bring your girl home. We can teach a thing or two in Kuchchipuram, can't we, Seshi? Only our girls make good wives for our boys—what if they go to foreign parts!' Rajam goes on, without waiting for a response from anyone in particular.

It is a morning for compliments and admiration. Criticism will come later, Malini knows. All the same, their tributes soothe her ruffled spirits.

'. . . And is yours there a big house, like the Collector's bungalow?' Seshi is curious to find out all she can about foreign houses. She has heard that houses there are so sparkling that you can eat off the bathroom floors. Rajam catches the word 'Collector' and butts in:

'Have you all heard the news? The new Collector has arrived. A brahmin boy and not yet married! Think of that! What a change after that drunken infidel, Vilayat Khan!'

'Malini has no need of new Collectors, brahmin boy or not!' Seshi, peeved at being interrupted, shoots a new question: 'And, Malini, your son-in-law—where will he be working?'

'In Delhi Tourist Office only. He is M D.' She rolls her head as she replies, to make sure that the prestige is not lost on them.

'In Del-hi? Janaki's daughter also lives in Delhi too. In winter it is so cold there, she tells me, the very oil on your hair freezes!'

'It is a lot colder in America. Why, even the tap water freezes.' Malini is not going to be outdone by mere northern cold.

Lakshmiyamma shouts from across the hall: 'Why doesn't something freeze here? This heat! And it is only the month of *Tai*! —Rukku! Bring the table fan and put it somewhere where it can't blow the pappadums off. We can all stand here chattering, while the day disappears in a trice!'

The women take the hint and seat themselves on the ground in a large circle. Some sit cross-legged, others, the heavier ones, with one leg outstretched and sarees hitched up to the thigh. They begin rolling out the dough-marbles into wafer-thin yellow moons.

Nitya joins them, and, much to their surprise, sits cross-legged ('She learns yoga, you know, from an American guru!' Malini explains). Nitya sits idly, drawing patterns on the flour kept for dusting the dough, till a shadow falls across her.

'Aparna! At last!' Nitya jumps up, scattering flour over the heads of the women, who are too deep in gossip to notice the girl who stands hesitating by the door. Seeing Nitya rush to her, they stop in mid-sentence, and look at one another, exhaling significant sighs.

'Mmm!' Deaf Rajam is the first to speak. Swaying back and forth with the rolling-pin, she launches into a volley of blessings on Nitya, darting significant glances to make sure that no one misses what she means: 'May the gods protect this child from evil eyes! May the goddess preserve her husband, may she grant him long life! May she bless them with many children . . . !'

'That'll do.' Lakshmiyamma's curt interjection brings the tirade to a halt.

During the deaf woman's outburst, the girl at the door has stood still, calm and unruffled. Slightly taller but distinctly darker than her cousin, Aparna is clad in a white handloom saree. Her long hair is tied in a loose knot. No kumkum adorns her forehead, no gold her neck. Everything about her proclaims her widowhood.

'Sorry I am late, Nitya! Here take this. It's for you.' Aparna holds out a green banana-leaf packet to her cousin.

'What is it? . . . Oh, how lovely! Jasmines!'

'The creeper was loaded this morning, more than what I needed for the gods. Normally I take them to the temple, but today they are for you. Do you have jasmines in America?'

'Yes, we do—but not this plump kind.' Nitya puts an arm around her cousin and, pushing her back a little, surveys her. 'Anyway, no one braids them as you do. You haven't changed much . . . well, not much . . . apart from being like this.' Nitya cannot bring herself to name the name, to call her a widow. Instead, she sweeps her arms vaguely over Aparna.

'I am all right. I do miss some things—jasmines, for instance. Otherwise, all right.'

'How can you be so calm?' Nitya's brows knit in annoyance.

'There's nothing I can do, anyway. Look at grandma, she has survived, hasn't she? So shall I.'

'How can you talk like this? Grandma is nearly eighty, and you are . . . you are only, what, twenty-three? —four?'

'Shush, Nitya! Come with me and I'll fix the jasmines in your hair, and let us talk. You tell me all about yourself. We must only talk about happy things, and your wedding. Come, come!' And raising her voice a little, Aparna turns towards her grandma with a coaxing smile. 'I won't be long, grandma. I must catch up with Nitya, it's been so long.'

Aparna guides her cousin past the women into the courtyard. It is bare, except for a few white sheets spread out in the sun, ready for drying damp pappadums. They sit, facing each other, on the 'crow-watch' bench along the wall.

Nitya's face brightens as she takes her cousin in. 'I am so happy to see you looking well. I was afraid you might have changed. I don't know what I expected. It's nearly five years since we left.'

'And you are a grown-up young lady, so polished and clever—and about to be the best bride in town.'

'Selfish of me, I suppose, but I am glad you are still as beautiful as ever, for I long to see you perform at my wedding. Will you do the peacock-dance? It's my favourite.'

Aparna is slow to respond. 'I am sorry, Nitya. I don't dance any more.'

'What! Why?'

'I only teach—a few local girls, and sometimes at the church school. I don't perform.'

'But why? That's terrible.'

'I can't explain. You won't understand. You have been away from all this too long. You saw those women when I came in. If it wasn't for you, I wouldn't have come here today.'

'Why, Aparna-Gauri, you surprise me.' Nitya assumes a school-mistressy posture. 'It is very wrong of you to bury your gift like this, just because some foolish old women tut-tut. I always said your talents were wasted here. You should have come with us to America.'

'No, I'm not wasted here. What will father and grandmother do without me? Here is where I belong, to Kuchchipuram. And I know Kuchchipuram is not Washington. Anyway, it is not the old women. It is my choice.'

'Your choice? What choice?' Nitya pouts.

'You look even prettier when you sulk.'

'Don't humour me! You are hiding something, though you smile. I want a proper explanation.'

'All right then. It is unbecoming for me, a widow, to get up on stage in all that finery, silks and jewels, and dance like a courtesan.'

'You never thought like that before! Now you are talking like grandma. Next you will be telling me that you are going to shave your head and make yourself ugly like she has!' Nitya's voice grows tearful as she continues: '—And you are not telling me the whole truth, I can tell. This is not it, is it, all about silk and jewellery? Why won't you trust me? I promise I'll be serious.'

'No, you can laugh if you want to, but you must promise you will get auntie to engage a good dancer, someone my Guru Ramiah recommends, for the wedding-reception.'

'Don't change the subject. I don't care about my wedding-reception. It's you I care about. Tell me why ? Why, truly?'

'Well, it is like this. When I got over the shock—as you know, it was a shock, I had known my husband for a month, and so much of that time was taken up with visiting people, my mother-in-law's relations, and then mother was so ill . . . I was just beginning to get adjusted to being married, then the accident happened, and I had to start adjusting to being a widow. It was all so sudden, and just shock upon shock. I sometimes wish *sati* had not been abolished. In some ways it would have been better!'

'Aparna! How can you say that? You *are* bitter.'

'I'm sorry. Not at all. That was a silly fantasy, I confess. Adjusting has been difficult, but not impossible. Now, nearly two years after, I am all right, more than all right.'

'How can you be all right when you can't or won't do the one thing you are made for?'

'You are sweet, Nitya, to think so highly of me as a dancer. But I have had a chance to grow up, really grow up, see through the illusion we call life—happiness.'

'Stop this! I would rather you were bitter or angry. Yes, angry! This resignation chills me. I hope you don't mean what you say.'

'No, Nitya. I am serious. Father says Gandhiji used to call widows, "*jeevathyagis*", "life-sacrificers". . . . I am beginning to understand what he meant. It is strange, but it is not horrible as you imagine. . . . Now, enough of this. We must see how we make you the best bride ever. Rukku will prepare some henna-paste for your palms, and I myself will apply it. I'll trace patterns on your feet too. It will itch, but you musn't scratch. I'll tell you tales to distract you! Now I must go to grandma. She is bound to be agitating. She's so used to having me around. Ah! Here comes Aunt Malini with those gorgeous sarees we shall deck you in. Come!'

Aparna stands up, holding out a hand to pull her cousin up.

CHAPTER TWO

Dusk was falling as Aparna walked back from her grandmother's house. The sky became a spangled mass of blue, gold, vermilion and grey, the piercing light giving way to softer shades, soft but still intense. The sky reminded Aparna of the wedding sarees Aunt Malini had displayed earlier that day. The dusk-light made everything bearable, even the open drains swarming with mosquitoes, the piles of uncleared rubbish in front of discoloured houses, those dirty, half-naked children scampering across: they were real yet not real, no more than a facet of the general phantasmagoria of existence. But the sky, the sky with its sea of colours—so real, so intense!

. . . Yes, she was right to refuse Nitya's request. And she had done it so calmly, so philosophically, that even father would have been impressed. But . . . Aparna quickened her pace. They were there, her own collection of silk sarees, sarees worn during her *bharatanatyam* performances, and the almost-new wedding sarees—all untouched since then, gathering dust in the wardrobe. She hurried home, the spangled clouds driving her on.

Vedam Iyer was not back from the temple. That was a relief. She couldn't do what she was about to do in his presence. Vedam Iyer, her beloved father, advocate and scholar much venerated by the town, lived a simple life, was even a Gandhian at times. How could she, the daughter of whom he was so proud, give way to something so impulsive? It would be a betrayal. Betrayal of what, of whom, she could not tell. Yet she knew that her father, fond as he was of her, would be dismayed to see her indulging such a girlish whim.

The teak wardrobe had belonged to her mother, a gift from an uncle who was a timber-merchant and had made his fortune in Burma, before he was driven out and had to walk all the way from Rangoon to Assam. The wardrobe stood as an emblem of endurance in that camera-room which came to be Aparna's after her mother's death. It was dark: the only window faced the street and had to be kept shut, for passers-by could not resist looking in, and stray children were for ever jumping on and off the raised verandah outside.

Aparna unlocked the wardrobe. A blended aroma of coffee, sandalwood and toffee exuded from the teak. Her mother had been in the habit, as was *her* mother, of treating the wardrobe as a lock-up sanctuary for precious goods—coffee, toffee and sandalwood soap. 'Who knows if you can trust the servant-girl these days? She might be tempted, so better these be under lock and key!' Poor mother!—always waiting to be robbed or cheated and never was, on little things.... Aparna had long removed those items from the wardrobe, but the smells lingered on. She stretched to the top shelf and brought down a large bundle of sarees, all neatly folded and wrapped in tissue-paper. She took the bundle out into the courtyard, struck by an impulse to spread them out under the evening skies.

The gold-vermilion nine-yard saree had been worn only once, during the wedding, at the time when her husband took her from her father, and tied the sacred knot. The deep blue one, chequered with silver and gold, was for the reception. How everyone had admired her in that—and the colour had come out particularly well in the photographs! She trembled as she unfolded saree after saree on the bench; the gold on the borders lit up the wall behind, blending with the dancing rays of the setting sun. Finally, she unfurled her favourite, the peacock-blue-and-green shot-silk, and sat in the midst of yards of silk, revelling in a sea of colour, glitter and smoothness. What if her father should come home early and find her thus, in the middle of this silken heap? Her heart missed a beat when she caught sight of a figure darkening the doorway.

'Is this advocate Vedam Iyer's residence?' A tall young man in immaculately laundered whites, as though he were just off to play cricket, was addressing her.

Aparna rose, trailing yards of silk, but too dazed to respond.

He pulled back a step, and with a quick motion, rested one arm casually over the low lintel. '—I'm sorry. I seem to have startled you. I am looking for Vedam Iyer.'

'Yes, yes. This is the advocate's house. Please come in. Excuse me. I must clear this mess.' She looked at the glittering heap, half-smiling, half-frowning.

The visitor's gaze rested on them. '"Mess"? They look magnificent to me—especially that shot-silk in this light! Peacock-blue, isn't it? I prefer to think of it as peacock-green.'

'That's . . . or, rather, it *was* my favourite.' She paused, still mesmerized by the brilliance. How was she to explain what she was doing? '—They needed airing. So I brought them out.' She blushed as she uttered the excuse.

'Yes, of course.' He stood there nonchalantly, studying her white-clad, kumkumless figure; then, with an abrupt shift of stance, he shed the faintly ironic tone and, in a voice charged with compassion, added, 'Yes, of course.'

Aparna winced.

She was conscious of being assessed as she gathered up the sarees. She started folding them rapidly in an attempt to regain her composure; but to her dismay, the silk kept slipping from her hands. Who was this stranger, that she should feel so exposed to him?

His grave expression gave way to a smile that softened somewhat angular, chiselled features. '—Pardon me! I haven't even introduced myself. I am Raghavan, Mani Iyer's son. My father went to school with the advocate. I have just been posted to Kuchchipuram as the Collector.'

'Oh! the new Collector!' —With that she could distance him. 'Father shouldn't be long. He has gone to the temple. Please take a seat.' She pointed to the cane chairs scattered around the bench. 'Or you can wait upstairs, in the office.'

The office was the largest and most modern room in the house. Vedam Iyer, having decided to keep the noisy world at a distance, had built himself an upper storey which overlooked South Car Street on one side and the central courtyard on the other. He was particularly proud of the verandah that ran the length of the office-cum-library: 'Bengali-style, and ideal for pacing up and down when one has a difficult case to think about!'

Aparna would have liked to have sent the visitor upstairs, but he forestalled her.

'No, not the office yet. This is only a social call. I may well need his office later, one day!' Raghavan laughed, nervously brushing his hair back with a wave of his palm.

'It's getting dark; I still haven't lit the lamps. I must go.' Gathering up her bundle, Aparna disappeared into the camera-room. As she locked up the sarees, she took a deep breath as if she were about to plunge into a river, and crossed the courtyard to reach the kitchen without once looking at the visitor.

Raghavan sat down on a chair facing the front door, and picked up *The Hindu*. He noticed that sections of a report on a religious discourse by Variyar were underlined. He put the paper down and stood up, stretching his arms and breathing in the perfumed air; as he walked about the silent courtyard, his heart surged with excitement at the prospect ahead.

How clean the air felt here, and how spacious the houses were! Not like Madras, where the evening air was charged with the fetid smell of drains, mosquitoes and DDT. . . . This was what was so good about this country-town. Despite its size, it still remained a village, and the ways of the people leisurely. Backward and blind, no doubt, riddled with superstition and crippled with custom; but that was a challenge he was ready to take up. Whatever the hurdles he might have to surmount, it would be well worth the struggle, to get away from the cramped, stinking, humid hell-hole that Madras was becoming. How glad he was to forget the raggedy, ill-built concrete tenement which went by the name of home, where the walls sweated salt, and, at night, oozed with the blood of squashed bed-bugs—where he, with his brothers and sisters, along with the numerous progeny of neighbours, were penned up like cattle, and were no better off than the cattle that prowled around wasteheaps! But here, here the air was balmy, and charged with freshness and promise . . .

'What's this lovely perfume in the air?' asked Raghavan, seeing

Aparna emerge from the kitchen. She was carrying a little earthen lamp, shielding the flame with her right palm, which she held gracefully arched over the wick.

'It's the *parijata* tree over there.' Twisting her neck with the practised ease of a trained dancer, she directed his attention towards a carpet of coral-pearl flowers that lay under the raised flower-bed in the courtyard.

Having placed the lamp in an alcove by the front door, she stood by, still and silent, looking into the distance. As the last rays of the sun withdrew, she too withdrew into herself, her face becoming a mask.

Raghavan sat down and cleared his throat: 'It's good to see this custom still being kept up. In Madras most people have gone so completely over to electric light one doesn't notice the sacredness of dusk.'

'Oh, yes. —But here I see father, just turning the corner.'

As soon as she sighted Vedam Iyer, her duties to the visitor were over, and she could disappear into the kitchen without seeming rude. The very curve of her back suggested that she did not wish to be drawn into any further conversation with him.

Vedam Iyer broke into the silence like a clanging bell. Since his wife's death, the advocate had become loquacious, especially after a visit to the temple to hear a discourse.

'Wonderful in so young a pundit! Sivaram Pundit is only in his forties, you know, and he reels off verses in so many languages! Not just Sanskrit and Tamil but Malayalam and Hindi. He was quoting Tulsi Das today. Do you read Hindi? Aparna does, a little. I myself prefer our Kambar—or Valmiki. No one can compare with the great Valmiki—or Kalidasa. Have you ever read Kalidasa?' The advocate pushed his spectacles down his nose and looked straight at Raghavan, and without waiting for a reply, continued, 'Come, come, I am so forgetful. How's everybody in Madras? How is my friend Mani? You must forgive an old man who gets carried away by a good discourse. At my age, that is my delight. Come, come! Don't get up! Sit down! —Aparna! Aparna-Gauri! Bring some coffee, my dear! We have a visitor, my old friend Mani's son!'

Vedam Iyer lowered his heavy frame into a large wooden chair with carved arm-rests, and leant his stick against it. '—She doesn't know you were coming today. I received Mani's letter only this morning. Then I was looking through so many affidavits I forgot to tell her.'

Aparna returned with two silver tumblers of steaming coffee, placed them on a small cane-table and stood by her father's chair, twirling the ends of her saree.

'Aparna, dear! You must come and listen to Sivaram Pundit. He is as good as some of our veterans. What voice! What rhythm! What wisdom! What explication!'

'So I have heard. Grandmother also likes his discourses.'

'Ah, yes! Your grandmother! A wonderful woman! —You must meet her, Raghavan. She'll like meeting you. Her husband was at the court of the Maharajah of Mysore, you know, and then he became a district judge feared by the British! Splendid old lady she is! Aparna is her favourite—but then Aparna is everybody's favourite.'

'Father! Please!'

His excitement died. '—And how is everybody in the other house? What news from your aunt?'

'Aunt Malini is not happy about the arrangements for the groom's party. She asked if we could help her find somewhere better.'

'Ah, the wedding!' Vedam Iyer pulled down his spectacles again and peered at Raghavan. 'My sister-in-law's daughter is getting married. They are all from overseas, you know! How they can live in those god-forsaken places, I don't know! All the same, they have come back here for their daughter's wedding, and we must do what we can. —So your aunt wants me to find somewhere, eh?'

'Perhaps we should talk about this later.' Aparna had noticed that Raghavan had suddenly discovered something very interesting in the newspaper, and, with a barely suppressed smile, seemed intent on reading it whilst the conversation took a domestic turn.

Vedam Iyer was glad to be let off. Aparna gathered the empty tumblers and returned to the kitchen.

'—Now tell me, Raghavan, when did you arrive? How are things at your office? Have you still that sleepy Kittu with you? My clients keep complaining about him—very tricky, very tricky he is. Your predecessor couldn't do much about him; but then *he* was a drunkard, and in the pocket of politicians. I don't envy your job. Bad enough being a lawyer, but you have to be a god himself as Collector!'

From the kitchen Aparna could see her father firing questions at Raghavan. She began preparing supper. Being Friday, Vedam Iyer required only a meal of semolina *upma*. The mustard crackled, the chillies darkened, and as she poured water over the toasted semolina and cashew nuts, the soggy mixture hissed and plopped; she recollected with a stab of pain and excitement her awkward encounter with the visitor. She should not have been so weak; surely by now she should have more self-mastery.

The *upma* was ready. When the whirring of the primus ceased, she could hear them talking. She could have joined them, but the kitchen window was a better place to study the visitor. Whatever it was that provoked him to speak so vigorously, his face was athletic with an energy that made him look more handsome than he had seemed at first. She moved closer to the doorway to catch their conversation.

'Mani writes you gave up a good post to come here, to Kuchchipuram?'

'Yes. I was a lecturer in History at Loyola College, my old college.'

'Loyola? Very sharp, those Jesuits, sharp and crafty. What did you teach?'

'Everything—the Cholas in particular.'

'Great builders of temples they were too. You'll find this district is rich in them. And with such incomparable shrine-myths.'

'Precisely! We have too many myths and too little history. One day I hope to complete my work on the factual histories of these temples, and clear the haze.'

'Facts can obscure vision. They were visionaries, those emperors. Great were the days when the Chola empire spread out across the southern seas.'

'No doubt. The more one dwells on our past the more angry it makes one about the present. It became a terrible let-down daily, after holding forth on the glorious reign of the Cholas, to step into the grime and stink of Madras. I decided it was time I did something about the present.'

'You have your father's zeal. He was a more devout follower of Gandhi than I ever was. He got beaten in the salt-march, you know. If only we had all been more faithful to the spiritual precepts of the Mahatma. *Ahimsa!* Who believes in it now? Sad, really sad!'

Raghavan delayed, leaning well back in his chair; and then lunged forward as if he were re-entering the ring for a second bout.

'I must confess I have little time for Gandhi. Gandhi-cap has ruined Gandhi for me. It sits too easily on mealy-mouthed politicians who spout spiritual waffle at the slightest pretext.'

'True, alas, too true. Still, Gandhi was the last living saint this country has been blessed with.'

'"Saint"? A shrewd politician, strong-willed, no doubt—but "saint"? He was mixed-up like any other, and his sexual guilt drove him to do some very strange things. A very strange saint who slept with his nieces to "test" himself!'

'That? It is much misunderstood. It was a form of *tapas*, penance.'

'Penance? Only a supreme egoist would indulge in such a "spiritual" experiment without any regard to the feelings of the young women. When you consider . . .' Raghavan stopped, seeing that Vedam Iyer was looking into the middle distance. He turned round sharply, and found Aparna listening from the kitchen doorway. When he ceased, she looked up; the pained expression in her face clearly betrayed that his words had disturbed her. Beneath that statuesque beauty, Raghavan saw a vulnerable, hurt child.

*   *   *

'How refreshing to have someone intelligent to talk to in this place!' Vedam Iyer ambled into the kitchen. 'I would have asked him to supper, but thought perhaps next time, to a proper meal.'

'He's gone then.' Aparna placed a plank on the floor for her father. She could have saved herself the bother of livening up the semolina dish with expensive cashew nuts: Vedam Iyer couldn't chew them, and she did not care for *upma*.

'He'll be coming again. He's knowledgeable and interesting. A little outspoken, but that's just young blood talking. I've asked him to join me at the temple to hear Sivaram Pundit. And we must read Kalidasa together. He is keen, just like his father. How we used to swot verses from Kalidasa, instead of reading our law books! It was a sad day when he left great learning to become a school teacher!'

Vedam Iyer sat down and, after a quiet recitation of evening prayers, resumed: 'By the way, Raghavan has offered the Collector's bungalow for your aunt's guests. He is going on tour next week, I believe, and won't be back for a while. That should please your aunt. She can accommodate all her foreigners there. See to the arrangements, my dear. He is expecting you all there on Sunday.'

'Sunday! So soon!'

She wished she had not mentioned her aunt's problem in front of the visitor.

CHAPTER THREE

When Mirza Ghazi plundered Kuchchipuram, he spared the temple of Shiva. Legend has it that, as the Mirza approached the temple, brandishing his sword in the name of Allah and crying *jihad*, he was flooded with light, with such intimations of the mystery of the secret sanctum that he went blind, temporarily. So he had spared the temple and contented himself with mutilating a few *apsaras* on the west *gopuram* and renaming the town 'Ghazipur'—'Ghazipur', before that, 'Koochipuram', the 'city of sticks'. The pariahs and the *sudras* still call it 'Koochipuram' as they gather firewood from the straggly casuarina trees on the slopes of Tillai Hills along the banks of Valli River. 'Ghazipur' did not last either. Light-struck Mirza went crazed and could not tell a *khayal* from a *bhajan*, and so as to drown his sorrows in women and song, kept the booty, and was caught—sniffed out by the shrewd Tiger of Mysore, Tippu Sultan; and the Mirza's nose joined others on the platter that the loyal son sent in tribute to his wily old father, Hyder Ali, in Srirangapatnam.

And soon Mirza Ghazi lost his beloved Ghazipur to the newly-arrived whiteskins. While Captain Clive and Captain Drayton clambered up the muddy banks of Valli River, heaving great guns and carriages, and while soldiers, French from Pondicherry, and English from Cuddalore, fought their way playing hide-and-seek, with muskets and drums in the dark of Tillai jungles, the northern-southern brahmins of Kuchchipuram, the *dikshitars*, held council to save their sacred city. And on *Maha-Sivaratri*, 'the great night of the Lord', from the Thousand-Pillared-Hall of Shiva-Nataraja Temple, they proclaimed: 'Mother Ganga shall save us! The pristine waters of sacred Ganga shall wash away the taint of Islam, ward off the taint of the incoming whiteskins!' So Gangotri water, pure melted ice from the locks of slumbering Himavant, was brought; brass pot upon brass pot, and their lead seals broken in street after street, roof after roof, and the temple washed and cleansed and purified of the taint of Islam, and the taint of the whiteskins sealed off. Believe it or believe it not, Captain Clive and Captain Drayton, who had camped on the outskirts of the town, moved on, trembling with fever, to Devikottai by the sea, where the Pretender, Prince Shaja, awaited them. And with great jubilation, the *dikshitars* renamed the town as 'Kashipuram', and for the white friends of the Pretender it became 'Kashpur'. 'Kashi, Ghazi, Kash—brahmin, mussulman, and *parangi*—what's in a name? The sins of our births and previous births are still with us, here in this "city of sticks", and our lot is the same yesterday, today, and will be the same tomorrow, be it Hindu, Muslim, or *parangi*'—So mutter the poor folk, as they bend over their brooms, swishing them across the outer precincts of Shiva-Nataraja. 'Kuchchipuram! Pure Dravidian! So it shall be!' cried the new politicians of DMK and ADMK. And so it was. Kuchchipuram, before that Kashipuram, Ghazipur, way back Koochipuram, 'the city of sticks'.

'... And what is the forbidden mystery of the secret sanctum? Is there really a mystery?'—Raghavan had risked sounding sceptical when Vedam Iyer filled him in on local lore.

'Oh, yes, there certainly is. And it is a great mystery, hence forbidden to the merely curious.' Vedam Iyer closed his eyes as he spoke. 'A mystery that only a true seeker shall comprehend.' Slowly emerging from his reverie, he gazed at Raghavan to fathom if he were a true seeker. 'You'll find out for yourself. It is best that way. Truth is not for report but for discovery.'

* * *

Today as he sits in his office, facing a work-table loaded with zig-zag piles of files, Raghavan has only reports to confront. In this kingdom of Kuchchipuram he is now the Mogul prince, his minister the portly assistant Krishnamurthy, alias Kittu, and his entourage the elusive chauffeur Kabir, and the ever-obliging peon-cum-gardener, Thambiah. They all treat him with deference, with a great deal of bowing and scraping; but the supply of facts is meagre.

Kittu, dark, heavy and bald, his lips stained red with constant chewing of betel leaves, reminds Raghavan of a sleepy buffalo, serene in neck-deep pond water, only occasionally twitching its tail to ward off besieging flies. For Kittu, who has slipped into middle age without ever discovering youth, the mere effort of moving from his own desk to the Collector's is heroic exertion.

'Here are the files Collector Sir requested. And sir may wish to visit the flood area.' Kittu places in front of Raghavan a well-worn folder, bulging with papers frayed at the edges.

'Tell me, Mr Kittu, all that you know about this case—*all* that you know.' Raghavan pulls the chair forward as if he is about to extract a tooth; getting information from his assistant is not dissimilar.

'They were mostly fisher-folk. Their *bastis* got washed away when the floods came—that is, when they opened Puliyur Dam up west and Valli River here burst her banks at Meyyur.'

'Only Meyyur? Was there any warning beforehand?'

'Who can tell? Some say there was, some, there wasn't. Who can tell? There may have been; but then, there may not have been—difficult to say.'

'The damage must have been considerable.' Raghavan is about to flip open the files, but changes his mind. He must make his assistant a little less vague. 'Mr Kittu! I want to know what *you* think. What is your estimate of the loss?'

'Well, they say the fishermen lost everything—huts, nets, boats—even children got washed away, so they say.'

'What do *you* say?'

Kittu blinks before he answers. 'Me? . . . What I know is what they say.'

'Then you would agree this is a clear case for compensation?'

'Collector Sir, it is not for me to say, sir. It's all in the file, sir.' Kittu bends forward to gently push the file toward Raghavan, adjusting his top-towel as it slips off his shoulder. He straightens up and continues pursing his lips as if he is still feeling inside his mouth for the remnants of betel nuts. 'If I may say, sir, a visit is always recommended in these circumstances. A visit does good.'

'What good, without a clear decision? These people need money.'

'Yes, of course, sir; but nothing can be done yet.'

'Why not? It's a long time since the floods. When was it? August? September? Now it's January.' Raghavan's features grow taut.

'Yes, Collector Sir; but it is difficult to tell who has claim and who hasn't.'

'Difficult? Aren't we here to solve difficulties?' Seeing Kittu flinch, Raghavan relents: 'All right! I'll visit Meyyur. Put it on my tour agenda. —What next?'

'The Minister for Agriculture, Veerappan, is coming to Angambadi, for the by-election.'

'And so?' Raghavan can see another befuddling cloud threaten his perception of facts.

'We are making arrangements for his visit, and he will want Collector Sir to go with him.'

'I am only the Returning Officer, not his lackey. I can't waste my time escorting politicians.'

'With all respect, sir, I wouldn't advise that.'

Raghavan pulls his chair back. Kittu is right, Kittu knows he is right.

Kittu continues in a drone that blends with the whirr of the ceiling fan above. 'It is not easy these days, sir. Politicians expect so much when they come to the district. Vilayat Khan, your predecessor, went everywhere with them. He never failed in that,'—Kittu pauses—'however drunk he was! Moreover, this Veerappan could create trouble with your compensation case, Collector Sir!'

Kittu manages to sound as if the compensation case is a private indulgence of the new Collector, as drinking was of his predecessor—and the minister might spoil the fun.

'The Meyyur case has little to do with by-election politics. It's not even in his area! As far as I can see, it is the right of the people to receive compensation for what they lost.'

'Yes, of course, Collector Sir. But not if they are not the right people!' Kittu grins.

'What do you mean?' —Good thing he didn't lose his temper:

for all Kittu's sleepy demeanour, his assistant is no fool. 'Please explain, and tell me everything you know. —I mean everything that's not in these files.'

'Well, sir, I don't know much, but they say that Aarumugam, you know, the communist member of the Meyyur Panchayat, they say he is moving his people in to agitate for compensation. And they *say*, some are dismantling their huts deliberately. As for lost children, there are evil rumours . . . good money to be got selling organs. We don't know what the truth is, sir.'

Having made a long speech, Kittu grins again. His wide-open, betel-stained mouth reminds Raghavan of a sinister circus-clown. How is an inexperienced young Collector, determined to be professional and progressive, to work with this cross between a clown and a *yali*?

'What else do you know?'

'That's all, Collector Sir. May I be going now?' Kittu looks at the clock on the wall. Portly Kittu, not used to standing for so long, has been distinctly uncomfortable. He casts a weary glance at his seat at the far end of the room, but it is nearly time to go home; his wife will nag if he doesn't do the evening shopping on the way back.

Raghavan realizes that, in his eagerness to extract truth, he has forgotten elementary courtesy. 'Yes, yes, Mr Kittu. Thank you. I am sorry to have kept you standing. And, please, could you send the petitioners away? I'll see the rest on Monday. I have some visitors tomorrow. And do get the peon to pluck some bananas from the garden for your family.'

* * *

'*Truth is not for report but for discovery.*' A wry smile flickered over Raghavan's features, emphasizing their angularity. A fine philosophic quip indeed! What would Vedam Iyer say to this temple dedicated to manilla folders and frayed files?

Raghavan shut the desk and stepped out. All was quiet but for the scrunching sound of trowel on gravelly soil. The peon was busy at the marigolds and snapdragons in the border immediately below the front verandah. Thambiah was proud of his handiwork; so he smiled, and summer-lightning flashed from his pitch-dark face. Raghavan could only manage a grimace in return. The garden, for all its cool green shades, felt like a compression-chamber, and the peon's grin followed his every movement.

He went inside and turned on the radio. An untutored male voice was wailing out, in Dhanyasi Raga: *'Mee-e-e-e-e-na-a-a-a-lochani, O beauteous one with fish-eyes!'* —Why compare female eyes to fish? No, her eyes reminded him of a frightened doe; and they were so luminous, like black grapes newly washed.

He switched the radio off. Her eyes had been moist with the tears she was holding back—surely his words had touched some deep wound. Years ago, when her story had reached Madras—'Poor advocate friend of yours,' so mother had put it to father, 'to be saddled with so young a widowed daughter!'—he had listened and reacted to the tragedy as he would to any newspaper report of a man-made disaster. Her story only served to fan his smouldering anger against the callousness of society. How typical of mother to imply that the girl had somehow brought misfortune on her father! But to see that girl turn flesh and blood, to see so much youth and beauty condemned to a living death by custom and taboo . . . His mind shrank from contemplating her plight, and yet he could think of little else.

How like a goddess she had been in that sea of silk—a bemused goddess, in anguish. Yet there was a serenity about her that spoke of hidden depths. She reminded him of Valli River, whose calm, elegant undulations held unpredictable reserves of energy—so different from the city-bred college-girls he had jostled with in crowded buses. A bunch of predictable butterflies they were, all powder and paint, but brittle as the bangles that they strung along their shapely wrists. It was his misfortune to see through their battery of feminine tricks; and, all too soon, the things that had first attracted, those childish giggles, allusive whispers and postures of studied neglect, simply became wearisome. . . . But here was someone shrouded in mystery, and hiding from him like a hunted gazelle.

He had almost accustomed himself to the belief that he would never meet a woman worthy of courtship. The women he had known as colleagues or students during his lecturing-days fell into two categories: well-upholstered dollies with candy-floss brains, all giggle and pop; or sharp-witted prissy-missies of such sour demeanour that one glance or word from them was enough to quench all passion and romance. If they weren't the kind that lived on a diet of Georgette Heyer and Marie Corelli and mooned after the latest film-idol beckoning to them with outstretched arms from every pillar and post, they were the meek, submissive sort, too well-brought-up in traditional homes to even acknowledge, let alone voice, any feelings—poor dumb sheep prepared for barter in the arrranged-marriage market.

His body and soul yearned for some princess worthy of great passion, a Sita or a Draupadi for whom emperors and young princes might enter the contest, to bend an awesome bow or to pierce with arrows an elusive target; or, better still, a Pandya princess worthy of Chola conquest, whose neck glistened with the sheen of pearls and who was kept jealously guarded by *Yavana* attendants plying palm-fans.

Clunk! A bucket hit the slate floor: Annamma, the maidservant, stood by the door, with her daughter Prema beside, both armed with brooms and tattered, damp rags. 'Can we sweep this room now, sir?'

'Yes, yes, I am just leaving.'

Chauffeur Kabir was polishing the blue Ambassador, casting a furtive glance at him every now and then.

'The car is ready, Collector Sahib! Where shall I take Sahib? There is a new film running at Paradise Cinema—*Desert Moon*, very romantic, lots of song and dance, and Radhika and Kamal too.' Arms folded, a spotted red rag dangling from one hand, Kabir halted before him, with one foot planted slightly forward.

Raghavan found the chauffeur's stance disconcerting: only he could manage to look so deferential and defiant at once. Kabir was amiable enough, the car was maintained well, and he knew the district. He was said to have been close to Raghavan's predecessor; but then Vilayat Khan had needed liquor. Though prohibition was no longer in effect and liquor shops had sprung up in even the sparsest of villages, the northern-southern brahmins, the mighty *dikshitars*, had kept liquor out of city bounds. So Vilayat Khan had needed Kabir, and the chauffeur liked being needed. Raghavan found that irksome.

'Thank you, Kabir, but I won't be using the car this evening. I intend to walk. You may go.'

Kabir snapped the red rag, though there was no dust on it.

His peevishness riled Raghavan. That was the trouble with this country. Everyone behaved as if he were a personal slave. No distinguishing the personal from the professional. Until they learned that, there could be no progress.

As he walked past the disappointed chauffeur, Raghavan relented. 'Is the car fit for the tour? Plenty of driving to do for you soon. There's no point in taking the car to where I am going now.'

'Yes, sir, certainly, sir.' —Kabir, with a ready smile of forgiveness.

Raghavan opened the front gate and stepped on to Old Bridge Road. The bridge was a hardy stone edifice built by the East India Company, and not much in use since the advent of a more modern structure by the railway station further west of the river—that is, not much used by the fast *mofussil* buses and fearsome lorries belching diesel-smoke, but good enough for the fishermen of Meyyur to bring their daily catch to Kuchchipuram market.

Should he turn right or left? To the left lay the route that was becoming daily more familiar, past the police station, the courthouse, the market, and through Flower-Bazaar to East Car Street, a route that inevitably brought him slap against the towering east *gopuram* of Shiva-Nataraja Temple. But according to Vedam Iyer, the westward river-path, though longer, offered a delightful prospect.

Raghavan turned right, towards Old Bridge. He was still seething with ill-defined irritations. He stopped on the bridge and leant over the rugged parapet. The river was majestic in her quietness; in full flood she would no doubt turn into a veritable Kali.

Laughter tinkled across the water; it came from the southern bank, which was a stretch of rich green, lined with groves of coconuts, palmyras, plantains, mangoes, and jack-fruit. A group of women, after their evening bathe, with wet, wrung-out sarees slung over their shoulders, were filling great brass pots with river water. Their dark skins glistened in the evening sun. Who were they? Surely they could do better than that, for drinking water?

Raghavan resisted the impulse to rush down and question them. They would probably giggle, and ignore any lecture on hygiene he might be tempted to deliver.

'*Oi, oi, oi!*' He was startled by a herd of cows, buffaloes, and goats. Cowherds, mere lads of six or seven, were heading home after a day-long spell on Tillai slopes on the northern side of the river. They must have been out all day, sitting idly under the trees, testing their twig-switches on dragon-flies, while the cattle grazed and munched. Almost certainly illiterate. 'Who will mind the herds if the lads go to school?' he could hear the elders protesting. Something must be done to get them to read and write. . . . But first things first. His head might swarm with a thousand and one schemes; but before he could hope to launch any of them, he must first find a way to relax, to quell the nervy restlessness that was sweeping over him ever since he had seen that girl in white, rising from a sea of silk.

He decided to explore his kingdom, beginning with the temple. But where was the river-path?

He approached a cluster of huts nearby that resounded with the clamour of men, women and children round a municipal pump; they were squabbling, clashing and splashing alongside a queue of brass pots, aluminium vessels, and plastic buckets.

'Is this where the river-path to town begins?' A hush fell on the crowd. Raghavan recognized Prema, the maid-servant's daughter. He repeated the question.

She did not reply but gave him a shy smile. More heads appeared in the cavernous doorways of huts.

'*Namaskaram*, Collector Sir!' An old man came forward from the throng. He was vaguely familiar. Emboldened by his presence, the crowd left the pump and clustered round Raghavan. It was beginning to look like an official visit.

'I am looking for the path to town.'

'Oh, to town? The path to town is there!' The old man pointed towards Old Bridge Road. 'That's the way to town.'

'Yes, I know, but I am looking for the river-path.'

'The Old Bridge Road and Market Way is the better way to town. Why walk through here? It will be dark soon.'

Some women giggled. The children looked at Raghavan with great curiosity, as if to say, 'Why, indeed?'

Raghavan wished he had some sweets. He could have dispersed them with dignity. 'Isn't there a river-path?' His tone had become sharper than he intended.

'Ah, the river-path. Collector Sahib wants the river-path, can't you hear?' The old man clapped his hands as he would to chase chickens, and the children scattered. 'Collector Sahib should go through the palmyra grove, and coconut grove, go past the horses of the Aiyanar Temple, and then through Ibrahim's betel-plantation—Ibrahim grows the best drumsticks, and snake-gourds also, but *dorai* must look out for those wily snakes that sometimes hang alongside mimicking the gourds. When *dorai* comes out of the betel creepers, he will see the railway bridge, and that is the sign to turn south and he will soon be in North Car Street.'

Raghavan recalled who the old man was: Velan, the head-potter. He had waited under the mango tree in the bungalow compound, waited all day with a petition to be heard. 'Something to do with river-clay, to sculpt horses for their god Aiyanar; but there's more to it than mere clay'—so Kittu had mumbled, and postponed the hearing.

The old man finished.

'Thank you.'

'That's all right, Collector Sir.'

Making a mental note to reprimand his assistant and speed up the petition, Raghavan headed in the direction of the coconut grove.

CHAPTER FOUR

'But Saturn doesn't look like that. Saturn can't be a god. It is only a planet. I saw on TV.' Seenu can barely wait till they emerge out of the poky, dark 'Shrine of the Nine Planets'.

'Shush, Seenu! You must stop saying things like that. Learn to behave in temple!' Aunt Malini is in no mood for science or theology. She has so much to think about, so many arrangements to make, what with priests, musicians, jewellers, cooks, flower-sellers and so forth, and the wedding only a week away.

'But it's true! Nitya saw it too, when NASA sent a probe past it. Here he sits in a special niche, eating sesame rice! How crazy!'

'Shut up, Seenu! Don't upset mother—and stop jumping about like a monkey with that camera of yours. Look at you, coming to temple like a Japanese tourist.' But it is true: she also has seen Saturn on television.

'Coward! All you can say is "Don't upset mother!" I'll ask Aparna.'

Seenu runs to catch up with Aparna, who is walking ahead with Rukku.

'Aparna! Aparna!! Tell me why we have to do *puja* to this dumb planet!'

How is she to explain the process whereby a far-away planet becomes a god with an evil grip on mortal life? The boy is right. But so also are grandmother and Acharya the family astrologer.

How can they ignore what the planets bode, especially after what happened to her? If only she had not been rushed into a wedding when Mars was dominant, who knows what she might have been spared . . . ?

'Listen, Seenu! According to our ancestors, planets influence lives, and Saturn bodes evil. We don't want any trouble at Nitya's wedding, do we? Today is Saturday, sacred to Saturn. So grandmother has sent us to propitiate him—just a simple *puja*, that's all.'

'I still think it's dumb!'

'Come, come. I can see you are bored. Let's see what we can find. How about an elephant ride?—that's if the temple-elephant likes you. He's rather choosey!'

'I'm not a baby.' Seenu draws himself to his full height. Too true—he is too tall for the elephant.

'Let me think! What about a swim in the temple-tank? But you'll have to be careful. It's very mossy and slippery.'

'Yuk! If I swim in that pea-soup, I'll come out looking like a green monster.'

'—You are a monster already!' Nitya has joined them. Ambling along, they reach the Thousand-Pillared-Hall.

Malini stops. 'Oh, dear! I forgot to pick up the *prasadam*. And the temple-cooks make such good sesame rice, too! —Nitya! Seenu! Wait for me here! —Aparna! Watch them, dear. —Rukku! Take me to the kitchens! No one is to wander off! It's getting late.'

'. . . Wow! What *is* this spooky place? —A set for "Dungeons and Dragons"?' Seenu clicks away with the camera, arrested by the granite magnificence of the Thousand-Pillared-Hall.

Nitya's eyes brighten with mischief. 'Oh, Aparna, do you remember how we used to play hide-and-seek here? We frightened ourselves with our own echoes! Let's have a game. Knowing mother, she'll be *ages*! Come on, Seenu! Let Aparna catch us!' Without further ado, Nitya races up the steps and disappears into the darkness beyond the entrance.

Seenu runs after her, shouting : 'Aparna! You mustn't turn till you have counted to a hundred!'

—What will Aunt Malini say? Dear aunt, so full of bustle and chat! Ever since her arrival, nobody can sit still for a moment, such a whirl of activity she has plunged everyone into.

Father is right, how can one preserve one's equilibrium without detachment—and how can one be detached with Aunt Malini around? And Nitya, so child-like, and Seenu, so impulsive and outspoken—none of them understands what this temple is all about.

Aparna sits on the top step, which is still warm from the day's heat. Her spirits begin to revive as she watches the distant coconut palms sway caressingly over the east *gopuram*. 'The temple is the very body of God, the image of the cosmos he creates, preserves and destroys'—so her father is fond of saying; and how right he is. And how magnificent they look, these vast structures ahead of her: paved pavilions, pillared halls, domed shrines, ranked platforms, extending from the 'womb-house' to the outer corridors, every inch teeming with life! All life is there, at once solid and ethereal, benign and malign, woven in stone, fold upon fold, the rich tapestry of this illusory world. MAYA, no doubt. —Yet how rich the web! Tier upon tier, on the seven-storied gateways, in niches and on walls, in friezes and on stairs, on panelled pillars, and on spiralling domes, wherever the eye lights, in endless variety, there they all are—animal, human, divine! Shiva, Parvati, Ganapati, Kumaran; *devis*, *devas*, rishis rapt in adoration; demons, monsters, crocodiles, swans, elephants, keeping watch; trees, flowers and creepers encircling man, beast and god; and, from amidst this sacred profusion, the dancers fly heavenward, drummers in train! —Yes, fly heavenward, their solid, curvaceous forms seemingly so light, borne aloft in ecstasy! . . . So she too had been borne aloft, in the days before darkness sealed-up her life. Her grace-infused limbs, lithe in rich, golden silk, had curved and twirled, stepped and leapt to the melodies that streamed from the singers; her poised feet, banded with clusters of ankle-bells, had rung out the sorrow and the longing, the joy and the thrill of living, to the beat of drums and the clang of cymbals. But now . . . now she has to be mute, to be calm even as these stone statues are calm; now, she must shake off illusion, discard *'the idle longings of an undisciplined heart'*. . . . What does the *Gita* say? *'Be of steady mind, be still, even as the unflickering candle-flame in a sheltered spot.'*

*   *   *

Aparna shook herself; and following along the band of celestial dancers carved on the elegant *citrakunda* pillars, started looking for her cousins.

The Thousand-Pillared-Hall, dimly lit and exuding a potent smell of grease and burning oil, seemed immense: distorted shadows, now lengthening, now collapsing, enlarged the spaces within. Which way had they gone? If they had gone through the hall to the cloisters by the temple-tank, she could be stuck there searching all evening.

Aparna halted and listened. In the eerie silence, she could sense a presence. Holding her breath, she glided towards the centre of the hall, and there it was—the tell-tale fluttering of a shirt-sleeve against the side of a pillar. Tiptoeing carefully towards her target, she snatched at Seenu's shoulder with her right hand, and swinging round, pinned him by his other arm to the stone.

'Caught you, at last!'

'You certainly have.'

She stopped, paralysed. She was staring at Raghavan.

The blood drained from her arms. She stood transfixed, as though by a hooded cobra about to strike. A thin scar-line on Raghavan's right cheek flickered into a smile. She released his arms as if she were holding red-hot coals. Stepping back, she began wiping her hands on her saree repeatedly, all the while talking fast: 'I'm sorry. I was looking for my cousins. We were playing hide-and-seek. I thought it was Seenu—he too is tall. They must be here somewhere, still hiding. Seenu was bored, and it was Nitya's idea.' She stopped peering round the columns, and looked at him with reproach. 'Usually, no one comes here at this time.'

Raghavan straightened. He had been leaning against the pillar, one foot tucked behind him and his back arched, in an effort to decipher an inscription overhead—it was an extremely awkward position in which to be caught and pinioned. His back smarted.

'I was retracing the steps of our Saivite poet-saint, Shekkilar, who, I believe, composed his *Periya Puranam* here, in this very hall.'

'Him? —It's Father who knows all about Saivite poets and Chola kings.' Aparna wiped her brow and continued in a hectic tone: 'But did you know that Shekkilar received his opening phrase here: "*Ulakelam*", "In all the world"? —From one of these pillars? A divine voice spoke to him from a pillar. I wonder *which* pillar!' She looked around and, cupping her palms, sang out the phrase in a lilt: *'Ula-ke-lam.* —What an echo! How could anyone have followed his recital, with so much echo? Now the other hall, Nrittya Sabha, the Hall of Dance—have you seen it?'

'No, not yet.'

'That is different. Not so big as this, but no echo. You can hear a dancer's ankle-bells, clear and round. The great Balasaraswati has danced there, did you know?'

'No, I didn't.' He found it amusing, this diversionary tactic of hers, so typically feminine: she was flooding him with information, determined to erase what had happened. His arms were still throbbing from her fierce assault.

Seeing him smile, she stopped. 'I should be going.'

'Please don't. Do go on. Tell me more, I need a guide, to see this at its best. Don't stop. Please.'

'I don't know much, really. —What was I saying? Oh, yes. Balasaraswati came and performed when they re-dedicated the Hall after it was restored. You should have seen her, she's the queen of dancers—every tiny movement so full of *bhava*, such soulfulness, that everyone was in tears.' Her eyes grew bright with recollection. She paused, and then turned to him with child-like candour. 'But why am I bothering you with all this? Father tells me you are a scholar.'

'Did he? That's a bit of an exaggeration. I am compiling a history of Chola temples. I'd heard about these inscriptions. Kulottunga Chola II—or is it III? There's some dispute among historians.'

'I'm no use with inscriptions. You'll have to ask father. Did he tell you about the secret of the sanctum?'

'He didn't tell me what it was. He said I should discover it for myself. I've tried, but the sanctum was shut. So I came here.'

'You must go during a *puja*, especially a festival *puja*, then you'll see and hear . . .'

'Hear?'

'Yes, hear the music for the divine dance, and then . . .' Her face became still and shiny, like a pond covered by water-hyacinth.

'And then?' Raghavan asked in a gentler tone, sensing that she had entered some trance of memory.

'And then you see him . . .'

'Him? Who?'

'Why, Lord Nataraja! At Arudra Festival. It's cold, the priests bring out the two of them, Lord Shiva and his consort, they're so glorious in their floral palanquin, and . . . and for all his matted hair and snakes and tiger-skin and skulls, Shiva is serene, gentle, not at all terrifying. Then the musicians arrive and the bathing begins: the god is bathed right here, and the *music* . . . well,

> "*Out of the silence, the drumbeat and music,*
> *Out of the music, the dance and the dancer.*"

The dancer is the one they call Swayambhu, "Himself", the "formless one". . .'

He watched her. There was something in her trance-state that disturbed him.

'You seem almost at home here.'

'I grew up here, more or less. Mother used to bring me almost every day, and during festival time, I often woke up in the temple at night. Then my guru brought me here, to study and learn those dance-postures that are carved on the east *gopuram*. The temple is like a second home—that is, if I don't count grandma's . . .' Shaking her head free of reminiscences, she gave him a surprised look, and abruptly weaved her way out. Raghavan followed her.

She rushed down the temple steps.

'—*There* you are! What took you so long? We gave up.' Nitya's voice dropped to a whisper. 'And who's *that*?'

'That is the new Collector.'

'Call me Raghavan, *please*!' There was a distinct sharpness in his voice: after all that talk, how dare she make him seem a mere official!

'—Oh? Mr Raghavan! We are very fortunate to meet you here.' Aunt Malini was beaming. 'It is very kind of you to let us have your bungalow for our wedding guests. I have so many coming, the bridegroom's family, friends from abroad, I was worrying so much about where to put them all, they are so used to comfort, and in this town, do you think I could find anywhere decent? Then Aparna brings me the good news, you are so kindly giving us the bungalow. This is my daughter Nitya who is getting married, this my son Seenu, he is having sacred-thread ceremony, and this,' Malini added as an afterthought, 'is Rukku. What would we all do without Rukku? —Pardon me, here I am chattering, while the storm-clouds are about to burst upon us. What *shall* we do? No umbrellas with us.'

They had reached the east gate. Raghavan stopped and turned to the women. 'Please wait. I think I can help.' He had spotted Kabir, nonchalantly leaning against the blue Ambassador as he chatted to Muniya, the cobbler under the peepul tree. So his chauffeur had been tailing him: this effrontery of driving around in the office-car without his superior's knowledge must be nipped in the bud.

But the pleasures of gallantry won out against the urge to discipline Kabir. 'My car is here. The driver can take you all home.'

'—Collector Sahib! I see the thunder-clouds. I bring the car for Sahib. And I see Sahib's shoes under Muniya's tree.' Kabir grinned, feeling that his mission had been a total success.

'I see. Take these ladies to Vinayak Street, and come back for me.' Already, the line he had hoped to maintain between professional and private was breaking down.

'Yes-sir.' Kabir jumped towards the car. Seenu leapt into the driver's seat and started inspecting the vehicle. Malini and Nitya got in. Rukku hesitated, but seeing that Raghavan was holding the other door open for her, she felt emboldened to get in also. Raghavan looked back towards Aparna; but she waved him aside.

'Not me, thank you. I am waiting for father. The discourse will be starting soon.'

Aunt Malini put her head out of the window. 'Be early tomorrow morning, Aparna. —Thank you, Mr Raghavan. It is very kind of you.'

'That's all right. I'll send the car round in the morning. It's a long walk to the bungalow.'

A group of women, old and young, pushed past him towards the temple door, hurrying to get to various shrines with offerings of coconuts, bananas, betel leaves and flower-garlands. Raghavan lost sight of Aparna. When she came back into view, she seemed absorbed in studying the sculptured dancers on the *gopuram* wall; he could not decide whether she was reminiscing, or just avoiding conversation.

'—There you both are!' Vedam Iyer's ringing voice cleared the way. He strode towards them, his forehead shining with sacred ash. 'Raghavan, what a pleasure! I am glad, very glad. Have you been seeing the temple? Looks like rain, doesn't it? Let's go in, it's nearly time for the discourse to start. I like to get a good seat without any pillars blocking my view. Come, Aparna! How was the Saturn-*puja*? Have they gone, your aunt and family?'

'Yes, father.'

'Good! That's good. Now to the real things of life. As I say, *bhakti*-yoga, devotion, in the morning, *karma*-yoga, work, during the day, and *jnana*-yoga, knowledge, in the evening—that is my philosophy! What do you say to some *jnana* now, Raghavan?' Vedam Iyer's face crinkled with laughter.

'Most certainly.'

They could hear the instruments tuning up for the invocatory song. As he accompanied father and daughter to the Hall of Dance, Raghavan felt a twinge of envy.

—How good it must feel to have life so tidily ordered!

—Would he ever attain to such clarity of vision?

—And should he, after all?

CHAPTER FIVE

'Good looking, isn't he, in a gaunt sort of way?' Nitya, sitting with her knees drawn up, can observe her cousin in the oval mirror.

Aparna is combing Nitya's hair. Her face is set. She is determined to straighten Nitya's springy curls so as to make her plait long. Soon it will have to be sewn up in a shield of *pandanus* petals. Two years ago, when it was her turn to be a bride, Aparna herself had submitted to such ministrations; sister-in-law Meena had cajoled her into obedience with much laughter and love. It had been torture to be weighted down for days by a stiff, prickly plait; but she had borne it so that her hair could be impregnated with the sweet perfume which the yellow petals gave out as they wilted and browned. Ah, the *perfume!*—it had lingered on for weeks: she could catch an unexpected whiff even after her kumkum had been wiped off and her bangles broken to usher in widowhood. . . . Now it is Nitya's turn to grow heady with excitement; and, understandably, she is restive as a colt about to bolt.

Aparna prods the small of Nitya's back to make her sit upright.

'Ouch! You are hurting me! What is wrong?'

'Nothing. You *must* keep still.'

'—Well? Don't you agree?'

'Agree with what?'

'That he is handsome, the Collector—what's his name?'

'Raghavan.'

'It must be the scar on his cheek that makes him look so severe. Did you notice how his face changes when he smiles? You didn't let on you knew him.'

'I *don't* know him. He called to see father, offered to help your mother. That's all.'

'Oh!' Nitya smiles indulgently. 'He did seem keen to help.'

'Why not?' The comb gets stuck. Aparna frowns as she disentangles the knot.

'Come on. You know what I mean.'

'What *do* you mean?' Aparna stops and looks up, her head erect, her lips quivering slightly.

Nitya stops smiling. 'Sorry. I shouldn't tease you. I forget.'

Aparna resumes plaiting. 'Now tell me about your Kumar. You haven't given much away. Where did you meet him? What's he like?'

'You won't believe this. It wasn't at all a romantic meeting, in that ski-lodge café. I had gone with my college friends, and he with some chaps from his computer centre. You know, they work in this computer-ghetto in the middle of the desert, and escape every now and then to civilization. Anyway, there I was, having twisted an ankle on the very first day, hobbling about with a crutch, and scouring the menu, then who should walk in, also bandaged up to the neck, as it were, but Kumar! We just looked at each other and burst out laughing. Until then, I had felt such a fool. Somehow, he made me laugh, and everyone else seemed foolish.'

'—Where shall I put this *thalambu*?' Rukku walks in with a basketful of neatly-cut segments of *pandanus*.

'What have you been doing, Rukku? Your hands!' Nitya's eyes widen with astonishment.

'Grinding the henna for you. Not bad, is it?' Rukku spreads out her palms; they are dyed a reddish-orange.

Aparna turns round to inspect. 'Good quality, it seems, going by your colour.' When she undertook to beautify Nitya, she had forgotten how easily henna stained, and how long-lasting the effect was. *Her* hands would go the same colour—and to flash the vermilion hands that signify auspiciousness would no doubt be seen as offensive. Her memories were painful enough, without provoking comment from the elders.

'I think, Nitya, that *Rukku* ought to apply the henna to your hands.'

'Why?'

Before she can think of an excuse, Seenu bursts in. 'Come on, chatterboxes. Mother can't wait all day. Kabir is here.'

'Since when have you become so concerned about mother? What are you up to?'

'The Collector's chauffeur is a great guy. He's going to give me driving lessons.'

'Driving lessons! Seenu!', Nitya and Aparna cry in unison.

'Oh, please, Nitya! Please, Aparna! Don't dob me in. Kabir says it is safe near Old Bridge Road. Please don't spoil the fun. This is such a boring dump. It's all right for you, all this fuss.'

'Shouldn't you be with the pundits or something?'

'Not *that* drivel! I don't believe in all that nonsense.'

'But you can't escape.' Nitya sounds gleeful.

'—Children, children! Stop arguing.' Aunt Malini puts her head round the door, as she re-arranges the folds of her saree. 'Nitya! When are you going to grow up? Always fighting with your brother, and he so much younger than you!'

'Yes, mother. Tell her. She is always picking on me. Wait till I tell Kumar what a shrew he's marrying!'

'Don't you dare!' Wrenching herself free from Aparna, Nitya races after her brother, who has dashed through the door.

'I hope marriage settles that girl. She's such a tomboy.' Aunt Malini sighs philosophically. 'Come, Aparna! Let's go. Get a pen and paper! We must list everything we need. I like being methodical, nothing like method, I say. Now where are those two? Fooling around at a time like this! I'll be glad when their father arrives. I've so much to do, and he's never there when I need him. There's not a moment to lose. I am so busy, I couldn't even shut my trap to keep a fly out!' Aunt Malini sighs again, tucking-in the re-arranged folds of her saree and pleased with the effect.

Seenu is already in the car. Kabir holds the door open.

Aparna hesitates. It is tempting to find an excuse not to go.

'What's the matter, Aparna? Are you not feeling well?' Nitya looks troubled.

'Oh, nothing . . . just a headache. I am ready.' Aparna can feel her body tensing with vague fears as she gets into the car.

Why should she feel apprehensive about meeting him again? After all, what had happened at the Thousand-Pillared-Hall was an accident. What if she *had* grabbed him so? She didn't have to tremble with shame at the memory. It was a simple mistake, nothing but a mistake, a trifling folly, not a crime . . .

But however hard she tried to beat her thoughts into order, they returned, mocking her: fragments of that conversation throbbed in her head, a word or a phrase breaking loose, only to stab and sting with renewed force. 'Caught you' . . . 'You certainly have!'—'Caught you'—'You certainly have!': the exchange was still ringing in her ears, making them burn hot. Whatever had possessed her to chatter on? All those months of disciplined effort, keeping dangerous thoughts at bay, had just buckled under the surprise. During the pundit's discourse . . . —but *that* was sheer vanity, to think that his eyes were upon her simply because her back felt hot—though she had not turned round once. He was sitting behind, with father and the other men; and from what father had said, he had been intent on the discourse.

'—Here we are, already. Still distant enough from the temple for a good long pre-wedding procession.' Aunt Malini bubbles with joy as she sights the neat white bungalow nestling among lofty *ashoka* trees. 'Look, Nitya! Just what we need, a big garden for the reception—and there's Mr Raghavan waiting for us.'

The more Aunt Malini sees of the bungalow, the more it gives her the right feeling. With those verandahs so elegantly closed at the sides in bamboo and thatch—little tea-parlours they must have been—she can tell at once that only the British could have built it.

'This bungalow stands on the site where Captain Clive camped,' Raghavan explains, as they follow him from room to room, '—long before he ever dreamt of becoming Governor-General. It was built at the turn of the century by an eccentric Indologist, half-English, half-German: Franz, or *Frank* Mueller spent most of his time in the river—right in the middle of it. You can imagine what the village folk said. "Why does this white sahib want to stand in that mud and silt, digging, when he has servants? He must be mad to pick up broken bits of pottery and glue them together, when he could have brand-new pots from Velan." That's exactly what Velan, the head potter, said himself, until he found out about the money to be made from Roman remains. He became Mueller's assistant. I hear Velan is a fund of stories about the illustrious Mueller. Poor Mueller died of cholera, and the villagers believe it was Valli River's revenge.'

Raghavan is in high spirits, full of that affability and easy conversation which Aunt Malini finds so lacking in these parts. Raghavan addresses her all the while, occasionally directing a word or two to Nitya. Aparna is relieved to be spared.

They are back in the central hall. '—That's all. Whatever is here is at your disposal. I am leaving on tour on Thursday.'

Aunt Malini's face crumples. 'But, Mr Raghavan, *surely* you are not going to miss Nitya's wedding?' The thought of her eminent guest not being present when all her foreign friends are on show is too much to bear.

'I'll try not to. When is the wedding? Sunday? I may get back by then. —Here comes Thambiyah, my peon. He looks after everything.'

Thambiyah shuffles in with a tray of drinks. He is delighted both with the Collector's guests, and at the prospect of wedding festivities at the bungalow. So, without being ordered, he has prepared sherbet for them all.

Raghavan hands the sherbet round. 'The peon is also the gardener. If you need anything, just ask him.'

'Thank you, this sherbet is most welcome. It's getting hot again. The garden looks cool. What do you say, Nitya, which side should we use?' Aunt Malini steps out to admire the roses, the snapdragons, the hibiscus, and, especially, the crotons, as Thambiah points them out. '—Madam likes my garden? I like garden. Wet or dry, hot or cold, I am always here.'

'Plants need a lot of caring. Do you talk to them? I do. My window-box of geraniums is a picture! Your master is lucky to have a gardener who cares.'

'Collector Sahib? He is too busy to notice flowers and fruit.'

'Well, you make excellent lemon-sherbet.' Aunt Malini sips the last drops, and hands him the empty glass.

'Lemons grown with my own hands, too!' The grinning peon shuffles closer.

'No doubt, no doubt.' Aunt Malini draws herself up; she mustn't let the peon get above his station. 'I am very busy. No time for chit-chat. Show me the rest.'

As she surveys bungalow and garden, with the peon in attendance, Aunt Malini feels possessed by the spirit of the place. Her voice grows imperious as a memsahib's. 'Aparna! Go through the house and note what supplies we need. A list, I need a *list*. Nitya! Come and help me decide where to put the dais and awning for the reception-concert.'

'Coming, mother.' Nitya finishes her sherbet slowly. She mutters, out of earshot of her mother: 'Why bother? I'm not interested. Aparna won't perform.'

Nitya's parting shot cuts Aparna to the quick.

The moment she is gone, Raghavan turns to Aparna. The sparkle of the gracious host subsides. '. . . Your cousin seems upset.'

Aparna looks away. 'She shouldn't be. She can be a petulant, spoilt child, sometimes. She knows why I can't do what she wants.'

'Are you so sure? I haven't forgotten what you said in the Thousand-Pillared-Hall. It can't be easy, giving up that which matters to you most.'

'It's not.' She faces him. 'I am too weak. That's what makes me angry.'

'You have great cause to be angry; but surely not with *yourself*.'

'What's the use? Anger just wrecks one's peace of mind.'

'Quite the contrary. Anger can be a good thing, when it has a justified target. If we cease to be angry, we cease to live. Do you recall what the pundit said yesterday?'

'He didn't say *that*,' Aparna retorts.

'Yes, you are right. The pundit didn't say that—he should have; but the poet Valmiki *did*. It was a master-stroke of his to trace the source of poetic inspiration to primeval anger. I like the idea of his poetic gifts being discovered through cursing. According to the pundit, it was the volley of curses which Valmiki let loose against the hunter who had killed the love-birds that set him writing his great epic. How did he put it?—"So, by the river, the world's first poetry was born, from pity and anger".'

'It *is* moving, the beginning of the *Ramayana*.'

'"Moving"? The pity is a sop, while we are being brain-washed. We are invited to condone Rama's heartless behaviour towards his wife because of a *dhobi's* gossip, even though she has gone through fire to prove her innocence. We are to applaud his adherence to *dharma*! What kind of *dharma* is it that cloaks such cowardly barbarity?'

'. . . There was a time when I too used to get passionate about

Sita's plight. Now I no longer do. Now I understand why Rama acted as he did.'

'I can't see why. Tell me.'

'No just ruler can dispense with *dharma*; and *dharma* needs detachment.' Aparna throws her head back. 'Surely that's the case, whether one is an Emperor or a Collector?'

It was a challenge. *Snakes and ladders*. Just as you reach the top, there lurks the giant serpent. Raghavan feels as though he has slithered right down its throat . . . *How* is he, and *who* is he, to call in question her resignation, even if he dares? What can she do but seek detachment, beat a dignified retreat from a world where society condemns her to an unhallowed existence? Is his protest any more than arm-chair rage, something thousands before him have indulged in, and thousands will . . . ? What could he say to her that would not trivialize?

'I'm sorry.'

'There's no need to be sorry.' This time Aparna is quick. 'It's I who ought to apologize, for my foolish behaviour yesterday.'

One small ladder—and he feels he might surface from the pit. 'Ah!' Taking time, he rolls up his sleeves and, with an air of seriousness, examines his arms. 'See the bruises? You could have maimed me!'

'I *am* sorry. I had no idea!' She is overcome with confusion.

Raghavan unrolls his sleeves, laughing. 'Don't be alarmed. I'm all right. Perhaps you'll tell me more, some day.'

'More? As it is, I wish I hadn't talked so much . . .' She wishes Aunt Malini and Nitya would hurry. 'I must make my inventory.'

'By all means. Anything I can do to help?'

'No.' One might almost think he was pursuing her, the way he talks. But she mustn't give way to silly notions. He knows who she is, *what* she is. He is being polite, merely polite and good-humoured, that's all. —Where *are* they, Aunt Malini and Nitya? — Oh, *why* did she come?

A crash and a bang, and Nitya's voice in the next room: 'Oh, dear! . . . Aparna! Mr Raghavan! Look what I've done!'

They rush to the door, narrowly missing each other. Raghavan holds back to let her through.

Nitya is sitting on the floor, clutching her toes. 'I am so sorry, Mr Raghavan. I shouldn't have run. I tripped over a box or something and knocked all these off your desk. I *am* sorry.'

'Don't worry about the papers, Miss Nitya! I hope you are not hurt.'

'No, just my toes.'

'It's *my* fault. I should have removed these boxes. They are my books and research papers, waiting to be unpacked.'

'Oh, let me help.' Nitya starts clearing the floor. Aparna joins her.

Raghavan watches them with amusement. 'You are both so quick. I am hopeless. I can tidy everything else, except my own things.'

'Look at these, Aparna! —What are they, Mr Raghavan? They look creepy.' Nitya gathers up a sheaf of black-and-white photographs. Horned heads protrude from a vast expanse of water: dead buffaloes float with their bloated bellies up, their blank eyes staring at clear, bright skies.

'The aftermath of the Meyyur floods.' Raghavan takes them from her, and spreads them out on the desk.

Aparna, still down on her knees and gathering scattered papers, looks up. 'I remember the floods last year when Valli River burst her banks. She was magnificent. So much energy! So wonderfully terrifying! And such expanses of water, that it was as though the final dissolution had come!'

She rises and comes to the desk. 'Aren't they eerie, these scenes? And beautiful?' There is a strange glee in her eyes.

Raghavan cuts in sharply. 'Beautiful as *photos*, yes. But the reality wasn't. I am hoping to arrange full compensation for the victims—but it is very hard to get at the facts. The stories differ, depending on who I talk to.'

Aparna sobers up. 'Have you talked to the padre?'

'The padre?' —*Snakes and ladders*. It is ladder-time once again.

'Yes, the padre at St Joseph's Church. You should speak to him. He knows the Meyyur people. They used to come to him, even to the church school. I have seen them sitting outside the school-gate, all hunched up in rags, waiting for him.'

'That's odd. My assistant Kittu didn't even mention this padre.'

'Maybe he thinks the padre is a communist. A lot of people do. Not everyone likes him.'

'Do you?'

'I don't know him well. Father believes he's a menace. But I've heard good things too. I sometimes help at my old school. He is Correspondent there.'

'—Where are you all?' Aunt Malini waddles in, escorted by a subdued Thambiah. '—Aparna! You must come at once and look at the back of the bungalow. Just by the well, I am finding the right place for the cook's tent. We *must* keep a cook here. We can't keep sending coffee, *idli*, and whole *thalis* of food all the way from Vinayak Street. You agree? —Oh dear! It's past eleven o'clock. We musn't keep Mr Raghavan waiting on us all morning. He is very kind.'

'That's all right.'

'There's nothing much in your kitchen. Why don't you come back with us, and have a proper meal? Then you can meet their grandmother also. You *must* meet her.'

Raghavan looks towards Aparna. 'Thank you. But I have some urgent work to do. I've just heard something that might prove the very lead I'm looking for.' —If he left soon, he might catch the padre after Sunday service. First, he must thank her—but how? What was he to call her? 'Miss Aparna' would sound strange: she wasn't a 'miss', not in any sense. 'Mrs . . .'—*what*? He didn't even know her dead husband's name. He could ask, but then he would have to call her by that man's name. It might be an unpleasant name; and surely it would stir up unpleasant memories.

While Aunt Malini gives further instructions to Thambiah, Nitya breaks loose and races towards the car. A game of chess is in progress on the car-bonnet. She peers over Seenu's shoulder, who lays his finger on her lips.

Raghavan joins Aparna on the steps. 'Thank you for that suggestion. I am going to see the padre right away. And . . . I have a petition for you. Will you listen?'

'Yes?'

'Don't refer to me ever again as "the Collector". My name is Raghavan. —And may I call you "Aparna"?'

She looks into the distance as she speaks. 'I must go. They are waiting.'

CHAPTER SIX

'Stop, Kabir! Stop right here!'

Raghavan lurched to one side as Kabir pulled the car up by the level-crossing.

'But Collector Sahib, there's still a long way to St Joseph's Church. The road is rough, but I can manage.'

'Road? It's only a dirt-track, not fit for even a bullock-cart, let alone this new car. You wait for me here. I'll walk.'

'Yes, sir.' Kabir yawned. The Sahib was right. But there was nothing to do here; if he watched the steel-tracks glistening in the heat too long, his eyes would hurt. As soon as Raghavan was a safe distance away, Kabir donned his sun-glasses and pulled out an ancient copy of *Filmfare* that he kept reserved for emergencies such as this.

Raghavan set out on the winding track that formed a causeway among the paddy-fields, connecting the railway-line to an island of trees in the distance. But for the white bell-tower rising from amidst the palmyras, he would not have guessed that there was any human habitation there, so thick was the vegetation.

How would this padre receive him? Would he find what he needed to know? 'Not everyone likes him,' she had said. . . . Would *he*? A steamy heat-haze rose from the paddy-fields, bearing aloft an oppressive blend of odours: mud, dung and rotting reeds. The sun was almost above him; it was no time for a stroll through the countryside.

Raghavan shrugged his shoulders to free himself from the damp shirt that clung to him. His heart was pounding as it had when, as a young lad, a mere stripling of a brahmin boy with sacred thread, he had taken the short-cut to the village school through forbidden *bastis* of pariahs. But these people were surely not all pariahs. What were they? Churches in Madras he could handle: colonial relics that Anglo-Indians kept going. It had been fun teasing the proselytizing Jesuits on the electric trains. But what would he find here, in this country outpost? . . . It was too late to turn back.

A cool breeze greeted him as he approached the shady grove. The harsh white glare of the noonday-sun softened to a myriad bronze beams. It streamed through the emerald-green banana palms with their pale yellow scrolls of tendrils; the light acquired a coppery glow as it filtered through sticky-soft, young mango leaves. Raghavan's doubts began to subside.

St Joseph's Church had no architecture to boast of. A squat, whitewashed, rectangular structure with an ageing coconut thatch that had seen many monsoons, the church reminded Raghavan of his village school. And as he climbed up the steps leading to the front-entrance, over which hung faded mango-leaf festoons and crêpe-paper chains, he felt very much an unwelcome school-inspector.

Service was still in progress. The padre, a dark man in his late forties, small and bird-like, was in full flow—his sing-song voice, now rising, now falling, not loud, but always emphatic:

'. . . By all means enjoy *pongal*-festival! Bring the harvest in, decorate your cows and bulls, your calves and buffaloes, with sandalwood-paste and kumkum-powder! But remember: *pongal* is only a harvest festival, and you are the harvest our Lord comes to harvest! You are the new creation! The grass grows, it flourishes and withers, but you are made for everlasting life! Celebrate *pongal*, rejoice in the harvest, for the Lord feeds us with good things, and it is right that we should thank the Lord; but never forget the everlasting bread that no *pongal* can give! Beware! When the sheaves are gathered, the chaff is thrown into the everlasting fire. For you, Jesus gives new life; and new life you must proclaim. You must show your Hindu neighbours what new life means. They boast of many gods; but their eyes are blind, their ears are stopped, their hearts are darkened, for they know not our Lord Jesus . . .'

Suddenly, the padre leant over the lectern and fixed his eyes on a scrawny youth in his twenties. 'And you, Raju! Do you know what they tell me? Why they made you a policeman? Well, *do* you? I'll tell you why. Because you are a Christian, for Christians, they say, are honest, reliable. *Are* you? You are a Christian, you are a new man, and you must show it is true. If you cheat, if you take bribes as they do, you are bringing disgrace not just on yourself and on your forefathers, but on all of us Christians here, and on our Lord Jesus Christ. May the Lord forgive you!'

Heads turned towards the unfortunate Raju, whose large eyes, rolling in dismay at being so hounded, rested on the visitor by the door, pleading to be rescued; all eyes followed him. The padre wiped his brows and, adjusting his stole, joined his congregation in inspecting the intruder.

There was only one way to dislodge himself from so many silent, staring eyes: Raghavan took off his shoes, and walked in.

Middle-aged men on a bench along the wall moved to make room, nodding their heads in approval. Someone handed him a *Book of Lyrics*. The padre cleared his throat and resumed the sermon. More on 'new life', and on the 'old leaven' in government offices. The sermon frequently turned into a quiz in which a group of modish youths sitting on the floor participated energetically, shouting out the right texts: 'Ezekiel!'—'Corinthians!'—'Math*the*yah . . . !'

Alien words. Alien faith. But nothing alien about the faces. Some were familiar from the jostling crowds of Flower-Bazaar. There was Mr Samuel from the railway colony, with his fair-skinned Anglo-Indian wife; he had been quick to call on the

Collector. Those sleek-haired young men who, with a harmonium, *tabla* and guitar, formed the orchestra and choir, must surely be the activists Mr Samuel had warned about. There was no mistaking the sober, stern matrons, clad in stiffly-starched pale-coloured sarees, who asserted their middle-class superiority by occupying the benches on the far side—without question, they were teachers from the church school.

But it was the motley crowd seated on +loured straw mats on the floor who absorbed his attention. By their sturdy biceps and sinewy backs, half-bare, he could tell that they be-longed to the land. Some of them were women from the group he had seen by the river. There was clearly a tacit dividing-line between the benches and the floor. Directly under the padre's observation was a cluster of care-free teenage beauties. Distracted and distracting, in their bright half-sarees, bold kumkums, long, oiled plaits dangling with yards of flowers, they were no different to the girls he had seen at the temple—could they be catechumens? Despite the padre's stern looks, and the fiery frowns of the bench of matrons, the girls were nudging each other and suppressing giggles as they peeped at the visitor from under their shared lyric-books.

As soon as the service had finished, the padre came over to Raghavan, who was trying to recover his shoes from an assortment by the door. Raghavan extended a hand: 'District Collector Raghavan.'

The padre greeted him, palms together in traditional fashion. '*Namaskaram*, Collector. Padre Yesudasan. We are honoured. Such a surprise.'

'May we talk, somewhere quiet?' Raghavan looked uneasily at the men, women and children hovering behind the padre and eyeing the new Collector in fear and wonder.

'Excuse me a moment.' The padre went over to Mr Samuel and whispered something, then darted back into the crowd. 'No more lingering now. Be back at sundown, all of you—we must get ready for the bishop next week.'

He rejoined Raghavan. 'A lot of christenings next week. And the bishop is only on a whistle-stop tour! Still, our people always give him a grand welcome. I am sorry to keep you waiting. Let's go to my house. It is that hut behind those oleanders.'

Raghavan could sense that the padre was on guard; he must somehow gain his confidence. 'This is only an informal visit.'

'As the Lord said to Abraham . . . ?' The padre looked up with a suspicious twinkle.

'"The Lord"? . . . Oh, I see. No, no sacrifices demanded.' Raghavan laughed. 'I am just a Collector trying to do my job. I am looking into the compensation-case for the Meyyur flood victims. I heard . . .'

But before he could proceed, the padre grabbed him by the sleeve. '"COMPENSATION"? Did you say "com-pen-*sa*tion"? Did I hear right?'

Gathering up his robe like a skirt, he ran back towards the few lingering by the church. 'Eh! Muniya, Raju, An–tho–ny! Whoever there is, whatever you are doing, come at once! Bring the Collector a fresh green coconut! Such a hot day! To think of it, *compensation* at last!'

As they approached the hut, he explained: 'Pardon me! You see, Mr Raghavan—I hope you don't mind me calling you Mr Raghavan—you see, for the government, Meyyur is just a "problem", just one more of those natural disasters. What are they doing about it? Nothing much. Just a few token hand-outs, a bag of rice here, a few old blankets and rags there, and a visit from some big-wig to console the poor! —Pardon me! I have nothing against visits. I visit people all the time. But to treat Meyyur floods as natural disaster, as if that's what it was—who are they fooling? But, I heard you saying "compensation". That is the first time I am hearing the right word in all these months. At last there is someone recognizing the people's rights.'

'"People's rights"? One moment, padre!' Raghavan had become alarmed at the speed with which the padre was adopting him as champion of the people. 'The issue is by no means as clear-cut. I'll be blunt. There's talk of communist agitation.'

'That's just slander,' said the padre quickly.

'Are you sure? Can you prove it?'

'Meyyur has its share of mischief-makers. The poor suffer.'

Raghavan believed him—he *wanted* to believe him: justice should not be choked by half-truths. 'That's why I am here. I need facts so that I can sift the facts from fiction. I need names, reliable identifications. I am told you know the Meyyur people. I must meet them. I mean the *right* people!'

Raju brought in two green coconuts, sliced them at the top, put straws in and handed them to the padre and the Collector. As they sipped the refreshing juice, the padre grew solemn. Raghavan began to regret puncturing his exuberance.

The padre waited till they had finished the drink, then spoke quietly: 'Please come in. I want you to see something.'

They passed through an outer room which served as an office, and entered an inner room. It was furnished with a camp-cot and a table. In one corner of the room stood a massive crucifix, rough-hewn, gnarled and dented: it bore no marks of carpentry.

'I call it my carbuncular cross: made of driftwood, a souvenir from the floods. One day, when we rebuild our lost church, this will be housed there. Meanwhile, I live with it here.'

The padre pulled out a trunk from under the cot, and, squatting on the floor, took out a bundle. 'Taking photos is an obsession with me. I was a journalist before I became a priest.' He put them on the bed. 'Here are the people: the *right* people you are looking for. I took these when we built St Andrew's for the fishermen of Meyyur. There they are, your *right* people. Dead now.'

Raghavan confronted a throng of weather-worn faces lined up in front of a white-washed hut. They were smiling.

The padre's eyes grew dim as he continued: 'St Andrew's is no more, washed down the river along with the fishermen and their huts. Down, down they went, the church with her people.' He wiped off a tear.

Was he mourning for the building, or for his congregation? Raghavan dismissed the suspicion as unworthy, and continued looking through the photos: surrealist scenes of devastation; tree trunks, branches with tangled bodies of cows and buffaloes jostling with pots and pans and broken beds on vast expanses of water; wizened old men and women, their faces frozen in terror, clinging to branches protruding from amidst the floating debris— as were kites, carrion-crows and vultures.

Some scenes were familiar. 'I have seen these photographs before.'

'Good! Are they still there? I feared your assistant might have dumped them. I sent them—that was when I still hoped to persuade the authorities. I needn't tell you; nothing happened. You see, Collector, I can identify the dead. It's the living who need help.'

The padre rose from the floor. They stood facing each other. Raghavan met the padre's gaze. 'I'll see what I can do.'

'That's good. I believe you can.'

The padre cleared the bed. As he returned the bundle to the trunk, he pulled out an album.

'Now, this is what I call my "good-news folder". You see, Meyyur was a beautiful village before the floods. The river went berserk so suddenly, with no warning. The next thing we knew, Meyyur was no more. MEYYUR! What a name! "Truth-place". It was a village full of peacocks. Come to think of it, Meyyur could be a corruption of "Mayur"—"peacock-village". Look at these; you'll see what I mean.'

Scenes of villagers in festive attire: young girls in a circle performing a stick-dance, the whirlings of their skirts vying with the peacocks in the background—a riotous display of green, gold, blue and purple.

'The peacocks screeched and screeched that night. They always do, before it rains; but this time, no one knew they were screeches boding death.'

There was little that Raghavan could say about those images of beauty and terror. He snapped the album shut. Something fell out. One more peacock?—no, a dancer turned peacock: Aparna. Wrapped in shimmering blue-green silk, she was transformed into a peacock. A massive fan of feathers spread behind her, as she leant backwards, knees bent and apart, inclining to one side. The slender arms that had bruised him were spread up and out, their hands turned inwards, to enact a dancing bird in ecstasy.

'—Is anything wrong?' The padre's watchful eyes were observing him.

'No, nothing. Just that I know that girl.'

'So you *know*. Sad case, sad case, the advocate's daughter. Doesn't she look magnificent? Such a charming girl, so artless that I think of her as a peacock herself. This was taken at a school cultural show, some years ago. She was a splendid dancer, as you can see. Not any more, I gather. Since her own disaster, I haven't seen much of her at the school. The advocate is orthodox. He's a learned man—worthy of respect. Of course, he and I don't see eye to eye on essentials.'

'—PADRE! PADRE!!' A group of children and young men came bursting in; the hut rang with their shouting.

'He is dead!'—'No, he is not dead, just fallen.'—'No, no, no, he is having a fit.'

'Shush, all of you! Stop this commotion! At *once*!' The padre silenced them with a sweep of his arms. '*Who* is dead or not dead? What are you shouting about?'

The cackle resumed, but the voices grew a little more distinct.

'Please, padre! You must save him. Muniya the cobbler is dead!'—'No, no, Muniya is not dead. He fell into the well.'

'Into the well? What well?'

Silence. Then the padre understood. 'Don't tell me he's been at that forbidden well!'

'He was only digging it for his brother Muththu, padre!' An old man took over. 'I am telling you. The well is ours, whatever they say. Why shouldn't Muniya dig? Muniya did not fall into the well. He was *in* the well. Dry it is, and Muniya is digging and digging, and, suddenly, "ping!" he goes: he's hitting something. Then he is screaming "I struck, I am struck. Death to me, death to all who touch me. I shall die, they shall die!"'

A young man ventured an interpretation: 'Treasure, padre, treasure! Muniya is finding gold, maybe!'

'GOLD!! Ahh!!' A hush fell on the crowd.

'Who says Muniya is finding gold? Let him come out! I'll stop his mouth! Liar! Tale-teller!' Muththu, the brother of the cobbler in distress, approached the padre and prostrated himself before him. 'My brother is dying, padre! He is not one of us, he will be soon, I promise by the grace of God. Please don't let him die in the well, padre! He is not listening to us. And they will kill him when they find out. *Please*, great one!'

Raghavan decided it was time he intervened. 'Who will find out *what*?' The crowd pulled back. '—Let's go there! This looks like something I ought to deal with. Which way?'

They walked along a rough path through the grove, and reached the site.

Muththu parted the crowd around the well. 'Make way, make way, you idlers! The Collector is here! The padre is here! — Collector Sahib! My brother is a stubborn man. He is not listening to me when I am saying this well is cursed, and there is no water to be got. He is digging and digging, saying water will flow if he keeps digging. Now the miserable wretch is digging his own grave.'

The padre put an arm around the wailing Muththu. 'There, there! Don't cry! We'll get him out, the foolish fellow!'

The padre bent over the brick-surround and called into the darkness below. 'Muniya! eh, Muniya! Can you hear me? We are lowering the rope. You come out at once. If you don't, I am sending Anthony, the "Monster Water-Rat", down. Do you want *him* hauling you up?'

When the echoes subsided, they heard a faint voice: 'Monster Water-Rat can hang himself! I am not coming out. I must die here. I am a god-killer.'

'A god-killer!' The crowd instinctively edged away from the well.

'A "god-killer"? What does he mean?' Raghavan peered into the dark well. 'Has anyone got a torch? What does he mean?'

'I can only guess . . .' The padre, clearly unwilling to speculate further, turned an angry eye on the nearest person. '—Didn't you hear? Run! Get a torch.'

Raju brought a torch and handed it to the Collector. Raghavan swirled the beam round till it picked out a lean figure, crouched in a corner, and shivering. Before him lay the torso of an idol, encased in sodden clay. 'Padre! Take a look at this! This Muniya has stumbled on something exciting.'

The padre trained the beam till it shone directly on the object—the unmistakable figure of a tarnished bronze god. Muniya was clutching a broken piece.

'I feared it might be something like this.' The padre sounded weary as he straightened up. 'First, let us get him out. He is not dying, just petrified.'

Raghavan took command. 'Listen, all of you! No one must go near this well! It is strictly forbidden. We are now getting Muniya out. Then experts will look into this matter. No one should touch anything—and I mean *anything*.'

'Monster Water-Rat Anthony' leapt into the well, and surfaced with Muniya tucked under one arm.

The padre shouted: 'A doctor, a doctor! Go, get our doctor before he leaves clinic!'

Stretched out on a mat, Muniya lay as though paralysed.

Covering his face with his hands, he began to whimper. Through his moans, they could hear him chanting. 'Muruga! Muruga! Muruga! Vel Muruga, shakti vel, vel shakti, shakti vel . . . take my life, before they take *me* . . .'

'He is terrified of something or somebody. What's he so afraid of? Could it be some hallucination?' Raghavan expected the padre to know the answer.

'It's no hallucination. He's afraid of the *dikshitars* of the temple. The well is in disputed land, and Muniya is a cobbler.' The padre looked at Raghavan as if that was all the explanation needed.

'. . . I see.' Muniya's adventure would be read as a deliberate provocation; when the *dikshitars'* ferocious piety was kindled and their wrath let loose, who could protect the outcaste cobbler?

'Padre! Could you keep him with you for the time being? I must contact the Department of Archaeology immediately. They will want to inspect the site, as well as the find. I'll set up a police-guard. That should keep the *dikshitars* quiet for the time being.'

The padre felt encouraged. Would he be on their side, after all? 'The temple-folk won't admit the land belongs to us. They don't recognize modern law. They still claim all this as theirs, because Chola emperors bequeathed the land to the temple centuries ago. The temple's flower-gardens used to be here. Muththu's family grows vegetables now. I am telling these people to keep off that waterless well, but they don't listen. Who can blame them when the temple-folk block off the canal from us, and drinking-water is so scarce?'

Raghavan feared the padre was involving him in another of his contentious causes. Should he allow himself to be dragged in like this? Yet Muniya needed protection, otherwise the temple-mob would lynch him. Who could protect him, if not the Collector?

Law and order. *Dharma*. Wasn't that what he stood for?

And *dharma*, as Aparna put it, requires detachment. He must stay detached from padres and *dikshitars* alike.

As the padre continued his account of the land-dispute, Raghavan led the way out. He made no further comment.

*   *   *

Many hours later, when they had all gone, and the moon was high in a cloudless sky, Muniya lay in the dark porch of his brother's hut. As he lay there, staring into the silent sky, neither awake nor asleep, still, and yet shivering, Muniya dreamed a dream.

It was a dream of fire. He saw the yellow glow of the porch-lamp grow rich and red, and leap into tongues of flame, circling and spiralling above him and around him. Beneath him he saw mounds of smouldering charcoal, heaped on either side of a burning pit that beckoned him. White sprays of sparks shot out like stars, and warmed his fear-chilled bones.

Muniya sat up. The shivers stopped. His limbs loosened, and his tongue broke free.

'Muththu! Selvi! Come and hear! Here, under this moon I take my vow! I shall firewalk! At Mariamma's temple I will firewalk for my Murugan! She shall guide me, he will cleanse me of my sin, and I shall live! Vel Muruga! Kartikeya! Son of Shiva! Six-faced Lord, born of holy sparks! This sinner who polluted you shall firewalk for you. You will save this worthless god-killer!'

Muththu and his wife Selvi came rushing out. They found Muniya standing upright, his arms lifted high in prayer, and his face shining in the darkness.

Muniya rolled up his mat and departed into the darkness beyond, muttering, *'Vel shakti, shakti vel, vel shakti, shakti vel . . .'*

CHAPTER SEVEN

Beep... Beep... Beep...

Toku... Toku... Toku...

The musicians have arrived. Reeds are being tested, and the buffalo-hides of drums are pounded.

Sundaram Pillai and party have arrived, the most renowned *nadaswaram* players in Tanjore District, heralded by a cluster of petromax lanterns hissing white light. Music from the street-*pandal* flows into the house: the pleading, whining, exhilarating melodies of Kalyani Raga, a serpentine river of nectarine sounds that carries in its wake the chants of priests, the clamour of children, and the hum of conversation.

Lakshmiyamma's house is brimming with people, with relatives from far and near: cousins, uncles, aunts, grand-uncles, grand-aunts, and innumerable children; children, children everywhere, running, tumbling, laughing, whingeing, crying; weary children tugging at stately matrons who bustle in rustling silks, their bangled arms encircling great platefuls of auspicious offerings: polished brass plates shining like gold and weighted with puffed-rice jaggery-cones, stainless steel plates piled high with coconuts, plantains and betel-leaves, silver plates with swirling pools of blood-red *aarti*. Young women, married and unmarried, clutch shapely silver bowls brimful with smooth sandalwood-paste and gather round Aunt Malini, waiting for the signal to proceed to the temple and bring home the bridegroom.

It is the eve of Nitya's wedding, and procession-time.

Soon Kumar will be escorted by this array of women and priests through the streets of Kuchchipuram in an open motor-car, and will arrive at the house to be ceremonially engaged to Nitya.

'—Aparna! Aparna!! —Where *is* she? —Nitya is asking for you, Aparna! We are leaving now.'

Aparna can hear Aunt Malini calling above the tumult and the music.

Should she go to her? She is safer in the kitchen, surrounded by tired toddlers left in her charge. Dare she leave, and risk those significant sighs, those venom-charged glances from the stately matrons? . . . If Nitya hadn't insisted, if grandma didn't need her so, if the children didn't cling to her like this, would she be there at all? . . . But the music, the music is so enchanting, and the whole house is tuning up, charged to the brim with auspicious sounds, smells and sights.

—All the more reason why she should not be there.
—It is no place for someone like her tonight.
—A green widow.
—Inauspicious.

—That is what they are saying, those women. She can hear them, those bulky, married matrons, their breasts heaving with weighty gold-chains, their foreheads emblazoned with large circles of kumkum, so proud, so confident, so assured in their auspiciousness, she can hear them whispering in corners, muttering under their breath, sometimes with token discretion, more often than not in loud tones so as to make sure their words reach her. She can hear their tongues clucking menacingly . . .

'—Bad enough it should be so with her! What has happened has happened! Shouldn't we make sure nothing goes wrong, this time, at this wedding? Who can quarrel with what's written on her forehead, her *karma*? She shouldn't be here, hovering around the bride like this. It's not for me to say, and who listens to me these days? But surely . . .' Grand-Aunt Vasu rolls her eyes as her bosom balloons in a sigh.

'Shush, Auntie! Not so loud! Aparna can hear you, and what is she to do? Nitya wants her here.' Sister-in-law Meena has interposed.

But Grand-Aunt is not to be silenced. 'So what? These modern misses, so headstrong and wilful, what do they know about what's auspicious and what's not? What does this convent-school Nitya know about what's sacred and what's holy? It's all Malini's fault. She is too indulgent—but then what do you expect? That's what living among pig-eating foreigners does to you—fills your brain with filth!'

Sister-in-law Meena is right. Aparna can hear Grand-Aunt Vasu's every word.

—She should defy her, and go to Nitya.

—But . . . why, *why* is it that the words that ought to sting do not sting? Is she really so impervious to such petty superstitions?

—If so, why does she feel that she deserves them?

Aparna peeps out of the kitchen, like a nestling unsure of its first flight.

The matrons are lining up for the procession. A few, acting as ladies-in-waiting, are administering last-minute embellishments to Nitya's bejewelled forehead.

Two years ago, she too had waited, as Nitya does now, in the same room, decked in silks and jewels and rose-garlands. She too had waited, surrounded by solicitous women, her heart astir with strange feelings.

She has no right to intrude into that circle of auspiciousness.

*   *   *

Aparna slipped out while no one was watching, climbed up the stairs leading to the roof-balcony and slumped into a deck-chair. Here she could give herself up to the eddying whirls of Kalyani Raga, undisturbed.

'*Ammaravamma*—Mother, oh mother . . . !' Sundaram Pillai launched into the song.

It had been her mother's favourite. Many a time, her mother had petitioned her from her sick-bed: 'Aparna, dear! Bring the *veena* and play me *Ammaravamma*!' Mother, poor mother! Always sick, always undertaking vows, ever since Aparna could remember, always propitiating the gods, always staggering through to a new illness! It was her illness that led to everything else . . .

'Good family, good job as manager at Canara Bank in Madras, Seshi gave me this horoscope of her brother's son in Madras, and his horoscope agrees well with our Aparna's, the astrologers say so, not just our Acharya but others too—so why wait? They seem a good family. They promise to let Aparna continue her *bharatanatyam*, she can perform in Madras, have better chances there than in this country town. All I am asking is to see my only daughter settled before I close my eyes forever . . .' So mother had pleaded with father.

Vedam Iyer kept stalling, adjusting his spectacles and saying no more than: 'Hmmm! All in good time!'

Mother persisted. One day, when his spectacles slid down further than usual, he was weary with resisting, and gave in.

He summoned Aparna to his office, and suggested, as he would to a litigant, that it was in everybody's interests, particularly her sick mother's, if she agreed to the match. 'The boy seems intelligent, he has a good education, comes from a good family, and you can continue with your dancing as now, so why object? What's to be lost?'

He did not force her, he did not order, it was a plea for peace. She had never seen him look so bewildered and helpless. She felt cheated. She couldn't argue. So she blotted out everything except the thought of launching into the big world as a dancer: the chance of performing in Madras and beyond was the only thing that mattered, the rest was irrelevant.

The wedding was like a dream—a dream that turned into a nightmare.

She could not recollect clearly her husband, Balu—Balachandran was his name, but everyone called him Balu. She had to look at the wedding photographs to remind herself of what he looked like—and, for that matter, of what she had looked like. She rarely opened the album.

Did she love him? It was an absurd question to ask. Does one love a jellyfish? Perhaps, after years of self-mortification, she might have learnt to tolerate his fleshy face, his large docile eyes, his slow, meandering ways. Placid, soft-spoken Balu had wanted to please, to please everyone, as she soon found out. 'Yes, Aparna! Of course, you must continue your *bharatanatyam*, you must perform, never mind what mother says'—so he had assured her. And she had believed him, until she overheard him assure mother-in-law in almost the same words: 'Of course, you are right, mother. We cannot have our family name compromised by having your daughter-in-law dancing on the public stage, stared at by all and sundry. It won't happen, no matter what my wife says. Your word is my command.'

Bland-faced Balu proved too slippery a target for questioning. He did not know, nor cared to know, how she felt, how her outraged self yearned for purgation through the sacred dynamism of dance. How could he, he who had taken her body, invaded it, possessed it as a matter of course? What right did he have to plough through her life and leave her desecrated . . . ?

It was still bitter, the memory of that 'first night', so carefully prepared for by ritual and sanctioned by ceremony; they could not have done it better had it been a sacrifice. Not that he was violent: such passion was beyond the reach of his plasticine temperament. He had talked, not words of love, but about himself, discoursing on his own excellence in circumventing beggars who had bank-accounts; and then, having polished off the sweetmeats one by one, he had dropped off to sleep, leaving her free to puzzle over the strangeness of it all, the roses, the perfumes, the soft bed and her complacent companion. Then, in the early hours of the morning, he had surfaced from some amphibian dream, his body heavy with torpor, had crept into her like a great sea-slug, and hugged her, heaving and snivelling till his eyes bulged out, while she had lain there, stricken with shame and horror at having yielded to that loveless penetration. Where would she find an antidote to the still lingering taint of pollution which that night had engendered?

She had suffered him only a month, but it made no difference. One night was enough. Her inner core, the self from which her creative energies sprang, felt soiled. Now Balu had gone for ever, having deprived her of the one thing she had no hope of recovering—her innocence. Why shouldn't she be cast out?

They were right, the ancients: there was no hope of purity now, except through fire. A century ago—why, even now in some parts of the country—the funeral pyre would have summoned her. Would she have resisted the call? Would she have been *'sati'*, the 'true one'? Perhaps Balu was still calling her, from the ashes of his burnt-out pyre . . .

'—Ah, here you are! Gosh! I thought I could never escape. The ceremony is over, for the moment.' Nitya, all a-glitter, was addressing her. 'Isn't it cool here? It's so hot downstairs, and wearing all this makes it worse. You can come with me now. You are quite safe. Those women have gone to look after the dinner-guests. I'll forgive you for deserting me this evening; but tomorrow you mustn't abandon me to those busybodies. Promise?'

'Promise. But now I must go home and sleep.'

*   *   *

It is after the funeral.

Balu has gone, reduced to cinders on the pyre, and they have set her floating down the river. Her limbs are immobilized, her eyes closed; she drifts with the current, along with bits of charred firewood that have escaped the flames. Her saree gets caught in a tangle of twigs, and she stops moving. The water flows past her and then begins to drain. The sun is climbing up: up and up the noon-sky, drying the river, leaving the river-bed exposed—parched, dry mud, cracking like an old woman's wrinkles. Branches and twigs shrivel and blacken.

If only she could reach water, if only she could wash off the dry mud clogging her pores, if only she could move . . .

Soon her flesh will dry up, her bones will be laid bare, and the sun will bleach them, burn them, and turn them into pure white ash.

White ash is sacred ash.

Vibhuti: 'all-pervasive'.

Ultimate.

Nothingness.

. . . Then she is in a cool forest, walking fast, grabbing what she can, shielding her lamp and treading softly, lest she rouse the cobras lurking in the undergrowth.

It is dark, dark as only Tillai jungles can be; and the only light is from the ornamental lamp in her hand. Then a cool breeze blows, and the lamp goes out.

She bumps into trees, and the trees turn into pillars. Smoke-fumes from the extinguished flame, coiling round her neck, turn into creepers. Oh, how they choke!

If only she could breathe, if only she could grasp some air, then she could still the echoes, the echoes of mocking laughter from the 'man-lion', Lord Nrisimha, sculpted on the tree-pillar. . . . Would he tear her flesh too, break her bones upon his knee and lap up her blood, as he did the demon-king's? If only she could see, if only she could break loose into open country . . .

*   *   *

'Aparna! Wake up! Wake up, Aparna!'

Sister-in-law Meena is shaking her. Aparna sits up, throwing aside the Panipet bedspread. She is drenched in perspiration.

'What time is it? Where am I?'

'It's five in the morning. —Here, at home, of course. This is your Meena here, can't you see? You were talking in your sleep. It scared me, the way you were struggling, as if you were wrestling with demons!'

'What was I saying?'

'Nothing clear. Just prattling, and your voice choking. You don't have asthma, do you?'

'No.'

'Just a bad dream, then.' Meena smooths Aparna's hair. 'There, you are all right now. I have to go soon. Malini is expecting me early, for the "swing-ceremony".' Meena pauses, and lifts Aparna's face gently by the chin. 'Why don't you take your time and come later, bring the children with you? —Look at them! Sound asleep! Nothing bothers them, hot night or not!'

It is touching, this concern from her sister-in-law. It is tactful of Meena to hint like this that she should keep away from the 'swing ceremony', away from those matrons as they sing sacred songs to bride and groom, who will be seated on a plank-swing erected under the street-*pandal*. Balls of reddened rice will be wafted, thrice this way, thrice that way, and plates of holy *aarti* will be whirled about, then thrown aside: thus the couple will be blessed, and evil eyes warded off. It is another auspicious moment at which her presence could only cause alarm.

'I don't want to go at all. I feel sore in the head.'

'My poor Aparna! Don't say that. Nitya is fond of you. Aunt Malini is broad-minded. It will all be over soon. Then, as I was saying to your brother, you should come with us to Madras. The children adore you, and you can do so much there. Now, go and brush your teeth; I'll pour out some coffee for you. There!'

As Vedam Iyer's only daughter-in-law, Meena has taken charge. She has been up since four o'clock. The advocate likes his coffee early.

Aparna heads for the backyard. She hauls bucket after bucket of cool water from the well, and bathes. The stiffness eases from her limbs; but the centre of her forehead continues to hurt, as if it has been gouged.

*   *   *

She was just in time for the 'bride-giving'. The camera-room was full of women.

'Here you are, at last! Please hand me some talc and cologne. All this turmeric and oil is making me suffocate!' Nitya stood amidst a throng of matrons who were twisting her this way and that as they wrapped and secured nine yards of yellow silk about her.

'—Shush, Nitya! You mustn't say things like that. Just a little patience! Watch what I am doing. You'll have to do this one day without help. Now step on this bit to keep it down!' Aunt Malini pointed to a fold of silk covering Nitya's right leg. 'Now it won't ride up.'

Before Aparna could pass her the cologne, Nitya was led out.

'*Ghetti Melam! Ghetti Melam!!* Loud drumming! Loud drumming!!' the priests shouted above the vibrant din of music and chanting.

Nitya was seated on her father's lap, her collyrium-lined eyes demurely cast down, her neck bent submissively to Kumar. The drumming grew frantic, the wail of the *nadaswaram* crescendoed to a climax. Kumar tied the *tali* thread round his bride; no more a bride, but a wife.

Aparna joined her grandmother, who was sitting by the door of the camera-room. From there, out of view, the two widows could watch the couple being brought to the ceremonial fire, the ends of their garments knotted together. Under the guidance of the officiating priest, Kumar ladled out clarified butter on to a heap of cowdung-cakes and sanctified twigs. The fire burned fitfully, and smoke-haze filled the whole house. Grasping his wife's hand over the fire, and with eyes streaming from the smoke, Kumar repeated the mantras after the priest, word by word, phrase by phrase. It was as though he were being taught a new alphabet. '*I seize thy hand that I may gain fortune: this am I, thou art that; I am the words, thou the melody; I the seed, thou the bearer; the heaven I, the earth thou . . .*'

Panigrahanam: 'hand-grasping'.

Thus had Balu . . .

Thus had Balu seized her hand over the fire; and thus too had *Agni*, the fire-god, been invoked at her own wedding, two years previous.

Agni, the fire-god—sanctifier, purifier, many-tongued guardian of home and hearth; *Agni*, the oblation-bearer, who paves the way to the heavens, to the abode of gods; *Agni*, the witness.

Beside the same *Agni* she had sat with Balu, round the same *Agni* she had circumambulated three times and taken the 'pledge-of-seven-steps'. On the seventh step, her foot firmly planted on a grindstone, she had pledged herself to be his faithful, chaste wife, forever and forever. With that seventh step, she had become his, irrevocably . . .

How could vows taken before such a fiery, holy presence be made null?

How weak and foolish she had been to be tossed into such confusion! Why heed the cravings of the body and the mind, when the spirit could be cut free? Blessed be *Agni*, the purifier! Blessed be *Agni*, the saviour!

As she watched the flames grow and leap under a steady stream of clarified butter, her resolve grew stronger. No more weakness, no more vacillation, no more reaching out for moorings in others—and no more mocking laughter from the gods. She would indeed be *sati*, the 'true one'.

'—He's here, he's here!' Seshi came bustling in towards Lakshmiyamma. 'Over there! That's him, the new Collector! Look! Tall he is, and not dark either!'

'Where?' Lakshmiyamma put on her spectacles to inspect. Aparna moved quietly into a darker corner of the room.

Raghavan stood overlooking the central courtyard, scanning a sea of white *veshtis* for a familiar face. Vedam Iyer beckoned to him, patting a space beside him, and waved away his neighbour so as to make room.

'Come, come, Raghavan, sit by me. —How was the tour?'

'Not over yet. I had to break it off. Some experts from the Archaeology Department are arriving today by the noon-express. You must have heard about the bronzes.'

'Who hasn't? It is the talk of temple and town. I suppose you know?'

'What *should* I know?'

'The idol—I believe it is Kumaran—he really belongs to the Shiva-Nataraja Temple. It's a long story. To think that his sanctum in the south-west portico has remained bare all this while! —Just as in Kalidasa's epic, *Kumara-Sambhavam*.' Vedam Iyer chuckled as he emphasized the title with his index finger: '"Kumara—Sambhavam"—meaning "the auspicious epiphany of a young god". —And he was found well and whole, I hear. Just as of old, when the six wives of the rishis found him in the fiery bush beside the golden pond. A gracious blessing indeed! Indeed a blessing!'

'It was certainly a relief when we hauled the bronzes up. Muniya hadn't hit the main figure. The broken piece he was clutching comes from one of the other two images—a hand holding a lotus. The locals insist that the two damaged bronzes are Murugan's wives. I don't believe so. They seem more like attendants or *apsaras*, though they could be anything. Only one thing is certain: they are unmistakably female.'

'But Kumaran is a perpetual *brahmachari*. These ignorant folk have taken over the Aryan god, and, not content with calling him Murugan, have given him wives!'

'I thought it was the other way round. I'd read that a powerful tribal deity could not be suppressed, and so has been Aryanized.'

'Where did you read that? That's just anti-brahmin propaganda.'

Raghavan allowed a pause. '. . . The locals want to build a shrine on the spot. The *dikshitars* want him in the temple.'

'What are you going to do?'

'I've called in the Archaeology Department.'

'Don't tell me about archaeology experts! I know what they'll do. They'll take away this sacred idol and dump him in some corner, in a museum. There the god will languish, gathering dust, neglected; or the rogues will sell him to some foreigner! No, no, a god's home is his temple. The temple is where he should be.'

The priests were calling: '*Asirvadam! Asirvadam!!* Holy blessing!

Holy blessing!' Vedam Iyer handed flower-petals and rice-grains to Raghavan.

'Here, take this! —And I tell you again, Kumaran belongs with Lord Shiva!'

While the priests intoned, a shower of petals and rice-grains fell on the wedded couple.

Raghavan scanned the packed courtyard. She must be there, somewhere.

'Well?' The advocate had noticed his attention wandering. 'What is it?'

'I thought I'd better warn Mrs Subramaniyam that these men from Madras will have to stay in the bungalow. Since her guests are there . . .'

'Oh, is that all? Why not tell Aparna, she looks after that sort of thing. —But here comes my sister-in-law herself, with her husband. He's a diplomat, you know, waiting for a new posting.'

When Seshi's message reached the women, Aunt Malini had immediately broken loose from them, leaving them to envy her acquaintance with the new Collector.

'—Oh, Mr Raghavan. I am so pleased you could come. You must meet our son-in-law; and, of course, Nitya's father.'

She introduced her partner, a taciturn man, distinguished-looking in his gold-rimmed spectacles and neatly combed, white hair, but somewhat ill at ease in a *veshti* tied in ritual style. He put out a hand. 'Malini hasn't stopped talking about you. Pleased to meet you.'

It was a time for meetings and partings, before the feast. Aunt Malini led the way to the far end of the courtyard, where the ceremonies were just concluding.

Raghavan handed a parcel to the bridegroom. 'A small gift, to mark this happy occasion. Congratulations!'

'Delighted to meet you at last. My family appreciates your hospitality.'

'It's nothing. The place would have been just empty.'

'You should see your bungalow now!' Kumar laughed readily. 'It's like an airport lounge, bodies and bags everywhere. You won't recognize it! —Oh, here is someone very eager to meet you, my friend Gerald.'

'Hi! It's "Gerry" to friends!' A lanky, blonde American, camera in hand and tape recorder slung from his shoulders, shot up from among the circle of priests.

'Gerry is a budding anthropologist,' Kumar explained, patting his friend on the back. 'He knows more about temples and rituals and all that sort of thing than any of us here. He's doing a Ph.D.'

'What a fascinating town you have here in Kuchchipuram—fascinating temple, simply fantastic. You know, Collector, these priests are just amazing. Here they are, chanting mantras the same as *four thousand years* ago, when the "*A*-ryans"— no, let me get it right, you say "*Ah*-ryans"—landed up by the Ganges. Just incredible! Isn't it marvellous how time doesn't flow in India? We in the west . . .'

Raghavan looked at his digital watch. 'My time *does* flow, I'm afraid. I have to meet a train. Must go. Excuse me.'

'—Oh, *no*, Mr Raghavan!' Aunt Malini interposed, frowning. 'You can't leave before the feast. The first sitting is just starting.'

'I'm sorry, Mrs Subramaniyam, I clean forgot. My two archaeologists from Madras will be using my office, and sleeping in the room next to it. I am sorry to have to do this to your guests.'

'No, no, it is *your* bungalow. Don't worry, we can look after them. They must be tired and hungry after their journey. Why not bring them to the feast?'

'Thank you. That's very thoughtful of you.' Raghavan edged his way out. Gerry sidled up to him.

'Mr Collector! May I come with you? I just heard about these statues, and I'm dying to see them. I am heavily into temple-myths, collecting material for my thesis. This is just fantastic . . .'

'Later, perhaps. Not just now.'

It was Kabir who came to his rescue. 'We must hurry, sir! The train will be entering the station any minute now, sir!'

The insistent Gerry, with his irritating nasal twang, was likely to prove a further complication. And Raghavan's detour had been pointless, he hadn't managed to even see Aparna. Where *could* she be hiding?

*   *   *

'Hmmm!' Lakshmiyamma sighed.

'What's the matter, grandma?' Aparna was tidying up the

room, folding discarded sarees. All the matrons had left, to supervise the feast.

'Pity! Two years too late! And just right too!'

'What is, grandma?'

'Nothing, girl, nothing!' She looked hard at her granddaughter, and sighed again.

'... Oh, *grandma*! How *can* you? Good thing no one heard you!'

'So what? I know walls have ears, but today they are not listening to me.'

'The past is past. We must let be.'

'Listen to her, the *jnani* talking! Don't lecture me, enlightened one! These eyes of mine have seen more life than you ever will, my poor child! What a fate ...! —And look who is here at *last*!'

Nitya and Kumar prostrated themselves before the old woman. Her eyes filled with tears as she blessed them.

'—Look, Aparna, what Mr Raghavan gave us.' Nitya opened the parcel.

Aparna stiffened. It was a bronze lamp, a replica of a dreamy *apsara* from a temple-frieze.

'Isn't it beautiful? It reminds me of you, when you do your dance with the lamp, *deepanjali*. I wonder where he found this?'

Aparna stood staring at it. It was as if the lamp in her dream had been snatched from her hand.

CHAPTER EIGHT

My dear Raghu,

    Blessings. We hope you are keeping well, as we are. Your money-order came just in time for Radha's college-fees. Why are you not writing to us? I am not wanting money only from you.

    I am your mother. It grieves my mother's heart thinking you have no one to look after you, that a boy of your age and position should be still without a wife. What are you doing for meals? How thin you were looking when we last saw you! Daily so many good families are pressing on us with horoscopes. The other day only, our **Sastrigal** came with many, many auspicious horoscopes—girls from good brahmin families, well-educated, making very suitable matches. When will you be listening to us? We are not selecting for you. We are very happy to be finding what you like. I am just asking you to write and tell what type, what colour, what build, what education. You leave the rest to us.

    We well know you have views on dowry, but you must be considering your sister Radha and your other sisters too. With four daughters to be married, and your father a poor school teacher only, how can we be refusing dowry? All these families are rich and wanting to give dowry. Who will not, for a Collector son-in-law?

    Think about these things and write. Your father sends his blessings. Write soon.

                                                  Mother.

A heavy lorry roared past, raising a muddy spray from the gutter. Raghavan jumped aside, took out a handkerchief and mopped himself. The letter lay crumpled in his pocket. —That one thin paper should weigh so heavy! Not since his school-days, when he had secreted dragon-flies in his pocket for training, had he felt such discomfort.

His shirt was drenched. He ought to return to the bungalow. But the wedding-guests were packing to leave. He was in no state to countenance all those good-byes, thank yous and pressing invitations.

He headed towards Flower-Bazaar. It was not when he bought that bronze lamp from the artisans' co-operative on Tillai hills and bought another for the bungalow because it reminded him of her, no, not even when his body grew taut searching in vain for her at the wedding, but only when he opened mother's letter, bracing himself once again to fend off her familiar plea, that the truth hit him. Mother had slapped him awake.

He could never fulfil his mother's dream, dowry or no dowry. He was no longer free. He had strayed into forbidden territory and been caught. Without him realizing, Aparna had become an inner presence, an enigmatic goddess in a neglected sanctum.

Was this what they called falling in love, this delectable ache at the mere mention of a name? Aparna. The recollection of being pinioned by her in the Thousand-Pillared-Hall set his pulse racing...

'Saridon! Saridon for headache! Always take Saridon! Saridon, Saridon, Sa - *ri* - don!' From the tea-shop came the call of Radio Ceylon, that unctuous purveyor of pop-music to an eager mainland audience.

> '—*O queen of my dreams, where are you hiding?*
> '*In vain do I seek thee with this garland of love;*
> '*The breezes of dawn bear my sigh,*
> '*The blushing dusk my melting heart,*
> '*The waves of the sea roar my complaints;*
> '*O lady in hiding, speak to me!*
> '*O queen of my dreams, come to me,*
> '*For I wander in vain with this garland of love!*'

The bazaar loud-speakers were blaring out a hit from the latest film, *Desert Moon*. It came from the tailor's shop—the disabled ex-army orderly who doubled his income by hiring out film-records to weddings and festivals. The singer crooned the refrain over and over, to a tumbling cascade of shrill orchestral sounds.

It had been so easy in the past to scoff at such things; he alone among his friends had luxuriated in a lofty disdain. What would they say if they saw him now, wandering up and down Flower-Bazaar envying the saccharin croonings of a play-back singer?

Yet it was no teasing matter. Their mirth would freeze from the moment they discovered who she was, what she was. '*Pardeshi*'—'mendicant alien'—that was their nickname for him. It had never seemed apt till now, as he wandered up and down Flower-Bazaar, seeking vainly to disperse the sense of foreboding that oppressed him. Not all the clamour and carnival of Flower-Bazaar could drown the aggrieved voice of mother within. 'Oh, Raghu! Raghu, my eldest and only son! How could you *do* this to us! What calamity! What woe!!' In every passer-by who brushed past him he read her reproachful look.

Flower-Bazaar was the same as ever: its covered walkway burst with flowers of every shape, size and colour. In stall after stall, deft hands were busy transforming mounds of roses, jasmines, chrysanthemums and greenery into garlands to grace wedding-couples or wily politicians. Like other newcomers to Kuchchipuram, Raghavan had been spell-bound—entranced like the crowds who now gaped at the floral sculptures displayed on stall-fronts, sculptures that would eventually deck the floats of temple-gods. The bazaar, its lanterns ablaze, was charged with mingled smells, sweet and foul: a heady perfume of jasmines drowned the stench from partly-covered sewers; oil-fumes from frying food overpowered gusts of incense burning under the gilt-framed pictures of Shiva, Rama, Krishna, Murugan, and Lakshmi. There were gods in plenty in all the shops, in saree-shops, in bangle-shops, in hardware shops, and in the kitchenware shops that spilt their glittering array of stainless steel goods out on to the pavement—gods of all shapes, sizes and demeanours, to watch over every bobbing head in that hubbub of men, women and children who ambled along, their garments fastidiously hitched up, picking their way past placid cows, begging urchins, crushed sugar-cane and puddles of filth; gods who gave them life and strength to laugh, haggle, shout, and raise their unabashed voices above the tumult of film-music that competed with the temple-chant blaring from loud-speakers mounted on its east wall.

>'Nata-raa-ja, Nataraja
>Nardana sundara Nataraja.'

A *bhajan* was in progress. The pious audience of hundreds repeated after the pundit:

>'Nata-raa-ja, Nataraja
>Nardana sundara Nataraja . . .'

NATARAJA: 'Lord of dance'. A beautiful god, a joyous god, a wild god. Also, the god of the cremation-ground, a god of destruction, of dissolution. For the chanters in the temple, just one more name to be invoked; but for her, how much more! How could this graceful, wild, mystic Lord of dance to whom she had dedicated herself have betrayed her?

Anger choked him. A young lad selling sugar-cane juice from a barrow caught his eye.

'Dry, sir? Fresh sugar-cane juice here, sir. With ice, sir? Very clean, all sealed, sir.'

'How much?' Raghavan held out a five-rupee note. The lad fed a fresh purple cane to the crusher, and juice frothed into a glass. The dry, white pith fell away.

The salty-sweet juice hurt as it slid down his throat.

'—Hullo!'

Raghavan turned round. It was Padre Yesudasan. In a flowing white cassock, astride an antique bicycle, and so near the temple, the padre cut a quaint figure. What was he doing there?

'—A glass of juice for the padre, boy. And don't bother with the change.'

A quick, bird-like hop, and the padre was beside him. 'Thank you. —How was the tour?'

'Good! I got to see the Meyyur folk, including the trouble-makers. I found out what they were up to. Ingenious, some of them—pouring boiling water down the walls of their huts to simulate storm-damage! You were quite right: the innocent have to suffer on account of the rogues. I have a lot to tell you.'

'*I* need to talk to *you*.' The padre looked around uneasily as he finished his drink. 'Fairly soon.'

'Well—why not now? Shall we go in here?'

The smell of coffee and frying pancakes had floated across from Udipi Hotel.

'Why not?' The padre parked his bicycle near the lamp-post. A boy immediately took charge. Whipping up his robes, the padre produced from his trouser-pocket a few coins for the beggars who were rummaging through banana-leaf platters dumped in the cement-bin outside the hotel.

Raghavan made for a table beside the window.

'—Upstairs is better. We could find a quiet family room up there.' The padre led the way.

A server appeared on the landing. 'Yes, sir? *Upma, idli, vadai, bhajji, bhonda, rava dosa, masala dosa* . . .' He made the menu resound like a mantric chant.

'Just a coffee for me.' Raghavan turned to the padre. 'And for you?'

'I haven't been here for a long time. Mr Samuel used to bring me here for a *masala dosa*. Udipi Hotel's *masala dosa* is famous, you know.'

'Then why don't you have one ? It's on me.'

'Oh. Thank you.' The padre's uncomplicated delight was touching. 'You too should have one. I strongly recommend the *masala dosa*, very crisp and tasty.'

'Perhaps I will then.' Raghavan called the server back. He had decided to put the padre at his ease.

Yesudasan checked a glass to make sure it was clean. 'How's your family? They're in Madras, aren't they?'

'My family . . . ? Oh, all right. I had a letter only this morning from my mother.' Raghavan gulped at the glass of water before him. It tasted bitter. 'Tell me what you wanted to talk about.'

'It is about Muniya, the cobbler. He is back at his stall outside the temple. I've just been to see him.'

'Is he all right?'

The server slapped down plates and cups. 'Two *dosai* and two coffee.' The coffee wobbled and spilt.

Yesudasan waited till the server was well out of earshot.

'That's what I'm worried about. He *thinks* he is. May be he is, for the time being. But it won't be long before trouble breaks out.' He munched his crisp pancake noisily. 'Already, alarming things are happening. This morning, his pictures were slashed. You know, Muniya sells pictures of gods and goddesses—even used to sell "Sacred Hearts" and "Mother Mary", till I put a stop to it.' The padre laughed, then recollected himself. 'You know they call him the "peepul-tree pundit": he likes holding forth. Well, someone has scratched "Clear off, god-killer!" on his tree.'

'"God-killer". That's what he kept calling himself. Who would have done it?'

'You might have a word with the *dikshitars*. I can't approach them. —Then there's his vow.'

'*What* vow?'

'Muniya has taken a vow to Murugan that he will firewalk. He's set on it. —Have you seen firewalking?'

'No. How brave of him!'

'It's a mind-boggling spectacle. But it whips them up—rather dangerously, at times.'

'You don't approve?'

'How can I? It's against our faith. But I have to admit it's a puzzle why they don't get hurt.'

'Sometimes they do. So I've heard.'

'Rarely. And then there's more than burns to cope with.'

'How come?'

'Well, then they blame themselves, get crippled with guilt, because it's a sign that the god has rejected them.'

'I see why you don't approve.'

'My people are of such fragile faith. Already, since the discovery in the well, things are changing. Some of them are getting secretive. I have my fears.'

There was a pause. So that was what was troubling the padre. Muniya's firewalking would only make apostasy worse: the fragile flock would slide back into its 'benighted pagan ways'.

'I see your problem.'

'There must be some way round.' The padre gulped his coffee and wiped his mouth. 'The sooner the figures are removed—and I don't care where they go, whether it's temple or museum—but the sooner they go, the better for us. Then there's this American fellow—have you met him? He's turning up there every day, encouraging the people, filling their heads with nonsense, and now they're clamouring for a shrine on the site. The *last* thing we need is another shrine!'

He could hardly have been blunter.

Raghavan smiled. 'I think I can look after that. The experts have nearly finished their report. It's been an exciting excavation. Besides the bronzes, they've uncovered an underground tunnel. It may lead to the river—probably an escape route for kings of old. I'd have thought a full-scale dig was called for. . . . And as for Gerry, I admit he's irritating, but he's quite harmless. *I'll* deal with him.'

They finished their coffee. The padre seemed reassured. Raghavan braced himself; now was the time to ask. All through their conversation his brain had been seething with schemes to realize the objective that had obsessed him from the moment he met the padre. Somehow he must secure the photograph of Aparna; the padre had no right to it.

He settled for a casual, official tone, as being the least likely to rouse suspicion.

'—By the way, that folder you showed me, the "good-news" folder—could I borrow it? I need a better idea of what Meyyur looked like, in case my development project gets approved. Your photos seem to be the only record.'

'Oh yes, certainly. You are welcome to keep it as long as you like. And I am glad something is being done at last. But . . .' The padre hesitated, looking at him intently.

Raghavan shifted uneasily.

'. . . May I ask if the plans include rebuilding my church?'

So that was it. Raghavan pushed back his chair and stretched. 'Well, as you know, that is difficult. Even impossible.'

'I feared so.' The padre stood up. '—Thank you, all the same. Please call on me any time. It's a privilege and a pleasure. I'll send the folder along. And thank you for treating me to *dosa* and coffee. Real pleasure. God bless you!' Smiling, the padre extended a hand.

*   *   *

It was some hours before Raghavan returned to the bungalow.

The guests had departed. The bungalow was in darkness, but the moon behind the swaying *ashoka* trees lit up the verandah. Raghavan began pacing up and down.

. . . That padre, with his sad, smiling insistence—why did he make him feel that he was letting him down? Why should he concern himself with a destroyed church? What was there to choose between all these gods, anyway—Nataraja, Murugan, or that dubious, pale-faced import from overseas? They were all the same: inscrutable, demanding, misleading—all betraying poor, deluded humanity into dreams of meaning, personal significance, special providence. . . . What meaning, what significance was there in *her* life . . . ?

Unless . . .

Unless meaning could be created. . . . Raghavan stopped and looked up at the pale sky, seeking confirmation. The moon had disappeared behind a dense pocket of cloud. The trees had stopped swaying.

Could he shift the weight of taboo, shatter the bands of age-old guilt that held her?

Jules Verne's hero had snatched a young widow from the burning pyre itself. Even the poor cobbler had courage sufficient for his fiery ordeal. —Why should he, Raghavan, hesitate?

But would she respond? Would she *allow* herself to be rescued, set free?

Or would she retreat still further behind her mystic mask?

CHAPTER NINE

'Ta—Ta—Ta . . .
  'Ta-*ting*-gi-na-thom . . . Ta-*ting*-gi-na-thom . . .
  'Ta-ka-*tai* . . . Ta-*ri*-ki-ta-tai . . .
  '*Ta*-ta-ka-tai . . . ta-*ri*-ki-ta-tai, ta-*ri*-ki-ta . . .'

Aparna, sitting cross-legged on the black mosaic floor of the main hall, sang the drum-syllables to a rhythmic clash of tiny hand-cymbals. A plump goddess Lakshmi on an overblown pink lotus smiled from the wall. Two teenage girls, identical twins, were dancing, their ankle-bells ringing to the ordered pattern of their steps.

'Ta-*ri*-ki-ta-tai, ta-*ri*-ki-ta—no, no, *no!*' Aparna stopped. 'Not like that. Are you dancers or robots? You are meant to be the most beautiful, entrancing, divine couple, and you are plodding like puppets, clackety-clack!'

The twins giggled in relay, one burst following another.

Aparna frowned. 'Now, Kamala and Vimala, watch me carefully!' Hitching up her saree, and tucking the folds in, she demonstrated. 'Now, Kamala, you must never forget who you are—Kaama, the god of love. And you, Vimala, are his wife, Rati. Now, Kaama, this is your bow of sugar-cane, and this, your arrow of mango-blossom, your "arrow of desire" which you will aim at Shiva. You are heavenly beings and must move like heavenly beings—like this.' With a single, curving sweep of arms and shoulders, Aparna conjured up the playful agility of a youthful god preparing his daring attack.

'Now let me see you both go through the whole thing again: slow, medium, and *drut*, fast. —What do I say?'

'"Dancing is not just tapping out steps, any monkey can do that."' The twins laughed in unison.

'All right, all right. Let's start. Whatever you do—bend, turn, advance, pull back—say to yourself: "I am beautiful, I am irresistible". —Here we go!'

'—She is wonderful, isn't she?' Nitya whispered to Raghavan, having signalled him to enter quietly. She was perched on the window-seat of the *rezhi*, a dark corridor stacked high with sacks of paddy, and exuding a musty smell of jute. Kumar stood behind her, his arms resting on her shoulders.

Aparna's back was turned to her unseen audience. She was wearing an off-white saree with a bright ochre border and matching blouse. Her hair was pinned up high, and stray curls lay matted on her elegant, damp neck.

Raghavan pulled back. She was altogether too close. Had it not been for the bars on the intervening window, he might have reached out and grabbed her by that slim, bare small of the back— a shiny expanse that extended with each curved movement or outward stretch, as her saree-blouse rode up.

'I really think I ought to go away and return later,' he murmured to Nitya.

'Why?' Nitya did not turn her head. '—Oh, look! A new character.'

A third dancer emerged from behind a pillar.

'Now, Raji, your part is Shiva, that is the most difficult. You have to sit still for a long time, deep in meditation, while the others dance. —Where is our Parvati? What's happened to Rani? Still not here. Does anyone know?'

'Rani was coming. They were going to the Mariamma Temple. Her brother has chickenpox.'

'Oh, dear! —Vimala? You stand-in till she arrives. Where was I?'

'Lord Shiva, Miss.'

'That's right. Here, Raji. You sit in deep meditation, like this, while Kaama dances to tempt you. Then you stir awake, just for a moment, knowing that Parvati is before you, adoring you; and then the music changes, strikes the note of alarm—*tat*, tat-inginathom! You open your Third Eye and whoosh!—Kaama becomes *basmam*, reduced to a heap of ashes. Absolutely simultaneous it must be: you, Shiva, opening your eyes, and you, Kaama, collapsing. —Now start from the beginning.'

Aparna turned on the tape-recorder. The girls went through the whole sequence.

'No, no, no.' She stopped the music. 'This won't do. Raji! You are closing your eyes as if you were playing "I Spy". —Oh, girls, what am I going to do with you?'

The twins giggled. Raji pouted. 'Sorry, Miss. It's boring. Am I not to dance?'

'Later, later. Not now. You *know* this is not the story of the dancing Shiva, not yet. Shiva is a yogi here, in deep sleep, like this. Watch me!' Aparna took the lotus-posture of a yogi in meditation. Head erect, back upright, she closed her eyes, and the deep peace of *yoga nidra* suffused her face.

'Let's creep in now.' Nitya was enjoying the situation.

Raghavan hesitated. 'Are you sure?'

'Ssss! Just follow us.' He obeyed. After all, he had a right to be there. Vedam Iyer had repeated the invitation three times, for him to come and read Kalidasa with him that Sunday afternoon. Why should he hover on his own in that dark corridor?

The girls spotted the trio tip-toeing in, and covered their mouths to suppress sniggers.

'There's nothing to laugh about! Whatever is the matter with you all today?' Aparna swung round and saw the intruders. 'Nitya, Kumar, and . . . and YOU. How *could* you?'

Raghavan felt the full blaze of her anger, though she was unable to name him: Shiva had opened that Third Eye.

Nitya grabbed her cousin's hands. 'Oh, *please*, Aparna, don't be angry. What were we to do? We couldn't sit there all afternoon. And don't blame Raghavan, he was wanting to go. It was entirely my fault. I *made* him stay. And you were so magnificent—wasn't she?' Nitya looked round, seeking support.

Aparna ignored Nitya and turned to her pupils. 'Now, girls, be going. No more rehearsals here. For the next one, I'll meet you at the school. Meanwhile, *practise!* Only two weeks before the performance. Off, now!'

'Yes, Miss.' The girls quickly untied their ankle-bells, eager to escape. This new dance-drama was much too demanding, and their teacher was clearly not pleased with them.

Aparna began packing her paraphernalia. Nitya knelt beside her and shook her by the shoulders. 'Come, Aparna! Don't take it so badly!'

'Who says I *am*?' She looked up.

Raghavan seized his chance. 'I *am* expected today, am I not?'

'Father is upstairs. I . . . I'm sorry. I forgot.' Biting her lips, she concentrated on pushing the tape-recorder back into its battered vinyl-case.

She looked too much like a trapped tigress to be left unbaited.

'Am I right, that the dance-drama segment we saw just now is from Kalidasa's *Kumara-Sambhavam*?'

'Canto Three.' She flung the recalcitrant case aside and sat back exasperated, unpinning and reknotting her hair, before making a fresh attempt.

Raghavan picked up the case. 'Here, let me. Pass that tape-recorder.' He disentangled a flap that had blocked the way, slipped the radio in, and zipped it up.

'Oh, Raghavan! Before you go . . .' Nitya whispered something in Kumar's ear. Kumar nodded. '—We are going to the cinema later this evening, Kumar, Aparna, and me. Why don't you come with us? I have a spare ticket. Seenu can't come.'

'Why not, Raghavan?' Kumar beamed. 'We are leaving tomorrow and it will be fun to do something together, all the lot of us.'

'Are you sure?' Raghavan looked at Aparna.

'Of course we are. It's so difficult to get Aparna to go anywhere. But she's promised this outing. We came to make sure she didn't back out of it. You won't, will you, Aparna?'

Whatever her inclination, there was no escape. 'If you insist.'

'Good! Seven o'clock then. We'll get a taxi and fetch you both. Ta-*ta!*'

Nitya and Kumar left. Aparna ignored Raghavan and continued clearing up.

He made his way up to the advocate's office. But half-way up the stairs, he stopped and turned back, resolved to try and regain lost ground. 'Aparna!'

'What now?'

There was no way he could proceed. His mild-eyed Pandya princess had turned into a village fury, eyes flashing, hands propped on slightly swaying hips, as if she were about to launch into some rumbustious folk-dance.

'Tell me. According to Kalidasa, after Kaama's death, his ashes were scattered through the world so that no human heart could escape him. —Is that right?'

'Since you know, why are you asking me?' Her face darkened as she turned away.

'—Is that you, Raghavan? I thought I heard your voice.' Vedam Iyer emerged from the office. 'No, no, let us go downstairs. The office is no place for reading poetry. For that we need the courtyard. It's cooler there, isn't it? —Aparna, dear, how about some coffee? —This calls for a celebration. It is so long since I drank the nectar of Kalidasa. Come, come.'

'My Sanskrit is very rusty. But I am looking forward to being enlightened.' Raghavan leafed through the book that Vedam Iyer handed to him.

'Don't worry about that. So long as you can read well, there is nothing to worry about. Poetry is all in the reading—the reading and the rhythm, the rhythm of your breath. Reading Kalidasa is like breathing in a draught of pure Himalayan air. You'll see what I mean. You do the reading, and I'll do the explaining. That is what we used to do, your father and I. —Or was it the other way round? No, as I remember, we took turns. That's right, we took turns. We should be able to do that ourselves soon. —Aparna, dear, have you anything to do? Why don't you sit down for a while and listen to Kalidasa?'

Vedam Iyer clearly saw this as the first of many Sunday afternoon sessions in his courtyard.

* * *

Paradise Cinema, a solid concrete building with fading pink paint, stood on the corner where Flower-Bazaar ended and Old Bridge Road began. Poised between temple and cinema, the life of the town flowed through the bazaar. The posters of gods and goddesses under Muniya's peepul tree took their likenesses from the heroes and heroines of the silver screen: Shiva had the smile of Kamalahasan, and Lakshmi boasted Radhika's rounded figure. Outside Paradise Cinema hung large oil paintings of the film stars themselves, shimmering and glittering within frames of blinking lights, lit up like deities in their sanctum. Temple and theatre drew devotees by the hundreds; and in the tumult of Flower-Bazaar, no one could tell or cared to tell where the pious *bhajans* ended and the film-songs began. The gods and the stars were not rivals but cohabitants in a single fantasy world.

'—Are we late? It's five years since I saw a Tamil film. I don't want to miss anything, not even the advertisements. Let's hurry.' Nitya led the way, dragging Kumar along. Aparna and Raghavan followed.

The lights were already dimmed. A sombre political voice extolled the virtues of the number 'Two': a documentary on family-planning was in progress. They made their way through a row of hisses.

'Here. These are our seats.' Kumar halted, pushing Nitya down.

'Thank God, no one has taken them.' Nitya made herself comfortable next to Kumar. Aparna followed, like a sleep-walker in the semi-darkness.

The main feature began with an enormous steam-train rolling across the screen. As it stopped, a young man, city-bred from his clothes, emerged from amidst the steam and smoke, greeted the green fields around him, and burst into song. It was the time-honoured story-line: wicked landlord, oppressed peasants, widowed mother, unobtainable lady-love . . .

After some minutes, Aparna registered how close she was to Raghavan. She withdrew her arms from the arm-rest and sat tight, her hands clasped in her lap. But however rigidly she sat, she could not avoid his sleeve brushing against her when he moved, as he did frequently, crossing and uncrossing his legs. Anticipating the next shift, she lost all contact with the film. A faint smell of camphor exuded from his crisp white shirt. Her body grew tense in an effort to resist the sensation of being sucked into a weir. His strong features in the darkness beside her revived childhood memories of a fear-filled encounter with the rock-carvings of Mamallapuram.

The story unwound itself. The heroine, it turned out, was the wicked landlord's good daughter. Clandestine meetings in father's banana plantation were the cue for further song.

'—A-a-a-a-ah!' The crowd let out a wail of protest as the air-conditioner ground to a halt. 'Not again!'

The air grew heavy with odours: cheap *bidi*, chewed tobacco, jasmine, and the sweat of talc-besmeared bodies.

Hero and heroine began singing a duet, singing and dancing, accompanied by a chorus of friendly farm-hands. A close-up of the smiling hero amidst a V-shaped array of turbaned heads caused Aparna to shudder in her seat. *Balu!* That smooth, fleshy face staring at her from the screen was Balu!

She got up, clutching the pit of her stomach, afraid she would be sick. Raghavan jumped up immediately. Kumar and Nitya turned round in alarm.

Raghavan leant over her. 'What's the matter?'

'I feel sick. I'll have to go.'

'All right, then, follow me.'

'—Hey, you there, what are you doing, blocking us like this? Sit down.'

Raghavan grabbed Aparna by the hand and led her out. Nitya and Kumar followed.

Once out of the building, Aparna snatched her hand free. 'I'm sorry, Nitya, Kumar. Please go back and see the film. I'll be all right. I don't want you to miss the story.'

'Look. It's the interval. Everyone is coming out. We're not missing anything. How do you feel now?' Nitya put her palm on Aparna's forehead. 'You seem hot. Are you running a fever or something?'

'I don't think so. It's just the crowd. I can take a rickshaw and go home. You must all see the rest of the film.'

'No, not when you're unwell.'

'I will take her home.' Raghavan's words seemed more of a command than an offer. 'You two stay and enjoy the film.'

'No, no. There's no need.' Aparna felt herself falling into concentric rings of darkness and light swirling in front of her.

'I insist. You look faint.'

They stood, silent.

Nitya and Kumar exchanged glances. Nitya brightened, and turned to Aparna. 'Raghavan is quite right. Kumar and I won't go in unless you do what you are told.' Marriage had given her authority.

'All right then.' She felt too weary to argue. The rings were closing in.

Raghavan led the way through a mass of staring eyes, and they reached a cluster of cycle-rickshaws alongside the compound wall.

The rickshaw-wallahs were dozing, curled up in their vehicles. It was at least an hour or two before the crowd would begin to spill from the cinema.

'Shall I wake one up?'

'No, please don't. I'd rather walk. I need the air.' Sitting next to him in the theatre had been bad enough; riding home with him, crammed together in a cycle-rickshaw, in full view of the crowds in Flower-Bazaar—what a god-send that would be to gossip-mongers! Why had she ever left the house? The ancients were right. She should have kept behind locked doors and not gone gadding about.

'You shouldn't walk that far. My bungalow is only a few yards away from here. Could you manage that? Then I'll get the car and drive you home.'

'Yes. Thank you.'

Old Bridge Road was deserted, but for a pariah dog barking at the full moon. Raghavan slowed to let her keep pace. They walked in silence.

Torchlight shone into their faces as they approached the bungalow: Thambiyah, gathering up his *lungi*, stood up, scratching his head sleepily, torch in hand.

'It's all right, Thambiyah. You can go home now. *Amma* here is feeling unwell. I am driving her home.'

'Whatever you say, Collector Sir.' Thambiyah retrieved his top-towel and shuffled out of the compound, nodding his head from side to side, and grinning.

'—Shall I get you something? Coffee? Aspirin?'

'No. Just some water.'

Raghavan went inside.

Aparna stood by the pillar. Why was that film called *'Desert*

Moon'? There was no desert, not much of a moon. Whereas here, in this compound, the shrubs were drenched in liquefied silver, and the ground looked like a bleached rug. Where was the moon moving to so fast?

When Raghavan returned with a tray, he found her sitting on the steps of the verandah, staring at the sky. He placed the tray between them, and sat down. 'Here, have some buttermilk. Good cure for a queasy stomach.'

She sipped the buttermilk, and spluttered, choking. Away from father, away from all those voices whispering, maligning, cavilling, chiding, away with the moon, racing helter-skelter through the cloudless sky to somewhere in space where there was no past, no future, no memories, no pollution, no disgust, no Balu . . . If only Balu could be purged away, and she could be free, this might be the beginning of her life . . .

The tears that had been welling for days, months, years began to flow. Soon she was shaking with sobs, burying her head in her knees.

CHAPTER TEN

It was the fifth time, Kittu counted, the fifth time that Raghavan had jumped up from his seat and walked round the room. Once, twice, or thrice, Kittu could ignore; but when the folds of his flesh were made to start and shudder for the fifth time, how could he just pass it over?

'Sir?'

But he might as well have addressed a stone pillar.

Raghavan stood by the window, tapping the frame with pen in hand, staring into the distance, his eyes intent yet vacant, as if he were undergoing some out-of-body trance. It was perturbing to see a young man usually so neat, brisk and alert, now with a crumpled shirt and dishevelled hair—and in no fit state to receive their visitor.

Kittu cleared his throat noisily. 'Collector Sir!'

'Yes? What next? Another batch to sign?'

It was a relief to get a response. 'Here, sir! The papers you asked me to sort out, the ones to do with the potter's claim to dig river-clay.'

Raghavan returned to the desk and signed the papers put before him, without asking any questions; that was odd, the failure to double-check, considering what trouble lay ahead, now that the Collector had approved the potter's claim to dig river-clay where brahmins bathed. Kittu began be worried.

'Sir, it's nearly eleven o'clock.'

'So?'

'Mr Gautam will be here at any moment.'

'Who?'

'Mr Gautam from New Delhi. It is all there in that letter we received last week.'

'Oh, him! Is he coming *today*? Has Kabir gone to fetch him?'

'Yes, sir.'

Raghavan resumed tapping. Kittu took a closer look. Something was certainly wrong. Twisting his elephantine frame solicitously, he ventured: 'Collector Sir, may I inquire if anything is wrong? Has the Collector received bad news from the family, or something?'

'Bad news? Family? —No, Mr Kittu, all is well.' Raghavan picked up his tie from the back of the chair, put it on, combed his hair, and repeated in firm, clear tones, as though to wake himself up: 'No, no, all is very well with them.'

'All well? That's good, sir. It is good that all is well.' Kittu mopped his face with his top-towel, untwisted himself and tried again. 'May I be asking if all is well with Collector Sir?'

—BEEP! BEEP! BEEP!

The car-horn was blaring under Kabir's insistent thumps. Raghavan took the opportunity to ignore his assistant's question. '—Right, Mr Kittu. Here he is: Mr Gautam. Where is Thambiyah? Send him to get some eats and some orange-soda!'

'Yes, sir.'

Raghavan braced himself to greet the man from the north who was visiting Kuchchipuram on a cultural shopping-spree. —Just as well Kabir arrived when he did, or Kittu might have continued probing. It must be quite transparent, the state he was in, for Kittu to make such an effort.

What could he have told him?—that something had happened last night to set his nerves a-jangle?

Last night: Raghavan could feel his heart pounding. He could not recall how long he had sat on that verandah, holding Aparna, absorbing her sorrow and her softness, while her tears drenched his shirt. When the courthouse clock chimed, they had come to, and his grip had tightened round her as she tried to wrest herself free. The herbal perfume in her hair-oil still hung about him this morning. ... All the way back in the car, she had sat silent. She had disappeared through that dark doorway without a word. And in this harsh morning-light, against the incessant drone of the grasshoppers, he was struggling to beat down tides of fear: the fear that, by trying to touch, hold, comfort, to break down centuries of taboo, he had lost her for ever. ... If only he could sweep aside this stale mound of papers and staler people, rush to South Car Street, beat on that door till she answered it, and then be reassured. . . . Instead, here he was, having to make polite conversation with Mr Gautam, Cultural Counsellor to the Festival of India Committee, Export Division.

'—South India! Land of green fields, grand temples, and gorgeous women in sarees! And with big *idlis* too!' Mr Gautam guffawed as he jigged cupped hands under his chest, and his laughter rippled through a mane of silvery hair, carefully coiffeured to conceal baldness and to recall India's genius of the sitar, Ravi Shankar. From his embroidered *jibba* in Lucknow-muslin down to his curly Ali Baba slippers, Mr Gautam exuded culture. His flowing white garments, the image of artistic ethereality, billowed over the solid contours of a sensualist in his late fifties; dark rings under his eyes and heavy eye-lids witnessed to many a night spent at dubiously cultural soirées.

Raghavan extended a hand stiffly, then signalled to Kittu. 'We are most pleased to have you here. Welcome to Kuchchipuram.'

Kittu garlanded the visitor. They went inside.

'Thank you, thank you.' Mr Gautam sniffed the flowers as he lowered his ample frame into the sofa. 'I love visiting the South! As I am saying always, the South is the heart of Hindu culture; and culture is my business. There is little about this culture-business that your Mr Gautam here does not know.'

It suddenly clicked: the fellow reminded Raghavan of old-style village *zamindars*, men who were known to frequent, even to own, temple-dancers—that same heaviness, the same aroma of self-love and corrupt wealth.

Raghavan handed him an orange-soda and held out a plate of sweets and savouries. Watching Mr Gautam munch and gulp, he could see that it was going to be a hard day of culture-crunching. Yet to offer any slight to a central government bureaucrat would only bode trouble for himself, and for his district. Exercising *dharma*, he had to tell himself, meant curbing one's gut-reactions; he must swallow his distaste and be gracious.

'Where would you like to start? There's the Shiva-Nataraja Temple, famous for its Dance of Shiva figure. Then there are the newly-dug up bronzes—and, of course, anything else you'd like to look at.'

'Where should I start? Let me see, let me see.' Mr Gautam wiped his mouth and, jerking with burps, put on his rimless spectacles to inspect the itinerary that Raghavan held out. 'Temples I have seen by the dozen, and I can't transport temples, only bits of them. We are already doing reproduction-Khajuraho. How can it be an Indian exhibition without our most notorious erotica, Khajuraho? No trouble in getting an audience if we have those. Who would want to miss such images of ecstasy? Seeing is believing. I am often asked if the erotic gymnastics of the Kama Sutra are feasible. I send them to see Khajuraho! Ha, ha, ha, ha!!'

Raghavan waited for the ripples to subside. 'How about our finds? The main one, of Kumaran, or Murugan, is a rare Chola bronze of astonishing grace.'

'Yes, yes. I am certainly keen on anything rare. Next to erotica, go for rarity and novelty, I say. But to tell you the truth'—Mr Gautam leaned towards Raghavan and gave him a friendly slap on the shoulder—'do you know what I am really after? Folk-art is all the rage these days in the west, especially *live* folk-art! Makes good import-export. I am here to capture and transport *live-culture*! *Live-culture* makes the best exhibit of all!'

Raghavan shuddered to think of some cultural zoo: Mr Gautam, whip in hand, imprisoning village-folk behind bars, and bellowing at them to be *'live-culture'*.

'I don't know if we have anything that would fit that description.'

Mr Gautam's bushy brows shot upward. 'You have horses!'

'Horses? Oh! You mean the clay-horses of Aiyanar Temple?'

'Precisely! You don't understand me yet, it seems. Let me explain. What I am seeking is not just some clay-horses.' He waved his hands and shook his mane dismissively as he built to a climax.

'I want to capture the artist at work, the spirit of rural India!'

'That would mean Velan the potter and his son. I have to warn you, they don't think of themselves as artists. For them, making those horses is an act of worship.'

'That's the beauty of it! —Can't you see? Where else would you find an unselfconscious, primitive artist, communing with the incommunicable?' Mr Gautam chuckled, relishing his paradox.

'Let me see if Velan is here. He usually hangs around in the compound. He'll have to walk with us to the grove.'

'Splendid! I am ready for an amble through the countryside, after that bus-ride. I could be travelling by car, or first-class train—why am I travelling by bus?' Mr Gautam paused; Raghavan waited to be illumined. 'Because it is in our crowded buses, crammed full of men, women, children, and chickens, that I see real India; that's where I commune with Mother India, like Bapuji. Do you understand?' There seemed to be tears in Mr Gautam's eyes.

Mother India in a smelly bus: Raghavan's brahmin nose twitched. Fellows like Gautam would keep Mother India cooped up there for ever, just for the sake of an aesthetic thrill, while they indulged in Havana cigars and imported whisky in their expansive, air-conditioned mansions! . . . But he bit back his anger, and let the exporter of live-culture gush on, unrestrained.

Velan was found, and led the way. The Aiyanar Temple lay deep in the arecanut grove. The temple was no more than a tumbledown brick sanctum, sprouting banyan roots from broken walls. Flanking each side of the path that led towards the fearsome deity stood an array of terracotta horses. In their fading ochre-and-white, there they stood—mute, giant toys, bearing witness to some mysterious presence, imperial, awesome, eerie.

'Wonderful! How majestic! —And the size!' Mr Gautam rubbed his hand over the flanks of a larger than life-size figure, and turned to Raghavan. 'Ask him, your potter, why he makes these horses.'

Raghavan translated the question. Velan shook his head.

'—He says his son makes them now. He can no longer knead clay.'

'Never mind, never mind. —Ask him why his *son* makes these horses.'

Raghavan duly repeated the query, and the reply. '—He says, isn't it obvious to "northern sir"? A warrior needs horses. How else can Lord Aiyanar patrol the demons?'

'A *warrior*-god? How fascinating! And demons too! Just as I say in my lectures—this is another case of folk-art celebrating the creative forces of the demonic!'

'"Celebrating?" —From what I've seen, it's more like plain terror. The village-folk can't even tell whether this Aiyanar is a conqueror of demons, or the chief demon himself! And you can surely guess what *that* means: blood-sacrifice, animal, most certainly, but even human, in the past!'

'Oh, why worry about such niceties? I am sure the villagers don't. They know how to live at peace with a mystery-paradox. Why should we spoil it with questions?' Mr Gautam bestowed a smile of benign understanding on the assembled crowd. 'Does the potter know why I am here? Tell him, tell him the good news. His son shall travel overseas! To England, with his horses! Foreign travel! He will be famous!'

Mr Gautam's forehead shone in anticipation of Velan's wonderment and gratitude. The old potter listened quietly as Raghavan translated, and rolled his head from side to side. Then he spoke, without animation.

Raghavan smiled a little. '—Velan says, his son is welcome to it. Even a boat on Valli River makes his stomach turn. He wants to know who will look after his son.'

'Of course, *we* will—the committee will.'

A further pause, whilst Raghavan conveyed this assurance. '... Velan says he is worried because you are all northerners. Your ways are not our ways, your food is not our food, and his son can't talk your language—and what will he do in a cold country where he is bound to fall sick?'

'The old man doesn't trust me? Peasants! Always suspicious. Give them gold, and they bite on it with their rotten teeth!'

'I'm sorry, Mr Gautam. But you can see why he is concerned. So would I be if I was sent to some jungle tribe and hadn't a clue about what they were doing or saying, whilst my fate was being decided. I can just picture him, locked up in some concrete horror, cold and bewildered, longing for a kind word and a bit of home-cooking.'

'Oh, I understand, I understand.' Mr Gautam tried again. 'Tell him how *privileged* his son is to serve Indian culture, what a great *honour* it is to be going to England.'

This time Raghavan could report a more favourable response. '... Velan says he is happy it is Mueller Sahib's country. Mueller Sahib's country is blessed to be seeing Aiyanar's horses. — Mueller, by the way, was the famous Indologist who lived here. He dug up Roman remains. Velan knew him well in his youth.'

'Sure, sure.' Mr Gautam began to sound weary.

'Collector Sir!' Velan's son came forward, seeing that the old man had finished. 'Collector Sir. What about clay?'

Raghavan passed on the query.

'Tell him it is all taken care of.' Mr Gautam yawned as Velan's son persisted. Raghavan translated the heavy sibilants of Tamil into acceptable English.

'Velan's son says the horses turn out right only with Valli River clay. He is asking if they have any sacred rivers over there?'

'Sacred rivers! Ask the British for a sacred river? What a joke I'd be! Tell him not to worry, everything will be taken care of. He can have the finest sculpting-clay. We'll get a *pujari* to bless it, if he likes. Sacred rivers! What next?'

Mr Gautam had plainly had enough of this particular cultural encounter. Raghavan decided it was time for another gastronomic interlude.

'Lunch at Udipi Lodge, then the temple or the bronzes.'

Lunch with the Cultural Counsellor proved to be a leisurely exercise. Enthusing over his plate of rice, *sambhar*, *rasam* and curries, Mr Gautam regained his self-importance, and held forth. 'This I call the "cultural politics of food". When the Indians colonized South-east Asia, what did they do? They spiced up Chinese food; so we have a culinary extension of culture in Singapore, Malaysia, and even Thailand. Of course, you wouldn't know, being a vegetarian brahmin; but ah! what you are missing, what you are missing. —Waiter! Another *paan*!'

Raghavan began to be anxious. If Mr Gautam continued in this fashion, he was bound to miss his bus to Tanjore, and that could mean being stuck with him for the night.

'Sorry, Mr Gautam! We must leave now if you want to see those bronze-statues.' Raghavan looked at his watch. It was nearly four o'clock, and the last bus was due in an hour and a half.

'Of course, of course. All good things must come to an end. — That was a superb *paan*! I didn't know you Tamils could make sweet *paan* such as those. —I am all yours now. Where are we going?'

'To the courthouse; that's where the bronzes are being kept. Safety reasons.'

*   *   *

The main room of the courthouse, which adjoined the police-station, had become a shrine overnight. Townsfolk brought offerings of incense, camphor, betel leaves and bananas, leaving them outside the window through which they had caught a glimpse of their exiled god. Marigold and oleander garlands were draped round the steel bars that obscured their vision of him. An assorted crowd of urchins and shoppers on their way to Flower-Bazaar loitered outside the police-station.

The general buzz indicated a heightened excitement.

The policeman on duty parted the crowd. 'Make way, make way! Collector is here! Collector!!' Raghavan saw it was Raju, the bony young man from St Joseph's who had looked to the Collector for help when the padre began hounding him.

Mr Gautam pointed to a saffron-clad, emaciated figure, clinging to the bars of the court-house window. 'Who is *he*? A local sadhu or something?'

It was Muniya, the cobbler. Raghavan pushed through. 'What's going on here?'

'They are watching Muniya, Collector Sir,' Raju explained, shoving aside some youngsters with his baton.

'He shouldn't be here. Doesn't he know that this is government property?'

'He won't budge from here, Collector Sir. Day and night he is here, sir, ever since his stall under the peepul tree was wrecked.'

'Stall wrecked? Do the police know?'

'Yes, sir. Police are looking for the culprits, sir.' Raju hadn't quite identified with his new role.

'Muniya can't stay here. This is neither the temple nor the bazaar.'

'I told him, sir, but he won't move. He says nothing, sir. He can't.'

'This won't do. Muniya! —Hey, Muniya!!' Raghavan approached the cobbler, and shook him by the shoulder.

Muniya turned round. Raghavan shuddered and stepped back.

'*Muniya*! What have you *done*?' Raju was right. Muniya could not but be silent. A three-pronged skewer was stuck through his tongue. Two others were threaded through his ear-lobes. A smaller trident was across his neck, piercing the skin of his Adam's apple. There were larger tridents through his arms.

Raju explained. 'It's his vow, sir. For the firewalking.'

'Firewalking! What a piece of luck!' cried Mr Gautam, coming forward to join Raghavan. 'I have heard about holy-torture, and this time I am seeing it. What luck!' He got out his video-camera, ready to add another slice of live-culture to his collection.

'Excuse me, Mr Gautam. I must first do something about this. I can't open the door to the bronzes with Muniya in this state. Who can predict what he or the crowd will do?'

But while he was speaking, Muniya pulled back from the bars. He prostrated himself before the god, picked up his brass-bowl and stick, and made his way through the awe-struck crowd; the skewers dangling from his tongue, neck and ears swayed ominously.

'What a pity the show is over so soon!' The Cultural Counsellor put his camera away. 'And what a dumb show, *what* a dumb show! Just like a silent movie!'

*   *   *

Raghavan slumped wearily in his car as the Tanjore bus took off in a cloud of dust. Mr Gautam was safely on board.

'Where to now, Collector Sir?' asked Kabir, ever ready for the great adventure.

'Where? . . . To the temple, Kabir.'

It was more than time he confronted the *dikshitars*. Surely, they were behind the cobbler's plight? Who else would drive him demented with anonymous menaces?

And yet—who was he to call the cobbler demented, when his own state would hardly bear scrutiny? The day had drained him of any exhilaration he might have felt on account of last night; his limbs seemed to be drying up. Every chance word grated. He felt himself sinking into some heavy malaise, rather as his feet might sink into the sands of Valli River when the stream dried up in summer.

Raghavan entered a dark, low-ceilinged room, its granite walls wet with moisture. The *dikshitars*, all twenty of them, were in council, their bare chests and arms shining with sacred ash and sandalwood, their tufted hair knotted not at the back but on the side of their heads. Undoubtedly, they were an impressive group. As his eyes adjusted to the gloom, he spotted Vedam Iyer in their midst.

'—Ah, it's you, Raghavan. How fortunate! I was just explaining to the *dikshitars* that it is all here in these deeds of the temple, everything about our Kumaran.' The advocate flourished a sheaf of dry palm-leaves, whose contents he had been deciphering. 'Come in, come, come. I'll show you. Here it says clearly that, "resplendent on his bejewelled peacock-throne, Kumaran resides in the southern sanctum of the Shiva temple . . ." That's it! That clinches the legal claim. As I said before, those bronzes belong to us. "Resplendent!" That means the Lord was adorned with emeralds and sapphires. Not any more—that infidel Mirza must have plundered them when he wreaked havoc here!'

'I demand to know who wrecked cobbler Muniya's stall.' Raghavan's words resounded from the walls like dry thunder.

The *dikshitars* looked at one another as if he had uttered some profanity. Raghavan directed his attention to the leader of the assembly, a venerable old man with overhanging dugs, his sacred thread dangling across a paunch that had seen many a dinner at weddings and festivals. The old man slowly raised his eyes. 'What have we to do with that pariah?'

'Who else could have done it?'

'There are all sorts of rogues and vagabonds about—communists, atheists, brahmin-haters, Christians—any one of them could have done it. You should think before you speak, young man. What have we to do with the likes of him?'

Vedam Iyer tried to restore peace. 'Saint Nandanar was a pariah, yet he saw the glory of Shiva.' He nodded affably.

'This cobbler is no saint. He is a sinner of many births. He has maimed an idol. Who knows what goddess she is? He will never wash away his iniquity, even after seven re-births!' The paunchy *dikshitar*, having put Vedam Iyer in his place, turned to Raghavan with an oily smile. 'However, we are blessed with an auspicious young god, and the Collector should see that the Lord is promptly installed in his sanctum. Just now we are considering an auspicious day for the purification-ceremony. We are very fortunate that we have a *brahmin* Collector in our midst. A god should not be kept in jail.'

'It's not a jail, merely a safe-room. But before you get too far on with your plans, there's something you ought to know. The bronzes may be needed for an exhibition overseas.'

'Shiva, Shiva!! As if it is not enough that the god lies languishing in a well, is found by a pariah and knocked about, then is put in a jail like a criminal—now the unbelieving government is wanting him to cross the seven seas. What for? Sin of sins! It must not be . . .'

'It will *have* to be, if the Delhi government orders so. You'll be hearing from me soon. *Namaskaram*.' Raghavan stepped out of the clammy room.

'—Wait! Don't go yet.' It was Vedam Iyer. Raghavan stopped, and the advocate ambled up to him. 'Don't worry about the *dikshitars*. They'll agree. I'll see to that. After all, I *am* preparing their claim. As for the pariah, I hear he is undertaking harsh penance. What can one do? Untouchable as he is, he still has much faith, much fervour. He seeks his god in his way, we, in our way. Stones, trees, serpents; Rama, Krishna, Kali—there is room for all kinds of worship, the higher and the lower. Brahman is one, and is all things to all people.' The advocate took a deep breath. 'I am going to the *bhajan* now. Will you be coming?'

'No. I'm weary.'

'Then I'll see you on Sunday for some more nectar of Kalidasa.'

'Yes, of course.'

*   *   *

The door of the house was closed, but not locked. Raghavan walked in.

'Aparna! . . . Aparna!!'

'Who is it?' Her voice came from the kitchen.

'Me. Raghavan.'

There was silence.

He crossed the courtyard and entered the kitchen. It reminded him of stepping into an inner sanctum.

She was bent over a cast-iron brazier, toasting pappadums on a charcoal fire. Her fingers were deftly tossing the dry pappadums one by one over the glowing charcoal, then retrieving them as they curled, before they could char. Her face glowed from the heat.

'Father's out.' She spoke without looking up.

'I know that. In fact, that's why I'm here. It's you I've come to see.'

Aparna concentrated on the pappadums.

'Aparna! Look at me! I *love* you.'

'Please don't say that.'

'I have to say what I feel. I'm not clever with words. I love you. I want to take you out of this. I want you to belong to me. Do you love *me*?'

'It's not a question I can answer. What you call "love" is an illusion. You'll get over it.'

'It's *not* an illusion and I don't *want* to get over it.' Raghavan stepped closer. She moved away. 'Why won't you face me? You are afraid of the truth. At least your tears spoke the truth. Last night . . .'

'Please don't mention last night. You must forget it. You mustn't even think of me.'

'How can I forget? And why should I?'

'You must. I was tired and weak—confused. That film reminded me of . . .' She stopped, then resumed toasting. 'It can never be, this love you talk about.'

'Why not? I'm not afraid. I want to marry you. If we stick together, we can defy the world.'

'Oh, it's not just the world.'

'What is it then?'

'It's me. Can't you see? It's me. You deserve something better than me, someone fresh and pure. I'm unclean, soiled, polluted, just a mere cast-off fit for burning. They ought to have put me on that funeral pyre.'

'Aparna! Stop!'

'Why? It's the plain truth. I'm a widow because of my past sins. I'm defiled. I'm no better than that pariah, Muniya. I understand how he must feel. He only maimed a statue, but I . . . Do you know what my in-laws think? They think . . . they say, that I . . . that my stars killed their son.' She seemed to be choking. 'Please go. Father will be back any minute. He mustn't find you here with me.'

'Why not? I want to talk to him. Does your learned father have any *idea* how you feel? Does he know how sick you are, sick and deluded? I must talk to him.'

'I beg you, don't. He likes you. He likes you very much. He's enjoying reading Kalidasa with you. So am I. Please don't spoil everything. He'll be shattered. I like things as they are. Listen to me, I beg you.'

'"As they are?"'

'Yes, as they are.'

'Do you have any idea how much of a torment it will be, both for me and for you?'

'All life is a torment. Isn't that what the Buddha says?' Aparna turned to face him. 'Life is a torment if we let our passions sway us. One *can* contain them. I should know.'

'What kind of a life is that?'

'Exhilarating!—Like this, see!' She bent down and picked up a piece of glowing coal, then rolled it in her palm before dropping it back into the brazier.

'What are you doing?' He reached forward to catch her hand, but missed. She slipped it behind her back, and after wiping the palm on her saree-end, held it out. 'See! I'm not hurt.' She laughed.

'You play childish games.'

'But there's nothing childish about what I am saying. —Shush! Can you hear them, the drums?'

'If you mean that rumble—yes, I can, just about. —What about them?'

'They are beating the drums at Mariamma Temple. They must be hoisting the flag for the firewalking.'

'What of it? —Why are you changing the subject?'

'I'm not. You must go and watch. Then you'll understand. You, me, that poor pariah—we all need to firewalk. We can tread the hot coals, even dance on them, if we trust the gods.'

'We might get burnt.'

'Not if we trust the gods. We have to trust.'

'I don't see any gods *to* trust.'

'Then you must find out yours.'

'You sound just like your father. Much as I respect him, I don't agree. All these gods are a delusion. Gods in temples, gods in the jungle, gods behind bars—what's the difference? I see them all. They might be amusing if they weren't so menacing. Don't let them delude you!'

'It's not them that delude me. But I *am* deluded. Otherwise, how can I explain my behaviour last night? I am still this side of the black curtain.'

'Black curtain?'

'I mean the one in the temple. You've surely seen it, the black curtain that hangs in the inner sanctum.'

'Well?'

'It's the curtain of *avidya*, of ignorance, delusion, call it what you will, what separates us from . . . from . . .' Her face brightened.

Raghavan stood stupified.

He had been afraid he might lose her. But now he realized that he had never gained her. He had been poised to rescue her from the world; but as he watched her rapt face, it dawned on him that he must first free her from the gods.

'It's time you went,' she said.

CHAPTER ELEVEN

Ever since the Meyyur floods, whenever Padre Yesudasan could no longer stave off the urge to have a bout with his God, he turned to his "carbuncular cross". Clutching the base of the gnarled piece of driftwood in the corner of his bedroom, the padre was pleading aloud.

'Lord, O Lord, why are you trying me so? Why are you letting these idolaters mock you with their unseemly daring? Are you not the Lord of consuming fire? Why then do you not consume their ignorance, their folly and their *wilful* superstition? Why do you let my flock slip and slide, lusting after that fearsome female? Do you not *hear* what they are saying, those ignorant backsliders? "—She must be placated, our goddess Mariamma must be adorned with golden eyes. We must cool her angry eyes," they say, "otherwise, our children will be struck down with smallpox." . . . How am I to convince them it is otherwise, when Mariamma seems to grant their boons? Why do you let her triumph? Why do you let your people be so swayed, so possessed by that evil goddess? Why? Why? Why? . . . You know I do not wish this Muniya any harm; but can you not see that the cobbler must not triumph today?'

There was a knock at the outer door.

The padre paused, and cupping a palm behind an ear, listened hard. His hearing was poor today. It was the din of those drums at the Mariamma Temple. They had been going on for ten days. Try as he would, whether by silent prayer or loud lamentation, he could not shut out that incessant, low rumbling. A menacing drone infiltrated houses, trees, fields, penetrated every nerve and fibre, blotting out other sounds, and pulsating with the heat of the fire-pit.

'Who's there? Come in.' His knees hurt as he rose.

'Collector Raghavan.'

'Welcome! Welcome! This is a pleasant surprise. Please take this chair. There is no one about'— he laughed wryly—'all off at the firewalking. —Do you like tea? Will you partake?'

'Yes, thank you.' Raghavan seated himself in the easy chair the padre pushed towards him. His face looked tauter than ever.

'. . . You look weary. Have you been walking in this heat? —Working too hard?'

'No, no. Just a short walk from the railway-crossing. Kabir brought me. I was on my way to see the firewalking. I brought your folder back.'

The padre grew attentive. The young man would hardly have come all that way just to return a folder. He could have sent his peon. 'Are you sure you don't need it any longer? —How much sugar in your tea?'

'Two spoons, please. There *is* one thing . . .' Raghavan paused as he sipped the strong, sweet tea. He put the cup down and came to the table where the padre was standing. 'Did I tell you, I spoke to the *dikshitars* about Muniya's stall?'

'What did they say?'

'I rather rashly presumed they were responsible for wrecking it. They denied having anything to do with him.'

'They would.'

'You don't believe them?'

'No, no. I believe them. I believe them all too well. They certainly would have nothing to do with him. How could they, being superior brahmins? —But that does not mean they are not responsible.'

'So you think they arranged it?'

'That's the usual way.'

'Wait, padre. We don't have any proof. This is all guess-work, just guess-work because you dislike the *dikshitars*. Why *shouldn't* I believe them?'

'You may, of course. —But do you? Do *you* like them?'

'It's not a question of whether I like them or not. It's a question of finding the real culprit or culprits, whoever they are. We have to look at all possibilities. Does this Muniya have any enemies?— personal enemies, I mean.'

'He could have. He's quite quarrelsome—not like his brother, Muththu. Muniya likes getting into arguments. His wife ran away, a few years ago—went to Madras to become a film star. Heaven knows what became of her. Most likely, she's walking the streets—that's where most of them end up. Ever since she left, Muniya has got very pious: more devout than the caste Hindus. He hopes to be born a brahmin in his next life. He listens avidly to the pundits— and can quote them too, against me and his brother. He hasn't forgiven me for his brother's conversion. His brother's family is all he has got; he still hasn't given up trying to win him back.'

'And how does his brother react?'

'Muththu's peaceable—but Muniya is very clever. That's why they call him the "peepul-tree pundit". Do you know, he has the cheek to ask, "Why does your padre want you to worship a sickly-looking foreign god who wasn't even able to defend himself, when we have so many, healthy, strong, beautiful gods to choose from?"'

Raghavan laughed; but seeing the padre's solemn face, he restrained himself. '—I'm sorry. But I can see there's something in what he says. —Do you think he will come through unscathed today?'

'How can we tell? I'm going myself, just to see how he fares. It has to end, this tussle between us, one way or another. I'm afraid for Muththu. I might as well be honest with you: if Muniya gets burnt today, I shall not be sorry.'

Raghavan scrutinized the padre for a moment.

'. . . I appreciate your frankness. Now it's my turn to be frank. I didn't really come here to discuss the cobbler—though I *am* concerned about him.' He sat down, and drew the chair closer to the padre. 'That folder I borrowed from you—do you know why I wanted it?'

'You said, to see Meyyur as it was.'

'That wasn't the major reason. It was your photograph of the peacock-dancer—Aparna. I wanted it; I've got it here. —Could I keep it?' Raghavan drew the photo from his pocket. 'I want to keep it, because I love her.'

'I see . . . I see.' The padre chuckled, rubbing his chin. 'I see . . . —Would you like some more tea, something to eat? I see . . .' He started busying about.

'No, thank you.' Raghavan sunk back into the chair. '—I had to talk to somebody. The past few days, I've been in turmoil, not knowing which way to turn.'

'I understand. Really, I understand your problem. What are you going to do? The advocate may be a learned man; but he's not going to break with tradition.'

'Her father knows nothing as yet. She wouldn't let me say anything to him. —Anyway, I can face that. But it's Aparna who is the problem. She's full of guilt—false guilt, in my view, but I can't convince her. She says she's defiled, that feelings of love are an illusion— something to be overcome. She even held a piece of live coal in her hand, just to prove it.'

'Oh, all that Hindu talk, I know it too well. Very alluring when life becomes too much of a burden.'

'I'm sure I could rescue her. She's deeply hurt and needs love. The other evening, she broke down and wept in front of me. —I'd seen her, practising some dance-steps with her pupils. She's a natural dancer—and all her life is ahead of her. But she's determined to suffocate in guilt, while denying that she's suffering. How can I reach her? What am I to do?'

The padre listened, rubbing his chin. Finally, he put a hand on Raghavan's shoulder. 'Dare I say what I'm thinking?'

'Say what you like. I'm beginning to lose hope.'

'Well, take comfort. I admit it's rather strange comfort. But whatever she may say, the urge to life is likely to win. If you've kindled love, it will hurt her to reject it. She's going to suffer. That's your hope.'

'How am I to take comfort in hurting her *more*?'

'You'll have to forgive me for being blunt. You Hindus prefer to by-pass suffering; you postpone the problem with theories of *karma*, ignore it or deny it altogether, write it off as illusion—whereas we...'—the padre looked sharply at Raghavan before proceeding—'... our faith insists that we face it. Only through suffering can we discover ourselves. Aparna has to suffer—*real* suffering, not false guilts. So must Muniya. So long as he seeks to placate false guilt, as he's doing today with this firewalking, he'll never find real deliverance. That's why I won't be sorry if he gets hurt.'

'But what if Muniya *doesn't*?' Raghavan stood up. '—Shall we go and see? Can I take you there? —I may not understand all you say, but I'm grateful to you for listening to me. I'm sure I can trust you to be discreet.'

'Rest assured. It's my pleasure and privilege to keep a confidence. Let's see what happens to Muniya. —Aren't these drums a nuisance? They're getting louder and louder. The procession must be nearing the temple.'

*   *   *

Vedam Iyer looked up from his newspaper, and saw Aparna putting on her sandals.

'You're going somewhere, my dear?'

'I'm going to the Mariamma Temple.'

'Oh, why go there? Always clogged with the primitives, so *rowdy*—all sorts of ragamuffins loitering about.'

'I want to see the firewalking.'

'Oh, *that!*' Vedam Iyer sniffed. 'The ignorant seeking sensation. You ought to stay clear.'

Aparna hesitated. '... Father, I said I'd go. My pupil, Rani—her family are doing special *puja*, for chickenpox.'

'Well, just take care, take care. You never know at these gatherings *what* will happen—so much hysteria about!' He returned to his newspaper. 'Are you going alone?'

'Rukku is meeting me. . . . Father, grandmother's bailiff is doing the sacred-pot dance this year. He's the best, that's why I thought...'

Vedam Iyer looked up at her over his paper. 'My dear, you look just as you did as a little girl, when your mother wouldn't buy ice cream from the cart on the street-corner. You didn't know then it was dangerous, that it might bring on typhoid; you don't know what's dangerous now. *How* am I going to look after you?' He shook his head. 'All the same, You are a grown woman. Not for me to stop you. Go. —Go, by all means. But be careful.'

*   *   *

'Big sister can't come. "Went distant" this morning—wrong time of the month.' Rukku's brother had caught up with Aparna outside the north *gopuram*. 'I am to go with you, if you want me to.' The boy looked wistfully at the *bidi*-shop across the street, where his companions were engrossed in a contest of spinning tops.

'You don't have to, Pichchu. I can manage on my own.'

The boy lingered for a while, and then moved away.

Aparna set off towards the Mariamma Temple. She did not feel secure in this part of town. She rarely came into North Car Street or crossed the new railway bridge to Mariamma's temple. The goddess guarded the northern boundary of the town.

The crowd swelled along North Car Street, surging forward in the dusk like an incoming tide at full-moon. Sturdy peasants surrounded her. When they glared at her, she was tempted to turn back, but pushed on. She must see how Muniya fared. She could hardly retreat now, not after what she had said to Raghavan about the firewalking. And he might be there. She pushed forward briskly.

'Mind my child, lady! Look where you're going!' A peasant woman with a toddler on her back had swung round at her. Aparna just missed the shower of betel-juice the woman spat out. She tried to slow down, but found that she had little control over where or how she moved: the crowd was carrying her, pushing and pulling to get ahead of the firewalkers. The procession turned the corner.

There they were: a daring, defiant row of saffron-clad bodies, smeared white with sacred ash, the steel spears and tridents skewered through their arms, necks, ear-lobes and tongues dangling menacingly, threatening to split the flesh open—yet the only red visible was the vermilion of outsize circles of kumkum on their foreheads. With clay pots of burning camphor balanced on their heads, they paced forward in unison to a swinging step, bodies yielding but not flinching, as the *pujaris* behind them lashed their backs and sides with hemp-rope whips. Priests and penitents were flanked by arcs of peacock-feathers carried aloft on the shoulders of *kavadi* bearers who danced themselves into trance, the whites of their eyes bulging upward as they swayed and lurched to the staccato beat of drums. The crowd gasped as the dancers wove in and out of the procession in a frenzy of adoration, chanting *'Vel Muruga, vel Muruga, shakti vel, vel shakti'*. A medley of chants rose over the din of drums.

'—*Maa-ri-a-mma, Maa-ri-a-mma, enga-muththu Maa-ri-a-mma, enga-muththu Maa-ri-a-mma* . . .'
'—*Vel Muruga, vel Muruga, shakti vel, shakti vel* . . .'
'—*Jai-Shakti, jai-Shakti, jai-Shakti, jai-Shakti* . . .'
'—*Shiva-Shiva, hara-hara, Shiva-Shiva, hara-hara* . . .'

As the crowd spilled over Railway Bridge, the sun was setting behind the Mariamma Temple, scattering orange-and-blue clouds, fringed with silver. Mariamma, the golden-eyed goddess, a squat, stone figure of indeterminate shape, draped with a sash of brilliant yellow crêpe, stared from her pitch-dark sanctum into forty feet of blazing charcoal before her. Heat from mounds of red-hot coals that were stacked high on either side of the fire-pit, ready to be raked in to enhance the blaze, kept spectators well back. One by one, dazed firewalkers and entranced dancers began their ordeal. Propelled by a rising crescendo of chanting, they stepped lightly into the pit, and, keeping an even pace, walked, hopped, or danced along the burning path toward their goddess.

All eyes were on the treading feet, and on the embers that cushioned them. Aparna, wedged between groups of weavers and potters, waited for Muniya to take his turn . . .

*   *   *

Whoever said he was walking on fire? Muniya could not see any burning charcoal. Fire-pit? Who said it was a fire-pit? No, it was mother Mariamma's 'flower-pit'.

Black coal	*dark stems*
Yellow flames	*clusters of chrysanthemums*
Orange glow	*rain-fresh marigolds*

> Red-heat . . . . lithe hibiscus
> White-heat . . . . cool camphor
> And at the end of this carpet of livid flame-flowers, there in the trench of turmeric water, lay liquid gold distilled from the ascending moon.
> Whoever said he was walking on fire? No. Couldn't they see he was treading goddess Mariamma's golden 'flower-pit' . . . ?

*   *   *

Muniya walked the fire three times. As he dipped his feet for the third time in the water-trench to cleanse them, one of the *pujaris* removed the skewers and tridents from his tongue, ears, neck, and arms.

Muniya was free—free of guilt, and jubilant. He prostrated himself before the goddess, muttering: 'Whoever says she is ferocious Kali? No, Mariamma is a benign mother. She is mother Mariamma, Murugan's mother, Muniya's mother, the mother of the whole world . . .'

'—He's through! My brother is through! Muniya is through! No burns, no burns at all!' Muththu came running towards the padre, his skinny face bursting with joy.

The padre glared, seized him by the shoulders, shook him. 'He is through, is he? No burns, you say, you are quite certain? Tell the truth.'

'I *am* telling the truth, padre! I am no liar. Muniya is through without a burn.' Muththu wriggled to get free.

Raghavan pulled the padre off. 'Let him go! We can check for ourselves.'

The padre released Muththu. 'You are quite right. We must. You never know what lies they harbour.'

Muththu ran ahead to warn his brother.

'—They are coming, our padre and the Collector! The padre wants to see you.'

'The padre? What does he want with me? Can't he see I am saved? Look!' Muniya held out his hands and stuck his tongue out. There was no sign of a wound or blood where the tridents had been. 'Let him come and see! He can see for himself how my Murugan has saved me!'

'The padre wants to check your feet.'

'Does he now? You unbelievers, you're all the same! You don't believe, even when you see. It's plain as daylight I am not burnt. Let him come and check my feet! Not a mark, I tell you, not a mark! He won't find anything. He can look and look!'

Seeing that the padre was accompanied by the Collector, the *pujaris* surrounding the penitents cleared the way.

'—Hi there! Hullo, Collector! Hullo, padre!'

Raghavan recognized the high-pitched nasal twang. It was Gerry, Kumar's American guest. Gerry had called at the bungalow once or twice, his head full of theories about the newly-found bronzes, and Kittu had eventually been instructed to choke him off.

'I had no idea you were here still. I thought you had left.'

'You're right. I did leave, then I didn't—if you get my meaning.' Gerry winked—and so also did the cameras and tape-recorders slung over him like cobras over a snake-charmer.

'Where have you been?'

'All over the district. Having a great time, temple-crawling, and collecting myths. Absolute gem of a district this, for work like mine. You should see what I've gathered. And my, what tales! Did you know, for instance,'—Gerry dropped to a conspiratorial whisper—'did you know that this Mariamma these folks are worshipping is really none other than the "boundary-Kali" of the Shiva myth? Could you have *guessed* the connection? When Shiva defeated Kali in the dance contest, she was installed here, on the outskirts. *Do you know why she is here?* —Libidinal energy, that's what she is; and these folks know you can't just wish her away. They daren't repress her energy. So she is ensconced here, demanding her dues. Isn't it wonderful, how it's all worked out? Respectable spouse in the temple sanctum—and this lawless lady out here: both acknowledged, both worshipped! Your people had it all sorted out, the id and the super-ego, long before Freud even thought of it!'

Raghavan was impressed. 'I know the story—but I never heard it explained quite like this. How did you manage to arrive at this? Anyone helping you?'

'The pundits and the *pujaris* at the temples. They tell the stories, and I find the meaning. They're marvellous chaps. What's more, now I can talk like your folks. Just listen!' Gerry turned to Muniya and said something in broken Tamil. '—Sure way to reach the people, learning the lingo—though I must say, speaking your

Tamil is like rattling pebbles in my mouth!' Gerry laughed, cameras and tape-recorders clattering.

A bewildered Muniya was asking his brother: 'Who is this pink sahib? What does he want?'

Raghavan translated Gerry's Tamil: 'The pink sahib is an American pundit. He wants to know what you felt, firewalking. What *did* you feel? We want to know as well, the padre and I.'

'Nothing. I thought nothing.'

'Nothing?'

'I was walking no fire-pit. Don't you see? It is mother Mariamma's "flower-pit". She saved me.'

'Quite a wit!' Gerry flicked open his spiral book to jot it down. '"Flower-pit"! Just listen to that! What an amazing fellow! I tell you, this fire is no joke. I dropped my handkerchief, just to check, and it burnt out in no time. Some fellow over there put his toes in, and was squealing with pain. This is some fire! It's fantastic what some folks can do! How do you think they do it?'

'I thought you knew that too.'

'Well, I have my modest theory. No offence meant—but I think it's a biological thing, a racial characteristic, if you get my meaning. These fellows have thick soles, they've been used to walking on hard things barefoot.'

'But do you really think that's adequate? It seems too simple an explanation for what we've just witnessed. What's your verdict, padre?'

'Verdict? I have no verdict. Muniya is unhurt—as this fire is fire. How and why, God knows!'

'He doesn't seem all that happy about it.' Gerry leant towards Raghavan.

'He's not. He has lost.'

The padre walked away. He cut a sad, lonely figure in that jubilant crowd. Raghavan moved to join him, but was distracted by a piercing shriek.

A woman was running across the fire-pit, her saree burning. She collapsed by the water-trench and lay there writhing, clutching her feet, shrieking and wailing.

'*Ayyoh Mariamma! Ayyayoh Mariamma!* Sinner of sinners I am, Mariamma! *Ayyayoh Mariamma!*'

Raghavan joined the spectators about the victim. *Pujaris*

flocked round her, splashing turmeric-water with bunches of neam-leaves.

From the whispers, mutterings, and knowing head-shakes of the crowd, Raghavan could piece together the woman's story. She has been coming to the firewalking every year, for some years now, trekking by foot from the next village across the rice-fields. Her husband had left her for another woman. She had kept her vow year after year, praying for his return. Never before had she been burnt. Something was surely amiss, this year. Maybe she had broken her fast, maybe she didn't keep all the purity-rules, maybe the other woman had put a curse on her, maybe *she* had put a curse on the other woman, maybe, maybe . . . It was plain, as anybody could see, that the goddess was angry. The wrath of Mariamma had fallen upon this guilty sinner.

When Mariamma turns wrathful, where can one flee?

'—She has second-degree burns. She ought to be taken to the clinic immediately.' Raghavan was addressing one of the *pujaris*, who carried on wafting his neam-leaf branch as though he hadn't heard.

Someone brought a bamboo-stretcher. The woman was carried off, her loud wails clearing the way.

Raghavan caught up with the padre, who had stopped to watch.

'Well, padre, there's a clear casualty for you. What do you make of it? Bewildering, isn't it? It's obvious that some get hurt, like this poor woman, while others like Muniya go through unscathed. How do you explain it?'

Raghavan might have been talking to himself. The padre walked on towards the bridge, then stopped and shook his head, muttering: 'Of course, of course. I should have known. I should have realized.'

'Known what?'

'It's *him*, behind it all—Shaitan, the Evil One.'

'You don't really believe that these people are evil?'

'No, not the people, no, no. I pity them. They know not what they do—literally. This is Shaitan's doing. It's him, all the time, behind this mass-hypnosis. It's one gigantic spell cast by Shaitan.'

'What about the woman who got burnt?'

'Just think: for all her firewalking, year after year, her husband still doesn't return to her. She must have begun to doubt. I hope that now she's cured of this delusion. It solves no one's problems.' The padre paused. 'You look doubtful yourself.'

'It seems rather convenient, to invoke the supernatural: God or Shaitan.'

'We live in a world surrounded by the supernatural. We ignore it at our peril. As Luther said, if God doesn't ride us, the Devil will! —You still don't believe?'

'If that's the case—where does Shiva-Nataraja come in? Surely you're not going to say *he* is Shaitan?'

The padre's face clouded again. 'I can't answer that—not yet.'

They had reached the bridge where Kabir was waiting. He was holding a handful of kites and balloons—presents for his children. Now that Mariamma's awesome ceremonies were over, the fun had begun in earnest: the crowds, animated by a full-moon, were bursting into carnival. It was as if Flower-Bazaar had been transported to the north of the bridge: pipes and drums were giving way to film-music blaring from loud-speakers mounted on mobile vans. Clusters of women and children thronged around gipsies who hawked brightly-painted toys, beads, ribbons, combs and brooches. Raghavan searched for Aparna.

The padre extended a hand. 'Good night! The moon is lovely still, even after man's been treading all over it. We are surrounded by mystery—the moon is a mystery, so is the wearer of the crescent moon, your Shiva. I concede that much.'

'Can't I take you back?'

'No, no. I need to think. I'd rather walk. We shall see what we shall see . . .'

What did he hope to see? Raghavan could not tell. Nothing had been resolved; yet the padre seemed to be regaining some buoyancy of spirit. Was it just the habitual rebound of the professionally pious?

Half-way across the bridge, with Kabir scattering pedestrians by persistent blasts on the horn, Raghavan suddenly leant forward. 'Kabir! Take me to South Car Street. I won't ask you to wait. I don't know how long I'll be.'

*   *   *

The door was ajar. Music poured from the courtyard. Vedam Iyer was listening to the radio. Hearing footsteps, he called out.

'Is that you, my dear? I was getting worried.'

'I'm sorry, it's me: Raghavan.'

'My dear boy, come in, come in. I couldn't tell, in this darkness. I like listening to music in darkness, don't you? Aparna is still not back. She set out on her own to that Mariamma Temple.'

'I've just come from there. I didn't see her. I was . . .' Raghavan broke off, not willing to confess he had been looking for her.

'It's old age. I get anxious about her. She was going with some family I don't know.'

'Shall I go and look?'

'Well . . .' Before Vedam Iyer could complete his sentence, Raghavan had left.

He turned from South Car Street into Flower-Bazaar, and saw Aparna coming towards him, running rather than walking.

'What happened?'

She shook her head, breathing fast and looking back in agitation. 'Not here, not now. I must get home. Father must be worrying.'

'So he is. That's why I've come looking for you. What happened?'

Once they were in South Car Street, she slowed down. 'Oh, just a gang of youths who'd hit the bottle, whistling and teasing—they started following me from North Car Street. I couldn't shake them off. It's foolish of me; but I get frightened easily.'

When they entered the house, she faced him. 'Please don't say anything to father. My companions didn't turn up. He mustn't know that. Please don't say anything to him. He wasn't very happy that I went.'

Raghavan followed her into the courtyard.

'—Ah, there you are, my dear! I needn't have worried. — Raghavan, why don't you eat with us and stay for a while? There's a good concert on at nine o'clock, direct from Music Academy. Stay and listen.'

'I was going to Udipi Hotel . . .'

'Too much lodge-food isn't good for you. —Which reminds me: I had a letter from your father today. Your mother has been busy. Mani has sent me two horoscopes for our family astrologer to look at. They're right. It's time you became a householder.'

'My mother? And now my father too!' He had caught Aparna's expression. 'How many times do I have to tell them, I have no intention of marrying yet?'

Vedam Iyer pulled down his spectacles, somewhat taken aback. 'Steady! Steady! They're doing no more than what seems right to them. We all feel like that, at first. I remember when I was young—only twenty when my parents started looking for a suitable match. These things have to be done in good time. You'll have nothing to regret. As the Vedas wisely say, of all the *ashramas*, the householder's is most eminent. Now, the four stages of life, as you know, are ordained . . .'

Raghavan looked at Aparna once more. She was watching him intently, her lips tight, her eye ironic. She must not be left with the wrong impression: despite all this nonsense from his parents, he was still a free man. He must somehow talk to her alone.

Vedam Iyer was already far distant; eyes closed, he was chewing over the sentiments he had just uttered, as was his wont.

Raghavan stood up. 'I feel very hot and sticky. I need a splash before supper—may I?'

'Mmm? —Of course! Certainly! You know where the well is. — Aparna! Give Raghavan a towel and a *veshti*.'

Raghavan took off his shirt, hauled water from the well, and bending over, began splashing himself. It was some while before Aparna came out into the courtyard with his towel. She put down her bundle, averting her eyes. The cotton *veshti* she had brought looked new—perhaps not even the advocate's.

'Stay! Don't go yet.' Raghavan came across to her. 'You were laughing at me, weren't you?'

'No. Why should I? Father's right. You *should* be a householder.'

'That's enough of that. —Where were you at the firewalking? I searched and searched.'

'I saw *you*. You seemed preoccupied. Anyway—what was the point? We both saw Muniya triumph. So I left.'

'The woman got burnt. You surely heard her screaming?'

'Oh yes. I admit that was terrible. It must be shattering to fail.'

'Is that what you call it—"failure"?'

'What can one say? She must be guilty in some way. Poor soul.'

'Aparna! How can you talk like that? She was just a desperate woman, taking a crazy risk. She was deluded—but so are you. I *must* speak to your father.'

'Oh, no! Don't do that!'

'Why stop me? What are you frightened of?'

'Don't you realize what it means, telling father? If you really care about me, you must never say a word.'

'Why ever not?'

'Do I have to spell it out? Didn't you hear him quoting the scriptures? He'll no doubt find some more . . . If you speak as you say you must, that will be the end. I'll never be able to see you again.'

'Then you *do* care.' Raghavan dropped the towel and attempted to seize her hand.

'I don't know—I don't know what I feel. Seeing that woman run like that, screaming, and her saree burning—it could have been me. There's no glory in pain.'

'Aparna! Listen to me! It doesn't *have* to be you. All you have to do is simply say "yes" to me.'

'You don't understand. You can't understand. You don't know what it is to feel as I do about myself. Let me be. I can hear father in the kitchen. I must go in.'

CHAPTER TWELVE

'Grandma?'

'Mmmmm! —What are you wanting, my girl?'

'May I ask you something?'

'Ask! Ask! Why all this stretching and twisting? What is this big secret you are wanting to know from this wizened one?'

It was Sunday, three days after the firewalking. Aparna was sitting with Lakshmiyamma, picking stones and specks from off a mound of rice-grains. Vedam Iyer was away in Madras, presenting an appeal in the High Court. She could have gone with him, could have seen brother Gopal and his family.

But there were many, many reasons why she couldn't, why she didn't, why she said 'No, not now, not just now; another time will be better, certainly not now.' When her father looked surprised, she added, 'Grandmother needs me. Rukku can't be with her till Sunday.'

What she hadn't told father was that the school cultural-show was due on Tuesday. There were posters everywhere: *'The Dance of Kaama*, choreographed by Aparna-Gauri'. Her pupils were performing, and they were nervous. She couldn't abandon them. There would be such commotion. From behind the scenes she must be their heart and soul. She must make them perform their best—the whole town would turn out and the chief guest was to be the Collector. . . . No, she could not have gone to Madras at a time like this.

'Well? I am waiting to tell.' Lakshmiyamma could see her granddaughter was day-dreaming again.

'Grandma! When you were married, how long before it happened—grandfather's going?'

'How long? Let me think! What a question!—Long enough for me to have borne him two daughters and a son. What with nursing your mother through whooping-cough—always sickly she was, your mother—what with running hither and thither after your uncle—such a prankster he was—and with Malini, Malini meaning trouble always, what with all this, was I sitting down and counting my days? How long? Fifty years ago it must be, fifty or thereabouts!'

'So long! What was it like, being a widow for so long?'

But Lakshmiyamma was not listening. Once her memories were switched on, there was no stopping the flood.

'. . . I still remember, as if it were just yesterday, the judge waking up, waking up and bathing—he always headed straight for the well as soon as he got up, never had his coffee till he bathed—I still remember him telling me, telling me without worry, without fear, just telling me about that dream. That dream! It was an omen. The family priest had come to him in the dream, saying, "Come, judge, sir! We must go to the river to perform this new-moon ritual for the ancestors". NEW MOON. He knew straight away, when he heard that. What else could it be but a call from Yamaraja, the Lord of Death? Then the next night he was gone, your grandfather, gone in his sleep to join the peace of our ancestors, leaving me like this—gone, gone before he touched forty. He never had to grow old, while I . . . I . . . They broke my bangles, tore my *tali*, shaved my head—and here I am still, fifty years on, still bearing my curse. . . . Why be talking about it now? That was another life—and this, another one yet. —Watch out! What are you doing, girl, mixing up clean grains with stone-ridden ones?'

'Sorry, grandma! I wasn't looking.'

Sad she might sound, lonely she was not—not Lakshmiyamma. Hair shorn, shunned as inauspicious, she had, with growing years and grown-up children, accrued enough power and dignity to put them all in their place.

... What did she, Aparna, have to look forward to? Father was getting on, and after him lay a long stretch of guilt-laden loneliness. Could she really bear that?

Yet she had never looked at it like this before—at the bare facts. Not that she didn't know them; but they hadn't mattered—or rather, she had attempted to will them into non-existence, had even regarded them as an asset. To be free, free of the bonds that tied you to the world, to be spared the pain of loving and losing— she had considered herself blessed. 'Be *yogayukta*', 'be an athlete of the spirit'—those words of Krishna to Arjuna, hadn't they been her strength, her goal, her source of inspiration? To be free, free from the clogging weight of the world, to make her body a supple vehicle for the spirit—wasn't that what she had longed for, even when she danced? Why be dragged back now? Why should it change now, just because ... just because ... ?

'—*Aparna, listen to me! It doesn't have to be you!*' Raghavan's words were a challenge; they had lodged in her like arrows. She must pull them out, break their spell before it was too late. She must not allow him to step any closer, she must get right away, if necessary.

Aparna shook herself. Had it really come to this, that she needed to run? What was she running from—and to where?

The grandfather clock chimed.

Four o'clock.

It was his usual time to arrive for his Kalidasa session. Not today. Vedam Iyer had sent him a message to say he had been called to Madras.

'What's the matter, girl? Why are you fidgeting so?'

'Nothing, grandma.' Pushing the cleaned grains to one side, Aparna stood up. 'I must go home for a while. The roses need watering. Also, I must get a book to read.'

'Where's that Rukku? Never here when you need her! —And you are off as well! It's four o'clock, and the cow is starting to moo already. What am I to do?'

'Rukku will be here soon, I am sure. I won't be long. I'll be back straight away. Please!'

Aparna walked fast, shielding her eyes against the glare of the afternoon street. Her head was a mass of sensations.

She needed to think. She needed to sort out her thoughts from her feelings, her fears from her fantasies. She needed to be back where they had taken shape, had grown, and were now threatening to disintegrate her. She must recall, recapture, re-live what she had felt, exactly as she felt it while he was there.

She hurried along South Car Street as if pursued. Her hands trembled when she unlocked the front door.

A musty smell of hay hung in the darkness of the *rezhi*. Paddy-sacks stacked high on each side of a wide central runnel gave the corridor the feel of a banked canal.

It had been a favourite childhood-haunt. It was here that she had sought refuge from misery: when brother Gopal ruled her out of the all-boys game of dacoits; when the gawky young calf, a docile pet, was taken away from the cow; when her mother fell ill, spreading an eerie hush that seeped into the very walls of the house. Many an hour she had lain hidden among these sacks, as in an enclave of warm, friendly creatures, waiting for someone to notice her absence—and many a time she had eventually crawled out, fearing that no one would.

Aparna slowly sank to the floor, sliding down the sacks. The rough gunny scratched her back. She closed her eyes, and let go.

She could feel a shaft of silence opening within her, from brow to heart. It was a familiar, fearful descent down into that darkness. Down she slid, with the inevitability of a stream tunnelling through a gorge, plunging into an interior cavern that seethed with memories.

A gekko bleeped overhead, chipping in vain at the silence that lay on the house. The walls were mute, recouping from the ceaseless lapping of the advocate's ringing tones. She also was glad to be released, even if for only a brief while, from her father's eloquent certainties.

It had been refreshing to hear Raghavan. His voice had a vibrancy that she had come to associate with the rustle of crisp white paper.

'You don't have to be like her.' . . . He had made it sound so easy, so simple, as if all she had to do was to walk away, step from *her* past into *his* present. He was calling her as if he were all in all. As if . . .

Who was he? What was he?

A Collector.

A neat, handsome young Collector, full of zeal for tidying up messy situations, messy lives—an old-fashioned District Collector such as the Raj might have been proud of.

That had been her distant view. Would that it had remained so! But distance had collapsed at a touch, a stroke, a tight embrace. Like a skilled surgeon, he had snipped off the bandages, and, forceps in hand, was pushing and probing at a wound she had sealed off. And his compassion was turning to passion.

What lay behind the passion? What needs, what fears, what hopes, what darkness? What was he, in truth?

And what was she now?

A mere shell—or, rather, a derelict house that harboured a guilt-inflicting ghost.

What was there left to give? The sap of life, that divine energy which had filled the hollow of her bones and rippled through her limbs and glowed at the tips of her poised feet as she executed an intricate *pada*, or shone through her henna-stained fingers when she defined a *mudra*, no longer flowed through her body, as it had before the advent of Balu. Instead, she was a dull ache from brow to heart.

'You don't have to be like her.' It was not so easy, or so simple.

What had grandmother said? About the dead and their summons?

Irresistible.

Raghavan was not the only presence; beyond him was another, the shade of Balu.

The porpoise-bulk of Balu surfaced—a muddy stirring that always left her awash with guilt.

Could she ever be freed from the pollution that clung to her?

Even if she could, what would it be for? For a mirage called 'love'?

There was a rattling noise from the courtyard. Aparna jumped up in panic.

A burglar? At this time of day?

She tiptoed quietly to the door and, keeping herself well-hidden, peered out into the bright light.

She could see nothing. Perhaps the burglar sensed she was there.

The tiles rattled again, this time louder than before.

No burglar worth his salt would make so much noise. She pushed the door fully open and walked out. The noise came from the eastern side of the roof.

A monkey.

Perched on the slope of the roof, his small, lithe body glowed a translucent pink in the heat. He was holding a faded rose-garland, and with great solemnity pulled its petals off, prising them through their glitter-thread wrapping and scattering them around, with an occasional pause to lick or bite a petal or a succulent stem. Now and then he wriggled from side to side, and was forced to dig his feet frantically into the crevices between the tiles, dislodging them in the process. That was the rattle she had heard.

What should she do? She looked around, found a prickly-broom and made towards the monkey.

Her throat was dry. So much silence had entered her that no word, no noise would come out. She stood by a pillar and waved the broom at the creature.

Seeing her, the monkey dropped his garland, with a swift swing broke off a coconut branch that overhung the roof, and began mimicking her.

They stood looking at each other, partners in an absurd ritual that led nowhere.

Aparna dropped the broom and burst out laughing.

The startled monkey dropped his branch and began running. As he leapt, he kicked the garland, sending it spinning in the air. The garland fell at Aparna's feet.

Roses.

She had forgotten them.

Aparna picked up a bucket and went towards the well.

She was just returning from the well, her bucketful wobbling, when she heard a knock at the front door.

Rukku walked in, panting. She must have run all the way.

'Aparna! Aparna! Did you hear the news? I came straight away when grandma told me you were here. I saw Rani's mother in the market. Then she told me. I said to myself you'll need help. I didn't wait a moment. Rani's mother was so worried, not finding you.'

'Why? What's happened?'

'Rani's mother wanted to tell you herself; but then the house was locked and these mud-brained neighbours told her you were in Madras. She was so relieved when she saw me in the market, and told all.'

'Told what, Rukku?'

'Rani has chickenpox. Very bad, very bad. She can't dance. You'll have to do Parvati yourself, so she says, the head-mistress. —What will you do?'

Aparna's arms went limp, the bucket fell from her, and water rushed in all directions like a river gone berserk.

CHAPTER THIRTEEN

The grandfather clock was creaking itself up to chime again. Aparna counted.

'One . . . two . . . three . . . ' She had counted like this, tossing and turning on the *dhari* mat, when the clock chimed twelve, one, and two.

If that monkey hadn't interrupted, she might have sorted herself out. But just when she was struggling ashore from a dangerous current, she had been flung back into a yet more menacing whirlpool further downstream.

What was she to do, with father away?

Without Parvati, there could be no 'Dance of Kaama'.

She must get them to cancel it.

Yes, she must tell them she could not perform. Surely it needed no explanation, surely they would understand . . .

It was inconceivable that they would cancel the event. How

could they, after months of preparation?—this one and only function of the year at which the whole town was expected, the wealthy *chettiars, mudaliyars* and *naidus*, all noted philanthropists and devout patrons of *bharatanatyam*?

... But to assume, to insist that she could go on, that she should reverse her life at a stroke, put aside her widow's garb and be transformed into a dancing girl—how could they expect that? The very thought made her shudder.

Suppose she dared, suppose she summoned the courage to adorn herself once again with kumkum, silk and jewels, could she really dance as Parvati should, her heart filled with expectant ardour? Could she ever command that innocence, that purity? Where was she to find it, how was she to conjure up what had perished in her?

They'd have to accept, she would have to tell them she could not.

The 'Dance of Kaama' would have to wait till young Rani recovered.

*   *   *

'Come in ! We have been expecting you only.'

The padre was with Principal Manikkam. His presence signified crisis.

Aparna hadn't anticipated him there. Her hopes of convincing them began to dwindle.

Mrs Manikkam's dentures flashed from her stern, ebony-dark countenance, which was half-hidden by silver-rimmed spectacles. 'Very good of you to be so prompt. That girl Rani's mother was getting frantic, not finding you. We were worrying too, you know. Now that you are here, we can drop all our worries—isn't that right, padre?' Everything about Mrs Manikkam was silver and grey: her hair, her face, her saree, even down to the anklet-bells she affected. When she spoke, her words cracked like sky-splitting lightning through monsoon clouds; whoever came before her instinctively looked for cover.

Aparna did not move from the doorway. 'Please . . . I am sorry, Mrs Manikkam. I cannot do it.'

'You cannot? How can you say that? Do I have to spell it out, what that means? Everything will be ruined. We'll never see those patrons again! Is it just some ordinary building-fund function like other schools have? You know what it is for, the whole town knows. Everyone knows how desperately we need a nursing-home at the clinic. No more babies dying in miserable hovels, no more mothers dying giving birth! How can you say this, you cannot help? Is it just, I am asking, is it just, hmm?'

'Not so fast, not so fast, Mrs Manikkam!' The padre pushed his chair back, lest the bewildered girl should class him with the wrathful matron. 'Please, Miss Aparna, do come in and sit down. —Mrs Manikkam! Didn't you tell me you have a geography class just now? Your students must rioting by now! Aren't they lucky to have you? What brilliant maps you draw! I can never resist looking at them as I pass by. Don't worry about this, we'll sort it out. And please, send the peon for some ice-soda. Miss Aparna looks hot and thirsty.'

Mrs Manikkam knew the padre's compliment was genuine. 'All right then! I am going. I hope you only get the right answer from this girl.' She picked up her handbag and strode out, keys, chains and anklets jingling.

'That's better.' The padre chuckled. 'She scares me. I don't know how her pupils cope. I gather they call her S.S. Is that right, S.S.?'

'It's said to stand for "Stainless Steel".'

'"Stainless Steel", eh? S.S.? Quite clever—and true too! . . . Where were we? Let me tell you first. I understand your difficulty.'

'Thank you.' Aparna sat down, wiping the perspiration off her face.

The padre watched her, cupping his palms and drumming his fingers, but saying nothing until the pepsi-cola arrived.

'The advocate, your father—keeping well, I hope?'

'Yes. Very well. He is away in Madras. High Court case.'

'Ahh! . . . I see.' The padre sipped his drink leisurely. 'One can easily get addicted to this in this heat, don't you agree?' He laughed.

It was as though she were still a five-year-old waiting at the clinic, enduring her pain; in just this way the doctor had held out camphor-white medallions of mint, before dabbing her swollen tonsils with a purple liquid that stung her throat and made her retch.

Placing his empty bottle on the desk, and without looking at her, the padre phrased his next question.

'I believe we have a mutual acquaintance—one might even say, a friend—Collector Raghavan?'

Aparna started, and the drink spilt on her saree.

'The Collector?—Yes. He's a family friend.'

'Yes, of course, of course. We are very privileged to have him as our chief guest. He is well-disposed to our worthwhile schemes. So you see, it all depends on you. What do you say?'

'What is there to say? I am sorry it is happening like this, but I cannot, really *cannot* help. I cannot perform, the way I am. I am sorry.'

'Are you absolutely certain you are making the right decision?' Eyeing her with deliberation, he added, 'What will Mr Raghavan say?'

Aparna rose from her seat, flushing. 'What has he to do with my decision?'

'Hasn't he?' The padre paused a moment. 'From what I heard, he might have everything to do with your decision—why, even with your life.'

'"From what you heard"? What *did* you hear? What has he been saying? I never thought . . .' Her voice grew hoarse.

'Don't be frightened! He hasn't been indiscreet, I assure you. It's just that I know—because he himself came to me—that he loves you and wants to marry you. He would, if only he could.'

'Oh, no!' Burying her face in her hands, Aparna sank back in her chair.

The padre walked up to the window and looked out till she had recovered.

'—I must go.'

'Don't, please! We have hardly begun talking. Then there is the little matter of what we are going to do about Parvati. If you ask me, I cannot but think of this chickenpox crisis as an act of Providence.'

'"Providence"? It's a disaster.'

'Some disasters have a way of becoming providential. You'll see what I mean.'

'I don't see any such thing.'

'Look at it like this. Remember the floods last year? That was a disaster. Many lives lost, cattle and farms ruined—and Meyyur, lovely Meyyur, just wiped out! Mind you, it was beautiful up on the hills with all those trees and plantations—but down by the river where the scheduled castes live, just a backward village, infested, with the poor in shacks and hovels! What right do we have to expect humanity in such conditions? Not surprising it breeds communist crime-dens. No proper houses, no schools, no clinic, no drains, nothing! Then the floods came, water creeping up and up until all had gone—no more shacks, no more lives, nothing, just nothing left! . . . Shall I tell you something? They say it's "an act of God"—a "natural disaster" they call it. I tell you, there was nothing of God or natural about it. Just plain human evil, that is all—original sin, that's all! Greed! Selfishness! Callousness! Corruption! If they hadn't opened that dam up-river without warning, well . . . what's happened has happened. What's the use of blame, blame, blame? The dead are not crying, only the living.' The padre shook himself and resumed. 'Now with this new Collector, there are signs of new beginnings. He showed me his plans for Meyyur. There are to be new houses—proper houses this time, brick-and-mortar homes, a school, and even a co-operative for the fishermen. New life, from wiped-out land. Perhaps we needed the floods after all. —So you see, a disaster can turn providential.'

'That may well be, with Meyyur . . .'

The padre waved her silent.

'Now take this chickenpox. This girl Rani gets it, no one but Rani. She cannot perform. No one else can. It is your dance, only you can do it. The dance is the most important event of the year, that's what they are all coming for. It means a nursing home for everyone in Kuchchipuram—everyone, not just the rich. So we have to go on, with or without Parvati. Without Parvati, it will be a poor event, a broken event, a non-event. What will happen? I'll have to get up on the dais and explain to a packed hall: "Due to chickenpox, the Shiva in the dance is without a Parvati."—"The 'Dance of Kaama' without Parvati? Is this a joke?"—I can hear the grumbles, the jeers, and the money-back demands. I don't know how many pledges of donations we will lose forever. . . . Now if you lay aside your scruples just this once, we shall not only save the situation, but with a bonus. Not just any young dancer, but the renowned Aparna-Gauri herself is to perform. I can see the cheques getting added noughts. And . . .'—the padre paused, and came close to her—'And, it is a God-sent opportunity for you to start living again. You *do* love him, don't you?' He was leaning over the desk as he put the question, almost in a whisper.

Aparna shrank back.

Laughing, he straightened up. 'I shouldn't be asking that. You do love *him*, don't you?—your Nataraja, the Lord of Dance? Every dancer is his devotee, am I not correct? Shouldn't you be doing this performance for him? Not for me, not for the Collector, or even for the good cause, but for him, Nataraja? He commands this city, he is the Lord of the Universe, he danced in rage when he lost his consort, Sati—is this not true? And who's Parvati, but Sati reborn from the ashes? —Am I right?'

Aparna was dumbfounded. This padre whom she had always thought of as being on the 'other side', believing in an alien god, proclaiming a strange faith—to hear him talking like her father!

'Do you really believe Nataraja is the Lord of the Universe?' The question tumbled out before she could consider the wisdom of asking it.

'*You* do. That's what matters.'

'What you said, just now—all that's true. But it's not easy to forget what I am—a widow. What hope have I of being Parvati? Parvati has to be pure, innocent, fresh. These I am not, nor can I ever be.'

'My dear girl! It pains me to hear you speak so. You are young, you are beautiful, and—forgive my presumption—in my view you are innocent, totally innocent.'

'Sometimes I feel one thing, sometimes another. I don't know what to think. If only I could be strong and not confused by feelings!'

'My dear child! Don't be afraid of feelings! To live is to feel. What would we all be without our feelings, our sorrows and joys? One must feel and feel till the heart burns with love, like a lighted candle. Love lights up our life. Do not be afraid of falling in love. Only love can give one the courage to live.'

They stood silent for a while.

'—Well? Shall we see you tomorrow?'

'I don't know. I need time to think.'

'You have . . .'—the padre looked at his watch—'a little over twenty-four hours. I am confident we shall see you as Parvati. Good-bye. God bless you!'

It was drizzling as Aparna stepped out of the school-compound.

Dring-dring, dring-dring: 'Rickshaw, rickshaw, cycle-rickshaw, Miss?'

Aparna walked on, ignoring the cycle-rickshaw that had pulled alongside her.

'Why not take a rickshaw, Miss? Have mercy on a poor man, Miss! No fare this morning, and my children's bellies are drying up with hunger.'

He was scrawny, and, as he pedalled, his muscles moved like worn pistons within a thin casing of skin. Aparna hesitated.

The rickshaw-man felt encouraged. 'See that scoundrel, Miss, with that customer? That customer should have been mine, he was coming to me, then this rogue swings around and whisks him off, right under my nose.' He pointed to a rickshaw behind him whose owner was obsequiously wiping the vinyl-seat for a bald-headed, well-to-do *chettiar*. Something about that customer's demeanour, the easy grace with which he gathered up his *zari-veshti* as he climbed into the vehicle, and dabbed his brow without disturbing the boldly-etched sandalwood caste-mark, jolted her memory.

—The *nattuvanar*, Guru Ramiah, the only person who could set her right in this dilemma.

Aparna turned round quickly. The disappointed rickshaw-man was moving back towards the school.

'Oy! Oy, rickshaw! Come back! Can you go far, as far as Meyyur?'

'God bless you, *amma*! Most certainly, most speedily! Like an arrow piercing the wind, like a kite tearing the sky!' Face beaming, the rickshaw-man flung his right arm out, mimicking some film hero. A pretty lady of light weight, and a good long distance—what more he could wish for? He crossed himself as he began pedalling.

'Where to in Meyyur am I taking *amma*?'

'Do you know Guru Ramiah's grove on Tillai slopes?'

'Who is there who doesn't know the great guru's place? Wait a moment! Haven't I seen *amma* before? . . . Well, if I am not beholding the advocate's daughter! Why, so you are. Don't you remember me?—rickshaw-Muththu? How many times I have pulled you along in this chariot since you were that small, to the guru's place! Remember me a little?'

Aparna looked at him. He had aged, and looked thinner than she remembered. It was plain that the passing years had not improved his fortunes.

'So you are: rickshaw-Muththu. I do remember.'

Muththu chatted as he sprinted along, Aparna punctuating his reminiscences with a rejoinder now and then. They reached Old Bridge Road.

'It is a long time since I had the good fortune to carry *amma* in this vehicle to Meyyur.'

'I haven't been there for a long time.'

They passed the Collector's bungalow. Muththu slowed down to let a herd of goats pass by.

To think she might be dancing before him tomorrow. She could barely listen to Muththu airing his opinions on local politics.

'. . . And there he was,' he was saying, 'the Collector, without any warning, at our Sunday service. We were scared at first, then it turned out he hadn't come to question or charge us. Our padre tells us that this new one is not like the rogue-politicians. He is doing everything for Meyyur. Our padre says he is young and not tired of the wicked world yet. He is even trying to help my brother Muniya. Does *amma* remember my brother Muniya, the cobbler under the peepul tree? Why, hasn't he mended many a shoe and sandal for *amma* and the advocate?'

'I saw Muniya firewalking.'

'So *amma* saw all? He wasn't burnt one whit, no, not our Muniya. The padre checked him too. But he, my brother, is a worry to us all.'

'Why? What's happened?'

'What it is we cannot tell. What with the firewalking and the hooligans breaking up his stall, Muniya has got very strange. Can one blame him? He loses his wife, he puts up with it; he hits an idol by accident and risks his life firewalking—and how do the gods reward him? They set hooligans on him, wreck up his stall. Now he has lost everything: tools, scissors, hammers, nails, leather; some customers are threatening to beat him up because of lost shoes. And to cap it all, his pictures are all torn up and scattered as if a tiger had ripped through. He sits there weeping over the shreds. He sits on our porch and says nothing day and night, hardly touches his food, ants crawl all over the rice and him—but he doesn't care. He's gone screw-loose.'

'I am very sorry to hear this. Perhaps he should see a doctor.'

'That's what my wife says. But where will I find money for medicine?'

'Can't you take him to the clinic? Surely the padre will arrange for the doctor to treat him. It must be all those shocks.'

'He speaks rudely to the padre—how can I take him there? It's good of *amma* to think of my poor brother. —Here we are.' They had reached the slopes of Tillai. Muththu hopped off his seat and started pulling the cycle up the narrow path that ended in Guru Ramiah's grove.

'Wait, Muththu! Wait a moment! Let me step down. I can walk up.'

'It's nothing. *Amma* is light as candy-floss. You should be seeing some customers, veritable sweet-shop *marwaris* they are, flesh upon flesh rippling like an elephant's!' Muththu laughed, and Aparna joined in. She resigned herself to being hauled up. If she jumped off the moving vehicle, she might injure a leg or sprain an ankle. All things considered, she'd better not . . .

What would Guru Ramiah say? She had not seen him these two years. He came to the wedding and, with tears in his eyes, had blessed her. Perhaps he knew even then what was to happen.

Patches of blue sky showed through over-arching branches of lace-leaved tamarind trees lining the path. Often she had scrambled up their sturdy trunks, tearing her skirt, and greedily devoured the sweet-sharp pods and tangy leaves. As the rickshaw bumped up and along the path, memory upon memory of a past before Balu began to unfold.

She could hear the cooing and cackling of birds from the grove. It had always been a haven for birds: ring-necked parrots and mynas fought over the mangoes, guavas, gooseberries and rose-plums. Even before the rickshaw passed under the entrance-arch overhung with jasmine creepers, Aparna could feel the smells and colours of the arbour reviving her: hibiscus, oleander, *parijata* and, above everything, the heady scent of *nagalinga* flowers from a giant tree that dominated the grove.

Valliamma was under the tree, offering *puja* to the Shiva-lingam. As Muththu clanked his way up to the thatched cottage, she looked up, shielding her eyes and screwing her face against the sun's rays, which penetrated even dense foliage. Her turmeric-stained, rotund face broke into a welcoming smile.

'Well, I am blessed! Who do I see? Welcome, welcome. My dear girl, how long has it been! —Guruji! Guess who is here!' Valliamma's short, plump body puffed up with excitement. ' —How have you been, my girl? What sorrow, what sorrow to bear!'

'What am I to say, Valliamma? I am as I am.' Aparna sprang from the rickshaw and stretched her arms towards the tearful woman.

'Here, take this!' Valliamma proferred a *nagalinga* flower that she had been clutching. 'I can't but think this is very special; it is coming straight from the Lord. Just as I was looking up to see who was coming, it happened: this flower fell on the lingam and rolled down towards me, as if the Lord were saying, "Take this, and welcome your child come home". The Lord is indeed returning our "flower" to us.' Valliamma's eyes brimmed with tears again.

'What an extraordinary flower *nagalinga* is ! So fleshy and delicate. There's nothing quite like it, is there, Valliamma? When I was little, I was too scared to pick it ever, for I used to think that this hood of a petal was going to turn into a real cobra and hiss at me—and the scent is so strong that I was convinced it would cast a spell that I could not wake from. It still makes me giddy. Oh, it is good to be back here. When I sighted those tamarind trees, I felt as if I was shedding skins.'

'How strangely you talk, as always.' Valliamma shook her head. 'But I am telling you, I knew something was going to happen. Last night I dreamt of a funeral. Funeral-dream means something good. Then this morning, a gekko spoke from the good side of the lintel—and just now, this gift from the Lord . . . Let me look at you.' Valliamma halted and turned around. The rickshaw caught her eye. 'Oy, rickshaw ! You wait for *amma*. How long she'll be I cannot tell. I'll send you some rice and curds.'

'Most delighted, lady!' It was as Muththu had hoped.

'Come in, my dear! Our guru doesn't say much, but I can tell how his heart is bruised, grieving for you. It has been like losing a daughter for us—we who have none. That such a thing should happen to his best disciple! Only the other day he was telling all to our V.I.P. guest. Guess who? None other than the famous lady from Adyar, Rukmini Devi. She was coming to see your guru all the way from Madras, and they were talking and talking. She is writing about our Kuchchipuram dance-tradition. It was then that I heard him talking about you—so full of grief my ears were singed.'

'Why be crying, Valliamma? I am here now. I can't tell you how good it feels to be here! I came with a burdened heart, but already I am feeling light—light as this perfumed petal.' Aparna held up the *nagalinga* flower, and its mauve streaks shone through a sun-drenched white.

Guru Ramiah was sitting cross-legged on a silk-straw mat, reciting aloud from a volume of Tevaram hymns, swaying back and forth toward the sandalwood book-rest. Aparna prostrated herself before him, touching his feet. Guru Ramiah took his spectacles off and blessed her.

'Rise, my child! —Valli! Sweep the hall, spread my mat, get ready everything! Don't stand there whimpering!'

'Right away?' Valliamma protested. 'The poor child hasn't had a moment to catch her breath. Who knows when she ate or drank? It's nearly noon. Shouldn't she at least have a morsel?'

'Valli, Valli! How can you think of meals? She has come, hasn't she? What should we wait for?'

'But guruji! You haven't even asked me why I am here.' Aparna was being thrown into the water and told to swim even before she could ask how.

'Why else would you be here, if you weren't sent by the Lord? Let us resume where we left off two years ago. It was a *tillana* in Vasantha Raga you were doing. I remember as if it were yesterday.'

'So it was! Most demanding . . . But, guruji—don't you realize? Have you forgotten I am not the same as I was? Do you . . . do you really believe . . . Am I hearing right? . . . I . . . I am . . . to dance again?' Aparna gulped each word, choking with fear and an elation that seemed to strangle her.

'My dear child, shall I tell you how I have wrestled with that question since that which happened happened? The same question day and night, hitting away at me like a woodpecker tapping. Tradition, custom, the ways of our ancestors—what does it all mean, I ask myself, pacing here, what does it all mean? Does the Lord wish it? If he doesn't, who then? I ask and ask, getting nowhere. Then comes this lady from Adyar, like a kingfisher bringing the light of blue waters, like a messenger from the gods. I am talking to her, telling her all and sundry about our dance-traditions: about the four hundred temple-dancers that belonged to Shiva-Nataraja, here in Kuchchipuram, about the sad corruptions, about the "minor-chain" *zamindars* who ruined the women who belonged to the Lord, about the rash white men with their ignorant missionaries who wrecked all with their talk of social reform, about this and that, talking away. Then I begin to see, see clearly for the first time, how wrong we were to accept blind beliefs as god-given law. What if you *are* a widow, does that make you any less the Lord's? You belong to *him*, to *him*—not to any man, but to Lord Nataraja! So did the *devadasis*; "deva - dasi"— what does it mean but "the Lord's servant"? . . . Come, let us begin. —Valli! Is the harmonium out? Have you found my time-stick?—and ankle-bells for Aparna?'

'She must not begin with her hair like this, knotted and messy. Come, sit down!' Comb in hand, and armed with a bottle of herbal oil, Valliamma gently pushed Aparna by the shoulders, positioning her to plait her hair. 'And here, while I do that, eat this—just a plantain.'

Guru Ramiah tuned the harmonium. '—Not ready yet?'

'Pardon me, guruji!' Aparna hastened to tie her ankle-bells. 'I am nervous. I feel like a raw pupil, just beginning.'

'All will be right, all will. The gift that the Lord gives, he does not snatch away. You'll see.'

Aparna bent down to receive his blessing; and before she straightened up and with eyes still focussed on the ground, she addressed him: 'There is something more, something because of which only I came here today.'

'What may be that? Speak, speak!'

'The school cultural-function is tomorrow. I prepared my pupils to perform the "Dance of Kaama".'

' "The Dance of Kaama"? Well, that's astonishing. The lady

from Adyar was telling me about her plans. She is setting the whole of Kalidasa's epic as dance-drama.'

'Is she? Really?' Aparna looked up. 'I am only doing a segment, the part of the story when Parvati comes to worship and woo Shiva and how the lord of love, Kaama, shoots his arrow at the yogic Shiva—Shiva opens his third eye and Kaama is burnt down. It ends with Rati's lament and a *tandava* dance by Shiva. I have adapted Kalidasa's verses to suit a traditional concert-range, beginning with *alarippu*, followed by *jatis*, *varnam*, *padam*, and even a *tillana* at the end.'

'It should be wonderful—just like my Aparna to be so inventive! What then is the problem?'

'The girl Rani, who is to dance Parvati, is sick. I have to do it. There is a long *padam* and a *varnam* for Parvati's solos, before Kaama arrives.'

'Very good, very good. Excellent idea! There's no end to the infinite shades of emotion that one can capture in a *padam*—and with leisure, ease and grace! And what colour, description, mood, dexterity of spirit can you not show in a *varnam*, I ask you? I see no problem.'

'I am fearful. I am not what I was. . . . How can I dance as Parvati should?'

'My child! Do not be afraid. Let it come, let it come. As you dance, you'll no longer be you. The moment you fold your hands in *anjali*, and invoke our Lord Shiva, his spirit will enter you; let him enter the courts of your heart, for he is the true dancer in us all. *Chidambaram*, where he dances his cosmic dance, is none other than our inmost heart. That's where he tramples our ignorant self underfoot and releases our spirit.' Guru Ramiah closed his eyes. 'Listen to this!

> *"Jata Joot Madh Kalak Katha*
> *Sesh Chandra Lalit Jhalak Katha*
> *Roondh Malah Galay*
> *Sesh Dharani Dhara*
> *Parvati Shiva Hara Har*
> *Parvati Shiva Hara Har.*
>
> "He with the matted locks,

> From which flows the Ganges
>   in a sparkling cascade;
> On his brow, the serpent, and the crescent moon;
> With a garland of skulls he dances
> On the earth upheld by the great snake;
> Parvati's Lord: Shiva, Shiva . . ."

—Hear the footwork? So clearly Kathak. I got it from a dancer from the north who came to study with me. It says all. —Come, my dear! Let's start, and I'll teach you that dance—my offering to your Parvati.'

So they began, the guru plying the bellows of the harmonium, keeping time with his stick, and singing in his cracked voice. Aparna eased into an *alarippu*: her hands, her eyes, her neck, then her whole body moved, flexing, twisting, folding and unfolding like a lily or a lotus in the evening breeze. To limber her feet, the guru took her through fast *jatis*, and they were about to continue when Valliamma announced lunch.

'The poor girl is wilting in this heat. She'll drop if she doesn't have food. I beg you to stop.'

Grudgingly, the guru gave in.

'—I made you some *poori* and *aviyal*. I know how much you like that.'

'I would rather not eat,' Aparna protested; but Valliamma ignored her and spread a banana-leaf platter to serve her.

'The rickshaw is still here. I have given him food. What are we to do with him?'

'Tell him to go!' Guru Ramiah shouted from the courtyard where he was washing his hands. 'Pay him and tell him to go.'

'—Wait, Valliamma! I'll write a letter to Rukku. He can take it. Otherwise, grandmother'll send a police search-party to find me!' Aparna laughed. As she wrote to Rukku, she paused. 'And, may I say I am staying on, sleeping the night here?'

'With pleasure. Of course.' Both spoke at once.

Muththu was despatched with a handsome fee and a letter conveying instructions for the following day.

At Aparna's insistence the guru yielded to a brief siesta, and then they resumed.

Her guru was right. It was as he had said. With each step, with each movement, each *mudra*, she began to shed herself from herself; her energies, long pent up and frozen, began to thaw in the dynamics of dance, cleansing and purifying. She was no longer the inauspicious widow, feared and shunned, but holy Ganga, uncoiling from the austere heights of Himavant and flowing through the locks of Shiva as healing water.

She danced until dusk.

While Valliamma prepared supper, she sat on the porch, counting the stars one by one as they emerged in a sky that darkened from luminous blue to indigo-black. Within her, it was Deepavali-time, hundreds of sparklers cascading pleasurable feeling.

Valliamma joined her. 'Here, drink this! You need the energy.'

'What is it? *Badam kheer*, almond-milk? Oh, Valliamma, I feel so happy I could cry. Look at this sky. Doesn't it seem like a velvet-spread someone has embroidered with pearls and diamonds? Yet you can see no trace of a stitch.'

'It is lovely—but not as lovely as your face shining so. Come, let us go in. The mosquitoes are starting *their* concert.'

'Wait a little, Valliamma! Can you wake me up early, can I go with you for a pre-dawn bathe in the river? I want to see the sun rise on the river. I remember it well, the sun popping up from behind the *bilva* trees, so suddenly, like a great big, burning orange, and spreading ripples of gold to shimmer up-river . . . Shall I tell you something? I used to think, whenever I saw that, why doesn't it sizzle, like when our blacksmith Kuppu plunges his hot metal in the trough, go bzzzzzzz, like *that*?'

'—What's all this laughing going on?' Guru Ramiah spoke from the inner room. 'Valli, what are you doing there, feeding her to the mosquitoes?'

They went in. After supper, Aparna stretched out on a mat. Valliamma sat beside her and massaged her legs till she dropped off to sleep.

That night, in her dream, the peacocks returned to the grove, and were dancing around her on a rainbow-coloured carpet of flowers.

*   *   *

'Now turn around and look! See if the hair-pendent is hanging right.'

Rukku stood back to admire, having fastened the tripartite, bejewelled gold-chain on Aparna's hair-line, and accompanying circlets of 'sun' and 'moon' on either side of her parting. '—Come on, have a look! I've nearly finished.'

Aparna, sitting on the stool with her back to the dressing-room mirror, did not move.

'I'd rather not.'

She had let Rukku do everything. Rukku had wrapped her round with the green brocade saree, and adjusted the pleated folds so that they would fan out during the dance. Rukku had combed and plaited her hair, lengthening it with black tassles, and covering the plait in a sheath of jasmines and chrysanthemums; then she had fastened the swan-patterned, ruby-and-pearl jewel on her chignon. With wide-eyed wonder, Rukku had taken the jewels one by one out of their cases, and fixed them: the neck-choker of glittering white stones and emeralds, the gold-leaf mango-garland, the diamond ear-rings with their golden, bell-shaped dangles.

All the while Aparna sat still, like a doll, as Rukku put on the make-up, the creams, the lotions, the powder, the rouge, the collyrium and the lipstick. Only when Rukku smoothed her forehead had Aparna stiffened. Would she *dare*? Would Rukku dare offend orthodoxy and mark a widow's forehead with the sacred kumkum?

Rukku, resourceful Rukku, had thought of that too.

'Look, Aparna! I am putting on this.' She held out a maroon circle of felt attached to a white card. 'It's all the fashion these days.'

Ingenious, Aparna had to admit. There was nothing auspicious about that felt, it could offend no one. Fashion had come to the rescue of tradition.

The piece of felt on her forehead nauseated her. Nothing had changed. She was the same widow as ever. Why, oh, why, had she allowed herself to go through this charade, this sickening cosmetic cover-up?

'—Are you looking or not? You are being childish. After all my work, don't I deserve a little applause?'

'Sorry, Rukku! You have been very patient with me.'

Aparna turned round, faced the mirror, and froze.

'—How's everything going here? All ready?' Mrs Manikkam had darted in. 'The hall is full. All the big patrons are here. The Collector has just arrived. Our padre is showing him round the school. Immediately after the speeches, the padre only will be announcing your dance. . . . —Oy, you three there!' Mrs Manikkam had spotted Rati, Kaama and Shiva, crowding near the stage-door. 'Come back in! At once! Don't be twitching the curtains and peeping-in before your time! —How's Aparna?'

'She's fine. I've nearly finished.'

'Good, good. I'll tell the padre. We don't want Indian punctuality before our new Collector. No delay, understand? The hall is like a first night at Paradise Cinema, absolutely packed full.'

Blazing a trail with smiles and sparks, Mrs Manikkam left.

Aparna continued staring at the image in the mirror. What illusion was this? . . . Where did this beautiful creature come from? . . . Who was she?

Parvati hara har, Parvati hara har . . . the sound-syllables of the Kathak piece that Guru Ramiah had taught her the previous day began clicking inside her. *Parvati hara har, Parvati hara har* . . . They fused with her heart-beat, like the phrasal rhythms that float up with steam and smoke from the wheels of a speeding train. Everything else—the girls giggling, Rukku chattering—fleeted past her like grazing cattle, hills and trees, paddy-fields and telegraph-poles. Stray sentences of speech boomed and crashed from the speakers on stage.

The wheels slowed down. Someone was finishing with a Sanskrit-flourish, Dr Radhakrishnan style. '. . . And as our Manu-shastra says, in the first Krita age the chief virtue is the performance of austerities, in the second, Treta, divine knowledge, in the third, Dvapara, the performance of sacrifices—and in our own blighted age of Kali, when *dharma* limps on one leg, liberality alone . . . So I say again, be liberal, give!'

The hall crackled with ear-splitting applause. Rukku joined others by the door. 'The Collector is going to speak now! Aparna, come! You can hear better from here.'

Aparna did not move. She closed her eyes. She too had defended *dharma* before him. She had been confident; but now the name of the ancient architect of *dharma* made her freeze. Manu, that law-giver from a mythic past, extended his steel grip across the centuries; he had little compassion for the likes of her. '*Manu dharmam, manava raksham*: Manu's law is the saving of mankind'— she could hear her father chuckle at his own quip. What would old Manu say to all this?

Could she go through with it?

Could she brave that rule-bound audience?

Raghavan had challenged *dharma*. He had been prepared to defy them all for her ...

'—Aparna! Aparna! Wake up!' Rukku was shaking her. 'That was really a short speech from our Collector. The singers are tuning up. The padre is announcing about Rani and you. Come, you must go now.'

Parvati hara har . . . Parvati hara har . . . The inner beat resumed. Aparna stood up, and gathering her troupe, stepped out on to the stage.

* * *

    'She is clothed in sparkling raiment,
    Her gentle breast rises and falls with a tender thrill;
    Her little feet with music mark rhythmic ecstasy,
    A smile divine faintly lights her face,
    And all the colours of nature
               have painted her with heavenly hue,
    To please the assembly of gods and goddesses:
    Parvati, Parvati, Parvati.'

    'Her twinkling feet almost speak words,
    They form a lilting song;
    Parvati, the pale Uma, dances as in a dream;
    Her mood sweeps all those present with her
    And fills the winds of Heaven.
    So gentle are the flowings of her body
    That like a serenade it joins with the music,
    And every cadence strikes sweet harmony
    With the beat of the drum ...'

So Parvati danced to awaken love in the ash-whitened Shiva.

Kaama, god of love, came to her aid, and was burnt. Rati, his widow, lamented. Shiva showed forth his ascetic glory in a *tandava* dance. The 'Dance of Kaama' drew to a close.

The dancers bowed to an applauding audience.

Aparna lifted her eyes and scanned the auditorium. The padre and Mrs Manikkam were in the front row. For a moment she did not recognize the chief guest between them. In his pale-grey suit and red-striped tie, Raghavan looked less like an official, more like a bridegroom at reception-time. He smiled, and it was a smile that took possession of her.

Once back in the dressing-room, Aparna peeled off the brocade saree and wrapped on her usual white. She undid the plait in a moment, and shook her hair free of the petals that clung to it. She stripped the felt kumkum off her forehead and flung it into the basket. She was taking off her jewels, tearing at them in a frenzy, when Rukku came in.

'What are you doing, Aparna? Why so soon?'

'Soon or late—what difference does it make?'

'Can't you hear the noise of the crowd? They are calling you back for more. —Girls, what are we going to do?'

The girls looked on, cowed by the frenzy that possessed their teacher.

'Rukku! Help me get this thing off!' Aparna was fighting with the back-clasp of the neck-choker. 'Don't be alarmed! I shan't disappoint them. I shall give an encore of my own.'

'What riddle are you making? How can you, like this?' Rukku attempted to gather up the scattered jewellery.

'Can't I, like this? The hypocrites, they've deserved it. I shall carry the story forward. I shall dance the dance of Parvati when in penance, the dance of "Aparna"—she "who partook not even a leaf". I shall appear as myself.'

Rukku stood staring, speechless.

'Go, Rukku! Tell the musicians all I need is the first verse of *Sambho Mahadeva*. I am ready. I want them to see me as I am—as Aparna.'

*   *   *

Silence fell among the noisy guests as Aparna followed Mrs

Manikkam into the staff-room where refreshments were being served to patrons and chief guests. The encore had caused a stir: there was much talking, whispering, tut-tutting and head-shaking at the strangeness of it. The padre cleared his throat noisily and, with a sweep of his arms, brought the gathering to attention.

'Ladies and gentlemen. Here is the star of our evening, Aparna-Gauri. Without her courage and generosity in circumstances we all know about, we would not have had our splendid performance. Let us show our appreciation.' He started clapping, and others followed.

Once the room filled again with a normal hum of conversation, Raghavan approached her.

'Congratulations! Your pupils do you credit. As for the teacher, how am I to praise her? Such splendour, power and grace, surpassing even my wildest imaginings!' He was making no attempt to conceal his ardour. 'To think that I was resigning myself to a boring school-function, and then I find you transformed . . .'

'I had no choice.'

'The padre told me. I hope this is the beginning of many more performances.' His voice dropped to a whisper. 'I didn't expect you to change back. Why? What was the point of such a display?'

'No display. According to our poet, Parvati became Aparna, didn't she? I danced as I should have, as Aparna. Do you think anyone here would accept me as anything else? Could I ever be any different? Why do you torment me with foolish dreams? Good-bye!'

*   *   *

They waited outside the school-gate. Rickshaw-Muththu should have been there half an hour ago. It was nearly eleven. Departing guests had emptied the rickshaw-stand.

'Why is he not here yet? It's so late. What are we going to do, Aparna? I am frightened, standing here, with all this.' Rukku nodded towards the suitcase she was carrying, crammed full of jewellery. 'Should we go on waiting?'

'He did say he would be here, didn't he?' Aparna felt irritable and tearful. She should have bitten back those words; now it was too late to regret them. It had drained her, the whole evening, especially the encore. She was on the edge of a deep weariness, when the clanging of the rickshaw startled her. Rickshaw-Muththu was carrying a passenger—a drunkard, it seemed.

'*Amma*! Don't be angry with me. This wretch, my brother, is sick, very sick. He is babbling nonsense. What am I to do? I put him in the cart and took him to the clinic, like you said, but there's no one there tonight. The night-watchman says all the sisters came here. Look at him! Oh, *amma*, please; help!'

Aparna peered into the rickshaw. 'The poor man! He must have a high temperature, he's so hot! Wait, Muththu! —Rukku! Let's go and get the padre. He'll know where to find a sister.'

They met the padre half-way across the playground. He was leaning on the Collector's car, saying farewell. He looked up, listened, and went in search of the nursing nuns.

Kabir approached them.

'Collector Sir says it's not safe for you ladies to be going home at this time of night. Please, ladies, I am to take you home.'

Rukku climbed in readily. Aparna followed, peeved to be caught helpless.

Raghavan sat silent.

'Where first?' Kabir was repressing his grin. Rukku leant forward.

'I can get off first. Maruthi Lane in Flower-Bazaar. Driver! Don't try to go in. It's such a narrow lane, the car'll get stuck in the gutter. I can walk from Flower-Bazaar. It's not far.'

Rukku was eager to be free of her awkward charge; such cutting looks and ominous silences were not to her liking.

It perturbed her for days.

CHAPTER FOURTEEN

The dawn train brought Vedam Iyer home.

He was weary. The case had not gone well.

'These bureaucrats in government, why do they want to be meddling in temple matters? What do they know, what do they care about sacred traditions? . . . It all started with the British. They were experts at meddling with things that were none of their concern. Now our petty little office-babus wag their tongues at the likes of us, fancying themselves as if they were Raj officers, meddling, meddling!'

Vedam Iyer sighed.

Aparna served him *rasam* in a bowl. Drinking it in one go, he resumed fulminating.

'As for the temple-folk, do they have any sense, quarrelling among themselves so much? And over what? Who should get the first offerings, who has the "coconut rights", who should sit where—"rights and honours", "rights and honours", that's all I hear! Their religion is in their bellies, as our beloved Swami so rightly says. If only they didn't fight, why would the government bother us?'

'Why, what's the government going to do?'

'Now they are threatening to bring our Kuchchipuram temple under their jurisdiction; this temple from the time of Chola kings has been managed by none other than the reverend *dikshitars*. If this case doesn't go right, soon we'll have some cigarette-puffing,

Western-suited manager in the sacred precincts, dictating to us brahmins what we can do, what we can't. What would such "leg-shaking" no-goods care about? Certainly not holy things, only the tithes and the bribes!'

Vedam Iyer burped.

It was a pity that the appeal-case was running into the ground. Aparna had put off breaking her news till meal-time. She dare not leave it for him to discover from others, as he was bound to as soon as he set foot in the street.

'—Well, my dear! How have things been here? At least there is always peace in this house.'

Aparna's courage sagged. 'I had a letter from Nitya.'

'What news?'

'They are both well, and settling into their new home. She is inviting me—that is, us—to visit her. Auntie and uncle got their new posting. They'll be leaving soon for Australia.'

'So they are off on their pilgrimage. It's not *"hara hara Sambho"* any more but *"hara hara* jumbo" these days!'

'Nitya has a job now. She is a receptionist at a big hotel.'

'The things they do these days, Hindu girls from good brahmin families!'

With each response, Aparna tensed, and the words stuck in her throat.

'Father!'

'Yes, my dear?'

'I have to tell you something. Last week, my pupil Rani fell sick. At the school function I had to dance her part—Parvati.'

Vedam Iyer was cupping his hand for the curds she served. Shaking his hands free, he stood up, breathing heavily, and stared at her. The whites of his eyes bulged. 'You? . . . *danced*?'

Without a word, he made towards the backyard, washed his hands, and climbed upstairs.

*   *   *

She stood at that waist-high stone-slab all afternoon, rubbing an oblong block of sandalwood on its pepper-brown surface, moistening it every now and then with water. Her hands were cool with the soft, perfumed paste that oozed from the hard wood; her eyes brimmed with tears, hot drops falling on the paste which she gathered into a silver bowl from time to time. Later that night, it would join other such bowls at the Shiva-Nataraja Temple and cool the third eye of Shiva.

It was the eve of *Maha-Sivaratri*, 'the great night of Shiva'. The silence shrouding the house felt a fitting prelude to that approaching festival of penitence and purification.

Eyes burning, Aparna looked anxiously at the clock. It was nearing four. The advocate was still upstairs, behind locked doors.

What if Raghavan should walk in?

Was father expecting him this Sunday?

What was she to do?

She had not seen Raghavan since that night at the school. Her good-bye had been a calculated rebuff. It pained her to recollect how hurt he had looked.

Why did she have to be spiteful to him, of all people, the only one who had seen her suffering, and offered love?

It was painful to reject that love—but even more painful to accept it.

If she yielded, wouldn't that mean being coerced into being something she could not be in clear conscience? How could she, with her tainted past, ever be the wife he deserved? As Guru Ramiah said, she must live, if at all, not for any man, but for the Lord of Dance. To dance as she had that evening, and had since, every day of that week at Guru Ramiah's—there was the hope she allowed herself. No bonds, no claims, no guilts, no hurts, but pure bliss of movement, cleansing and healing the ache within. But now the angry silence of her father had splintered her dream.

The office door opened.

Vedam Iyer descended the stairs and, walking-stick clattering, began pacing up and down the courtyard. He wore the same expression as when a case proved difficult to unravel, when he could not decide whether his client was innocent or guilty.

The clattering stopped.

He cleared his throat, and said in a mellow voice: 'Aparna, my dear! What is this you have done?'

'I couldn't let them down. I saw Guru Ramiah. Then I agreed.'

'Do you intend carrying on? What's the idea?'

'With your blessing, father.'

'"Blessing"?' He struck his walking-stick hard on the ground. 'What are you talking about? Don't you see what it would mean? I don't have to tell you how Kuchchipuram loves gossip. Already, tongues must be wagging: "A brahmin-widow, of all things, the advocate's daughter, dancing like that; now she dances—what next?" Your behaviour will be read in the worst possible light. You will be seen as the commonest, commonest . . . do I have to say it? Is that what you want?'

'I hadn't thought of it like that. They were respectful at the school. The padre said everyone spoke well, and gave a lot to the clinic.'

'"Spoke well"? Another time, another place, the same people won't hesitate to drag you through the dust. . . . That padre! I know all about him and his "rice-Christians". He gets to my daughter when my back is turned, and she lets his honeyed poison twist her brain!'

'Father! It wasn't like that. It wasn't because of him. Guru Ramiah thought I should.'

'Him! I don't know what the world is coming to when those who should know better can't be trusted. What does he think he is doing, misleading you, nurturing foolish ideas. I had expected better from you, Aparna. I thought I had taught you well. I thought you were above such mundane fancies.'

'—That was no mundane fancy.' Ducking under the low-lintel, Raghavan stepped in.

Father and daughter looked at each other: they could not tell how much of their exchange he had heard.

'So you were there too!' Vedam Iyer eyed him as he might a suspect witness.

'Of course! I was the chief guest. I don't know of anything more spiritually uplifting than Aparna's performance. She was a divine Parvati, the most beautiful, the most ecstatic . . .'

'I see. . . . I have no doubt she performed well.' Vedam Iyer moved towards him. 'Aparna is not famous through the district for nothing. Still, I was never very happy about it all. Brahmin families taking on someone else's *dharma* brings nothing but trouble. It was her mother's doing: from the day she was born, she nagged and nagged till I agreed. Aparna was only five when she went to this guru. Then at eighteen, the first performance, all

Tanjore was there . . .' The advocate shook his head. 'Then the gods blotted her life. You see, my boy, it is not the same any more. Our tradition clearly forbids certain things for one like Aparna. Harsh it may seem, but ancestral wisdom is true wisdom. We ignore it at our peril. As Lord Krishna says, when women violate *shastra-dharma*, the world order suffers.'

'The only one suffering at present, as I see it, is your daughter. Deny her gift, and you might as well bury her alive.'

Vedam Iyer looked at the young man as if for the first time. Could it be, could it really be, that the heat of his words signified something more than modern youth's rash reformism? Could it be that these visits . . . The advocate looked at his daughter; she was bending over the sandalwood-paste, biting her lower lip.

. . . Surely, not Aparna. It was time he made peace.

'Now, my dear, as I was saying, I was only thinking of your good name and our family honour. Don't take it to heart, what I said. It's a father's unpleasant task to say what is right. What is done is done. Let us have no more of it. . . . Now, Raghavan, come, sit down. I have news for you from your mother and father. — Aparna! Bring that parcel for Raghavan in my suit-case.' He assumed his habitual good humour. 'Mothers will be mothers, always wanting to feed their sons! Your mother has sent you sweetmeats and pickles. She was insisting that I take them for you. She misses her eldest son!'

Aparna returned with the parcel. 'And this must be for him too.' She held out a thick envelope, already opened.

'Ah, that! That's what I am to be talking about. Your father, my friend Mani, made me promise that I use all my persuasive powers on you. "What are you a lawyer for", he says to me, "if you can't even make my son see sense?"' Vedam Iyer laughed, and rubbing his chin, handed the package to Raghavan. 'Come, come, open it, open it.'

Raghavan's brow darkened as he took out the contents. He had guessed right: horoscopes and photographs of prospective brides.

'Ah, now.' Vedam Iyer sifted through the horoscopes. 'Your asterism is *bharani*, right? "*Bharani*-born rule *dharani*"—the world, as the saying goes. So, you are a Collector—very apt. Now it is my task to scrutinize these, and yours to choose one of those. It was hard selecting, Mani was telling me. With no help at all from you, your mother is making the selection—but then women understand these things better, don't they, Aparna? What do you say? Which of these girls will make a good wife for our Raghavan?'

'That's it. Why not?' Raghavan sprang up. Holding the photographs fan-fashion, he thrust them before Aparna. 'What an excellent idea! Why doesn't Aparna choose for me? What does she say to this plump one? *"Name: Sundari. Age, 21. B.Com. Cashier in State Bank. Domestically trained. Home town: Mayuram"*; or this one, *"Name: Kalyani. Age, 25. Research officer at Binny Mills. Dowry no worry. Modern outlook"*—whatever that means. Rich and modern—what more can one ask? And look at this. *"Shobhana. Age, 22. Height 5'2. Fair. Renowned Tanjore family. Proficient singer, and Veena player. Only girl in a family of four sons."* Well, well! You can't better that. Such choice, such variety, beats Kuchchipuram market! Pity they've changed the law—I could have married them all! What do you say, Aparna? I await your decision. *You* must choose.'

Having crackled like hot mustard, Raghavan flung the photos on the bamboo table and sat down, his face flushed and dripping.

Vedam Iyer pulled down his glasses and wiped his face with his top-towel. He watched them both. That distressing question again: such anger and bitterness in one, and such visible pain in the other, what could it mean but . . . ?

He must not think any further.

As if the scandal of her dance-performance were not enough, how much more trouble would she bring him before the end of his days? Fathers with daughters—was there no respite for them from worry and vexation? What sins had he committed in his previous life that he was burdened now with this green widow of a daughter? Daily, her presence was becoming a reproach, and causing such anguish to his tired old heart. What was an old man to do with such a fate? O Iswara! When would there be an end to these wearisome fruits of *karma*? Where was the way out of this seemingly shoreless ocean of *samsara*? What sport of his was it that we are entangled in this web of maya . . . ?

Maya. Illusion. All is illusion: happiness and sorrow, life and death. Brahman alone is true, Brahman alone is eternal. This universe is a conjurer's trick, as Adi Sankara says. Strange, she seemed to have forgotten all that he taught her from the *Gita* and the Upanishads, from Plato and Seneca. He must bring her back to the right path before she strayed. He must make her see the truth. Before it was too late, he must open her eyes to the snares of passion, save her from this dangerous tempest, from this young man.

He must be firm. Tender, yes, but firm.

'Aparna, my dear! It's well past four. Isn't it time we had coffee?'

Aparna shrugged herself awake. She had been standing immobile by her father's chair, her knuckles whitening as she gripped its cane-work, striving not to flinch from Raghavan's sarcasm. He stung her like sand on sore skin; her limbs had gone rigid for fear of what father might say or do. And she could not take her eyes off those photographs. There they were, brides-to-be, immaculate, fresh, full of hope, mocking her with their coy smiles.

She spent a long time in the kitchen making the coffee. As she lit and fanned the charcoal brazier, a wave of depression swept over her. Why was she cursed with such a life—the dead and the living exacting their intolerable dues? —Balu, a ghost she could never appease, father, stamping out any flickering surge of life, and now Raghavan—he hurt most.

Did he have to be so bitter?

Yet that was only part of the problem. . . . *'Withering on the tree-trunk like torn bark half-consumed by a runaway elephant'*—those words of an ancient Tamil poet might have been written for her. But her body ached with an anguish that cried out a further truth. Try as she might, awake or asleep, ever since that night on the bungalow verandah when she had felt the comfort of his firm body against her, she could not tear him from her consciousness. Present or absent, he impinged on her, unsettling her with a new sensation, a painful, burning exhilaration which she feared and yet longed for.

The coffee was ready. Aparna looked out. All she could see was a wall of newspapers. There was something comical about the way the two men hid behind their copies of *The Hindu*: grown men sulking like children after a quarrel. Aparna smiled despite herself.

Coffee reduced the tension. Gathering up scattered newspapers, Aparna steadied herself.

'Father! Is there is anything you need before I go? I am delivering the sandalwood-paste to the temple for tomorrow's *puja*.'

'To the temple? You? Alone?' Vedam Iyer put down his paper. 'My dear, after what you have done, I do not think it is wise. I do not want my daughter reproved in public. Do you wish to provoke the *dikshitars*? Do you wish to be jeered at by all and sundry?'

'—But, sir, forgive my intruding.' Leaning forward, Raghavan lightly touched the advocate's feet. 'Forgive me for exploding as I did. But surely, you cannot be serious. You cannot keep Aparna confined in this house forever for fear of the public!'

Vedam Iyer's face sagged in a weary smile. He picked up his coffee. 'Young man! You mean well, speaking as you do, straight from the heart. But when you reach my age, you'll see the wisdom of not provoking the poison-tongued multitude . . . Now, Aparna! Listen to me! I am too tired today. Tomorrow we shall go to the temple. We will see if anyone dares open his mouth in my presence. We will rise at dawn, bathe in the temple-tank; we will worship, we will fast, we will keep the night-vigil. It is a glorious penance to be in the presence of Shiva on his "great night", keeping vigil, keeping our souls awake in the darkness of our being . . .' With each utterance, Vedam Iyer revived. 'And you too, Raghavan, I strongly advise you to do the same. What better time than this auspicious night to seek the benediction of our Shiva-Nataraja? His raised foot shall deliver us all.'

Vedam Iyer finished his coffee.

'—And today Raghavan, we shall set aside Kalidasa. I have for you something more elevating; it is a hymn addressed to our "Lord of the Golden Hall", composed by an illustrious ancestor of ours— my favourite prayer. Just listen to the rhythms of this saintly poet's heart-felt cry. We can all join in, seeing how our hearts are inflamed with worldly troubles.' Vedam Iyer began reciting:

> '"*Maulo ganga sashankau*
>   *karacharanatale komalanga bhujanga*
> *Vamebhage dayardra himagiritanaya*
>   *chandanam sarvagatre*
> *Ittam sitam prabhutam tava*
>   *kanakasabhanatha sodum kvashaktih*
> *Chitte nirvidatapte yadi bhavate*
>   *na te nityavasomadiye* . . ."'

'"On your head you have the cool stream of Ganga and the chilly moon, on your hands and feet there are many slimy snakes; the left half of your body holds the daughter of the snow-clad mountains, who is herself moist with mercy, and on your entire body, lo! here is the cold sandal-paste. Thus, O Lord of the Golden Hall! Where have you the power to bear this excessive cold, if you cannot resort for eternal dwelling to my heart which is ever ablaze with despair?"—"Ever ablaze with despair"—how right he is, how right! How we need the coolness of his grace! So tomorrow I will see you at the temple.'

*   *   *

Parting the silken, green film of algae that lay on the surface of the water, Vedam Iyer dipped down into the temple-tank for a third time. He could take only so much of crowded shrines, packed full as they were that day with bodies. All morning, he had joined the chanting of the priests who in clusters of eleven sat round the sacrifice-altar in the big hall, invoking the gods of this tenfold universe into ten sacred water-pots, and in the eleventh, the One beyond, Shiva himself, of transcendent glory. How it wearied him to sit among those townsfolk! Little did they appreciate the holiness of the rites, so busy were they with their noisy transactions, giving and receiving offerings.

Vedam Iyer emerged from the tank, and easing his way up the slippery steps, looked for a sheltered spot in the adjoining cloisters where he might meditate in peace.

'Om Namasivaya, Om Namasivaya . . .'

His lips began rolling the sacred five-letter mantra. His mind was wandering, much as he longed to tune into the pulse of holiness that could be felt everywhere in the temple on this eve of *Sivaratri*. The granite pillars rang with stentorian chords of vedic hymns, and every shrine and sanctum reverberated to the basstones of murmuring penitents. If only they could be just one disembodied sound, one transcendent OM. . . . Much as he relished the beauty of *pujas*, of the flower-offerings and camphor-flame and incense, he could not stand those clammy bodies for long; those puffy faces with bulging bellies, those skeletal rag-bags with eyes lost in deep sockets—they repulsed him one and all. There they were, pushing and pulling, poking and jostling, as if they were in Kuchchipuram market. It wearied him to watch them pleading for prosperity and plenteousness, as they elbowed their way to the priests lest they miss out on the blessed offerings. It was beyond him to know why anyone would wish to prolong their sentence in this flesh, in this loathsome 'abode of nine gates'. The only boon he ever asked was to be freed from this burdensome flesh. His flesh.

He had sent her home after the morning *puja*, noticing how frail she looked, overcome by the crowds and faint with fasting. The *dikshitars* had scowled. Words were ready—he could tell by their looks and the way some re-knotted their hair. So he had sent her home. She was to return later with her grandmother and join him at the main sanctum for the night-*puja*. *Dikshitars* or not, she must not miss that *puja* on this most holy night. The Lord would open her eyes, save her from this impending folly. 'Om Namasivaya. Om Namasivaya . . .'

*   *   *

'Collector Sir!' The temple 'guide' came forward, having spotted Raghavan hovering on the periphery of the throng in and around the main sanctum. 'Collector Sir shouldn't have to be standing this far out where he can see nothing. Your Honour's place is in there, right by the *dikshitars*. Won't they curse me if I don't do my duty? Please, sir, come. Let me have the pleasure of taking you in, sir. I only know the place where you can view the *puja* well and receive first offerings and blessings, as is your right. The *dikshitars* would wish that only.'

Raghavan did not move.

He had seen him around the bungalow, this dry-looking, middle-aged man with protruding teeth, shuffling around, for ever hitching up his crumpled, yellowing clothes. According to Kittu, he was from a respected brahmin family which had seen better times till they fell to litigation, wrangling over hereditary *mirasi* rights which, they claimed, the previous temple-management had taken from them. So the man hung around the temple, sour and depressed, roaring at all and sundry like a pensioned-off sacred bull; the *dikshitars* had let him style himself 'temple-guide' because they found in him an ideal menial, obsequious towards his brahmin superiors and belligerent towards all others.

The man repelled Raghavan. Yet what he said was true. It was no good trying to watch the proceedings from a discreet distance; all he could see so far were sweaty backs, bobbing heads and uplifted arms. And he had come not just to see but to feel and understand. Anger more than curiosity had impelled him to come. He must settle this quarrel with her god, once and for all.

The crowd parted in deference as Raghavan followed the 'guide'. He found himself stationed by the entrance, as close as anyone could ever get to the secret that lay beyond in holy darkness, where no commoner might enter.

A *puja* was in progress at the approach to the sanctum. A short stout priest was seated on the floor, legs crossed in lotus-posture. He tossed flowers, while intoning a sing-song catalogue of Shiva's hallowed names. An arc of pink, red, white and yellow petals lit the air before him, as flowers darted from his deft right hand and fell on the deity, made manifest in a crystal lingam.

*   *   *

Cool crystal, clear crystal, luminous crystal.

Vedam Iyer felt a shaft of radiance bathe his forehead as he meditated on the crystal lingam. Suddenly all became clear: colours showered upon the colourless, yet the colourless was the source of colour. Why didn't he see this before? Beyond the deity with attributes lay One without attribute. Beyond all this clamour and colour of *pujas* and priests was the Lord of the secret sanctum, colourless, formless, silent as the surrounding ether. And He, the Lord of exalted spaces, his formless splendour encased in the interlocking discs of golden mandalas, was beckoning him from that sanctuary, here and now, to join him at his heavenly abode, the cool Mount Kailasa.

Vedam Iyer closed his eyes again. 'O Lord in crystal! Cleanse my mind, that I may be even as you are: crystal bright, crystal clean, crystal strong. Take me away from this world of woes, of giving and taking, of writs and counter-writs, of marrying and begetting, of photographs and horoscopes . . .'

Vedam Iyer opened his eyes. Aparna had arrived and was standing beside him, head bowed and praying.

What was he to do with her but take her away with him? True, she was not old enough to accompany him all the way on his pilgrimage, but she could at least travel part of the way with him. The travel would cure her of her present distraction. 'Om Namasivaya, Om Namasivaya . . .'

*   *   *

She had come to shed her burden at the feet of Nataraja, the Lord of Dance. There he stood, in all his bronze and gold majesty, towering above the flower-smothered crystal. But she could not lift her eyes to behold his face—no, not tonight. The light of his countenance, the bliss of his smile, was too much to bear tonight. Head bowed, she would take refuge at his feet, seek benediction from the raised left foot or, better still, be prostrate under the right foot, crushed to death, even as the dwarf-monster. Tonight the only boon she would ask of the Lord of Dance was that he finish the joke he had begun. To be crushed, to be extinct: body and soul, she longed for oblivion.

*   *   *

He was no doubt a suave artist, this dancing god, Raghavan had to admit. He glittered in gold, diamonds and emeralds—and there was a daring grace about that much-adored posture of his, the left leg swung across and over the right in such elegant abandon, and that suave smile—'an enigma to be experienced not solved', as the advocate might say. —No, rather the smile of an artist, of a supreme magician. Why shouldn't he, this ascetic-erotic, wild play-boy of the heavens, smile when he could bewitch so many? Look at them! How their faces glowed, not just from the light of lamps and camphor-flame but from hunger for his divine provender, for that radiation of holiness which their souls craved! He had them all enthralled, with his promise of bliss, this dancing god—why shouldn't he smile?

He had trapped her too.

And here was he, a mere mortal, resolved to wrest her free

from the bronze-grip of this arch-conjurer, come what may—but how?

The bells clanged. A curving melody on the pipes swept up to the top register. The sanctuary was lit by flames of camphor spiralling from conically-decked discs in bronze. The priests' chants swelled to a chorus. The crowds surged forward.

Raghavan stood unmoved, his anger still seething. Oh, to sweep aside all this holy paraphernalia in one fell blow, as Mirza Ghazi should have done when he swooped down on Kuchchipuram!

Shiva, the destroyer—did he ever destroy his own holy clutter? Or does he wait for an alien Mirza?

'Honoured sir!' A priest was proffering sacred-ash and camphor-flame. Raghavan pulled back. What had possessed him, to pollute this territory of the holy with such profane thoughts? To applaud the mussulman, why, even to think of him at a time like this and in a place such as this . . .

How could he, with such unclean thoughts, receive the blessed offerings from a servant of Shiva?

In silence, Raghavan pushed his way out through the milling crowd.

CHAPTER FIFTEEN

'Are you still here, Thambiah?' In the new-moon darkness that shrouded the bungalow, Raghavan could hear the snores of his peon.

The shapeless bundle under the office window snorted, uncoiled, and lengthened out. 'Collector Sir? Here only I am, sir.' His peon stood up, sleepily rubbing his eyes.

'You may go now. I'll lock up.'

'Yes, sir.' Thambiah moved towards the gate, then turned: 'Oh, sir! Pardon me, there's someone waiting for you, sir, in there.'

'Someone?'

'That padre from St Joseph.'

'Oh!'

As Raghavan's eyes adjusted to the darkness, he could make out the contours of a rickety bicycle by the verandah post. What would bring him here this late, riding that thing in darkness over pitted paths?

Raghavan waited till the gate creaked shut and the peon was out.

'Hullo, padre! Why sit in this gloom?' He switched on a table-lamp.

The padre was sitting on an easy-chair with his back to the

window, smoking a cigarette. He hastily looked for somewhere to stub it. 'Excuse me. I don't do this very often these days. If it is too much for you, I'll throw it away.'

'No, no. Carry on! You must need it.' Raghavan dragged up a chair and faced him.

'It's late. You must be wanting your sleep. I am sorry to bother you, but . . .'

'I won't deny I am weary—but as for sleep, that's far from my mind. I came back to get my torch. I was going out again, towards Old Bridge.'

'Please don't let me stop you. May I join you, if you don't mind? And talk? Well may you wonder why I am here this late. I wanted to see you as a friend. In the morning I could only see you as our Collector.'

After rummaging through the desk-drawers, Raghavan pulled out an Eveready.

'Shall we go then?'

They walked in silence, following a dim pool of torch-light that bobbed and jerked on the rough moonscape of a street bespattered with mounds of buffalo-dung.

When they reached Old Bridge, Raghavan stopped. Leaning over the parapet, he trained his torch-beam on an errant stick that wandered down the lazily gurgling current. Here he should be able to shed the infection of the temple, its noise, lights, fumes; here he should be able to rid himself of the hot sweat of holiness. He had walked for hours before returning to the bungalow; but the glare and tumult of Flower-Bazaar had only increased the throbbing inside his head. He was still reeling from the violence of his reaction towards the temple and all its works.

The padre coughed and flung his cigarette-butt into the water.

'You must have heard about what happened at the temple to-night?'

'At the temple? Why? What happened?' Raghavan nervously flicked the torch-switch on and off. 'I was there earlier this evening. There was nothing unusual—unless you mean the special *pujas*.'

'No, not that. It must be an hour ago. It's Muniya, our cobbler—he went there.'

'Isn't he sick? I thought he was at your clinic.'

'He was. He is still. He would have lost his leg, the infection was so bad. The doctor says it was a neglected wound.'

'But he had no burns when you checked him?'

'That's right. He certainly didn't. I believe it to be a late reaction. The doctor, of course, disagrees. "Unscientific", he says—whatever that means. Who can tell? The fact is, Muniya had this infected leg and didn't want anyone to know. The smell made his sister-in-law suspicious. Then his brother brought him to the clinic. You saw, the night of the school-function.'

'I remember that night well.'

'Tonight being a great festival, Muniya gave the sisters the slip and went to the temple, to see his god and be healed.'

'So . . . ?'

'The temple-guide, you know . . .'

'That fellow! What did he do?'

'Well, seeing that this pariah had crossed the threshold and even dared approach the sanctum, he got into a rage. There was a scuffle. Muniya was driven out with sticks.'

'The criminals! They have no right to ban Muniya. It's illegal. Surely they must know that.'

'Legal or illegal, those brahmins don't like to see an untouchable in their holy premises. The pariahs know that. They never go in—only when some Congress-wallah drags them in.'

'Was he hurt?'

The padre fell silent.

'Tell me! I must know the whole truth.'

'He was beaten up. But, more than his swollen face, what hurts him is the pain of rejection.'

'Muniya must fight back. He must lodge a complaint. The courts are there to hear such cases of discrimination. And do you know, our state is one of the worst offenders? No doubt the temple will fight back.' Raghavan paused. Would Vedam Iyer plead their case? The thought of a public punch-up with the advocate was not wholly unwelcome.

'I don't think Muniya will complain. He stands in awe of those brahmins. Besides, he knows that no one will come forward to give evidence.' The padre shifted his elbows off the parapet and crossed his arms as if he were before a schoolmaster.

Raghavan was puzzled. Had the padre come all the way in

darkness to tell him about a scuffle in the temple—very likely, one leading nowhere?

The padre lit another cigarette. 'That's not why I came to see you. I have another problem. And I have to tell you what came to my knowledge. I now know how and why Muniya's stall was wrecked. I know who the culprits are.'

Raghavan swung round. 'You *do*?'

'Yes. They are good lads, lads of our "Joshua Brigade". They get carried away, so full of zeal they are to get converts. They feel we of the older generation are slack: we let be, we don't tackle things head on. . . . At first it was just a prank, a lesson to teach a "stubborn idolater"—for so they see Muniya. They raided his shop only to tear up his pictures of gods and goddesses—scribbled things to scare him into submission. Things soon got out of hand. Others, street urchins and hooligans hanging round the *bidi*-shop, joined them. That's not all. Some of those work for the temple-guide. He has an interest, you know, in the property. His family used to extort tithes from the tenants near the temple—that is, before they lost their rights. It's a long story.'

'Are you saying the temple is responsible after all for Muniya's plight?'

'You might say that. The *dikshitars*, of course, would deny it. They don't interfere. They just let things happen.'

'Now that you have told me this, what do you want of me?'

'Nothing. To do nothing.'

'How can I do nothing, knowing what I know now?'

'I believe Muniya won't go to court. And those giddy youths are now truly sorry. They came to me and confessed everything, when they saw what was happening to the cobbler. They have promised to help him. They will build a hut for him, and buy tools. —By the way, they didn't steal. That was someone else. They are making amends. And I am asking, as a favour, that you give them a chance. If the police come in and take them away, there will be nothing for anyone.'

'If the police find out this, I cannot interfere. Law is law.'

'Law doesn't always cure problems. Law will wreck their lives. Law strangles.'

Law strangles! The phrase had a familiar ring. It seemed a long time since he had spoken against *dharma* to her in the bungalow.

Raghavan ran his palms along the rough parapet. 'You are right. It *is* strangling.'

'Who do you mean? Aparna? How is she?'

'I wish I knew.'

'Why?—I was so pleased to see her free, that night at the school. What happened?'

'What happened? The predictable. When her father learnt about it, he put the chains back on. And began finding some for me too, lest I prove dangerous. Yet it seems there's nothing I can do.'

'I'm sorry. I'm very sorry indeed. Poor girl! As if she hadn't had enough suffering.'

'But I thought you believed suffering was good for her.'

'Forgive me. That's not what I meant.'

'I don't know *what* you meant. But she *is* suffering. That I can tell. It's not just on account of her father, either. . . . Do you understand the lure of holy-nothingness? My rival is no mortal, but that arch-destroyer, Shiva himself, who entrances them all. Tonight, when I saw her at the temple, it all became clear. That's why I left. Shall I tell you something? These lads of your "Joshua Brigade" have my sympathies. Why, tonight, at the temple, right in the middle of the *puja*, I felt like smashing something.'

'You? A brahmin?'

'Yes, me—a brahmin. Do you know, I even wished that Mirza Ghazi had razed everything to the ground!'

'That's no solution. It's not easy, getting rid of these gods. They have a way of springing up again. I should know. I'm battling with them all the time.'

They stood side by side, staring into the darkness below. The padre put a hand on Raghavan's shoulder. 'Come, it is nearly midnight. We should be going back.'

'What for?'

'There's no answer to be had here. You're tired. You must get some sleep.'

They began walking back.

As he mounted his bicycle, the padre turned to him.

'May I hope? For my people?'

'Hope? Why should I stop you? Isn't hoping your profession?'

'I understand why you're bitter. But you can help. You know you can. Good night. God bless you.'

*   *   *

In the early hours of the morning, when he could hear the tinkling of bicycles headed for the leather factory, Raghavan began to doze and dream.

... *The Assyrian came down like a wolf on the fold, and his cohorts were gleaming with* ... *gleaming with* ... how did it go? And what was it, the beat? Dactyllic? Trochaic? Anapaestic? ... And who were they, those riders on rippling brown, Arabian horses?

Not Assyrians, but Mirza Ghazi's troops, galloping at full speed along Old Bridge Road, their swords glittering in the noon-sun. Their horses were loaded with sacks from which the riders pulled out idols of bronze and stone, broken pieces which they swirled over their heads like discus throwers, before flinging them into the river. Raghavan had to duck to avoid being hit, and pressed his body against the hot stone parapet, so hot that it scalded him. His eyes were stinging with the dust kicked up by the horses' hooves. 'Souvenirs, souvenirs! We must collect souvenirs for our museum!'—Mr Gautam was shouting to some coolies below, who were hauling out pieces and loading them on to a cart. Male and female torsos, animal and human figures, lay in an indiscriminate heap. Raghavan shouted: 'Stop, Mr Gautam, stop!' He had seen them move, those stone and bronze limbs underneath the rubble, writhing to get free from lumps of plaster and splintered granite.

Parvati lay among them, her eyes closed and her rounded, heavy breasts heaving.

'Stop, Mr Gautam! Stop!'

The words died in his throat. Raghavan woke. He was hot. The sun was streaming in through thin curtains. He could hear the even swish of a broom outside—Annamma, sweeping his verandah.

His chest hurt with the shout that had not materialized. Yet the dream had brought him a curious relief. He lay back, and with head resting on crossed wrists, closed his eyes, to savour once more the longing that possessed his body. He was no longer angry, but taut with desire.

A commotion in the compound broke the spell. Rubbing his eyes, Raghavan looked at his watch. Eight o'clock. He sat up with a start. The noise outside reached a new pitch. Someone was haggling and shouting. Hastily tightening his *lungi*, he stepped out.

The cleaning woman, hands on hips, broom dangling idly beside her, had joined his peon at the foot of the verandah-steps. A cycle-rickshaw had just arrived. Its passenger, a thin, middle-aged woman with greying hair tied into a severe bun, was arguing with the rickshaw-man. Petitioners, early arrivals from neighbouring villages, began to gather round the rickshaw to see who would win the haggling.

Raghavan ran down the steps. The woman climbed out of the rickshaw, her face crumpling in displeasure as she counted out her coins, and looked up.

'Mother! What are you doing here?' Shirtless and still in his night *lungi*, he felt exposed before that early morning audience.

'Ah! You are here after all!' She surveyed the assembled throng. Raghavan flinched as she appealed to them. '—Do you hear what he says, my own son? What sort of a welcome is that for a mother who hasn't slept a wink all night, travelling in a smelly train?'

'I didn't mean that. It is such a surprise. Why didn't you tell me you were coming?'

'Didn't I? What are you saying, son? Raghu, Raghu! How I was waiting, looking for you only at the station till every one was gone. Then I thought, maybe he is on tour, maybe the letter didn't come. Then I took the rickshaw, the last one. The rogue knew I had to, a lonely woman with no one to meet me at the station. So what big fare he is asking, the scoundrel! How they are learning, these country rickshaws—no better than Madras cheats!'

The letter. It had arrived the previous morning. Seeing that familiar writing and guessing its contents, he had not opened it. He couldn't tell her the truth; but he couldn't lie either.

'I would, of course, have been at the station, had I known.' Avoiding looking at her, he stooped to pick up her luggage.

'No, sir, let me.' Thambiah dropped his watering-can and grabbed the green trunk, now it was clear that the haggler was his master's mother.

'Take it to the back-room, Thambiah.' Raghavan turned to her, attempting a smile. '—Anyway, I am glad you arrived safely.'

'By God's grace, here I am. Do you think it was easy, getting reservation? You know how it is. If you don't pass something under the counter to the clerk, to the TCR, you can't travel anywhere. Then, for all that expense, do you imagine the sleeper is any use? All night I am keeping awake for fear the "chain" thieves might break my neck—not that I wear much, but they don't stop at even the *tali* these days. How thin and dark you are looking! About time someone took charge of you! When was it since you last had a good meal?' She reached out with her palm and smoothed his hair. The audience smiled approvingly. Raghavan pulled back.

'Let us go in first, shall we, mother?'

She started at his stern tone; but seeing that his lips were set, she followed him quietly.

Once they were in, and he had shut the door behind them, he felt better able to face her. She cut a sorry figure in her crumpled brown saree and grease-darkened *tali*.

'Sit in this deck-chair. Be comfortable. I'll make you some coffee.'

She pushed the chair away. 'No, no. I haven't come here to sit around. This floor will do for me. I'll stretch out for a minute, the slate is cool. What a nice bungalow you have! You didn't even tell us. Last week when the advocate came and we were talking about you, and he was telling us how you are gladdening his days, then only I said to your father, why am I to be like a mother without a son? Radha is old enough look after them all—always books, books, that's all your sister cares about! How will she ever learn any housework while I slave day and night? So I decided to leave them all and put my feet up here awhile.'

'Hasn't she got exams soon, mother?'

'Oh, she will do all right. What is the use of a girl getting so much education? It only brings trouble. Educated girls don't respect their husbands.'

'Mother! You are not planning to stop her, I hope. *I* pay the fees.'

'You can keep your money. What good is that to me when water is so scarce and I am having to stand for hours, and sometimes in the middle of the night, to catch a few driblets from a spluttering tap? Who helps me then ? My feet ache so, and the soles are all cracked up. Do you know any good country medicine-man? I have had enough of doctors—allopathic, homœopathic, you name them, I have seen them all.'

'I have said this many times and I say it again, you must move house. Find a better place, with water—I'll pay.'

'No, son! We like it where we are, it's near the station and temple. We have been there all this while, know everyone. We are too old to move into new colonies.'

Same old arguments, same old excuses. It wearied him to hear them: she always managed to make him feel useless.

He placed the coffee before her. 'I must hurry, have a shower and start work. If you want anything, ask the peon.'

'Don't you eat before work? When does the cook arrive?'

'Cook? I don't keep a cook.'

'You don't?'

'I manage. The peon brings a carrier from Udipi Hotel sometimes.'

She sat up, poured her coffee a yard-high several times between cup and deep, stainless steel saucer, then shook her head. 'No cook, you say? There I was like a fool saying to myself I could stretch my legs like a rani, now that my son is Collector. No cook! Not that I mind cooking for you, but this place needs a woman. More of that later... I brought some Madras onions, your favourite. There, in that bag. Pass them to me, I'll peel them first and then bathe. What time do you come to take meal?'

'Depends on how many people are waiting. Not before midday. Don't wait for me. And here, take this.' Raghavan handed her a hundred-rupee note. 'You won't find much in the kitchen. Thambiah will get you all you need. I must go now.'

Before he left, Raghavan retrieved the unopened letter from his desk. He placed it inside a ledger and then read it. The contents explained mother's visit. It was not a sudden impulse but a shrewd perception that the advocate might not be effective in persuading him to a bride that had brought her to Kuchchipuram. The girl in Tanjore, the one with four brothers, had taken her fancy. She was determined to get her son to Tanjore for a bride-prospecting.

Raghavan hastily scanned his schedule. He must stall her. He could go on a tour again. The projects in Meyyur and beyond needed personal supervision. Surely, with the temple and bazaar to distract her, she could be kept at bay for a while—but for how long?

* * *

Valli River saved him.

His mother took to bathing in the river every morning.

The river was much to her liking. There on the steps leading down to the water, she found agreeable women, good gossips from whom she could learn all there was to learn about temple and town, and market-prices. And she could shine among them as the Collector's mother. What with the luxury of flowing water and undiminishing respect, she seemed almost to have forgotten what she came for. Then there was the bungalow: there was so much to do to make it what it ought to be, with little touches here and there, feminine, motherly and holy. The very first evening Raghavan noticed that the *apsara* lamp had been removed from his desk. He stormed into the kitchen.

'Mother! Where is my lamp?'

'What lamp, son?'

'The bronze one.'

'Here, of course, where it should be.' The lamp was lit and ensconced as a goddess, garlanded and glowing alive on the kitchen shelf where his mother had erected a little shrine for assorted idols.

He withdrew in silence.

Days passed by, with her bringing up the subject of the Tanjore girl on and off and Raghavan stalling her with excuses. Then one evening, as she sat by his chair to sort out the groceries the peon had brought in, he knew his time was up.

'That peon of yours, he is honest. But the cleaning-woman, she is a lazy one. She just wafts her broom here and there, leaving all the corners dirty. As for the vessels, I've to rinse them twice and clean half of them again. If she is like this when I watch over her, what is she like when there is no one to keep an eye on her? That's why I am telling you, this house needs a woman. Why won't you marry? You are a good age now. Soon you'll get to be thirty. Do you intend to stay a dry log of a bachelor?'

'No, mother.' Raghavan turned over the pages of the paper he was reading.

'Then what are your plans? When can we go and see this

Tanjore girl? Besides, you must think of your sister too. They have four sons. Who knows, one of them might like our Radha.'

'Then go ahead, marry Radha off. There's no point in my going and seeing that girl. I am sure I don't care for her.'

'How can you talk like this? Are we rolling in money? Who knows what they might ask in dowry? But if you marry that girl, then it will be different.'

So that was it. She was planning to barter her son for a son-in-law. How was he to escape these traps without shocking her with the truth? And the truth—what shape was it now? He had not seen either the advocate or Aparna for more than two weeks.

'What do you say, Raghu? Why don't we go to Tanjore next week? They are just waiting for a letter from us.'

'Hm? Tanjore, no. As for Radha's marriage, shouldn't she be asked first? When she is ready, I'll see to it.'

'What has happened to you? How dry you sound, as if marriage were a matter for a memo! Marriage is a happy event, an auspicious happening. A married woman lights up a house.'

'So do widows, according to this report. "*Woman ablaze—Sati in Rajasthan.*" The relatives didn't waste much time.' Raghavan threw the paper down and stood up, stretching.

'Why must you be ruining auspicious speech with unholy words?' She looked up, her forehead creasing in alarm. 'Raghu!'

'Yes, mother?'

'What's in your mind? Tell me plainly. You are worrying me.'

He looked away.

'Do you think I cannot see? You are not happy as you should be. All this work, work, you are doing—only a heart-sore man works like that. All I am longing is to see you happy, son.' She began to sniffle, wiping her tears on her saree-end.

'Come, mother! There's no need to cry. I am well, healthy, I'm enjoying my work. Kuchchipuram is an interesting town for a historian. Recently, we had some archaeological finds. I am preparing a report on that. There are exciting prospects for me here. What are you crying for?'

'What is a man without a wife? Why are you so stubborn? All I am asking is that you come with me and see this girl in Tanjore. Once you see her, I am sure you'll like her.'

Raghavan moved to the window, and leaning back against the

sill, looked at her steadily. Frail and worn though she was, she would persist. The blow must be delivered now and quickly—just one word to snap her foolish fancies.

'Mother! Listen to me. I do intend to marry. When I do I'll bring you a daughter-in-law surpassing all these ads in the matrimonial columns.'

'Oh, Raghu! Why didn't you say this before? Why cause all this agony?'

'But listen, mother, I haven't finished yet. No more of these horoscopes, Tanjore girls or whatever. Understand?'

'All right, son. Whatever you say. What is it to be? A "love marriage"?' Raghavan hesitated. 'It is, isn't it? Who is she? A college girl? What caste? What caste?'

'Ours.' The moment he responded, he regretted it: he was pandering to a bias he abhorred.

'Really?' She exhaled a distinct sigh of relief. 'Why didn't you speak before? As if your father and I can't adjust. Who is she? Fair or dark?'

'Dark . . . and beautiful.'

'Oh! . . . You are not dark—why choose a dark one? Still . . . what's her name?'

'That I cannot tell you yet.'

'Why? Why are you casting puzzles before me?'

'Because . . . because she hasn't said "yes".'

'Not said "yes"? Is it her parents?'

'No.'

'Are you saying it is the girl? Not said "yes" to a handsome young man like you? And a Collector too? Is she so rich? What kind of a girl is she, so stuck up? Passing strange, this. I thought only parents are supposed to give trouble for "love-marriage". Never heard of a girl being difficult. She likes you, doesn't she?'

'Yes.'

'I don't understand.'

'This isn't what you call "love-marriage".' Raghavan's voice grew sombre. 'She is a widow.'

'A *widow*?' His mother slapped her forehead with her palms and her eyes widened in horror. 'You don't mean . . . that girl, the advocate's daughter with strange name?'

'Yes. Aparna.'

'Oh, Raghu! Oh, oh . . .' She broke into a long wail, then loud sobs.

Raghavan watched her cry.

Suddenly the sniffles ceased. She sat upright, wiping her face. Her lips began to curl in a triumphant smile.

'You say she refused. She is a sensible girl. She knows what is right. It is you who must be sensible now. Besides, her father, the advocate, will never tolerate such a thing. They are of ancient stock. Does he know all this?'

Raghavan looked out of the window.

'Raghu! Don't turn your back to me! Answer me! Your mother is speaking to you.'

'Don't scream so! And shush! —I can hear someone calling.'

'—*Amma* ! *Amma* !' It was the peon.

'What is it? Can't you see we are busy?' She rose and went to the door, her anger finding a new target.

'That rickshaw is here again, *amma*.'

'That impudent fellow! —He came yesterday when you were at the project. He must give it to you, you only, whatever it is. How many times I was telling him who I was, he wouldn't listen. Stubborn fellow.'

Raghavan found it was rickshaw-Muththu by the verandah. The cobbler's brother prostrated himself. 'Oh, sir! I am happy to see you are here, sir. Now I can finish my task. I am to say nothing but give this to you, you only, sir. Orders are orders, what can I do? Please tell *amma* there not to be angry with a poor messenger.'

It was an envelope addressed to 'Collector Raghavan' and marked personal. The large round hand was unfamiliar. The padre again?

'Here, Muththu. You did the right thing.' Raghavan gave him some coins.

Pacing the verandah, he tore open the envelope and stopped midway as he read.

We are leaving Kuchchipuram soon. Father is going on pilgrimage to Badrinath and Kedarnath. I am accompanying him till Delhi. I will be staying with Nitya and Kumar. Please forgive me. I have caused you much pain. You must understand. It is best for you to forget me.

Aparna.

P.S. From today I am staying with grandmother in Vinayak Street. She is not happy about this trip. I must persuade her to go to my uncle in Madras.

Raghavan grabbed his sandals by the door, crammed his feet in and ran down the steps, ignoring the hail of questions that followed him.

'What is it? Why the hurry? What about supper? Who was it? And . . .' Before the inauspicious 'where' slipped from her, she stopped, much as she would have liked to know where her son was going in such hurry, and why.

*   *   *

'Someone there?' Lakshmiyamma's voice boomed from the kitchen.

'Raghavan.'

'*Who-oo-oo?*'

'Raghavan, the Collector!'

'Collector boy, is it? Push the door open. Come along in.'

Raghavan stopped by the kitchen steps. Her thin frame hunched double, Lakshmiyamma was putting things away in a wire-mesh cupboard which was propped up on basins of water.

'Like *barfi*?' Without looking at him, she flung the question at the nearest pillar. 'Sit down. I'll get you some. How is collectoring these days?' This time the question fell some feet in front of him.

Raghavan sat on the steps leading down to the kitchen. 'I work as well as I can.'

'Do they let you, those rogues in government?' She pushed a plate of coconut *barfi* towards him. 'In the judge's days things were different. You could walk through the fields even at new moon. No bandits to fear. The English Collector saw to that. Nowadays, bandits have become politicians. Such times we live in!'

'I have some such "bandits" to deal with. They give politics a bad name.'

It felt absurd, getting drawn into an old woman's nostalgia, when every impulse in him was to search the house for Aparna. His impatience did not escape Lakshmiyamma's notice; but she seemed determined to torment him.

'Don't you like *barfi*? You haven't touched it. Made it for this journey of hers. What does she need a pilgrimage for, at her age? I should be the one going to Kashi. Fate plays such tricks. They say we can't change what's written on our foreheads. Or can we?' She flung the question directly at him, and put on her spectacles to scrutinize his face.

'I believe we can—and we should.'

'Is that so? Times are changing. In our days girls were locked up even before they matured, not allowed out till they were yoked. Nowadays boys visit girls. You have come to see our Aparna, haven't you?'

Before he could reply, she continued, shaking her head: 'Too late, too late.'

'When did they leave?'

'Last night, by Boat-Mail.'

'But her note came just this afternoon!' Then his shoulders slumped. He remembered. Rickshaw-Muththu had called before, and been driven off by his mother.

Lakshmiyamma observed him quietly.

'A letter, I heard you say. Aparna wrote you a letter?' She chuckled. 'What are you going to do now?'

'How long are they away for?'

'Too long, too long. Four, five, six months—who knows? I shall be gone, dead and gone before she returns. Did you think she listened? So bent on this pilgrimage! Like father, like daughter—so lofty and pious, she thinks she is a *sanyasini*! Hmm!' Lakshmiyamma shook her head vigorously, and turned sharply to him. 'And you, are you pious? Who do you prefer, Vishnu or Shiva?'

'Me? Neither, at the moment. But I am not an atheist.'

'The judge was like that. He liked to read theosophy and that Englishwoman . . . what was her name?'

'Annie Besant?'

'Besant, that's the one. There's a picture of her in there somewhere. It was all mumbo-jumbo to me. My old head is too dense for such high-dry things. Over there in South Car Street, in my son-in-law's house, why, the very rafters belch out *vedantam*. Do you study such things?'

'I prefer action to speculation.'

'A *karma*-yogi then?'

'If you like . . .' Raghavan rose. 'I'd better be going.'

'Going already? I shall wander around like a ghost in this house. Rukku looks after me well enough; but without that granddaughter of mine around me, this place feels derelict.'

'What about going to Madras, to your son?'

'Who wants to die in that man-made hell? I would rather breathe my last here.'

'If there's anything I can do, please allow me!'

'Come and see me sometime—that is, if you have time to talk to an old thing like me.' She adjusted her spectacles and came closer, peering at his features. 'You have the countenance of a raja. God bless you! God bless you both!'

CHAPTER SIXTEEN

'Dhilli, Dhillika, Dehli, Delhi . . .
'Ghazni, Ghori, Khalji, Lodi . . .
'From the south to the north . . .
'Beginning at the beginning . . .
'Qut-ud-din-Aibak, Aibak, Aibak . . .'

Tossing her head from side to side on the arm-rest of the sofa, Nitya was attempting to memorize the litany of Delhi's rulers she had composed. She looked dainty, sprawled luxuriously on cushions of varying sizes and colours amidst the mock-leather. Her aerobically-trimmed legs were encased in tight stone-washed jeans, and under a grinning Mickey Mouse on her thin, baggy T-shirt, her breasts bobbed about in casual abandon. She looked cosy and provocative, as did everything about her. That doll's house of an apartment in Defence Colony was cosiness itself, a veritable capsule of coolness against the hot July winds. Panels of clear glass inset in the tinted French windows gave a glimpse of a world outside; but the casement was kept tightly shut to block off sudden putrid gusts from storm-water canals that served as open latrines for the slums nearby.

It was two o'clock on Friday.

'Qutb-ud-din . . . —Aparna! Won't you help me?'

Aparna looked up from the letter she was reading. 'What do you want me to do?' She had been trying for the past hour to ignore her cousin's prattle, but with little success.

'Here, take this marked map, and these handy-cards. I want you to check if I am getting it right.'

'All right then.'

'Where was I? Qutb-ud-din-Aibak, after him Shams-ud-din Il-tut-mish . . . What a barbaric name! He must have been a ruffian with a name like that. Good for spitting out with *paan* and betel nuts, don't you think? Iltutmish; after him, the Khaljis . . . Ala-ud-din Khalji, raider of the South, after him, Mubarak Shah, who grew fond of boys in middle age and was killed by his favourite, Khusrao Khan, Khusrao Khan beheaded by Ghias-ud-din . . .

'Then beginneth the line of Tughluqs . . .

'Ghias-ud-din-Tughluq, after him Muhammud-bin-Tughluq—"mad" king Muhammud, who would shift the capital and drag all his people south, and come a cropper. Was he really mad, or just ahead of his times? —That'll be a good talking-point. After Muhammud, Firoz-shah-Tughluq—sane, civilized Firoz of Firoz-abad, of our friendly Kotla . . . So much more to go before the Moguls. I can't wait to get to them . . .'

Aparna peered close at the map and cards as if she were short-sighted, to avoid her rising irritation becoming too apparent. It was typical of Nitya. Centuries of war and conquest, dreams, disasters, the making and breaking of kingdoms and of peoples, were being processed and packaged into quaint morsels for easy consumption by the tourists. Nitya was something of a conqueror herself—the Rezia Begum of the drawing-room, a consumer-queen *par excellence*. It was a novel, irksome experience for Aparna to discover that her butterfly-brained cousin had a gift for subjugating the rough-and-tough of life by a mere toss of her curls or a flick of her lacquered nails, falling just short of the callous. Nitya had created for Kumar as ideal an oasis of suburban perfection as any upwardly-mobile Managing Director of Tourism could wish for. Ever eclectic and entertaining in her choices, Nitya had wrought in that room a confluence of East and West. A touch of Mogul glory could be felt in the expensive but modest Persian rug on the floor, a nod towards tribal culture in the beaded hangings from Orissa that were draped over doorways. Crude pottery from Kidwai markets sat smugly with imported Swedish glass in a reproduction Georgian cabinet; on the mantelpiece, over a non-existent fireplace, there was lacquerware from Rajasthan flanking phallic figures from Africa. On the wall above, the modish chaos of Jackson Pollock posters complemented soulful eyes of village girls staring from Amrita Sher-Gil prints. Items used in Hindu worship added that special touch of Indianness which Nitya took pride in. Gods were in attendance, metamorphosed into ash-trays, book-ends, lamp-stands and door-stops. Only one was allowed to escape such a transformation—Lord Nataraja. In a tasteful reproduction of a ninth century Chola bronze, he occupied pride of place on the bookshelf, equidistant from the collected works of J. Krishnamurthy and Bertrand Russell. It pained Aparna to see her cousin cradle the figure like a favourite toy as she applied lashings of Brasso to make him shine. On occasion, he was honoured by an incense-stick—not that Nitya was troubled by piety; but in the absence of non-flurocarbon-propelled aerosols, incense proved an ozone-friendly agent for clearing a room of curry smells. However much Aparna tried to ignore it, the figure on the bookshelf exercised its fascination. Her disgust at her cousin's domestication of the Lord of Dance stirred a long-pent anger. If only she could demonstrate what Shiva was really like, if only she could show forth that power by which he burnt the cities of the Three Worlds, and reduced the universe to ashes . . .

'What's the matter, Aparna? You're not checking me?' Nitya had her usual capacity for benign puzzlement.

'What? . . . I am sorry. I was distracted. Where were you? Ready for the Moguls, I think.'

'Oh, good. Thank God the Moguls arrived. I love those grand names, so elegant, so expansive—they *deserved* to be emperors. Ba-*bur*, Ak-*bar*, Hu-maa-*yuun*, Je-han-gir!—Best of all, Shah-je-*haan* . . . mmmm!' She lingered on the syllables as though she were caressing them. 'Once we get to the Moguls, it's plain sailing—at least until wicked Aurangazeb.'

'He cared passionately about his religion. Does that make him wicked?'

'He was a fanatic! Like the Ayatollah! "Ayatollah Aurangazeb": AA for short. Isn't that good? I shall use that.'

'You'd better be careful who you say it to!'

'Don't worry—all our friends are liberal. After AA, muddle again. I think I'll skip the rest till the Mutiny. Silly old Bahadur Shah lost! Predictable! He should have never let himself be pushed to the front. The British packed him off to Burma, and began tidying up.'

'Exile must have been terrible for him. You've missed something there. It says on your card that the British officers butchered his sons and put the bodies on display.'

'In view of who my guests are, I'd better drop that. That was very naughty of the British, of course—but how else could they teach the natives a lesson?' Nitya laughed and sat up. 'Right, now I am ready.'

'For what?'

'For our guests tomorrow, Lord and Lady Rotherby. I hope no one asks me anything before dear Aibak.'

'I notice you leave out everything before the Muslim invasion—nothing on the Rajputs or on others before them. Did you mean to?'

'It's all a jumble of myths and legends, isn't it, before that? I shall look a right fool if I start telling them those, charming as some of them are. I am terrible when it comes to myths: I can't keep track of them; and when I do, I can't keep a straight face either. So many of them sound so absurd. —That reminds me, now that I've got you here, you can help me with this Hindu culture bit—you know, religion, rituals, festivals, why we do what we do *when* we do etc. —Questions, questions! I get them all the time, especially from Americans. I wish there was a ready-reference book, like Larousse. A receptionist at Oberoi has to be an epitome of Indian culture! Oh, what a treat it is to slum in my old jeans like this! You should try it sometime. You have the figure.'

Aparna frowned. '*Me*? Never!'

'Why not? It's not wicked, you know, to try something different. I'm sorry, I keep chattering while you want to get back to your letters.'

'It's all right. I can't write anyway.'

'That was from Raghavan again, wasn't it?'

'Yes. It came yesterday.'

'Oh . . . !'

'He has been seeing grandma. I wish she'd gone to Madras. She's not well. I am worried about her.'

'Really! He must be *very* concerned. Three letters in two weeks, all about grandma! I'm very impressed.'

'Nitya! I know what you're thinking.'

'*What* am I thinking? Do tell me. I've such a sieve of a brain.'

'Look, Nitya. You're shrewd. But there are things about me I can't understand myself, let alone explain to you. It's the same where he is concerned.'

'Perhaps *he* can. Kumar is very good at explaining me to myself. Give him a chance! I'll leave you in peace. I need a drink. The dust of Delhi's history has dried my throat.'

Aparna read the letters from Raghavan, and re-read his most recent one.

. . . I went to see your grandmother again. She is getting frailer each day, but her mind is very sound. She talks a lot, about you and about your grandfather. She gave me his papers and diaries to look at. They are invaluable for the history of this town I am compiling. His account of the day-to-day happenings during the early years of the Raj is an eye-opener. You can see why she says the kind of things she does. If it weren't for these visits to your grandmother, Kuchchipuram without you would be intolerable for me. The postcard from your father bears no news of you. All he says is that, despite the traffic-congestion, Benares is still the 'forest of bliss' for the devotees of Shiva. I try to imagine you among all those strangers, and am overcome with envy. Do you remember Kalidasa's 'Cloud Messenger'? I long for a word from you . . .

Pen poised, Aparna looked out of the window. Through an orange heat-haze shimmering over huts on the slopes of the storm-water canal, she could make out figures of *dhobis* and their women hopping along, with bundles of starched sarees and shirts perched on their heads, bobbing ominously. As her eyes followed the contours of those day-light ghosts trembling in the heat, she was back in Kuchchipuram with the firewalkers. A sudden fit of violence swept over her; she should be out there treading the hot asphalt in defiance—or, better still, tearing down the tight-shut casements and letting the desert-winds blast through Nitya's miniature paradise. Her head swam with memories: sights and sounds from that evening when the drums began beating for the firewalking. With much bravado and with eyes smarting from repressed emotion, she had pushed off Raghavan's words of love. Little did she know then how far from exhilarating it would prove, that willed resistance to inmost need. For all her struggles, she had scaled no heights of transcendence, seen no vision of glory; her smothered spirit lay on a hollow, rocky shelf encrusted with hard resolutions and inundated by tides of depression. Day and night her forehead throbbed as if she were being pulverized. She re-read the letters, trying to find her way back to the shore.

Nitya returned with a pail of water and proceeded to refill the air-cooler beside the dining table.

'Sorry, Aparna! I keep interrupting you. This won't take a second. —Whoops!'

The water dripped down the mat-backing and soaked the carpet. Aparna caught a whiff of a familiar perfume.

Sarsaparilla.

It was the perfume that pervaded grandmother's house, given out by the clump of root she always placed inside a clay waterpot which stood propped up on a bed of Valli River sand. She could picture Raghavan there with grandmother. What had grandmother told him about her? He did not let on, but his letters sounded a greater note of intimacy.

She must write. She closed her eyes for a moment, and then began.

Dear Raghavan,

Weeks of travel, waking up among strange voices, strange faces, in strange places, has so numbed me that I do not know where to begin or what to say.

You cannot help thinking I ran away from you. But what else could I do? I was not flinching from you, but from myself. When I set off on this pilgrimage with father, it was in the hope of finding peace in holy places. I longed to be free—free of guilt and self-disgust. I was pathetically glad when father included Balu in his rituals of deliverance for our ancestors. If Balu was set free by the mantras I could be free—such was my hope, until I woke up to Benares.

We spent five weeks in the sacred city of Shiva. For father, five weeks of uninterrupted spiritual adventure, among temples, priests and pandas; *for me, five weary weeks of struggle against a truth that Benares never lets one forget.*

Benares is a unique city, a junction between time and eternity, where the dead and the living jostle in holy traffic. While father was enjoying disputing abstruse points of advaitam *with the hashish-smoking* yogis *and naked* sadhus, *he did not want me around. I could explore Benares on my own. And the sights here are beyond my ability to describe. Just imagine the chants and* pujas *of Shiva-Nataraja Temple enlarged a hundredfold, and the bustle and colour of Flower-Bazaar intensified a thousand times, and add to it the magic, the illusions and rope-tricks of our gipsy street-show: there you have Benares . . . It was not these but the ghats that drew me again and again. The most popular (which I found the most repellent) is Manikarnika: it is the busiest marketing-place for the dead. I took to going to the quieter Harischandra Ghat, where once a king cursed to the rank of an untouchable had tended the pyres. It was there, as I fought to find a foothold in the oozing mud, that it began—my terrible awakening to Benares.*

It takes great courage or great stupidity, I still cannot decide which, to maintain that frenzy of life you see in the bazaars, for, not far from them, the dead queue on the banks of Ganga round the clock, waiting their turn to be lit. Some are lucky, their flames last to the end. Others get flung into the river half-burnt. So the dead clog Ganga, on shore and off. There is no escaping the odour of death that rises from the burning pyres. And they burn day and night.

For many, this odour of death is the odour of sanctity: to be extinguished here is to extinguish death. Who can blame them? What other way is there to ennoble this sordid reality, except ritual glorification? As I stared at the pilgrims worshipping kumkum-besmeared sati-stones, it occurred to me that I could have become one such altar. The widows who did not choose that path sit at gateways begging alms and waiting to die within the precincts of the sacred city. I am neither the one nor the other. What then am I?

With this question ringing inside me, I bathed in the river. I waded and bathed in the holy waters, dreaming the dream of pilgrims: to be cleansed of all ills, to be rendered pure—to be pure, let me confess, for you. But as I dipped and rose, I found the ripples around me floating with ashes from the freshly dead. I could not tell where they ended and I began. Mother Ganga bears witness to so seamless a flow of being that it is indistinguishable from nothingness. No doubt, by now, you will conclude that holy bathing has concussed my brains. I assure you it is not confusion but clarity that makes me say this. It was not just Benares, either.

There was a moment of lucidity that I can neither forget nor ignore. It was at the deer-park outside Benares where Buddha had taught. We stood there, father and I, under the trees, avoiding the guides. As we were drawn into the green stillness of the place, father turned to me, his voice choking as it had on the day of my mother's death: 'My dear, my dear child! He knew, the great Buddha knew the heavy penalty that our poor life on earth is. What suffering, what suffering our transient self sees! Our transience is our bane.'

His words fell like a blessing. What if he is right? What if there is nothing behind all this living, all this suffering—no meaning to be grasped, or possessed? Would we not be mere shadows, clutching each other against a void from which there is no escape? How can you or I find a stay against this?'

She had not intended to cut him off, but the only response she could summon was to write as she felt. She was trusting him with the truth. Benares could not be wished away. It would always be there, deep down inside her, with its pyres that burn forever, and its waters that wash over and dissolve the sandbanks of self.

She sealed the letter as she heard Nitya approaching.

Nitya handed her a glass.

'What is it now?'

'Iced tea!'

Aparna took a sip, and shuddered.

Nitya's face fell. 'Don't you like it? I thought you would, since you like lemon.'

'Not in tea. —Sorry, Nitya.'

'All right, I give up.' Nitya put down her empty glass and looked at her watch. 'Kumar should be back by now. Bad enough waiting at the airport; but he will have to listen to that wind-bag Gautam holding forth. By the way, Mr Gautam knows Raghavan.'

'Does he? How? Who is this Gautam?'

'He fancies himself as the cultural ambassador of India. He's no fool. Kumar has been seconded to him for this Festival of India Exhibition in London. They have gone to meet our V.I.P.s arriving from London today. If I am very nice to them all, it might mean a posting to London. I am taking time off work to do the sights with the guests. You should come too. You haven't seen much of Delhi yet.'

'I don't think I can cope with any more sight-seeing, in this heat.'

'Of course you can. You brood too much. It'll do you good to be out and with people. We shall have the use of the air-conditioned car. It will be from coolness to coolness. The Moguls knew how to build for this heat. How I wish I could live in one of their palaces, with the *hammam* forever flowing with water and covered in rose-petals. It couldn't have been too bad a life for those begums, bathing all day.'

'I doubt if it was all pleasure, being at the mercy of those tyrants.'

'Some of them were very romantic tyrants. They wrote poetry, built marble monuments to love. We women need a daily dose of romance.' Nitya patted her cousin. 'Sorry, I am prattling on while you are so miserable. What can I do to cheer you up? Some music? I shan't play Indian; it is bound to make you more melancholy. Let me play you something that will blast your blues right through. — Where *is* it now?'

Nitya knelt down beside the cabinet that held music from Paco Pena to 'M.S.', and flipped rapidly through her collection till she found what she was looking for. A faded photograph of the Statue of Liberty stared from its cover.

'Here it is! Dvorák's *New World*. He was only a peasant, you know—but absolutely divine. This became my favourite, ever since I heard it performed at the Carnegie Hall. Father took us to meet the conductor afterwards. He was a Parsi, and very good-looking—you could have taken him for a macho Mexican. The evening was all excitement. I still get a thrill just when I think about it.'

Nitya switched on the player and tip-toed softly to the sofa. 'It starts ever so quietly, and then—then all heaven breaks loose. Shush! Listen!'

Aparna waited, nervously clutching her chair in readiness for an onslaught of alien sound.

Seeing her tense as the orchestra launched into full swing, Nitya leant over. 'Is it too loud for you?'

Aparna shook her head. It was not the volume but the bizarre unpredictability of the music that was unsettling; the music seemed full of gaps, of melodies that branched off and disappeared into strange gullies, never to return, or came back at tangents, from unexpected angles.

'Not all of it is so loud. A little later, you'll hear soft solos from some of the instruments. You'll like that.'

It turned out as her cousin had predicted. In the midst of all that tempestuous roaring, there was one instrument, sweet as a *shenai* (it was called a cor anglais, Nitya explained) which sang so plaintive a tune that it seemed to echo the silent wail in her heart. But just as she began to trust the music, they returned, the unruly pack of horns, trumpets and trombones, blaring and screeching, discharging loud, shrill sounds all over the room. Seeing her flinch, Nitya laughed.

'Look at you! You look as terrified as if you were strapped to a fair-ground Big Dipper.'

'I do feel giddy. I can't take all this raucousness.'

'It's brash, I admit—but so are carnivals. Don't fight it. Let go, let the sounds wash over you!'

'I shall drown.'

'Oh, Aparna! What nonsense!' Nitya sounded distinctly peeved. 'On the contrary, it is *our* music which makes me feel as if I am drowning.'

'Our music reaches toward the infinite.'

'You can keep your infinity. I prefer to stay safely tethered to the finite.'

The conversation was taking a dangerous turn. For a moment Aparna was tempted to hit back. Her cousin was simply deluding herself: no one could stay tethered or safe in an ever-dissolving void. But she had no wish to quarrel with Nitya or to darken her life. In silence, each pursued her own train of thoughts.

The phone rang. Nitya jumped up and rushed to the corridor. 'I bet that's Kumar.'

She returned with the afternoon post. 'Just as I thought. The plane is delayed. Here, there's another letter for you. That should cheer you up. Nothing for me. I'd better leave you in peace to enjoy your letter. It's time I resumed my Indian persona. I shouldn't be caught like this, in case Kumar brings them back here.'

CHAPTER SEVENTEEN

One glance at the spidery scrawl on the envelope, and Aparna realized that it was not from Raghavan but from her father. It was more than three weeks since they had parted company; this was his first communication. She opened the letter eagerly.

My dear Aparna,
  This is the last letter you will receive from me. As I climb higher and higher in these mountains, it gets more and more difficult for me to find words, to form expressions. Down below, words came easily, they seemed weighty and consequent. Here, the words I find are like the breezes that blow at this altitude: they come and vanish as though they are no more than dewy whispers from the invisible gandharvas who glide in the evening air.

I cannot convey to you the infinite sweetness of the calm that increases in me as I leave the world below and enter this region of holy silence. I have been asking myself, 'Why do we suffer so foolishly when there is such balm at hand in this eternal abode of the gods?' Here is peace, here is all the beauty and glory you could ever wish for, in these mountains and forests.

My mind swarms with questions as I plod up the narrow, flinty path to Kedarnath. Answers light up briefly, like fireflies. I ask myself 'What is man?' —A bundle of flesh jolting along, shaking and aching, more of an ass than that which he is riding. I am entirely dependent on the wisdom of the beast I am mounted upon. He knows, not I, how to pick his way through the rubble along this steep mountain path. It is so narrow that, one slip, we'll be tumbling down, the donkey and I, down the sheer drop on our right and end up several thousands of feet below, a mere fleck on the glittering countenance of River Mandakini. From these heights, I see her: a modest, still-flowing, silver streak of a river—yet what a mass of explosive energy she is when you see her face to face! Such is the mystery of purusha and prakriti.

This is the abode of the eternal Shiva. On the snow peaks in the distance, the sun dazzles with amber and gold and then turns silver and bronze. At noon, the snow melts in streaks of grey for a moment, and then is covered up in white once again. It is as if the Lord weeps to see the world, yet soon closes himself within his own purity. How soiled and puny one feels in his presence! When I look up I see the golden disc of Gayatri herself, the face of truth on the icy panels of Himavan. Infinity looms before me. How could I have stayed so long in the world, foolishly concerned with its petty businesses? The last newspaper I read was in Hardwar. It was full of grim reports: slaughter in the Punjab, riots in Bihar, bombings in our own part of the country—ignorant, passion-blinded man, grabbing at phantoms. From these heights, what petty bickering it all seems. Here I can feed on the ambrosia of the gods. Why return to the murk below?

Earlier, I traversed the road to Badri. It is motorable, busy, and the Lord Vishnu is easy of access. Pilgrims make their way fast to him, their buses and cars hooting and screeching, and bringing to him many offerings with much clamour. Nothing silences them, not even narrow escapes from death when the road is hit by sudden landslides. It ought to make them ponder in awe, but they carry on with their brainless chatter. Fortunately, not many choose to travel this steep, rubbly path to

Kedarnath, only those driven by soul-hunger. At the top, one experiences pure advaitam—*serene, dispassionate oneness, where neither subject nor object exists.*

You see, my dear, which way my thoughts lie. If you do not hear from me again, do not grieve. I commend you to son Gopal. He'll take care of you. I have discharged my duties by the world. It is time for me to loose the bonds. I can no longer resist the call of Swami Sivananda at Rishikesh.

Blessings from a pilgrim.

The letter fell from her hands. She had been dropped down a lift-shaft. There was silence beneath and around, silence and darkness cushioning the pad of feet that seemed to come from way above her head. She could hear a shower running in the bathroom and Nitya singing, attempting to render the tune that the wild pack of brass had just stomped out in the music they had heard together. Taking their cue from Nitya's beat, the objects around her in the room began to spin and dance. The elephant door-stop, the heavy Malabar bronze-lamp, the miniature gods and goddesses in their disguise, all became animated as in some nursery-tale fantasy. They intoned at first an indistinct hum, but soon gathered momentum: '*Ma-yaa-jaa-lam, Ma-yaa-jaa-lam, Ma-yaa-jaa-lam*'. . . '*Ma-yaa-jaalam*': 'trick of illusion'—it was a favourite phrase in her father's philosophical armoury, one he readily used to bat off grief—'The Lord is a magician and the world nothing but a magician's trick . . .' The chanting soared to a high-pitched ringing. She put her hands to her ears, and her body convulsed in a spasm of dry sobs. It was as if she were fifteen again and in the grip of an undiagnosed ailment—dubbed, for convenience, 'prickly-broom' measles, since her body had erupted in tiny swellings that emitted needle-sharp pulses of pain.

The shower stopped, and with it the music. Nitya put her head through the door, her hair turbaned in a white towel. 'Well? Any news? Or are you going to keep it all to yourself?'

Seeing Aparna hunched over the table, shaking, she tucked in the folds of her blue Kashmir-silk saree and rushed towards her.

'What's the matter? Is it grandma?'

'No.' Aparna shook her head, and pointed to the letter on the floor. 'Read that.'

Nitya put an arm around her cousin as she read Vedam Iyer's letter.

'Oh, Aparna! —He does mean to do it, doesn't he?'

'I am no more his daughter but a stranger. A *sanyasi* has no ties.'

'... That's terrible! I didn't know uncle could be so heartless.'

'Do you think it is? I cannot tell. He has his reasons. Why should he not renounce the world?'

'Can't he do it without leaving you? Does he have to disappear like this?'

'What can he do for me? I'm a burden to him. He wants to travel light. I should have known.'

'What?'

'That it would be so easy for him. And so hard for me. It is as if I don't exist, never had. Yet I thought he cared. Since mother was sick often, he liked me doing everything for him. He doesn't need me any more.'

'I wish I could do something. I feel so useless.'

The phone rang. Nitya ran to the corridor. 'That must be Kumar again. He'll know what to do.'

She returned quickly, excited. 'Hurry, Aparna! It's for you.'

'For me? Who?'

'A real surprise! Quick! It's long distance.'

Vague hopes stirred her like pins-and-needles: perhaps father had not taken the fatal step after all; perhaps the letter was just an inspired effusion. If something had happened to him, he might still need her...

'Hullo!' Faint as it sounded, there was no mistaking Raghavan's voice. 'Hullo! Aparna? Can you hear me?'

'Oh, *you* ... I thought ... Yes. I hear you.'

'Are you sick? You sound weak.'

'No ... yes. I don't know... Where are you?'

'At Agra Station. I should have been in Delhi by now, but there's been an accident. A young man has jumped in front of the train. —Hullo, Hullo!!' The line was fading and he shouted.

'I can hear you.'

'I never thought I'd be obliged to Mr Gautam. He has appointed me as zone-director for the South and summoned me for a preview of his exhibition. I can be with you soon. ... Why haven't you written to me? Do I mean nothing to you?'

'I have written. There's a letter, somewhere. . . . And another.'

'What?'

They were cut off.

Nitya found her standing with the receiver dangling from her limp hand, staring. She eased it from her and placed it back on its rest. 'Just in case he rings again. —Well?'

'How far is Agra?'

'About two hundred miles, I think. I don't know. Is that where he is? . . . Did he tell you when he's getting here?'

'No. . . . I don't think so. I can't remember. My head feels like a sponge. I can't think any more. I hurt all over.'

'You need rest. Try and sleep. I'll get you some aspirin.'

Aparna allowed herself to be propelled into the bed-room. Nitya closed the partially-drawn curtains so as to darken the room. 'You lie down. If Raghavan rings again, I'll call you. Kumar should be back any minute. He'll know what to do.'

It was a relief when Kumar arrived, without guests.

'Their plane is held up in Bahrain with engine trouble. They won't get here till dawn.' Kumar flung his brief-case on the coffee-table and stretched out on the sofa. 'I'm exhausted. Drinking whisky on a hot afternoon doesn't agree with me. But there was no way I could refuse Mr Gautam.'

'Kumar!'—Nitya put on her most solemn voice—'I don't know what we should do. Aparna got this terrible letter from uncle. He's going to become a *sanyasi*.'

'A . . . *what*?' Kumar sat up.

'A *sanyasi*—a sadhu or whatever. Poor Aparna is shattered. With our guests arriving tomorrow, I don't know what to do. I hoped she would be able to help. But she is in a bad way. Raghavan rang and she barely managed to talk to him—the line got cut off too. What are we to do?'

'Oh, my God! What have we now? I can only think of one solution. Call Dr Bedi. He's a clever shrink.'

'But Aparna's not a nut-case!'

'I find your cousin strange enough, as it is. She doesn't seem to like me. She behaves as if being a widow is the end of the world.'

'Kumar! How could you? If you knew my uncle's family and Kuchchipuram and what she's been through, you wouldn't say that.'

'I'm sorry. I can't think of anything else to do.' Kumar lay back, picked up a copy of *Newsweek*, and patted Nitya on the bottom. 'Don't look so solemn, little one. It doesn't suit you. My manly intuition says she just needs some firm talking-to. I'm not the one to give it. Raghavan might be. He knows your uncle better than I do. When is he arriving?'

'We don't know. I'll go and ring the station.'

*   *   *

At 7 a.m. next morning Raghavan knocked on the front door. Nitya let him in. Her morning make-up barely concealed her anxiety. 'You don't know how glad I am to see you.'

'I got here as soon as I could. Thank you for leaving that message. How is she?'

'Very shaken—ill. I can't tell you what a nasty shock uncle's letter was. I thought it was from you. She was writing to you at the time. Where is it now? —Here, you might as well read both, while I get you some coffee.'

When she returned, Raghavan was still reading, his face muscles twitching like flick-blades. Nitya put the coffee down and sat apart. He looked up.

'Can I see her?'

'I'll go and see if she's awake. She was restless all night. We could hear her sobbing at intervals.'

Nitya returned with Aparna. Her eyes were puffy, her hair lank and dry as though it hadn't been washed for days. She looked as if someone had punched her in the face.

'Pleased to see you.' She pressed her hand down the side of her saree, before extending it to him as to a stranger. 'It's very kind of you to call. I can't see you much. The light hurts my eyes. —Nitya! Can we switch the lights off?' She screwed up her eyes against the morning sun.

Nitya gave Raghavan a quick, anxious glance: there were no lights on. She pulled the curtains closer. 'Is that better?'

'Aparna! It's me, Raghavan.'

'Oh yes, the Collector. "A brahmin boy and not yet married": that's what they say about you in Kuchchipuram—did you know?'

'Drop that nonsense. Tell me how you feel. We can't help you if you don't help yourself.'

'Feel? I don't feel anything. Nothing.' She clasped her hands in her lap and added, 'Well, a little tired. . . . I feel tired . . . and dirty.' She stood up. 'I think I'd better go and bathe. I must pull myself together. Kumar will be angry.'

She moved towards the door like a sleep-walker, then turned. 'Have you seen snow? I haven't. He's lucky. It must be so clean, up there in snow-land. I shall never know what it's like. Don't you think it's unfair? I'm not mad, you know.' She laughed a little. 'Kumar thinks I am. He wants to call a doctor. I know all about it. I'm not sick. I'm happy.' Her eyes filled with tears. 'If he can break the chains, so can I! It's freedom from now on. Isn't that right, Nitya?' She began sobbing as she smiled. 'I'm sorry. I'm making a right spectacle of myself. I promise, no more tears. I'll be fine when this noise in my ears stops. Nitya tells me they're trombones and trumpets. Why do they keep screeching? I think I need some sleep. Pardon me, I can't keep you company.' She put her hands together in formal greeting and went out, shutting the door behind her.

Nitya turned to Raghavan. 'You see what I mean. She's in a bad way.'

'She's clearly in a state of shock, therefore confused in her feelings.'

'Kumar said we should call Dr Bedi.'

'I'm not sure that would do any good. He'll only put her on tranquillizers. That'll depress her reactions even more. She's depressed enough already. We should let her talk as she feels. This decision of her father's has knocked everything from under her. I can see from her letter to me that this pilgrimage was a disaster. Her father has confirmed her worst fears about life.'

'I don't fully understand. I only hope you're right, about not calling the doctor.'

'I can't claim to be right; but I'm certain we mustn't depress her further. We must allow the injuries to bleed. She has to find a way of grieving for her loss—all her losses.' Raghavan looked at the wall-clock. 'I've got to report to Mr Gautam at ten.'

'Can't you wait till Kumar comes back from the airport? Mr Gautam is with him, after all.'

'Oh, well ! In that case . . .' He got up and walked about the room, inspecting its décor. 'Perhaps I'm wrong to think a doctor can't do much for her—but I fear it will be difficult to get her to talk to one; whereas she might open up to one of us, you or I.'

'I've tried; but she doesn't tell me much. I suppose she thinks I'm too simple-minded.'

'This isn't the only blow, you know, from her father. He already hurt her deeply when he reproved her for dancing at the school function. She was at her best that evening: a glorious, happy Parvati. He hit her with the axe of orthodoxy. I was there when it happened, and there was nothing I could do about it.'

'I didn't know that. She never told me. One thing I did notice, she wouldn't watch television when any dancer was on.' Nitya drew back the curtains and looked out. 'I thought I heard the car. Yes, Kumar is here.'

Kumar greeted Raghavan warmly. 'Hullo, old friend. Never more welcome than now. I'm looking forward to working with you. I just heard all about it from Mr Gautam. Lucky you, getting a trip to London. I'm green.'

'You're not going to London, are you? When?' Nitya sounded panicky. 'What are we to do about Aparna?'

'Give her some of this.' Kumar handed his wife a piece of paper. 'I called on Dr Bedi on my way home. Tried my best to describe the case to him. Being a friend, he gave a prescription for sleeping tablets. He advises that sleep is the first stage in recovery. Sleep and dreams. He'll talk to her if she's willing. And one more thing—she mustn't be left alone. Bedi reckons patients in this state have suicidal tendencies. When she's rested enough, Bedi suggests she has as much company as possible. There. See? I'm not as hard-hearted as you think—even though she doesn't like me.'

*   *   *

'Nitya! Nitya!' Aparna's voice was low but clear.

Raghavan pushed open the half-closed door and walked in.

'Nitya is out. They are dining out with their English guests. I'm your guardian this evening.'

Aparna pulled the bed-sheet closer to her chin and looked around, her eyes halting at objects in an effort to re-orientate herself.

'What day is it? And how come you are here?'

'Tuesday. I arrived three days ago. Don't you remember? Saturday morning?'

She shook her head.

Raghavan pulled a bamboo stool from under the dressing-table and sat a little away from her. She glanced uneasily at him, her eyes fearful. 'Have I been delirious?'

'No. You've been ill.' He paused till he could command her full attention. 'Yes, you've been ill ever since you received that letter from your father.'

Aparna flinched. She sat up, holding her head between cupped hands. 'It's true then. I thought it happened in my dream.'

'I'm sorry. It is true. I've spoken to your brother, and he received the same message.'

'Dreams, dreams—how they deceive one!'

'Dr Bedi will be pleased to hear you have been dreaming. He gave you tablets to help you sleep.'

'On and on they go, stomping on. I can't imagine how one head could hold so much. My head *hurts*.'

'Shall I get you something? You've hardly eaten anything since last night, when Nitya tried to force-feed you.'

'Did she? . . . I vaguely remember being pushed about.' Aparna smiled wearily and gestured to stop him moving. 'Don't go yet. I'm glad you are here.'

'So am I. And to hear you sounding more yourself. You are very weak. You must at least have a drink.'

'I shall. I wish I had a broom to sweep my head through. It feels like a cutting-room floor, littered with bits and pieces of film that I can't connect.'

'Oh no, you mustn't sweep them away. Keep talking, we'll piece them together—together we will.'

'What do you make of this then?' She pushed the bed-clothes aside and shook her crumpled saree straight. 'It's Kuchchipuram. I'm drawing water from the well. I let go the rope a minute, the pulley reels fast, and the bucket drags down. I try to reach for it, slip, and tumble in. I keep falling and falling. It's dark and airless—but comforting in an eerie kind of way. All of a sudden, it just drops away from me, just like that, the whole brick-surround, tumbling down like plastic play-bricks. And my clothes . . .'

She stopped to take a deep breath, and reddened.

Raghavan could see she was passing-over some detail. 'And?'

'And there I was, standing . . . standing in broad daylight all alone, with fires burning right round me—except that they were sheets of ice.' She shivered at the memory.

'Does the dream upset you?'

'No. Strangely enough, it was pleasant. I feel stiff though, all over.'

'You've been asleep a long while. Do you feel strong enough to get up?'

'I ought to. Otherwise, I shall end up like my mother. I've been a nuisance to everyone. Poor Nitya! She didn't deserve this.'

'You mustn't blame yourself. There's no cause, absolutely none.'

She let her feet touch the ground gingerly as if she feared it might slip away from her, then rose.

Raghavan held out an arm to support her. 'That's good. Soon you'll be strong enough to go out.'

She took his arm. 'Do you think so?' Her face froze as she looked at him. 'Oh God! Now I remember everything, Saturday morning—and before that. I wrote you a letter. Did I post it?'

'No. Don't be alarmed. I did get the letter. We'll talk about all that when you are better—not now.'

CHAPTER EIGHTEEN

The sky turned from orange to brown as the two cars drove towards the garden that enclosed Emperor Humayun's tomb. Through the tinted windows it looked as though early monsoon-clouds were gathering for a storm. But as the party stepped out before the gateway, *aandhi* struck: the blinding brownness of a Delhi dust-storm, hot desert-winds scattering clouds of fine dirt.

'Blast this *aandhi*! Hurry, everyone! Quick, into the building!' Nitya ran ahead, pulling her saree over her head and face, followed by Kumar and Mr Gautam. Lord and Lady Rotherby, gawky yet clumsily elegant in their safari-suits, strode across, holding their straw-hats down and clutching handkerchiefs to their mouths.

Raghavan caught up with Aparna. She had halted by the entrance while the others moved into the octagon. It was a week since she began to emerge from her amnesic illness. Following Dr Bedi's informal advice, Nitya was determined to make her sick cousin socialize. To her relief and delight, Aparna had agreed to join in the round of activities Nitya was organizing for her foreign guests. Nitya and Kumar had cause to congratulate themselves, for without any embarrassing or expensive trips to psychiatrists or clinics, they had averted a disaster.

Raghavan remained perturbed. What Nitya took to be Aparna's remarkable recovery he read as a cover-up: she was blotting out the pain of her father by a display of frenetic energy. But when conversation sagged, when she thought she was escaping attention, he could see by the tell-tale dark rings under her eyes that her good spirits were stretched over a chasm of desperation. She frustrated his attempts to see her alone; and in company, her attitude towards him veered between child-like trust and fits of aloofness. As he observed her silhouetted against the scalloped archway, he was at a loss to gauge her current mood. Risking one more rebuff, he approached her.

'Are you all right?'

'I'm fine. I've never seen a dust-storm before. I wanted to watch.'

'You'll choke to death if you stand here. Come this way, I know a more sheltered spot.'

He led her into the nearest corner chamber, one flanking the central octagon. It was dark. The carved trellis-windows let in very little light. Aparna stumbled over a mausoleum as she made towards the window.

'Whose is it?'

'No idea. Could be any one of Humayun's relatives or descendants: Haji Begum, Dara Shukoh—they are all buried here somewhere. Nitya might know.'

'Don't worry. I'm not that interested. It's this I want to see. Look!'

Raghavan joined her at the window, a delicate expanse of filigree in stone. The dust-storm had gathered momentum in a short while and made the sky and land one mass of billowing brown cloud.

'I can taste it, can't you?' Aparna licked the film of dust that had settled on her lips. 'It's salty.' She spoke to him as if they were truants conspiring.

'It's a thorough menace. You can't keep out the dust, no matter how hard you try.'

'This reminds me of Benares at dusk. The sky was just like this because of the smoke.' She turned round to face him. 'You never made any comment on my letter. You think I was unhinged, don't you?'

'No, Aparna. I didn't comment because it would have just made your problems worse.'

'Problems!' She moved away. 'I see. I'm a problem to you too.'

'You misunderstand me.'

'Do I? You're quite right. Why shouldn't you think of me as a problem? After all, that letter alone is enough to certify me—isn't that right?'

'Look, Aparna! No one wants to certify you—least of all, me. If you must know what I think, I'll tell you. You are not the problem, but what you believe in—or rather, what you have been indoctrinated by your father to believe in. You're not a unique case. As Dr Bedi says, it's the common Indian disease—dissociation, suppression, denial, elevated to a spiritual status.'

'It's Dr Bedi now, is it? I thought it was just Nitya and Kumar, sneaking to him for friendly counsel for their mad cousin. You have all decided I am morbid, a nut-case—is that right?'

'You do me an injustice. You should hear me out first. I do *not* think you are a nut-case. If you are morbid, it is understandable, for you have seen too much of death to tell it apart from life.'

'Morbid?' Even in the darkness, her eyes flashed. 'I'll tell you who is morbid: not me, but the people who built these things. Tombs, tombs and more tombs—this city *reeks* of them!' She flung her arms out in a gesture of disgust. 'At least the Hindus don't insist on clinging to decayed corpses.'

Raghavan's patience cracked. 'Listen, Aparna! Since you push me, I'll tell you exactly what I think. Come here!' He grabbed her hands and walked out of the chamber into the octagon, almost dragging her to the white marble cenotaph under its sandstone dome. 'Take a good look round! See this marble? It glows as if it were alive. These arches, trellises, pinnacles, the dome, this whole monument, is a tribute to life—to love, not death. Do you see those apartments up there on the second storey? Did you know they ran a college there? Do you still call that "morbid"? . . . Haji Begum buried her husband and got on with life. Do you know how? It's simple. It's called "definition"—distinctions. It's definitions such as these that defeat the void you speak of. The Moguls knew how to wrest life from death—a desert-dweller's secret. What do *we* do? We rush off to a river, to the all-consuming, all-obliterating Mother Ganga. We bathe and bathe; and for all that water and wet, as you found out for yourself, we are no better off. . . . You know why? Because we refuse to define!' He let go of her hands. 'The trouble with our religion is that we absorb and absorb till we drown all distinctions and choke in a mess of our own making!'

Raghavan mopped his brow and and walked away; he could not bring himself to see the effect of his outburst.

Aparna stood as if she had been slapped. Then she moved slowly towards him.

'That's the truth then. I should have guessed, the way you walked out of the Shiva-Nataraja Temple that night. Everyone was talking about it. Even I could not understand why. You hate it all, everything we believe in—you want it all destroyed, don't you?'

'No, Aparna! I hate the holy clutter, I hate your father's cult of holy-nothingness into which he's lured you. I love you. More than anything else I want to see you restored to yourself.'

'How do you expect to do that, when you turn your back on all that has made me what I am?'

Her voice had softened. Yet when Raghavan looked at her eyes, they were suffused with alarm. He saw in those immensely rich dark pools what he had put off facing in himself: the fear that in his crusade against holy-rubble, he might lose his way.

'—What have you two been up to? Not quarrelling, I hope?' Nitya was at their side and sizing up the situation. 'Lady Rotherby is still doing the galleries. The storm is subsiding. We should be able to leave soon. Isn't this white cenotaph lovely? —By the way, did you know it is empty? It's only a show-piece. Humayun's body is in the vault beneath, where all decent bodies should be. Be with you soon!' Nitya breezed out, seeing two straw-hats emerge from a chamber.

*   *   *

'"Composition" and "*dis*-position". Gentlemen! This morning we are finalizing how we compose our collection of art and artists, and how we "dis-pose". Now is the time to declare your thoughts.' Mr Gautam surveyed Kumar and Raghavan as if they might be carrying contraband.

Kumar coughed, and ventured. 'As liaison between our sponsors and the Tourism Board, I have to make sure everyone gets proper coverage. There's the Oberoi, Taj and, of course, Air India. They have posters, slides and even videos which they want displayed. Here's a list of their requirements.' He pushed a sheet forward.

'Mmm! I see.' Mr Gautam adjusted his spectacles and scrutinized the list. 'Unfortunately, we artists do need commerce—but on no account must these demands be allowed to jar with my noble concept. It will be a pure, complete aesthetic experience, a glimpse of Mother India that will uplift hearts and minds. Commerce must be her handmaiden; since we cannot do without her, we must disguise her discreetly. It's up to you to find the ways and means.' Mr Gautam flicked his fingers elegantly to free himself from the vulgar encroachment of money.

Kumar glanced at him anxiously before tabling his next question. 'Then there is the catering tender. What are we doing about that? The big chains are bound to compete.'

'"Tender"?' Mr Gautam sat up. 'We do not put out to tender. The Tea Board will handle that, as usual. The aroma of Darjeeling tea, floating down to meet incense and sandalwood—I can just imagine the kinaesthesia. Mmmm! . . . But we must not waste all morning on the peripheries of this exhibition. "Exhibition"! How I dislike that word! What we have in mind is a plastic, fluid, living artistic experience—not just a viewing of objects. We need a new word, a new word for our happening. What do you say, Mr Raghavan? You are the scholar among us.'

Raghavan was only half-listening. His mind was on another question—Aparna's question. The alarm in her eyes had brought her closer to him than ever before. He was seeing his own doubts, his half-formulated fears, through her. Crates, some still unopened, others half-exposed, surrounded them: pieces of bronze and basalt, sculptures of Ganesh, Shiva, and full-breasted Parvatis, sticking through straw and shredded paper—reminders of a tradition he was turning his back on. Was that necessary or inevitable? They would surely continue to haunt him. Nor could they be simply consigned to oblivion as dead remnants, for they lived on—in the works Mr Gautam had collected, in the arabesques that the coppersmith from Tanjore lovingly recreated, in the folk-songs of the boys from Rajasthan, and in the majestic clay-horses of Velan the potter. He could no more cut loose from the past than from the present. All around him was living evidence that the past still shaped the present. The words formed involuntarily: 'The past is the shaping spirit of the present.'

'"The shaping spirit" . . . Brilliant! "Shape", "shaping", "spirit"—just the cluster of associations I am looking for. Thank you, Mr Raghavan. I knew I could count on you. "The shaping spirit"—that shall be the motif.' Mr Gautam, warming to his notion, got up and walked around the large barrack-room they were sitting in. 'A statue here, a carved relief there—and beside them, the living artist carrying on his tradition. Now that we have the motif for our composition, let us turn our minds to the details of *dis*-position . . .'

'Sir!' A peon who had been hovering in the background at last caught Mr Gautam's attention.

'What is it?' he growled. How could this underling dare to arrest the flow of artistic ideas? The peon took a step back, extending a piece of paper.

'A message from the P.M.'s office, sir.'

'Oh! From the P.M.?' Mr Gautam's countenance changed in an instant. The puppeteer from Tanjore, who spun round the double-faced swivel-head of his marionette queen to mark her passage from anger to joy, could not have managed it more swiftly.

'It is from the Lady herself. She calls me. I must go, immediately. Excuse me, gentlemen.'

As soon as Mr Gautam left, Kumar pushed his chair back, yawning. 'There's no point in carrying on. He'll reverse anything we do. Time for a break, anyway.' He clapped his hands, and a peon took the order for drinks. 'I'll be glad to get back to my air-conditioned office. This barn of a place is hell to work in.'

Ice-sodas arrived. Sipping his drink avidly, Kumar winked across the glass. 'By the way, what's up between you and Aparna? Nitya tells me she heard you quarrelling—"one almighty bust-up", that's how she put it.' Kumar laughed.

'It wasn't quite like that.'

'Come on, old chap! When women start to quarrel without reason, you know what it means. Only one thing: attention. They want attention, some love-gesture. Here's an experienced man speaking.'

'If you're right, it's a strange way of proceeding.'

'But she *is* strange, don't you think? Surprising fire, under all that meekness. That's what I said to Dr Bedi. I spoke to him last night at the club, after tennis. Want to know what he thinks?'

Raghavan remained silent. He did not want any association with the opinions of that doctor. He mustn't give her any more grounds for accusing him of collusion.

'"Transference".' Undeterred by Raghavan's lack of response, Kumar continued. 'Transferred anger, that is Dr Bedi's view. She can't be angry with her father, therefore she is angry with you. Interesting, don't you think? It's a pity she wouldn't see him. He's distinguished. London, Middlesex-trained, very interested in the case. I told him a little about you. You could talk to him, by the way—why don't you?'

'No, thank you.' Raghavan had met the doctor briefly one evening at the club, a brown-eyed *sardar* with gleaming black beard, quietly confident—too confident to leave room for dissent. He had no desire to discuss Aparna with that man. While he let others haul her around in their conversations, reducing her to a 'case', time was slipping away—each moment widened the fissure between them.

'Excuse me, Kumar. If Mr Gautam returns before I do, could you tell him I'll be back in an hour?'

'Don't worry. It's nearly lunch-time. He won't surface till three.'

*   *   *

'"Janata Express"?' Nitya cried, on hearing of her cousin's decision to leave. 'You must be mad, wanting to travel by that cattle-train in all this heat. It takes three days to get to Madras. You'll perish!'

A suitcase was open on the bed amidst a jumble of clothes. Aparna crouched beside it, pulling out odds and ends from under the bed and throwing them into the case in a desultory fashion. Her face was drawn.

'I said "Janata" only if you can't get me reservation in any other. I must go back to Kuchchipuram—the sooner the better.'

'Why this sudden hurry?'

'I want to be with grandma. She might pass away any day.'

'Grandmother may last longer than you think. You're not strong enough to travel—even then, it's not safe to travel alone.' Nitya sat on the bed, and modulated her voice to a gentler register. 'Is it because of the argument yesterday? It's obvious he loves you. You should get married. Times are changing.'

'Marriage is not the solution to all problems.'

'Do you want me to believe Kuchchipuram is?' Nitya got up in exasperation. '—I'll see what I can do. I promised Kumar to meet him for lunch before I start work this afternoon. Will you be all right alone?'

'Of course. I'd better get some practice at it.'

Nitya met Raghavan at the door. He greeted her awkwardly as though surprised to see her there, and his dark glasses hardly concealed his embarrassment. Nitya put him at ease.

'Just as well you're here. I can't reason with her. She's packing. Do go in. I can't delay any longer.'

All the way there in the taxi, with his eyes following as the driver dodged his way through chaotic traffic, Raghavan's mind had overflowed with words. Perhaps he had caught the disease from Mr Gautam, for he could not stop himself searching for apt phrases. His brain churned out little speeches, declarations, confessions, then sharp, straightforward apologies for speaking as he had, as though he knew all the answers, held all the solutions—whereas one simple question from her had knocked down his certainties, left him like someone slashing his way through an overgrown thicket, without help. Yet her question had also betrayed her. 'I want to see you restored to yourself'—'*How do you expect to do that . . .*' All hope now centred on that reply. It had been tantamount to an admission. She still needed him, as he needed her. They would journey together. It would be a paradoxical journey: he would lead her forward, out and away from a painful past into a fresh future; and she, she would guide him back through the paths he had hacked himself out of, and help him recover all that was precious and living in the traditions he had discarded as wayside rubble. He would say all that, and much more. But the moment he crossed the threshold, the whole torrent dwindled, leaving him high and dry.

All week he had been engaged in unpacking statuesque goddesses in bronze and basalt: thin-waisted, wide-hipped, full-breasted Lakshmis, Kalis and Parvatis. They were his guests and he was their princely host. They had waited in demure silence to be positioned, while he had viewed, re-viewed, measured, polished and assessed—the task had left him in a pleasant state of arousal.

She was bent over a suitcase. Her hair had come undone and her white saree hung limp over a shiny black blouse—a living replica of the Parvati in basalt he had been considering all morning. His throat grew dry and his body tautened: he was seized by a strong urge to swoop down and carry her off like Ravana in some aerial chariot, and make love till he had crushed all the pain out of her.

But one false move, and all would be lost.

'Well?' Aparna shook her hair back as she shut the case and turned round to greet him.

'I came to apologize.'

'For what . . . ?'

'I was too harsh in what I said yesterday—and rash.'

'Were you? I'd rather know the truth.'

'What you heard was not the whole truth.'

'When is truth ever whole?'

Raghavan scuffed the carpet with his shoes. This wasn't the direction he had wanted the conversation to go. He must cut in before they got lost in abstractions.

'Aparna! No more of this. I need you. You know that.'

She looked away. He couldn't tell whether she was angry, or frightened.

'Please come with me.'

'Where to?' The suggestion seemed to amuse her. 'No more tombs, I hope.'

'No, no. Something quite different. You must understand me better. I want you to see this exhibition I've been helping with.'

'When?'

'Right now! The car is waiting.'

They found the barrack-room a flurry of activity. Mr Gautam

had sacrificed his lunch-break, and with sweat pouring down his back was directing all and sundry. A stage had been erected for puppet-shows, and embroidered canopies in saffron and green were being hastily slung over booths—booths that housed artisans picked up from bazaars, *bastis* and government-workshops. Peons had multiplied by the dozen, and they shuffled around, lugging precious bronze and basalt sculptures, placing them and replacing them according to Mr Gautam's ever-changing notions of 'composition' and 'disposition'.

'—Ah! There you are, Mr Raghavan—and with your charming companion too. We have just under two hours to set all this up before she arrives.'

'Who? The P.M.?'

'The P.M. — who else? She summoned me to report on progress. She's taking a personal interest in this, I'm glad to say. She has expressed a wish to view before she takes the plane to Andamaan Islands for her holidays. Now, if you supervise sections three and four, the East and South, we'll tackle these. In half an hour we are meeting for a joint-inspection.'

After Mr Gautam left, Raghavan turned to Aparna. 'I'm sorry. I didn't expect to be busy.'

'That's all right. I'm happy to watch. If there's anything I can do to help . . .'

'Yes. There is. Be my guide once again, as you were that night in the temple.'

Her cheeks dimpled as she looked around. 'This reminds me of our temple-festivals. —Look, a temple-car! When we were little, my brother and I used to make one, cover it with pennants and garlands, and drag it through the streets.'

'This one is a replica—neither a toy nor the real thing. And it doesn't look anywhere near as impressive as the original in Tanjore.'

'How can it be impressive when nothing is happening—no flowers, no priests, no devotees, no *pujas*?'

'Priests don't come under Mr Gautam's classification of "live-artists". Even if they did, I'm not convinced it would be any better. I am more at home with the bronzes. Take this one, also from Tanjore.' Raghavan picked up a small, shiny, black figurine, a Durga with multiple arms slaying the buffalo-demon, who was already half-metamorphosed into a human. 'A goddess who slays to save. I found her rather tarnished, lying in a corner of the museum. Where do you think she belongs?—alongside her husband Shiva, or with her sons Ganesh and Murugan?' Raghavan laughed as he held up the figure for Aparna to decide.

She remained solemn. 'Neither. She ought to be on her own. Durga acknowledges no kith or kin.'

'Done!' Raghavan put the figurine on a pedestal isolated from the other figures.

They moved on. Passing under a welcome-arch that opened into an arcade that framed coppersmiths, stone-masons, garland-makers, silk-weavers from the South, all in booths down either side, they reached a cluster of bronzes waiting to be set up.

Aparna stopped by a group of three. 'These are familiar. Aren't they from Kuchchipuram? Murugan looks different here. I don't recall seeing that smile before. But I barely got a glimpse through those crowds in front of the window at the courthouse.'

'He's been cleaned up. Once he gets installed in the temple, he'll be covered up in grease again, and the smile will vanish. It's the same with all the others here. I can admire them while they're here—but I can't see myself ever worshipping them.'

'Not even Shiva?'

'Ah! Shiva. He baffles me. I can't accept him, I can't dismiss him. . . . You see these Natarajas here?'—Raghavan pointed to two bronzes of identical posture but varying size—'The smaller one is a twelfth century Chola bronze, the larger one is an eighteenth century replica. Do you notice the difference? You can tell at once which was the inspired artist. The Chola Shiva is ecstatic; and the later one, though still a magnificent piece of bronze-casting, is just that—a casting. Something vital has gone. And as for the modern versions produced in our workshops and co-operatives, they are dead as dolls. You see my problem. I can see what Mr Gautam is attempting to do, but look at what it amounts to—this whole exhibition is a tawdry sham!'

Aparna watched his pained expression, then bowed her head before the two Natarajas in silent contemplation.

With her eyes still focussed on the figure, she said: 'When I see young movie-mad upstarts launching into dancing after six months of training in some dance-school, I feel as you do about this. Unlike the great masters of the past, we have become cheap—our spirit easily goes out of tune.'

Raghavan tipped her face towards him. 'But you're not. I've seen what you could be, that night at the school. Leave being Aparna, be Parvati! Then there's hope for you, for me—for us.'

'Do you think I've not dreamt of it? But that blow from my father, can I ever recover from it? How could he, who knows so much about things spiritual, be so blind as to demean what I did when I danced as Parvati? I might one day come to terms with him abandoning me; but as for that other injury, it's gone deep. It hurts here, constantly.' She pressed her fingers on her forehead. Her eyes brimmed with tears: it was the first time she had spoken of her father.

Raghavan waited till she recovered. 'I've been thinking, and I'm convinced that . . . in his strange way, he has released you. His scruples no longer bind him, or you. He's freeing you, don't you see? He's freeing you in the only way known to him.'

'"Freeing"? It feels more as if I've been left blindfolded in a wilderness. I despair of ever finding my bearings.'

Raghavan bit back a protest: words were proving too weak against her grief. He needed something more effective. He scanned the enclave. A hubbub was rising around them. The P.M.'s arrival was imminent. He remembered the potter.

'Come this way! I want you to meet someone.'

They ducked under the arcade and reached a relatively quiet part of the barrack-room. In a semi-circle against the wall stood an array of terracotta horses; they were arranged in serried ranks, graded according to size.

The potter was left on his own.

'Do you recognize him?' Raghavan asked in a whisper. 'Our potter, Velan's son, from Kuchchipuram. It was because of him I got involved in this whole thing. I needn't have worried. Look at him! He carries his world with him and nothing here disturbs him.'

Totally oblivious to the hubbub about him, the potter was serenely kneading clay. He was stripped bare to the waist, and his forehead shone with streaks of sacred-ash. He looked up, grinned, and then in an instant fell back to working the clay towards its intended shape. Slowly and steadily, a horse was born, a moist, new clay creature, with sinuous flanks and regal mien, ready to conquer the world.

Aparna squatted by the potter, her eyes brightening. 'May I watch? I won't disturb you.'

'Certainly, madam.' Velan's son proceeded to mould beads and jewels around the neck of the new-born beast.

Raghavan withdrew: the P.M. had arrived.

Aparna picked up a pitcher that the potter kept beside him to moisten the clay from time to time. 'May I help? This is beautiful. You are a genius.'

'No, madam. By God's grace, I am a potter. The gods play tricks. Sometimes a fine horse like this shatters in the kiln I build around for him. My heart shatters too.'

'What do you do then?'

'I roll up my mat, for I sleep by the kiln till all is over. I tighten my garment, go down to the river and wade till I strike the right clay, then I start all over again.' He grinned.

CHAPTER NINETEEN

The plane took off to the rumblings of dry thunder. From her window-seat Aparna saw the earth curve and diminish. As the plane gained height, she thought of her father, plying his steep path up to salvation. Soon he would snap the chords that bound him to the world and to her, and would throw open the road to freedom. She ought to rejoice. Instead, a great weariness descended on her, and her limbs were heavy with a nervous ache. The advocate, not always comforting or considerate, had been a substantial presence in her life. He had taught her, cajoled her, reprimanded her; and, on occasion, he had softened with compassion. Since the death of Balu, he had provided a bridle to rein in her inchoate feelings of guilt. But then the barrier had come down, that day he coldly rebuffed her when she most needed him to lift her with his blessing. Now he was slipping away, leaving her with a lostness that made her feel as insubstantial as the cotton-wool clouds they were traversing.

The plane shuddered. They had hit a pocket of turbulence.

'Frightened?' Raghavan offered a hand. '... If you would like to?'

She hesitated, but not for long.

She took his hand and folded her fingers through his. She found herself welcoming the turbulence, and tightened her grip as the plane dipped and jolted. She returned Raghavan's smile and leant back to savour long-forgotten sensations that revived her numbed body: she could feel his warmth and strength flowing into her, defusing the nervous currents that shot through her.

An elderly Telugu lady in the aisle-seat had gone green with fear. Raghavan tried to reassure her with an explanation of the phenomenon of turbulence. The old lady stared at him in blank incomprehension. Then her rubbery face relaxed. She was touched by his concern and began quizzing him.

'Any children?'

'Children? No.'

'Married long?'

'No, not long.' Raghavan shot a quick glance towards Aparna and shrugged his shoulders. She looked away. It was too much to expect him not to enjoy the make-believe.

'Your wife is beautiful. Does she know her kumkum is gone? See this?' The old lady took out a silver container from her bag. It had two compartments with sliding lids. 'One for kumkum, one for wax—and this wire circlet for pressing the powder on. A little something for my daughter. She has three children, all boys. Clever, isn't it? You wouldn't believe where I bought it!'

'Tell me.'

'Of all places, outside Jumma Masjid. They are very clever, those Muslim craftsmen, making Hindu things. Here, pass it to your wife. The kumkum is from the sanctuary of Kali-ma. May she bless you both!'

Raghavan passed the container to Aparna. She stared at the red powder. 'I can't,' she whispered. 'Tell her I don't have a mirror.'

'Let me then. Just look at me.'

She held her face still while Raghavan marked her forehead with a perfect medallion of red.

'There! Now your face shines as it ought.'

A tingling warmth spread from the spot where he had placed the kumkum. At that sacramental touch, it began to pulsate with an inrush of fresh blood. She instinctively lifted her hand towards her forehead—not, as Raghavan feared, to wipe off the mark, but to cover her third eye: she was quite convinced everyone would see the gash underneath bleeding afresh.

She held her hand in that position till the plane landed at Madras.

*   *   *

The sky was awash with monsoon clouds as their connecting plane descended towards Tiruchi. Paddy-fields around the airport were being flattened by strong winds.

Kabir was waiting for their arrival. With a jaunty swing he stashed their luggage into the boot of the Ambassador. As he picked up Aparna's bags, he broke into whistling. Raghavan recognized the tune: it was the latest hit from *Desert Moon*.

He glowered at the chauffeur. 'Don't dawdle! These winds might mean a storm.'

'Yes, sir!' Kabir doffed his red fez and started the car. The engine rumbled and stopped. 'Sorry, sir! Sorry, madam! I won't be a moment.' He got out, lifted the car-bonnet, and began poking around.

His dignity restored by the mishap, Raghavan could afford to be affable. He joined Kabir, and peered into the engine. 'Need some help? What's wrong?'

'No, sir! I will manage, sir. Please don't worry. That new mechanic is an idiot, sir. I had the car serviced just this morning after I got your message.'

Raghavan returned to Aparna. 'I'm sorry. I don't know how long he will be. A cyclone is predicted.'

'Oh, don't worry on my account.' Aparna opened the car-door and stepped out. 'I thirst for this.' She lifted her face towards the darkening skies to catch the first drops of rain. Her hair fell loose and blew about her face. Watching her under the wind and rain, Raghavan began to wish he hadn't asked Kabir to meet them.

The chauffeur came towards them, grinning confidently and wiping his hands on an oily rag. 'O.K., sir. All ready to go now.'

The rain came down in storm-waves. As they edged their way slowly over the bumpy, unlit road to Kuchchipuram, Raghavan's heart surged.

Lakshmiyamma's house was swarming with women. Having

heard that the grand-dame of Kuchchipuram was ill and alone, the 'gossip-gang' had assembled, ostensibly to keep vigil by her bedside. They were all there: Seshi, Deaf Rajam, Rukku's mother, and others whom Lakshmiyamma had barely acknowledged in the past.

Aparna and Raghavan swept through them, ignoring their whispers. Seeing her arrive in the Collector's car, and enter so boldly with him (and with a kumkum-mark on her forehead—what effrontery!), they scattered into dark corners, sensing that there would be much for keen eyes to observe and report.

Lakshmiyamma lay on a thin mattress—a concession to the seriousness of her condition. Her eyes were closed. Kunjappa, the country-quack, was beside her, taking her pulse.

'How is she?' Aparna knelt beside her grandmother.

'Pulse is very low. Very low indeed.' Kunjappa stepped back. The crinkly curls on the sides of his bald dome shook as he spoke. 'She is neither here, nor there. Drifting, just drifting. It is to be expected.'

'How long has she been like this?' Raghavan asked. 'When I saw her last, she could still sit up and talk.'

'I am attending her daily. Daily. This is the way she has been.'

'Are you giving her anything?'

'Only the usual.' The quack turned to Aparna. 'You know your grandmother. She will never have anything but Kunjappa's "little red pearls".'

'She looks very thin.' Aparna ran her hands over the frail frame.

'That is to be expected too. She is not eating anything, *amma*. She believes it is just another case of "bilious gas". Who can argue with her?' Kunjappa packed his vials into his leather pouch. 'Well, that is all I can do for her today. I'll call again in the morning.'

Raghavan waited till the quack was out. 'We must send Kabir to fetch the doctor from the clinic. Her condition is too bad to be left to that quack. He's just talk.'

'Is there any point in prolonging it? She really believes that one gets well if one chooses to. I shouldn't have left her. She has lost the will to live now.'

Lakshmiyamma opened her eyes. She stared at them both.

'—Ah! Aparna! Come close, my dear.' She wheezed as she

spoke. 'Lift me up! Let me see you. Your face is shining. Is that Collector boy? The dream is true then: the judge told me that boy would bring you back.'

They propped her up. With a feverish glint in her eyes, Lakshmiyamma looked around. '—What are they all doing here? I'm not ready for the kites yet. Am I to be an exhibition? Can't one die in peace? Tell them to go away! At once!' Exhausted, she fell back and drifted off.

Reluctantly, the women left one by one, skulking behind dark doorways, pillars and posts. Seshi was the last. She hung around.

Aparna repeated her words again: 'There's nothing to do. I am here now and I can look after her. She needs quiet. I'll sit by her while she sleeps.'

'But, my dear, don't I know that? It's *you* I'm concerned about. You are young and alone.'

'You're kind, Seshi-mami, but I've all the help I need. Please go.'

Seshi left, having first stared at Raghavan, her dark-ringed eyes almost popping with silenced rage. She had not forgiven Aparna for plunging her brother's family into great sorrow. Now she was getting brazen, this pretty widow of her ill-fated nephew, and ready to double-disgrace them with scandal.

'That woman's a poisonous gossip.' Aparna sat on the swing and kicked the floor angrily to start it. Raghavan stepped out of its path hastily.

'I'm sorry. I know I should have left—but I couldn't.'

'What does it matter now? They can say what they like. You are leaving soon, anyway. It seems my lot to lose and lose—father, soon grandma, and now you. My stars drive people away.'

'Aparna! I'm not abandoning you. I could curse myself that I agreed to go to London. But what could I do? You had gone off into deep silence. I couldn't but conclude you had cut me off. My mother and father were closing-in with their marriage-noose. It was intolerable: I had to escape. I'll be back—three months is no more than the time you abandoned *me*.'

'Who knows what further desolation I shall sink into in three months?'

'Listen, Aparna! You mustn't give up, not now. All you need is a little courage. You know what you should do.'

Aparna stopped the swing. 'To know is one thing, to be, another. To be a dancer again, I need more than what you call "courage".'

'What, then?'

'Inspiration, faith—call it what you will. I lack the readiness to be a channel for a higher power. I feel all choked up—my throat feels blocked with sore lumps. Lord Nataraja must lift me up; if he doesn't reclaim me, my life is worth nothing to me. *He* broke me, it is he who must make me whole. Then like Velan's son, I too can wade down and look for fresh clay.'

'I don't understand the ways of Shiva. He is suave, he is my rival—but I am prepared to plead with him for you. After all, he and I will be spending a lot of time together in the next three months.'

Aparna smiled drily. The clock struck twelve.

Raghavan shook himself. 'Good-night! No—good-morning. I must leave. Kabir is still waiting. The town will talk.' He drew her to him and kissed her on the forehead. 'Don't wipe off this kumkum. Promise?'

'I promise.'

After seeing him to the door, Aparna stretched herself beside her grandmother. She could not sleep. The day's events kept unrolling before her like a film-strip, to the tune Kabir had whistled. Just as she reached the kumkum-episode on the plane, she felt Lakshmiyamma move. She sat up and trimmed the oil-lamp.

Lakshmiyamma had stopped wheezing. Her face was bright once again and her voice steady and clear.

'What time is it?'

'Around three in the morning. Are you feeling better, grandma?'

'When did you return, my child?'

'Last evening, grandma. Will you take some broth? You should.'

'No, my girl. Stay with me. That's all I want.'

'I will. I'll never leave you again. I shouldn't have in the first place.'

'Hush, child! I was wrong. It was good that you went. He wouldn't have come here otherwise. It is good you are back, and that he brought you back. He knows what I think.'

'What, grandma?'

'You should live—live as you deserve to. Here, take this key. Go and fetch the black case from the safe.'

The steel safe in the front room had always been shrouded in an aura of secrecy. In her stronger days, Lakshmiyamma spent hours behind locked doors, inspecting its contents. She had never allowed anyone, not even her favourite granddaughter, to look in. Aparna approached the forbidden treasury in some trepidation. As she turned the lock, a smell of musty silk greeted her. Wrapped-up inside were sepia-prints: prints of grandfather dressed in court-robes and grandmother in surprisingly stylish palace costumes. No one wore such clothes, not even in those days. What could they possibly be? Aparna put the photographs aside and unfurled a scroll that lay underneath. It was an invitation to a formal ball—from the governor. So they had dressed up, the judge and his wife, as befits courtiers of the Maharajah of Mysore. Aparna looked out of the window. It was difficult to believe that the shrivelled-up, dying old woman had once been a beauty worthy of regal attire. Amidst a pile of assorted items of jewellery and turbans, silks and gold-embroidered shawls, she found the black case.

When she returned, Lakshmiyamma was sitting up.

'You found it. Good. Open it now. It's yours.'

Aparna obeyed. A heavy gold belt, richly inlaid with rubies and pearls, shone in the lamplight. It was an old-fashioned ornament, no longer worn by any but dancers.

'It was made by the Maharajah's goldsmith. I wore it at my wedding. I want you to promise you'll wear it.'

'But grandma—can I?'

'You can, my dear. You should. I say so. Don't bother me with questions. I'm tired. I want to sleep.'

*   *   *

It was the tenth day after the funeral. Lakshmiyamma's house was being washed from end to end; all utensils, clothes and items of furniture must be ritually purified, to signal the return to life after ten days of mourning.

Aparna wished she could join the other women in the kitchen as they prepared sweetmeats for distribution through the town. Instead, she had been compelled by uncle and brother to attend the reading of the will. They were more than a little perturbed to hear that not only the gold belt but the house itself had been left to her.

There was a knock at the door. Rukku, holding the door half-open, called back to her. 'There's someone to see you, Aparna! He can't come in.'

'Who?' Aparna rose, glad to escape the jealous little enclave that had formed round her.

It was the padre.

'—Please accept my condolences for your loss. I believe you were close to your grandmother.' Unfurling his wet umbrella and opening it on the ground outside, he looked about. 'I presume your relations are with you?'

'Yes. Only my brother's family and my uncle. The others left after the funeral.'

'Oh . . . !' The padre wiped his steamed-up spectacles, then looked directly at her. '—Can they hear if we talk here?'

Aparna shut the door behind her and leaned against it. 'Not now.' The street was quiet. A few children, late for school, were running, struggling with huge umbrellas against the strong downpour.

'Please sit down.' Aparna pointed to the bench on the verandah.

'I hope you don't mind if I talk freely. Just accept me as a friend who is very concerned about your welfare.'

'I understand.'

'Let me come straight to the point. What are you going to do now?'

'My brother thinks I ought to go to Madras with them.'

'Will you?'

'No. I have refused. They are angry with me.'

'So you are staying here, in Kuchchipuram. It is as I was told. —And what will you do?'

'I don't know. It has been blow upon blow.'

'Raghavan told me everything. He came to see me the day before he left for London. He has asked me to look after you.'

'Thank you.' She almost told him there was nothing he could do. Instead, she pulled her saree round her shoulders. 'It's getting quite cold here.' She waited in readiness to bid him good-bye.

The padre did not take the hint. He seemed absorbed in

thought, rubbing his chin with the palm of his hand.

'—Do you believe in angels?'

For a moment, she was taken aback. 'No.'

'I didn't think so. Few people do these days. But they still put them on Christmas cards—dainty white creatures, flapping lacy wings. The truth is, an angel could be anyone—anyone who brings hope. Even *I* could be. I take it you are familiar with the story of our Lord?'

'Yes.' Aparna stiffened. The padre's common sense seemed to have deserted him. He could not have chosen a worse moment for what looked like an ill-considered attempt at conversion.

'I'm glad. I don't have to be tedious, telling you what you know already. I have a proposal.'

'A proposal?'

'A challenge, if you like. Would you consider casting the story of our Lord's Passion, his suffering and crucifixion, into a dance-drama, as you did with the story of Kaama?'

Aparna reddened. He had quite wrong-footed her. The sheer daring of such a request was appalling. 'Tell me, padre—you puzzle me. I thought you were meant to reject all things Hindu. At best, you tolerate our arts as childish indulgence; at worst, you castigate them as evil sensuality. Your missionaries in the past very nearly destroyed our dance traditions. Yet here you are, asking me to make your Jesus *dance*. Why?'

'Forgive me. You have some reason to be angry. Perhaps you will understand if I say I have had a change of heart. —Do you remember Muniya, the cobbler?'

'I saw him firewalk. He got ill, didn't he?'

'Yes. Then he came to us. He became one of us. The boys of the "Joshua Brigade", who had wronged him, made amends. Muniya is well now. He works diligently; he is always in and around the church, doing something, polishing, sweeping, gardening. His faithfulness and devotion to our Lord should cheer the most downcast of us. But . . .' The padre sighed, and continued. 'The mainspring has gone. There's no *joy* in his heart. I never hear him hum a tune or chant with the zest and verve he once had. I never see him laugh. In his heart of hearts, he is pining.'

'Pining?'

'Yes. Pining for all the innocent beauty and joy of *bhakti* that he gave up when he became a convert. I feel like a robber. I want to see him sing and dance, with the same mad joy as when he walked that fire—except that this time it would be a real victory over suffering, not some hypnotic overcoming of false guilt. I want you to be the instrument of that joy—his and mine.'

'Why me? I'm too mangled to proclaim joy.'

'Precisely. We believe our Lord to have tasted the utmost in dereliction before his resurrection. You have suffered much, and the deepest joy comes from deepest suffering. You have been cast out, rejected, injured by your kith and kin, and—dare I say it?—even by your god.'

There was a long silence.

'... I have no wish to deny what you say. But if you are asking me to forsake Shiva-Nataraja, I cannot even begin to consider it.'

'Pardon me. I understood *he* had forsaken *you*.'

'I am just realizing how wrong I have been. Last time, when I went to my guru, he put me back on the right path—by reminding me that Shiva-Nataraja inspires those who surrender to him. I've been squealing like an angry child, too angry to give myself up—too angry with the world, my stars, my father—and even Raghavan. All that bottled-up anger has been souring me. For the first time, I feel ready to surrender.'

'I take it then you will consider my request?'

'It will be embarking on a journey with an unknown destination. There are so many questions to be asked and answered. To start with, we hold Shiva to be the Lord of the universe...'

'As we do Christ,' the padre cut in quickly. 'Ultimately, only he who serves most has a right to that title.'

'"Serves"?'

'May I remind you that even your *bhakti* poets speak of Shiva as willing to be the slave of his devotees?'

'Shiva is more than that. He is a wild god: unpredictable, reckless, dangerous, exotic, and—dare I say it—erotic. Can Christ be all that?'

The padre paused. 'I take your point. The Church has too often been frightened of eros. But that is only because she proclaims a greater love, the love of a suffering God.'

'How can a God who is all perfection *suffer*? That's reserved for the likes of me.'

'Ah, but' —the padre's eyes twinkled as he leaned earnestly towards her— 'Even your Shiva swallowed poison to save the world, and retained it in his throat. Christ, the son of God, died on the cross to save mankind. One is an image, the other reality. They must cohere, somewhere in our imagination, in truth. Without such coherence, there is not much hope for either of us. We must begin somewhere. Why not with this, here and now?'

'You are asking a great deal of me. There's so much I do not understand, that I do not know.' Aparna shifted uneasily, twisting and untwisting the tassles that hung at the end of her saree.

The padre sat silent with a wan expression on his face: centuries of fruitless longing washed over him.

She came and sat beside him on the bench. 'It will be a dangerous tussle between Shiva and Christ. I cannot predict what the outcome will be. But if you are prepared to accept that, I'll try.'

He stared at her for a moment as if he had not registered what she said. Then his features lit in with a smile. 'Thank you! Thank you! God bless you. I'll see you again soon.'

Aparna returned to the hall. The family was in conference. She could tell by their looks that they had been discussing her.

'I have decided to leave Kuchchipuram. Rukku's family can live here and look after this house for us.'

Gopal spoke first. 'Good girl! There's my sensible sister. Uncle and I were just saying that there are any number of things you could be doing in Madras: typing, accountancy—why, even computer-programming. Nice little packet of salary they all bring in. With our connections we could soon find you a job.'

'To Madras, yes. But not to do jobs. Not to live with you.'

'Aparna! Whatever are you saying? What will you be doing then?'

'I am going to Kalakshetra. I must study Rukmini Devi's work. I'll need a troupe of able dancers to train, and all the help I can from him above. I've just agreed to a most unusual challenge.'

CHAPTER TWENTY

'The question is—should I tell the *dikshitars*?'

Raghavan stopped before the brick building the padre had been showing him round, a simple structure that was to be consecrated as St Andrew's Church the following morning. The air smelt fresh with lime-wash. Perhaps it was the enervating effect of jet-lag, still lingering a week after his return to base; or perhaps, the white clarity of the bare interior he had been viewing—anyway, he was impelled to unburden. The question that troubled him ever since his return to Kuchchipuram had surfaced, even before he could consider the wisdom of seeking the padre's advice.

The padre was quick to tune in.

'What if they discover it for themselves?'

'They won't. It's a hair-line crack, not easily detectable. It was only discovered when the experts set to work on Murugan, and removed all the verdigris.'

'If you tell them, you know the consequences.'

'I know they have chosen Krittika Night next month for the installation, Krittika being sacred to Murugan. All their grand plans for celebration will be spoilt.'

'More than that. You'll be held responsible. They will accuse you of causing the damage.'

'That's nonsense. It's always been there. It's not something that happens by mishandling. Anyway, it's a microscopic crack: across the back between the sacred thread and some ornament—barely visible to the naked eye.'

'Nonetheless, someone might spot it—and then all hell will break loose. Who knows, beside you?'

'Only the people in London. They are not likely to bother the *dikshitars*. As I said, a very minor flaw in an otherwise superb piece of bronze.'

'All the same, a defect. A defective god has no place in the temple. You know that.'

'Are you suggesting that I should come clean?'

'I could hardly advise you to suffer an uneasy conscience.'

'"Conscience"? If I listened to my conscience I wouldn't let them have the bronze at all. It is not as if we don't have enough gods to worship. What's the point of more clutter, when we need less? It ought to be sent to a museum.'

'Why don't you?'

Raghavan paused. 'The state of our museums grieves me. Besides, it's too easy a solution. It lets them off. There's a side of me that would rather enjoy the irony of a flawed god in that temple. It's a small revenge for huge wrongs done in the name of religion.'

The padre scrutinized Raghavan's face before wording his response. 'The pleasure of rebellion is sweet. But when anger cools, weariness sets in. Protest doesn't sustain one—only the love of God does that.'

'"The love of God"! I have been trying to work out what that could mean—if anything at all. Aparna gave me a copy of some *bhakti* poets to read during my time away. It was to be my first step towards understanding the mystery of Shiva. I owed it to her. There's no doubt the religious experience of those poets was genuine. They are intoxicating to read. They *were* intoxicated, madly in love with Shiva—there's no other way to explain their pleas, longings and ecstasies. But to think that all that was induced by dream-images, derived from myths! Fine when the race was young; but now, in this day and age, how can one be sustained by a phantom-god, by a will-o'-the-wisp—an abstract ideal?'

The padre put a hand on Raghavan's shoulder. The rays of the evening sun glinted across his spectacles.

'You are tempting me—and I can't resist. *"The Word was made flesh and dwelt among us."* The incarnation of God in Christ is no myth but reality—flesh-torn, blood-dripping reality. Such suffering is the measure of God's reality, of his love for us. In a sense, I feel we had to nail him down to make him real for us.'

'It's hard to live by dead myths—but I find it even harder to accept your story.'

'Is it so difficult? After all, Hindus believe in *avatars* who rescue mankind from time to time.'

'Precisely. But you claim Christ as unique. Why should he be?'

'All right: either an immense illusion or an immense truth—it's for you to decide. That's his challenge to us: to me, to you and Aparna, to everyone whose spirit thirsts for the truth.'

'You're expecting too much from me.'

'No more than what I asked of Aparna.'

'I must confess it was a brilliant ploy of yours, getting her to undertake that project. There's no doubt the task is renewing her. She looks well. Kalakshetra suits her. When I saw her last week, she was so full of excitement: she'd had a major breakthrough—found someone to compose the necessary music.'

'It wasn't a ploy. I took what you call a calculated risk. I was prepared for her to turn me down. She nearly did. Then she changed her mind. I'll never know fully what made her. I can't flatter myself into thinking it was my persuasion.'

'That's easy. No real artist can resist a challenge. And she too is tired of dreamy myths, seductive as they are. You've prompted her to explore in dance real emotions, inspired in and by real people. I saw a little of her work. It seemed very fitting that she should have cast John the Baptist to look like an austere, brahmin *rishi*—except that this one is all passion, a mercurial character of fierce righteousness, anger, piety, and humility. He mesmerizes commoners and princes alike. I assure you, the beginning bodes very well for what is to follow.'

'I haven't seen her these three months. She writes to me from time to time, to get things clarified. She sent me the young man who is to do the role of Christ. He stayed with me for weeks, studying, and working alongside me in the parish. He had been instructed to look, learn, absorb—and live as Jesus did. The people here became so enamoured, I began to fear for him.' The padre laughed, and Raghavan joined in.

'Padre!' Muniya had appeared with a basket-load of flowers.

'Ah! —Raghavan, I want you to meet my new churchwarden. He is overseeing the preparation of the church for tomorrow's festivity. He has a free hand. —What is it, Muniya?'

'May we start, padre? The women are ready to do the *kolams*. Shall I let them in?'

'Yes, yes. You can begin. But no tinsel, no paper chains, only pure fresh flowers and greenery. Dress the church as for a wedding. Understand?'

'Yes, padre. All the flowers from the bazaar stalls are here with me, padre.' Muniya was beaming.

'All decorations must be finished before midnight. Then we lock the church till dawn.'

'Padre!' Muniya lingered.

'Yes, Muniya?'

'There's a rumour, padre, we are having fireworks—is that so?'

The padre thought for a while. 'It will be just like Deepavali then. Do you think we should have fireworks, Muniya?'

'Me? Padre is asking *me*?'

'Yes, Muniya, I am asking you.'

'I know a lot of us have already bought fireworks, padre. I can tell them it is all right to bring them then?' Muniya grinned and moved on.

'—See how excited he is! It's a great day for us tomorrow. When dawn breaks on Deepavali, we too shall celebrate. I've never thanked you fully for all your help—your personal donation, the land-lease.'

'You have repaid me well enough in Aparna.'

'When is she arriving?'

'The train is due just before 7 p.m.'

The padre's face clouded. 'Does she know who is in town?'

'No. But she will, as soon as she steps down from the train. There are posters everywhere. He calls himself "Swami Abhedananda" now.'

'Doesn't that mean "one who makes no distinctions"?'

'Something like that. It's typical of him.'

'What will you do? Isn't it customary to seek blessing from a sadhu?'

'You know me well enough! How many customs have I been keeping? I shan't see him. As for Aparna, I can't tell. He may call himself "Swami Abhedananda", but the face she'll see on the posters is still her father's. The only difference is the white beard and saffron robes.'

*   *   *

'"Bhaja Govindam, bhaja Govindam,
Bhaja Govindam mudamate..."'

The loudspeakers mounted on the outer walls of Shiva-Nataraja shuddered as they relayed Swami Abhedananda's ringing admonition. The chant was echoed by a thousand voices. A new cobbler sitting under Muniya's peepul tree dipped a piece of leather in water and delivered his hammer-blows to the swinging tune of the refrain.

'"Bhaja Govindam, bhaja Govindam,
Bhaja Govindam mudamate.
Samprapte sannihite kale
Nahi nahi rakshati dukrinchakarane..."'

'... "Worship Govinda, worship Govinda, all ye foolish ones! When you near the end of your time, the hour of your death, no hair-splitting grammarian will save you"—so sings the greatest of the great souls, Adi Sankara...' Swami Abhedananda paused to gather dramatic momentum. 'And whom does this *mahaguru*, this saint-seer *par excellence*, this noble embodiment of *advaitam* invoke? Govinda: Lord Krishna! Was he diluting *advaita* philosophy—or was he merely making a concession to weaker mortals? Such deep questions do not concern us this evening. Tonight we shall sing, we shall pray, we shall aspire to swim ashore from the sea of births. We shall seek that which few of us seek. —Those are not my words, but the words of the great Adi Sankara, who goes on to sing:

'"Balastavat balasaktah,
Tarunastavat taruni saktah,
Vriddah stavat stambah saktah;
Pare brahmani kopi na saktah..."'

'"Child seeks child, the youth seeks the young maiden, old age seeks a stick for support—but no one seeks the great Brahman!" So say with me again . . .' The Swami nodded to the musicians around. The drummer struck, the folds of the harmonium swelled, and the assembly responded with greater enthusiasm: *'Bhaja Govindam, bhaja Govindam . . .'*

Shoppers for Deepavali clogged Flower-Bazaar. Saree shops, sweet stalls, and firework-stands were busier than ever. Despite Kabir's relentless horn-blasts, the car crept inch by inch. Raghavan looked anxiously at Aparna. She had recognized the Swami's voice.

'I could ask Kabir to take us straight to Guru Ramiah's by the northern road. We can escape this.'

'No. I must see Rukku first. I have presents for her and for her family. I want them to have them at dawn, like everyone else.'

She seemed undisturbed by the temple-chant; but the slight frown on her face suggested that Rukku had provided a convenient pretext. Her ears were straining to catch every word that emanated from the temple.

'. . . A thousand lamps will be lit tomorrow at dawn, lit and worshipped. In that directionless flame we shall see the great Brahman who is colourless, odourless, formless, who is infinite and infinitesimal; and, in the words of Chandogya Upanishad, "He is my self within the heart, smaller than a corn of rice, smaller than a corn of barley, smaller than a mustard seed. He is also my self within the heart, greater than the earth, greater than the sky, greater than heaven, greater than all these worlds".'

Kabir pressed the horn again and the Swami's words were drowned out. Aparna turned towards Raghavan. 'Could you ask Kabir to stop here somewhere? I won't be long.'

'Must you? I'll come too then.'

'No, don't. If we go there together it is bound to attract attention. On my own, it will be easier to melt into the crowd. No one will recognise me now, dressed like this.'

She was wearing a yellow printed-silk saree, and a large kumkum adorned her forehead; the gold necklace around her neck and her ruby ear-rings caught the bazaar-lights and showered rainbow-colours across her face. She pulled her saree close over her shoulders as she set out in the direction of the temple.

The temple was caught in a fever of festivity: the excitement of their own locally-bred sadhu camping there had swelled the crowd of worshippers. Curiosity as much as piety brought them there: they had all heard of the vast learning of the erstwhile advocate, now they had a chance to see and hear for themselves—and they were not disappointed.

Aparna tagged on to a group from Tiruchi; they were pious strangers passing through Kuchchipuram and took her to be one also. From their conversation she gathered they were jaggery-merchants. Alongside their womenfolk she could stand undetected, and watch the Swami from a safe distance.

'Brahman is the Supreme Reality, Impersonal, Absolute, beyond death, beyond time, beyond good and evil. So, as our Acharya sings, "we awaken to freedom when we realize that our bodies are no more than borrowed clothes that we cast aside at death".'

The words were familiar. She had heard them from him on countless evenings, and he looked much the same. The white beard and saffron robes made him seem heavier than before, but the sliding spectacles, which he had kept, gave the same comic twist to his utterances as before. He was in fine form. And not surprising that he should be—to be able to discourse to a captive audience of thousands, uninterrupted, undisturbed by clients, by worries, by her reproachful presence . . .

'—Don't I know you?' A woman who had just arrived behind the group nudged Aparna. 'Aren't you . . . Isn't he, the Swami . . . your . . . ?' She stared, stuttering with astonishment. Aparna turned round to face her. It was her pupil Rani's mother.

'Yes, *mami*. I am Aparna still. But that person over there, he is Swami Abhedananda.'

Leaving the woman to gape at her, wide-mouthed, Aparna made her way out of the temple.

Raghavan was waiting for her at the gateway. He hastened to her. 'How was it? Did you speak to him?'

'No. It was like seeing someone you know taking part in a play on stage. He is and he isn't my father. What I don't understand is why he came back here. In that letter of his, he sounded thoroughly wrapped up in the bliss of the mountains. Why descend to the plains now?'

'Perhaps it is akin to what the Buddha did. After his enlightenment he was moved by compassion, and preached.'

'There's little compassion to be had from this Swami. He is urging them all to go the same way as he has done. Even if I'd plucked up the courage to face him after the discourse, do you think he would have responded? I am quite sure I would matter no more than any of the others there.'

'I am told he is pioneering a new type of *puja*: a "thousand lamps *puja*", to be performed not by priests but by ordinary people from all walks of life—*sudras* and *pariahs* are to worship alongside *vaishyas* and brahmins. The *dikshitars* didn't like the idea at all. They tried to ban it. The new temple-manager overruled them. Too much revenue, to be ignored—a hundred rupees per person and a thousand in each session! Still, the *dikshitars* managed to push the *puja* out to the outermost *prahara*. That's as far as any reform will get in this temple.'

Raghavan stopped. She had not been listening. There was a bitter-sweet smile on her face.

'I'm sorry. I've changed my mind. I don't think I can face Rukku or anyone else just now. Take me straight home, to Guru Ramiah's.'

* * *

Deepavali broke in on Kuchchipuram at four in the morning. The sky flashed with a thousand comet-streaks of aluminium-light, and reverberated to explosions large and small. Thus, the great *asura* of Hell was once again chased back to his dark confine.

'What would you like now?' Raghavan, who had arrived early at Guru Ramiah's cottage, was standing guard by the basket of fireworks near the door-post. Aparna's face had lit up with child-like delight when he presented the fireworks to her. Now she was concentrating on each one with such solemn pleasure that he began to wonder if she had forgotten his presence.

'One moment!' Aparna waited till the crackly sparkler she was holding in her right hand had died down, sputtering shafts of bluish-white light. As she pulled back from the edge of the verandah, the gold weave of her parrot-green silk saree glittered in the darkness. 'Any "flower-pots" left?'

Raghavan rummaged through the basket and pulled out a cone-shaped cracker with a florid wrapper. 'Here!' Aparna placed the cone on the furthermost step, lit the wick and hastened back. A fountain of white streaks jetted high, forcing up a shower of gold, blue, and yellow globules of light.

'—Do you know, some vendor who couldn't find the right letters for "flower-pot" in Tamil named it *"pulavar pattu"*—"a poet's song"? Seeing how they make your eyes sparkle, I think the man ought to be congratulated! Alas, that was the last one!' Raghavan peered into the basket. 'What would you like next? Wheels, rockets, Roman candles, China crackers—or the "atom-bomb"?'

'It's your turn. I've been greedy.'

'They are all for you. My pleasure is watching you.'

'China crackers then!'

Raghavan handed over a string of red crackers. 'Don't hold them too long! Be careful!'

'I promise.'

Aparna held the string of China crackers at arm's length and lit them. The end one began to smoke and bang, setting off a chain reaction; she held on till the bangs reached more than half-way up the string, before she flung it into the distance. As the crackers jumped and spluttered, pieces of tattered red paper covered the yard. A film of soot landed on Raghavan.

'Oh . . . Oh!' With a deft flick of her fingers, Aparna dislodged the bits of black ash from his shirt-front. 'Look what I've done. Smudged all over.' As she peered closely to inspect the damage, her perfumed hair, still wet after the morning's oil-bath, fell over him in shiny coils.

'Never mind that.' Raghavan gathered her into his arms. 'Now, my princess! I'm not letting you out till you name the day.'

'Stop it! Someone might come!' Aparna struggled but failed to wrest herself free.

'Who? Valliamma or the Guru? We already have their blessing. Now that he knows I'm no barrier to your art, he's no longer suspicious. What are we waiting for?'

'For the day you leave Kuchchipuram. I cannot live here any more. It has died for me.'

'All right, I shall then. A job is coming up at the India International Centre. Mr Gautam is keen for me to join his staff. I have no illusions about what it means, entering the jungle of higher bureaucracy. But as Padre Yesudasan would say, in this imperfect world no one can achieve anything by staying uncontaminated. Besides, there'll be plenty of scope for you there. It depends on you. Can you bear to live in that dusty city of tombs which you hate so much?'

'Anywhere but here.'

'—Aparna! Aparna!' Valliamma was calling out. '*Idli* is ready, my children! Shall I bring it out to you?'

Raghavan released Aparna.

'We are not hungry yet, Valliamma. And we still have some fireworks to let off before light breaks.' She turned to Raghavan. '—That's right, isn't it? You must light the "atom-bomb". I am too scared.'

'Right then! Stand well back!' Raghavan walked towards the *nagalinga* tree, put a sparkler to the wick of the globular firecracker, and doubled back to Aparna on the verandah. She had closed her eyes and stopped her ears, in anticipation of a loud bang. She was not disappointed. A mighty explosion shook the grove, setting the birds to screech in disarray.

When the echoes subsided, Raghavan relaxed his hold on Aparna. She opened her eyes.

'Look!'

The bottom of the grove was shimmering like a string of gold. A stream of people, each carrying an earthenware lamp and singing, formed an undulating snake of flame along the narrow lane.

Raghavan ran down to the gateway and called back. 'It's the procession to St Andrew's Church. The padre is expecting us at the consecration. Shall we go?'

'Just one moment!' Aparna reached for the earthenware lamp in the alcove by the door. 'Here. I'm ready now. Let's join them.'

SOUTH INDIAN COOKERY IN *THE FIREWALKERS*

INDEX TO DISHES

dish	*page of text*	*recipe page*
aviyal	137	239
badam kheer	138	246
barfi	171	245
bhajji	75	235
bhonda	75	235
chutney, coconut	69	233
chutney, mango	69	243
chutney, tomato	69	243
chutney, wood apple	69	243
curry, aubergine	94	240
curry, cabbage	94	241
idli	46, 227	230
kesari (sojji)	69	245
koottu	69	241
masala dosa	75	231
pachadi, cucumber	69	242
pappadum	1, 99	244
payasam	69	244
pongal	48	237
poori	137	233
rasam, pepper	145	239
rasam, tomato-lemon	94	239
rava dosa	75	234
relish, ginger	69	243
relish, potato-onion	69	231
rice, curds	69	237
rice, lemon	69	236
rice, sesame	30	237
rice, tamarind	69	236
salad, carrot	69	242
sambhar	69	238
sambhar, onion	94	232
upma	17, 75	230
vadai	75	234

Snacks and Light Meals

UPMA
This popular snack can also be prepared with vermicelli. Onions are omitted when the dish is prepared for an orthodox brahmin. The vermicelli version makes a good picnic treat.

Serves 4

1 cup coarse semolina
a silver of ginger, 1/2 inch
1 small onion, preferably shallot *or* Spanish
1 green chilli
1/4 teaspoon black mustard seed
1 teaspoon urad dal
2 tablespns cashew nut pieces
2 tablespoons oil
pinch of asafoetida
juice of 1/2 lemon
a few curry leaves
2 cups water
1 teaspoon salt

Chop the onion and crush the ginger. Heat oil in a wok or frypan, and as it begins to smoke, drop in the mustard seeds. When they finish crackling, add the asafoetida, urad dal, cashew-nuts, onion, ginger, green chilli, curry leaves, and finally the semolina. Toast well for ten minutes, add water and salt and continue stirring for another ten minutes or more, until the semolina is cooked. Add more water if necessary. The upma is ready when all the moisture evaporates and it separates easily from the pan. The dish should emerge with a light fluffy texture. Stir-in lemon juice.

IDLI
This ubiquitous breakfast dish can be tasted everywhere in the South, from wayside tea-stalls to five-star hotels. Successful steaming of idli requires a special idli-pan. A substitute can be arranged by placing small ramekin dishes or egg-poachers within an ordinary steamer.

Serves 4

1 cup raw, parboiled rice
1/2 cup urad dal
flat teaspoon salt
oil

Soak rice and urad dal separately for at least an hour. Grind rice to a thick, coarse-grained paste, using as little liquid as possible. Clean and wash urad dal thoroughly and grind to a fine-textured thick paste. Mix the two in a large bowl, add salt and leave for several hours in a warm place to ferment and rise. The mixture is ready when it becomes frothy and gives out a yeasty smell. Stir well. Grease the idli pans well with oil, place them inside the steamer, and fill each scoop 3/4 full with the mix. Make sure that the water-level inside the steamer is below the idli-pans. Steam over gentle heat for 10-15 minutes. Test by piercing an idli with a toothpick; if it comes out clean the idli is ready. Serve with coconut-chutney* and onion sambhar*.

MASALA DOSA

If you order this famous delicacy of the South in a restaurant you are likely to confront a crunchy, golden-brown scroll, more than a foot long across the plate. Even the best home-made dosa cannot compete with what the professionals can do. The reason is quite simple: in hotels and cafés the cooks use a large cast-iron flat pan which is kept hot over a long period. However, a good approximation can be achieved in the home-kitchen with a well-heated, heavy, cast-iron pancake-pan.

Makes 6

6 oz. raw rice preferably parboiled
2 oz. urad dal
$1/2$ teaspoon salt
oil to fry

Clean and wash rice and urad dal thoroughly and soak at least for an hour. Grind in a blender till you get a fine, thick batter. Add salt, put the batter in a large bowl, and leave in a warm place to ferment for a day. (Left-over idli batter to which some fine rice flour is added also makes a good dosa-batter.)

Heat the pan well. Sprinkle some oil and water and baste the pan before starting the dosa. Drop a teaspoon of oil at the centre of the pan, and grease the surface once again. Drop 2 to 3 tablespoons of batter and, using the back of the spoon, spread the mixture round thinly till it forms a large circle. Take $1/2$ teaspoon of oil and dribble it round the edges. As the dosa cooks, lift the edges to let the oil run in. Cook for approximately 5 minutes until the dosa becomes crisp and can be lifted by the slice. Turn over and oil the edges as before. Cook till it becomes golden-brown.

Fill the dosa with 2 tablespoons of potato-onion relish*. Serve with coconut chutney* and onion sambhar*.

POTATO-ONION RELISH

This relish is served as a filling for masala dosa, and as an accompaniment to pooris and chapatis. It is also popular picnic fare.

1 lb cooked potatoes
1 large red onion *or* 4 shallots
a sliver of ginger
1 green chilli
$1/2$ teaspoon black mustard seeds
$1/4$ teaspoon turmeric
$1/2$ teaspoon sambhar *or* curry powder

1 flat teaspoon salt
1 teaspoon urad dal
pinch of asafoetida
3 tablespoons fresh, green coriander leaves, chopped
juice of half a lemon
2 tablespoons oil

New potatoes should be scraped and boiled; old potatoes should be cleaned, boiled in their skins, and then peeled. Heat oil in a wok and drop in the mustard seeds. As they crackle, add urad dal, asafoetida, ginger, chopped onion, chilli, curry powder, and turmeric. Stir for a while till the onions soften and then add the cooked potatoes, breaking them with the ladle. Add salt, coriander leaves, and stir well for 5 minutes. Turn the potato mix into a stainless-steel or china dish before stirring in the lemon juice.

ONION SAMBHAR

Sambhar is a lentil-based tamarind concoction, halfway between soup and stew in texture. The quality of the tamarind and the quantity of toor dal and diced vegetables used in sambhar can make or break a family's reputation. Normally, a standard sambhar powder* is used; but for onion sambhar the spices are roasted and ground fresh, and there are three distinct stages of preparation.

Serves 4-6

Stage One

    4 oz. toor dal $1/2$ teaspoon ground turmeric
    2 oz. mung dal

Wash the dals, add the turmeric, and cook to a smooth but grainy pulp. This can be done easily with the dals and water placed in a container inside a pressure-cooker; but make sure the container is covered loosely so as to avoid clogging the steam-vent. Set aside.

Stage Two

$1^{1}/2$ tablespoons coriander seeds *or* 1 tablespoon ground coriander
    1 tablespoon oil   3 or 4 dried red chillies
    $1/2$ teaspoon black mustard seeds   1 teaspoon peppercorns
    2 tablespoons of grated coconut

Heat oil in a frying pan. Drop mustard seeds in hot oil and cover while they crackle. Add the red chillies, peppercorns, coriander seeds, and, finally, the coconut. Toast till the coconut turns golden-brown. Turn out the mix on to a paper-towel to drain the oil. Grind to a fine powder in a spice-grinder, or, alternatively, blend to a smooth paste in a liquidizer. Set aside.

Stage Three

    1 green chilli   2 tablespoons ground rice
    $1/2$ teaspoon black mustard seeds   fresh coriander leaves,
    $1/2$ teaspoon fenugreek seeds   washed and chopped
    1 tablespoon split peas   1 tablespoon oil
    pinch of asafoetida   2 flat teaspoons salt

Also
1lb of small red Madras onions, peeled. (French shallots or Spanish red onions make a reasonable substitute.)
A small fistful of tamarind pulp soaked in one cup of hand-hot water (*or*, one flat teaspoon tamarind essence dissolved in 2 cups of hot water). Squeeze the tamarind, remove seeds and fibre, and strain the liquid. Repeat the process till you get 2 cups of tamarind-water.

Heat oil in a heavy saucepan. Drop in the mustard seeds. As they pop, add split peas, asafoetida, fenugreek, green chilli, and, finally, the onions. Stir well for 3-5 minutes. Turn down the heat and add the tamarind water, salt and ground spices. Simmer gently for about 15 minutes, till the onions are cooked.

Pour 1¹/₂ cups of water over the cooked pulses, strain off the broth, and put it aside for rasam*. Add the solid dal to the saucepan. Mix the ground rice and 1 tablespoon of water, and add to the sambhar to thicken it. Cook for 5 minutes until the smell of raw rice-flour goes. Sprinkle chopped coriander. The sambhar is now ready to be served with a number of things: rice, dosa, idli, vadai, or even pooris.

POORI
Originally from the north of India, poori has now become part of South Indian cuisine, especially because it goes well with almost all South Indian vegetarian dishes.

Makes 15
8 oz. wholewheat flour *or* half wholewheat or soya and half plain white flour
also
¹/₂ teaspoon salt	¹/₄ pint warm water
2 teaspoon ghee *or* oil	oil for deep-frying

Mix the flour, or combination of flours, with salt. Work the ghee in, add water gradually, and knead to a smooth dough, firm but elastic. Cover and set aside for ¹/₂ hour. Divide the dough into 15 pieces. Roll each piece into a ball on the palm of the hand, and on a floured board roll out each ball into a thin circle. Deep-fry the poori by placing it in hot oil and ladling hot oil over the top so as to make it puff up. When it turns golden, lift out and drain well on kitchen paper. Serve with potato-onion relish* and coconut chutney*.

COCONUT CHUTNEY
When made with fresh coconut and green chillies, this chutney is a refreshing accompaniment to fried or steamed snacks.

3 oz. coconut, freshly grated, *or* dessicated	pinch of asafoetida
	a few curry leaves
2 tablespoons split peas	1 teaspoon oil
2-3 green chillies	3 oz. curds *or* plain yoghurt
¹/₂ teaspoon mustard seed	juice of ¹/₂ lemon
1 teaspoon urad dal	1 flat teaspoon salt

Heat oil in a small frying pan and drop in the mustard seeds. As they crackle, add asafoetida and split peas. Toast until the split peas turn golden. Remove from the oil and put in a bowl, with half a cup of water. Let this stand for half an hour, while you grate the coconut. If fresh coconut is used, split the coconut by giving it a hard bash with a mallet over a safe surface, or, alternatively, follow the traditional South Indian method, which is to bash the coconut over the edge of a granite slab till the coconut splits right in the middle, and then catch any liquid that flows, in a jug. This makes a refreshing drink. Strike the coconut along the split and it will fall into two neat halves. Scour the white flesh with a sharp knife and prise it off piece by piece. The pieces can then be grated on a cheese-grater. Cut the chillies. Place the grated coconut, chillies and soaked split peas inside a blender, and grind to a smooth texture. Remove, and add the yoghurt, salt, and lemon juice. Heat the remaining oil in the frypan and drop in the mustard seeds, urad dal, curry leaves, and toast until the urad dal turns golden. Top the chutney with this seasoning. Stir before serving.

RAVA DOSA

A quick recipe for a dosa with a very different flavour, ideal to prepare when there is no fermented batter.

Serves 4

¹/₂ cup fine semolina	¹/₂ teaspoon mustard seeds
¹/₂ cup rice flour	1 teaspoon cummin seeds
1 flat teaspoon salt	1 green chilli, sliced thin
4 tablespoons sour butter-milk *or* plain yoghurt	1 cup water
	oil to fry

Mix the semolina, flour, yoghurt, water and salt in a bowl. Heat 2 teaspoons of oil in a small frypan. Crackle the mustard seeds and add sliced green chilli and cummin seeds. Pour into the batter and stir well. Proceed as for masala dosa: using a heavy cast-iron pan, spread 2-3 tablespoons of batter for each dosa and cook till crisp on both sides.

VADAI

This South Indian savoury dough-nut is rich in protein and is considered a 'heavy' item in a mixed menu. To make it more easily digestible, the vadai is often served in its modified form as tayir or dahi-vadai. For this, the fried vadai are first dipped in hot water to remove excess grease and then soaked in a yoghurt sauce, made by blending grated coconut, green chillies, curry leaves and liberal quantities of yoghurt, topped by a seasoning of mustard seeds crackled in oil.

Serves 4

4 oz. urad dal	1 teaspoon salt
1-2 green chilli	6-8 peppercorns
¹/₄ inch ginger	oil to fry

Soak the urad dal for at least an hour. Wash well. Place in a food-processor with a very small amount of liquid, add chopped chilli, ginger, peppercorns, salt. Grind to a smooth, thick paste. It should be spongy in texture. Add some rice flour if the mixture needs thickening.

Heat oil in a wok. When the oil begins to smoke, turn down to a moderate heat. Take a tablespoon of mixture and place it on a dampened piece of grease-proof paper, or, if you have access to a banana-tree, on a green banana-leaf. Shape it into a dough-nut and, using your index finger, make a hole in the middle. Slide the vadai carefully into the oil, taking care not to splash hot oil over yourself. A less taxing method is simply to drop spoonfuls and then use a sharp knife to make holes in the middle. Fry well, turning over several times till the vadai turns golden-brown. Remove with a slotted-spoon, drain well and serve with coconut chutney* and sambhar*. Or, you may proceed to make tayir-vadai*, as described above.

BHONDA
This snack made of mashed spud is yet another instance of what the South Indian cook can do to metamorphose the humble potato.

Makes 18

Make potato-onion relish* using 1^1/$_2$ lb floury potatoes. Add a generous quantity of chopped cashew nuts, and mix well. Take two tablespoons of mixture at a time and shape into balls. Chill while preparing the batter.

Prepare a thick batter by mixing 1 cup of besan (split-pea flour), 2 tablespoons rice flour and ^{1}/$_2$ to ^{3}/$_4$ cup water. Add ^{1}/$_2$ teaspoon saffron powder, a pinch of bicarbonate soda and 1 flat teaspoon salt.
Heat oil in a wok. Test the heat by dropping in a tiny bit of batter. When it surfaces to the top readily, the temperature is right for frying.

Dip the potato-ball carefully in the batter, making sure it is coated thoroughly. An easy way is to place a bhonda on a large spoon, immerse it in the batter and lift out. Fry 3 or 4 bhondas at a time, turning them over frequently for 10 minutes or so, until they turn a rich yellow. Lift out with a slotted-spoon, drain off on kitchen towels, and serve with coconut chutney* or sweet tomato relish*.

BHAJJI
These vegetable fritters are popular as afternoon snacks and are served with coffee or tea. They are excellent served with other drinks.

Serves 6
For the batter, mix the following ingredients in a large bowl:
  4 oz. besan ^{1}/$_4$ teaspoon saffron powder
  2 oz. rice flour ^{1}/$_2$ teaspoon chilli powder
  pinch of bicarbonate of soda   pinch of asafoetida
  1 teaspoon salt   5 oz. water
also
a selection of thinly sliced vegetables: potato, onion, aubergine, courgette, large mild chillies, green pepper.
Oil to fry.

Heat oil in a wok. Dip the sliced vegetables one by one into the batter, and drop them carefully into hot oil. Fry well till the bhajji turns crisp and vivid yellow. Remove with slotted-spoon and drain on kitchen towels. Serve with tomato relish* or coconut chutney*.

Main Meals

Rice is the staple diet of the South. It is served in three stages. For the first course, it is accompanied by sambhar, a number of vegetable dishes, and salads. The second course usually features rasam, which literally means 'essence', and is a delicately flavoured thin soup made with the sediment of cooked dals. Rasam is usually taken with a small amount of rice but some prefer to drink it from a bowl. The last course is invariably rice and curds, and no Tamilian feels a meal to be complete without curds at the end. It is at this stage that hot or salted pickles are served. On special occasions, sweets such as payasam* are served between the second and third courses.

Though plain steamed rice is most commonly served during meals, there are a number of interesting ways of preparing rice for special occasions. The following are a selection that will be specially prepared for the river-side festival-picnic that is celebrated on the eighteenth day of the month of Adi to mark the 'swelling of waters', when the river that had dwindled to a thin trickle during the summer once again begins to flow full as a result of monsoon rains in the west.

TAMARIND RICE

1/4 cup oil (gingelly oil, or failing that, add a teaspoon of toasted and crushed sesame seeds to peanut oil. A more expensive but satisfactory substitute is cold-pressed, green olive oil).
1 cup of strong tamarind water made by soaking and squeezing a moderate fistful of tamarind pulp, *or* by mixing 2 teaspoons of tamarind essence and water.
Also

- 2 cups rice, cooked
- 1 teaspoon mustard seed
- 1/8 teaspoon asafoetida
- 1 1/2 teaspoon salt
- 1 tablespoon jaggery *or* brown sugar
- curry leaves
- 4 or 5 red chillies
- 1 teaspoon coriander seeds
- 1/2 teaspoon fenugreek seeds
- 1/2 cup peanut kernels

Dry roast coriander seeds, fenugreek, and red chillies and grind them together. Heat the oil in a stainless-steel saucepan. Drop in the mustard, asafoetida, ground spices, peanut kernels, curry leaves and, finally, the tamarind water. Add salt and sugar and bring to boil. Simmer gently until the sauce thickens. Use enough of the sauce, about three to four tablespoons, to coat the rice evenly. Taste and add more, as required. Store the rest in a jar and refrigerate. This sauce is an excellent relish for plain curds and rice.

Tamarind rice is usually served with a curds-based relish.

LEMON RICE

- 2 cups rice, cooked
- 2-3 tablespoons oil
- 1/2 teaspoon ground turmeric
- 1 tablespn split peas (optional)
- 3-4 tablespns cashew nut pieces
- 1/2 teaspoon mustard seed

1 teaspoon salt
1 green chilli, chopped
1/2 inch of green ginger, chopped and crushed
pinch of asafoetida
curry leaves
juice of a lemon
1/2 cup grated carrots (optional)
1/2 cooked peas (optional)

Heat oil in a wok and drop in the mustard seeds, followed by asafoetida, split peas, chilli, ginger, cashew nuts. When the cashew nuts turn golden, add the curry leaves, turmeric, salt. Pour into a stainless-steel or china bowl before adding the lemon juice. Stir into the rice and mix well. The addition of grated carrots and cooked peas enhances texture and colour.

SESAME RICE

2 cups rice, cooked
1 1/2 teaspoons sesame oil
1/2 teaspoon mustard seeds
2 dried red chillies
pinch of asafoetida
3 teaspoons urad dal
6 teaspoons sesame seeds
1 flat teaspoon salt
2 to 3 tablespoons oil to mix

Heat the sesame oil in a wok. Drop in the mustard seeds and, as they crackle, add the asafoetida, chillies, urad dal and sesame seeds. Toast till golden-brown. Turn out on a kitchen-towel to drain off the oil. Grind the mixture. Add salt. Mix it well with the cooked rice and mixing oil.

CURDS RICE

2 cups rice, cooked
1 cup solid curds *or* plain yoghurt
1 teaspoon mustard seeds
curry leaves
1 green chilli, chopped
a sliver of ginger, sliced
1 flat teaspoon salt
1 tablespoon oil

Mix the rice, salt and curds, prepare seasoning. Heat oil. Drop in mustard, followed by ginger, chilli, curry leaves. Stir into the curds rice.

PONGAL (SWEET)

This sweet rice has a long ancestry: from Vedic times, rice cooked in milk with sugar and ghee seems to have been regarded as fare fit for the gods. In the South, pongal is the name for sweet rice boiled in milk with jaggery; the making of pongal in a specially sanctified bronze-pot is central to celebrating the harvest-festival in the month of Tai.

Serves 6-8

1/4 cup split peas
1 cup rice
1 1/2 pints milk
1 pint water
2 cups jaggery *or* brown sugar
10 cardamom seeds
1/2 cup cashew nuts
4 tablespoons ghee
1/2 cup sultanas

Put split peas in a heavy saucepan and dry-roast for five minutes. Add the rice and continue to dry-roast for another five minutes or until the rice is parched but not brown. Pour in milk and water. Bring to boil, lower heat and simmer for half an hour, stirring frequently. Add jaggery or sugar and continue cooking for an hour, stirring frequently. Crush cardamom pods using a pestle and mortar, remove shucks and pound the seeds to a fine powder. Add to the pongal. In a small frypan, heat 4 tablespoons ghee and roast cashew nuts till they turn golden-brown. Add the sultanas to the frypan towards the end, and pour into the pongal. Stir well and cook till the rice and split peas are cooked to a mushy texture, adding more milk if necessary.

SAMBHAR

Sambhar can be prepared either with freshly ground spices, as in the case of onion-sambhar*, or with a ready-made sambhar powder. The commercial brands tend to be hot and lack the subtle flavour of the home-made product. With a spice-grinder, it is easy to prepare sambhar powder at home. With a slight modification, the same can be transformed into rasam-powder; it is worth the bother, for the commercial offerings that aspire to be rasam powder hardly ever have its distinctive flavour.

Sambhar powder

$1/2$ cup toor dal
$1/4$ cup split peas
$1/4$ cup coriander seeds

$1/8$ cup black peppercorns
2 tablespoons ground turmeric
6 tablespoons red chilli powder

Clean the dals by picking out any stones and dirt. Dry roast them in a heavy pan with the coriander seeds and peppercorns for about ten minutes or until they turn slightly brown. Cool for a while, and grind them to a fine powder in a spice- or coffee-grinder. Add chilli powder and turmeric and mix well. Store in an air-tight jar.

(Rasam powder

Add a heaped tablespoon of cummin powder to $1/2$ cup of sambhar powder.)

Most vegetables are suitable for making sambhar except cauliflower, cabbage, or other leafy vegetables. Aubergine, pumpkin, potato, beans, Indian drumsticks, carrots, green peppers are most commonly used. While it is customary to use one vegetable, a mixture comprising potato, carrot, onion, tomato, and green pepper is occasionally used to produce *kadamba* or variegated sambhar.

Proceed as for onion sambhar*. Instead of freshly ground spices, add 2 flat teaspoons sambhar powder to the tamarind liquid.

RASAM

This is the original of 'mullingatawny', which is a garbled anglicization of the Tamil word for a type of rasam called 'milagu-tannir' or pepper-water. It is, however, a misleading description for the most cherished rasams of the South, which require more than pepper and water.

TOMATO-LEMON RASAM
2 cups broth, made by adding water to $1/2$ cup cooked toor dal.
Also
2 large ripe tomatoes	1 teaspoon ghee
1 pint water	$1/2$ teaspoon mustard seed
$1^1/2$ teaspoon rasam powder	1 teaspoon salt
pinch of asafoetida	juice of $1/2$ lemon
coriander leaves, chopped	

Measure a pint of water into a large stainless-steel saucepan. Cut tomatoes into small pieces and add to the water, with salt, asafoetida, and rasam powder. Simmer gently for 20 minutes. Lower heat. Add the lentil broth and reheat very slowly until the surface becomes frothy. On no account must the rasam be allowed to boil. Remove from heat. Top with a seasoning of black mustard seeds crackled in hot ghee, and chopped green coriander. Just before serving, stir-in the juice of lemon.

A simple rasam is made with tamarind—in which case, the tomato and lemon are omitted and a small amount of tamarind extract, say from a walnut-size pulp, is added to the pint of water at the beginning.

For a plain lemon rasam proceed as above, without the tomato.

PEPPER RASAM
This rasam is tangy and hot and is regarded as a good antidote to colds and stomach upsets. It requires few ingredients, but the result is quite distinctive. Note that, in this rasam, curry leaves are used instead of coriander.

2 cups of strong but thin tamarind water made with a small fistful of pulp.
Also
1 tablespoon toor dal	1 flat teaspoon salt
1 teaspoon black peppercorns	$1/2$ teaspoon mustard seed
$1/2$ teaspoon black cummin	1 teaspoon ghee
pinch of asafoetida	curry leaves

Dry-roast and grind together the toor dal, black peppercorns, cummin and (if required) red chilli.

Simmer tamarind water with asafoetida, the ground spices and salt for 20 minutes. Lower heat. Add 4 more cups of water and reheat very gently. Top with a seasoning of mustard seeds crackled in hot ghee, and add curry leaves.

AVIYAL
Originally from Kerala, this coconut-rich dish has become very popular throughout the South. It is served as a side dish with a main meal but also as an accompaniment to poori and chapatis and flavoured rices. The vegetables need to be carefully prepared to get a good, non-mushy texture at the end. The more variety there is, the better the dish; but some vegetables like cabbage, cauliflower and spinach are incompatible. Onions are strictly out of order, for purely culinary, not religious reasons.

Serves 6
- 1 sweet potato, washed and peeled
- small piece of yam, peeled
- 4-5 small, new potatoes *or*
  1 large waxy potato
- 1/2 cup french *or* string beans
- 1 aubergine
- 1 carrot
- a piece of white pumpkin, *or* marrow; *or* a choko
- 2 courgettes
- 1/2 cup shelled peas
- 2 Indian drumsticks
- 1 1/2 teaspoon salt
- 1 teaspoon turmeric

For the coconut sauce

1 cup freshly grated coconut, *or* a mixture of coconut milk and dessicated coconut.

2 tablespoons split peas soaked with a tablespoon rice and 1/2 teaspoon cummin.

Also
- 2-3 green chillies
- 1 cup curds *or* plain yoghurt
- 1/2 teaspoon mustard seed
- 1 tablespoon coconut oil
- curry leaves

Wash and cut vegetables into strips, 2 inches long and 1/2 inch thick. Put the cut vegetables in a large saucepan in the following order: beans, carrots, peas, drumsticks, potatoes, yam, sweet potato, pumpkin, choko, courgettes and aubergine. Add a cup of water, turmeric and salt. Put the lid on and simmer gently for 10-15 minutes while preparing the coconut sauce. Blend the coconut, green chillies, soaked split peas, rice, and cummin. Add the yoghurt. When the vegetables are tender but not overcooked, pour the coconut sauce over them, stir carefully, and cook for a further five minutes. Add curry leaves. Prepare a seasoning of black mustard seeds crackled in a tablespoon of coconut oil, and pour over the aviyal.

AUBERGINE CURRY

The word 'curry' in Tamil has overtones of dry, stir-fried, fried, or charred food. To a Southerner it does not immediately suggest the rich, hot or spicy sauce that the name usually conjures up for most others. Vegetables cooked in sauces have different names, depending on the method of preparation. Aviyal*, for instance, indicates the slow steaming of vegetables in the cooking process; Koottu*, which is another sauce-rich dish, signifies the special process of blending spices that is required for that preparation. A curry is usually dry, sometimes hot, sometimes sweet and flavoured with coconut. This aubergine curry is a typical example of what a Tamil understands by a spicy curry. The best results are obtained from using thin, tender aubergines rather than the plump variety commonly sold everywhere, which thoroughly lives up to its name in Hindi, 'baingan', which is said to have derived from 'bae-goon', meaning 'no character'.

Serves 6
- 2 lbs of aubergine, cut into 2" by 1/2 " pieces
- 1 tablespoon split peas
- 2 dry red chillies
- 2 tablespns dessicated coconut
- 1 flat teaspoon salt

1 tablespoon coriander seed   3 tablespoons oil
½ teaspoon peppercorn

Sprinkle some salt over the sliced aubergines and set aside.

Heat a little oil in a wok and roast the spices till the coconut turns light brown. Remove with slotted-spoon, and drain off excess oil. Grind to a medium-fine texture. Heat the rest of the oil in the wok, put in the aubergines, and stir-fry for 5 to 10 minutes, sprinkling a little water now and then. Add salt and ground spices, and continue stir-frying for another five minutes or more, until the aubergines are tender and yet crisp on the edges.

CABBAGE CURRY

This is an appetising way of serving cabbage and is very easy to prepare. The same method can be used to prepare choko, beans, white pumpkin, and green banana which has first been peeled and boiled.

½ cabbage, preferably Savoy
1 tablespoon oil
½ teaspoon mustard seed
1 teaspoon urad dal
pinch of asafoetida

1 red chilli (optional)
½ cup grated coconut
1 teaspoon sugar
1 flat teaspoon (or less) salt
curry leaves

Wash and shred cabbage finely. Heat oil in a wok and drop in the mustard seeds. As they crackle, add asafoetida, urad dal, chilli, curry leaves and, finally, the shredded cabbage. Stir-fry over medium heat, sprinkling a little water now and then to make sure that the cabbage stays a good colour. It must not turn brown. When it is tender, add sugar and coconut, stir well and remove from the wok; turn out into a stainless-steel or china dish.

KOOTTU

Cooked pulses and spices are combined in a variety of ways in South Indian cooking, and this dish is yet another variation on the way coconut and roasted spices are used to enhance the flavour of certain vegetables. There are three stages in the preparation, and also a passable short-cut. My husband, however, can invariably detect when the short-cut is used!

Serves 4-6

2 cups diced courgettes, *or* beans, *or* shredded cabbage, *or* choko
1 tablespoon split peas
1 tablespoon coconut oil
pinch of asafoetida
1 cup water
For the coconut sauce
2-3 oz. grated coconut
1 teaspoon oil
1 tablespoon urad dal

4 oz. toor dal
2 oz. mung dal
pinch of turmeric
curry leaves
1 teaspoon salt
1 teaspoon sambhar powder

8-10 black peppercorns
1 teaspoon cummin seeds
2 teaspoon rice flour

For the topping
    1 teaspoon oil
    1/2 teaspoon mustard seed
    1 teaspoon cummin seeds
    twist or 2 ground black pepper

First, wash and cook the toor dal and mung dal together, with a pinch of turmeric and no salt. Set aside.

Next, prepare the coconut sauce, since the roasted spices need to soak for a while. Heat oil in a small frypan. Roast urad dal and peppercorns, and after a little while add the cummin seeds. Remove from heat as the cummin frizzles up. Put in the blender with a little water; and when the urad dal has softened a little, add the coconut and grind to a fine, smooth paste. Stir in the rice flour and set aside.

Heat the coconut oil in a heavy saucepan. Drop in the split peas and stir until they are golden-brown. Put in the diced vegetable and stir-fry for a while. Pour in enough water to cover, and add salt, asafoetida, and sambhar powder. Simmer gently till the vegetables are cooked. Add the cooked dals and the coconut sauce and cook for another five minutes. Remove from heat. Heat oil in a small frypan and drop in the mustard seeds. As they crackle, add urad dal, cummin seeds, ground pepper, and curry leaves. Pour over the koottu and stir in just before serving.

The Short Cut
Instead of preparing the coconut sauce, just add the coconut and cooked dals when the vegetable is half-cooked, and increase the amount of pepper and cummin in the final seasoning.

Salads and Relishes

The notion of salad is a relatively new importation; though raw vegetables, seasoned in interesting ways, figure largely in South Indian meals. Lettuce is virtually unknown. Carrots, cucumber, green or red peppers, tomatoes, beetroot, and onions are used to prepare refreshing accompaniments to main meals. Quite a few of these preparations get their distinctive flavour from that typical seasoning of the South, black mustard seeds crackled in hot oil to which a sliced green chilli has been added.

CARROT SALAD
    2 cups grated carrot
    juice of 1/2 lemon
    salt to taste
    seasoning of black mustard seeds and green chilli
    chopped coriander leaves

Prepare the seasoning and mix well with the rest of the ingredients. Instead of green chilli, a sliced green pepper may be added to the seasoning.

CUCUMBER PACHADI
2 Lebanese cucumbers *or* one ordinary ridge cucumber, peeled and sliced.

Also
- 2 tablespoons freshly grated coconut
- 1 green chilli
- 1/4 teaspoon black mustard seed
- chopped coriander leaves
- 1 cup curds *or* plain yoghurt
- salt to taste

Sprinkle salt over the sliced cucumber, and leave standing for a while. Drain off water, add the yoghurt and coconut. Top with hot seasoning, and sprinkle coriander leaves. Carrots and tomatoes can also be prepared in this way.

TOMATO CHUTNEY

1 cup mild tamarind water made by dissolving a 1/4 teaspoon tamarind essence in water *or* by soaking and squeezing out a walnut-sized tamarind pulp. *Or*, 1/3 cup of white vinegar may be substituted.

Also
- 1lb tomatoes, fresh *or* tinned
- 1 cup jaggery *or* brown sugar, the darker the better
- 1/2 teaspoon salt
- 1/4 teaspoon chilli powder
- pinch of asafoetida
- 1/2 teaspoon mustard seeds
- 1 tablespoon oil
- 1 green chilli (optional)

Put the chopped tomatoes and tamarind-water in a stainless-steel saucepan. Add salt, chilli powder, sugar, asafoetida, and boil gently till they blend and thicken. Season with mustard seeds crackled in hot oil, and sliced green chilli. Store in an air-tight jar and refrigerate.

MANGO CHUTNEY

- 1 green mango, sliced into small pieces
- 1 cup jaggery *or* brown sugar
- salt to taste
- 1/2 teaspoon chilli powder
- seasoning of mustard seeds, crackled in hot oil

Put the mango pieces with a little water in a stainless-steel saucepan, and add salt, sugar and chilli powder. Simmer till the mango is tender and the chutney thickens. Top with seasoning.

WOOD APPLE CHUTNEY

This is made from bilva tree fruit, which is larger than a tennis-ball, with a white, tough but crumbly shell and a rich brown pulp. It is occasionally obtainable in the West.

Mix pulp removed from 1 large wood apple with an equal amount of jaggery *or* brown sugar.

GINGER RELISH-1

- 1 cup of tender green ginger, sliced
- juice 1/2 lemon
- salt to taste
- seasoning of black mustard seed, crackled in hot oil

Mix ginger, salt, and lemon juice, and top with seasoning.

GINGER RELISH-2
1 cup tender green ginger, sliced
2 tablespoons thick tamarind paste
salt to taste

seasoning of black mustard seeds, cracked in hot oil

Mix ginger, salt and tamarind paste and top with seasoning.

PAPPADUMS
Good-quality pappadums can be bought ready-made. The so-called commercial brands are often home-made, produced by co-operatives. The South Indian variety is usually plain; but chilli, pepper, and garlic pappadums are available for those seeking more exotic tastes.

Pappadums can be toasted lightly over a charcoal fire or fried in oil. To fry pappadums, heat ample oil in a wok or deep frypan. The oil should be allowed to get very hot. Test by dropping-in a sliver of pappadum. If it goes white and surfaces to the top instantly, the oil is ready. If it goes brown, lower the heat a little. Fry one pappadum at a time. Place carefully in the oil, hold it down with a slotted-spoon, and smooth it out lightly, using a knife. When it frizzes out fully, lift out, and, using both slotted-spoon and knife to hold it, shake off excess oil.

Sweets

Milk pudding or payasam is the standard sweet served with a meal. This may seem unimaginative, so I hasten to add that the South Indian version of milk pudding is such as to convert even the most inveterate hater of the English equivalent. Other sweets listed below figure more as offerings with coffee or tea whenever there are guests to entertain or occasions to celebrate, and both opportunities occur fairly frequently.

VERMICELLI PAYASAM
Our Italian friends cannot get over the sheer daring of using pasta to make a sweet; but once they get over the shock, they enjoy the dessert very much. Payasam is also made with flaked rice, semolina, or sago. A very small amount of the base, say 2 oz., is recommended.

Serves 4
2 oz. fine vermicelli, broken into pieces
$1^{1}/_{2}$ pint milk
4 oz. sugar
6 cardamom pods

3 tablespoons of unsalted cashew nut pieces
3 tablespoons sultanas
2 tablespoons ghee

Melt the ghee in a heavy saucepan over moderate heat. Toast the cashew nuts in the ghee till they turn golden, and add the sultanas. As they swell, remove nuts and sultanas with a slotted-spoon. Lower heat and put the vermicelli in the ghee; stir well for 2-3 minutes. It should become bright white and crisp, not brown. Add milk, and cook over low heat for about 15 minutes, stirring occasionally. Add sugar, stir well, and cook for a further 20 minutes. Remove from heat and add crushed and pounded cardamom seeds, and the fried nuts and sultanas. Serve warm or chilled.

COCONUT BARFI-1
This recipe produces a soft-textured barfi and needs to be refrigerated. The second one is more like coconut-ice and does not require refrigeration.

Serves 4-6
$1^1/2$ cups of freshly grated coconut, *or* a mix of 1 cup dessicated coconut and $^1/2$ cup coconut milk.

Also
$1^1/2$ pints milk   5 crushed cardamom pods
8 oz. sugar   3-4 tablespoons ghee

Put coconut and milk in a heavy saucepan. Bring to the boil, and boil gently for $^1/2$ hour. Add sugar and continue cooking until the mixture thickens, stirring well. Add crushed cardamom and ghee, 1 tablespoon at a time. Keep stirring till the barfi leaves the sides of the pan easily. Turn out into a greased flat dish, let it cool, and cut into segments.

COCONUT BARFI-2

Makes 12 squares
6 oz. freshly grazed coconut $^1/2$ cup milk
8 oz. sugar   5 cardamom pods, crushed
$^1/2$ cup water   3 tablespoons ghee

Melt sugar in water and boil the syrup for 5 minutes. Add coconut and milk. Add ghee as the barfi thickens. When it leaves the sides of the pan easily, add cardamom and turn out on to a flat dish. Cool and cut into squares.

KESARI or SOJJI
In the South, when the male of the species is said to be on the 'Bhajji-Sojji round' it usually means that he has been on many a bride-prospecting visit, for these two items are invariably served to a potential groom, and are often prepared by the would-be bride herself. Despite the somewhat cynical associations that the name conjures up, this sweet is very popular, as it is easy to prepare and keeps well.

Serves 4-6
1 cup coarse semolina   6-8 tablespoons ghee
2 cups sugar   12 cardamom pods, pounded

¹/₂ teaspoon saffron powder
¹/₄ cup cashew nut pieces
¹/₄ cup sultanas
2 cups warm water

Melt 2 tablespoons of ghee in a heavy, deep frypan. Roast cashew nuts till they are golden, add sultanas, remove both with a slotted-spoon. Add one more tablespoon of ghee, and put the semolina in. Fry gently for 5 minutes till it absorbs all the ghee and turns grainy. Lower heat, add warm water. Stir well, breaking up any lumps with a fork. Add the saffron and keep stirring for five minutes. Add sugar and continue stirring, adding the rest of the ghee one tablespoon at a time. Add the crushed cardamom, and continue stirring for about 20 minutes until the kesari leaves the sides of the pan easily, adding more ghee if necessary. Mix-in the roasted cashews and sultanas, and turn into a bowl. Smooth out the surface. It can be cut into squares when cool.

BADAM KHEER
This is popular both as a hot or cold drink, for it is believed not only to refresh but also to revitalize.

1 cup ground almonds
1 pint milk
1 cup sugar

6 cardamom pods, crushed
and pounded

Put almonds and milk in a heavy saucepan. Bring to the boil, add crushed cardamoms, and simmer gently, stirring frequently. After 10 minutes add the sugar, and continue stirring. Simmer for another 15 minutes. Remove the cardamom shucks. Serve warm or chilled in glasses. Strands of toasted and crushed saffron soaked in a little milk may be added to refine the flavour.

GLOSSARY OF INDIAN WORDS IN
THE FIREWALKERS

aandhi: 'the darkener'; a dust-storm
aarti: a red liquid made by combining turmeric and lime in water and used in ceremonial welcomes, or to ward off evil
advaitam: non-duality; the identity of *paramatman* or Supreme Soul with *jivatman* or human soul
ahimsa: non-violence
alarippu: 'the opening of the bud into blossom', the first dance-item
amma: literally 'mother'; a respectful way of addressing women
anjali: a ceremonial greeting
apsara(s): a class of beautiful female divinities, frequently represented in temple-sculpture; they are said to inhabit the sky, but often visit the earth; they are the wives of *gandharva*s and have the faculty of changing their shapes at will
ashoka: a medium-sized tree with magnificent red flowers
ashrama: one of the four stages of human life
asura(s): the chief of the evil spirits
avatar: a manifestation of a god in bodily form
basti: a slum dwelling
bhajan: a sacred song or chant
bhakti: religious devotion performed with demonstrative fervour; it may include dance, song, music, prayer, and offerings
bharani: seventh star-constellation through which the moon passes
bharatanatyam: the South Indian school of classical dance; the word *bharata* used of this form of dance is believed to be composed of the first syllable of each of its three main elements: *bhava* or feeling, *raga* or melody, *tala* or rhythmic timing. *Natyam* means the combination of dancing and acting
bhava: feeling
bidi: cheap Indian cigarette, rolled in a leaf
bilva: aegele marmelos, the wood-apple tree; its fruit is used medicinally; its leaves are employed in the ceremonial worship of Shiva
brahmacharya: a young brahmin before marriage, in the first period of his life
chettiar: a sub-group of the merchant caste
Chidambaram: South Indian town renowned for its temple dedicated to Shiva, the dancer. The temple is regarded as the earthly locus of Shiva's cosmic dance

citrakunda: square-columned
deepanjali: a devotional dance with a lamp
Deepavali: the 'Festival of Lights', celebrating the victory of good over evil
devadasi(s): 'a handmaiden of God', normally, a term for a temple-dancer; but when used pejoratively, it means a temple-prostitute
devas: gods, thought of as the heavenly or 'shining ones'
devis: female deities
dharani: the Earth
dhari: a woven mat
dharma: 'that which is established or firm'; law; what is according to right rule; a decree; a duty
dhobi: a washerman
dikshitar(s): the 'consecrated ones', a sub-group of learned brahmins
DMK: Dravida Munnetra Kalagam, the Dravidian Progressive Party
(A) DMK: Anna Dravida Munnetra Kalagam, a breakaway party under the leadership of Annadurai
dorai: a respectful form of address to a male social superior
gandharva(s): heavenly choristers
Gayatri: a hymn composed in the Gayatri metre; a sacred verse, addressed to the sun, and repeated by every brahmin at his morning and evening devotion. The verse is personified as a goddess, the wife of Brahma and mother of the four Vedas, hence seen as the golden face of truth
Gita: the *Bhagavadgita* or 'Song of the Lord'
gopuram: a temple gateway-tower
gotra(s): lineage; a tribal subdivision; in the brahmin caste, forty-nine *gotras* are recognized. These are supposed to be sprung from and named after celebrated teachers such as Sandilya, Kasyapa, Gautama, Bharadvaja etc.
hammam: a bath
jati: a dance-item which concentrates on sets of rhythmic patterns
jeevathyagi: one who sacrifices his or her life
jibba: a lengthy, loose shirt
jihad: a Muslim holy war
jnana: spiritual knowledge
jnani: an 'enlightened one'
Kali-yuga: the last and worst of the four ages, the present age, the age of vice
karma: work; an accumulated burden from previous lives
karma-yogi: one who seeks liberation through a discipline of work
kavadi: an arc borne by one bearer, of bamboo and peacock feathers

khayal: a secular song
kolam: decorative patterns drawn on wet ground with rice powder, or on dry ground with rice paste
kumkum: red mark worn on the forehead, signifying auspiciousness
lungi: a sarong-like male garment, made by stitching the ends of one sheet of colourful material
madi: with ritually pure clothes (i.e. having no outside contamination)
mahaguru: a 'great teacher'
Maha-Sivaratri: the 'Great Night of Shiva', a festival of repentance held over a twenty-four hour period in February/March
mami: auntie
marwari: a man from Marwar; but colloquial for a trader or money-lender
maya: illusion, unreality, fraud, deception, an apparition; a trick
mofussil: used of anything relating to country districts
mirasi: a right by inheritance
mudaliyar: a respected sub-group of the merchant caste
mudra: stylized dance-gesture
nadaswaram: a long reed-pipe, an oboe-like instrument
naidu: a respected sub-group of the merchant caste
namaskaram: a reverential salutation, bringing the palms together, chest high, fingers upright
nattuvanar: a venerable teacher of classical dance
paan: rolled-up betel-leaves and nuts, often sweet and aromatic
pada: a fluid dance-gesture
padam: a finely chanted lyrical song of love; or the dance to such a song
panchayat: a local council
panda: a temple-priest who guides pilgrims and officiates at rituals by the River Ganges
pandal: a festive awning
pandanus: an aromatic, cactus-like plant
parangi: literally, 'a pumpkin', a foreigner or white man
parijata: the coral tree, *erythrina indica*
prahara: the outer corridor of a temple
prakriti: Nature; the personified will of the Supreme Being in creation
prasadam: the food presented to an idol
puja: an act of worship of the gods
pujari: a priest who performs *puja*
purusha: a man; the Supreme Being as the Soul of the universe; the Spirit as passive and a spectator of the *prakriti* or creative force
rezhi: an entrance-corridor, from the front door to the interior

rishi: a religious sage
sadhu: a holy man
Saivite: belonging to Shiva
samsara: mundane existence; secular life, worldly illusion; colloquially, one's wife
sanyasi (m); sanyasini (f): an ascetic monk
sardar: a colloquial term for a Sikh
sastrigal: a ritual priest attached to a particular family
sati: a faithful wife who burns herself with her husband's corpse; or the act of so doing
sati-stones: stone altars erected to commemorate widows who burnt themselves on their husband's pyre
shastra dharma: a compendium of rules prescribed by authoritative religious texts
shenai: a reed instrument similar to an oboe
sraddah: religious dedication
sudra(s): the lowest of the four castes; manual labourers
tabla: a drum
Tai: the tenth month in the Tamil calendar; it falls between January and February
tali: a sacred thread, yellow in colour, dyed in turmeric, tied round the neck of a wife
tandava: an energetic, even frenetic, dance
tapas: bodily mortification, penance
thalambu: the Tamil word for *pandanus,* an aromatic, cactus-like plant
thali: a plate
tillana: a very energetic dance with statuesque postures and intricate footwork, executed with speed and dexterity
vaishya: the merchant caste
varnam: 'colour'; a highly elaborate dance-conception incorporating technical brilliance, richness of melody and artful interpretation
vedantam: a leading system of Hindu philosophy
veshti: a male garment, a sheet of fine-spun white cotton, wrapped round the middle
yali: a demon guardian, often found in effigy at entrances
yavana: a Greek
yoga nidra: deep meditation
zamindar: a feudal landholder
zari: a gold-embroidered border to a saree or veshti